PRAISE FOR LARA ADRIAN'S MIDNIGHT BREED SERIES

DARKER AFTER MIDNIGHT

"Adrian pulls out all the stops as she makes the move to hardcover. After ten edgy and passionate books, the final confrontation between the Order and Dragos is at hand. Over the course of this terrific series, Breed warrior Sterling Chase has been on a downward spiral as he battles against Bloodlust. . . . Adrian ensures readers are taken on a redemptive journey filled with passion, treachery and danger. Awesome!"
—*RT Book Reviews* (4.5 stars, top pick)

"*Darker After Midnight* is Sterling Chase's book, and while I felt like I had been waiting for it forever and was afraid that I had put too high of expectations on it, I should never have worried. . . . This book was fantastic—everything I was hoping for and SO much more. *Literal Addiction* gives *Darker After Midnight* 5 skulls and feels like that isn't even adequate for the gift of this book. We recommend it to everyone—paranormal romance lovers, urban fantasy readers, anyone who loves fast-paced, action-packed, intense reads with gripping characters and spectacular storylines woven into a phenomenally crafted world. If you haven't started the Midnight Breed series yet, we highly suggest that you bump it up to the top of your TBR list and get started today."
—*Literal Addiction* (5 skulls)

thor, you will soon find yourself completely and utterly caught within these magnetizing pages."

—Coffee Time Romance (5 cups)

"Lara Adrian has penned another wonderful addition to her Midnight Breed world that keeps the suspense of the series going strong and fans of the series wanting more. She has continued to bring excellence to the world that she has created with even more fantastic characters and heart-pounding intrigue. . . . This is a book that I'm definitely adding to my keeper collection. I am delighted to recommend this book to others who love this genre and who would love this story."

—Night Owl Reviews (5 stars, top pick)

TAKEN BY MIDNIGHT

"Keeping a long-running series evolving in an intriguing manner is no easy task, but Adrian pulls it off with seeming ease. It will be interesting to see what's next!"

—*Romantic Times*

"A thrilling addition to the extraordinary Midnight Breed series!"

—Fresh Fiction

"*Taken By Midnight* . . . holds you hostage. . . . I couldn't put it down and I bet you won't be able to either."

—Joyfully Reviewed

SHADES OF MIDNIGHT

"[Lara Adrian] once again serves up a blockbuster hit. . . . With a fast-paced tale of romantic suspense and intense and realistic characters . . . Lara Adrian compels readers to get hooked on her storylines, and that's why *Shades of Midnight* deserves a Perfect 10."
—Romance Reviews Today

"[A] rapid fire story . . . Besides delivering wonderful paranormal romances, the Midnight Breed series also continues to add complexity. . . . A twist at the end could prove quite interesting. This is time well spent!"
—*Romantic Times*

ASHES OF MIDNIGHT

"*Ashes of Midnight* will scorch its way into your heart."
—Romance Junkies

"Lara Adrian continues to kick butt with her latest release. . . . *Ashes of Midnight* is an entertaining ride and as usual kept me riveted from page one."
—The Romance Reader Connection

VEIL OF MIDNIGHT

"Adrian's newest heroine has a backbone of pure steel. Rapid-pace adventures deliver equal quantities of supernatural thrills and high-impact passion. This is one of the best vampire series on the market!"
—*Romantic Times*

"*Veil of Midnight* will enthrall you and leave you breathless for more."
—Wild on Books

MIDNIGHT RISING

"Fans are in for a treat. . . . Ms. Adrian has a gift for drawing her readers deeper and deeper into the amazing world she creates. . . . I eagerly await the next installment of this entertaining series!"
—Fresh Fiction

"Packed with danger and action, this book also explores the tumultuous emotions of guilt, anger, betrayal and forgiveness. Adrian has hit on an unbeatable story mix."
—*Romantic Times*

MIDNIGHT AWAKENING

"This is one of the best paranormal series around. Compelling characters and good world-building make this a must-read series."
—Fresh Fiction

"One of the Top 10 Best Romance Novels of 2007."
—Selected by the Editors at Amazon.com

"Ms. Adrian's series just gets better and better. . . . *Midnight Awakening* was exactly what I hoped it would be then so much more. . . . I'm intrigued and without a doubt completely hooked."
—*Romance Junkies*

"Vengeance is the driving force behind this entry in the intense Midnight Breed series. . . . Things look bad for the characters, but for the readers it's nothing but net!"

—*Romantic Times*

KISS OF CRIMSON

"Vibrant writing heightens the suspense, and hidden secrets provide many twists. This dark and steamy tale . . . is a winner and will have readers eager for the next Midnight Breed story."

—Romance Reviews Today

"Hot sensuality with emotional drama and high-stakes danger . . . [Adrian] ensures that her latest is terrific supernatural entertainment."

—*Romantic Times*

"[Adrian] pens hot erotic scenes and vivid action sequences."

—The Romance Reader

KISS OF MIDNIGHT

"Evocative, enticing, erotic. Enter Lara Adrian's vampire world and be enchanted!"

—bestselling author J. R. WARD

"*Kiss of Midnight* is dark, edgy and passionate, an irresistible vampire romance."

—*Chicago Tribune*

By Lara Adrian

Kiss of Midnight
Kiss of Crimson
Midnight Awakening
Midnight Rising
Veil of Midnight
Ashes of Midnight
Shades of Midnight
Taken by Midnight
Deeper Than Midnight
Darker After Midnight

eBook
"A Taste of Midnight"

Books published by The Random House Publishing Group are available at quantity discounts on bulk purchases for premium, educational, fund-raising, and special sales use. For details, please call 1-800-733-3000.

Darker After
Midnight

MIDNIGHT BREED SERIES
BOOK TEN

LARA ADRIAN

DELL
NEW YORK

2012 Dell Mass Market Edition

Copyright © 2012 by Lara Adrian, LLC
Excerpt from *Edge of Dawn* copyright © 2012 by Lara Adrian, LLC
"A Taste of Midnight" copyright © 2011 by Lara Adrian, LLC

All rights reserved.

Published in the United States by Dell, an imprint of The Random House Publishing Group, a division of Random House, Inc., New York.

DELL is a registered trademark of Random House, Inc., and the colophon is a trademark of Random House, Inc.

Originally published in hardcover in the United States by Delacorte Press, an imprint of The Random House Publishing Group, a division of Random House, Inc., in 2012.

This book contains an excerpt from the forthcoming book *Edge of Dawn* by Lara Adrian. This excerpt has been set for this edition only and may not reflect the final content of the forthcoming edition.

ISBN: 978-0-440-24612-2
eBook ISBN: 978-0-345-52929-9

Cover design: Jae Song and Scott Biel
Cover illustration: Christoph Rosenberger/Photographer's Choice/Getty Images

Printed in the United States of America

www.bantamdell.com

9 8 7 6 5 4 3 2 1

Dell Mass Market Edition: November 2012

To my amazing readers and online communities
both in the United States and abroad,
with deep appreciation and humble thanks
for all the enthusiasm and support
you've given my books. I hope you enjoy
the rest of the adventures still to come!

And to John, always,
for more than any words could say.

CHAPTER
One

"The charges are set, Lucan. Detonators are ready whenever you say the word. On your go, it all ends right here."

Lucan Thorne stood silent in the dusk-filled, snow-covered yard of the Boston estate that had long served as a base of operations for himself and his small cadre of brothers in arms. For more than a hundred years, on countless patrols, they rode out from this very spot to guard the night, maintaining a fragile peace between the unwitting humans who owned the daytime hours and the predators who moved among them secretly, sometimes lethally, in the dark.

Lucan and his warriors of the Order dealt in swift, deadly justice and had never known the taste of defeat.

Tonight it was bitter on his tongue.

"Dragos will pay for this," he growled around the emerging points of his fangs.

Lucan's vision burned amber as he stared across the expansive lawn at the pale limestone facade of the Gothic mansion. A chaos of tire tracks scarred the grounds from the police chase that had crashed the compound's tall iron gates that morning and come to a bullet-riddled halt right at the Order's front door. Blood stained the snow where law enforcement gunfire had mowed down three terrorists who'd bombed Boston's United Nations building then fled the scene with a dozen cops and every news station in the area in close pursuit.

All of it—from the attack on a human government facility, to the media-covered police chase of the suspects onto the compound's secured grounds—had been orchestrated by the Order's chief adversary, a power-mad vampire called Dragos.

He wasn't the first of the Breed to dream of a world where humankind lived to serve and served in fear. But where others before him with less commitment had failed, Dragos had demonstrated astonishing patience and initiative. He'd been carefully sowing the seeds of his rebellion for most of his long life, secretly cultivating followers within the Breed and making Minions of any humans he felt could help carry out his twisted goals.

For the past year and a half, since their discovery of Dragos's plans, Lucan and his brethren had kept him on the run. They had succeeded in driving him back, thwarting his every move and disrupting his operation.

Until today.

Today it was the Order pushed back and on the run, and Lucan didn't like it one damn bit.

"What's the ETA at the temporary headquarters?"

The question was aimed toward Gideon, one of the two warriors who'd remained behind with Lucan to wrap things up in Boston while the rest of the compound went ahead to an emergency safe house in northern Maine. Gideon glanced away from the small handheld computer in his palm and met Lucan's gaze over the rims of silvery blue shades. "Savannah and the other women have been on the road for nearly five hours, so they should be at the location in about thirty minutes. Niko and the other warriors are just a couple hours behind them."

Lucan gave a nod, grim but relieved that the abrupt relocation had come together as well as it had. There were a few loose ends and details yet to be managed, but so far everyone was safe and the damage Dragos had intended to inflict on the Order had been minimized.

Movement stirred on the other side of Lucan as Tegan, the other warrior who'd stayed behind, returned from the latest perimeter check. "Any problems?"

"None." Tegan's face showed no emotion, only grim purpose. "The two cops in the unmarked stakeout vehicle near the gates are still tranced and sleeping. After the hard memory scrub I gave them earlier today, there's a good chance they won't wake up until next week. And when they do, it'll be with one hellacious hangover."

Gideon grunted. "Better a mind scrub on a couple of Boston's finest than a very public bloodbath involving half the city's precincts and the feds combined."

"Damn straight," Lucan said, recalling the swarm of cops and reporters who had filled the estate grounds that morning. "If the situation had escalated and any of those cops or federal agents had decided to come banging on the mansion door . . . Christ, I'm sure I don't need to tell either of you how fast or how far things would have gone south."

Tegan's eyes were grave in the rising darkness. "Guess we've got Chase to thank for that."

"Yeah," Lucan replied. He'd lived a long time—nine hundred years and then some—but for however long he'd walk this Earth, he knew he would never forget the sight of Sterling Chase strolling out of the mansion and squarely into the aim of a lawn full of heavily armed cops and federal agents. He could have died several ways in that moment. If the adrenaline-fueled panic of any one of the armed men assembled in the yard hadn't killed him on the spot, spending longer than half an hour under the full blast of morning sunlight would have.

But Chase apparently hadn't cared about any of that as he'd allowed himself to be cuffed and led away by the human authorities. His surrender—his personal sacrifice—had bought the Order precious time. He had diverted attention from the mansion and what it concealed, giving Lucan and the others the chance to secure the subterranean compound and mobilize the evacuation of its residents once the sun set.

After a string of bad calls and personal fuck-ups, most recently a failed strike against Dragos that had inadvertently landed Chase's face on the national news, he was the last of the warriors Lucan would have turned to for answers. What he had done today was nothing short of astonishing, if not suicidal.

Then again, Sterling Chase had been on a self-destructive path for some time now. Maybe this was his way of nailing that coffin shut once and for all.

Gideon raked a hand over the top of his spiky blond hair and exhaled a curse. "Fucking lunatic. I can't believe he actually did it."

"It should have been me." Lucan glanced between Tegan and Gideon, the warrior who'd been with him when he'd first founded the Order in Europe and the one who'd helped him establish the warriors' home base in Boston centuries later. "I'm the Order's leader. If there was a sacrifice to be made to spare everyone else, I should have been the one to step up."

Tegan eyed him grimly. "How long do you think Chase would have been able to keep his Bloodlust at bay? Whether he's in human custody or loose on the streets, his thirst owns him. He's lost and he knows that. He knew it when he walked out that door this morning. He had nothing left to lose."

Lucan grunted. "And now he's sitting in police custody somewhere, surrounded by humans. He might have spared us from discovery today, but what if his thirst gets the better of him and he ends up exposing the existence of all the Breed? One moment of heroism could undo centuries of secrecy."

Tegan's expression was coldly sober. "I guess we'll have to trust him."

"Trust," Lucan said. "That's a currency he's come up short on more than once lately."

Unfortunately, right now, they didn't have a lot of choice in the matter. Dragos had demonstrated quite effectively just how far he was willing to take his enmity toward the Order. He had no regard for life, human or his own kind, and as of today, he'd shown that he would take their power struggle out of the shadows and into the open. It was dangerous ground, with impossibly high stakes.

And it was personal now. Dragos had crossed a line here, and there would be no going back.

Lucan glanced at Gideon. "It's time. Hit the detonators. Let's get this done."

The warrior gave a slight nod and turned his attention back to his handheld computer. "Ah, fuck me," he muttered, the traces of his British accent punctuating the curse. "Here we go then."

The three Breed males stood side by side in the crisp, cold darkness. Above them the sky was clear and cloudless, endless black, pierced with stars. Everything was still, as if Earth and the heavens had frozen in time, suspended in that instant between the silence of a perfect winter night and the first low rumble of the destruction unfolding roughly three hundred feet beneath the warriors' boots. It seemed to carry on forever, not some great bombastic spectacle of furious noise and spewing fire and ash but a quiet yet thorough annihilation.

"The living quarters have been sealed," Gideon reported somberly as the thunder began to ebb. He touched the screen of his handheld device and another series of deep growls rolled from far below the snow-covered ground. "The weapons room, the infirmary . . . both gone now."

Lucan didn't allow himself to dwell on the memories or the history that was housed in the labyrinth of rooms and corridors being systematically exploded with a touch of Gideon's finger on that tiny computer screen. It had taken more than a hundred years to build the compound into what it had become. He couldn't deny that it put a cold ache in his chest to feel it being pulled down so neatly.

"The chapel has been sealed," Gideon said, after pressing the digital detonator another time. "All that remains is the tech lab."

Lucan heard the slight catch in the warrior's low voice. The tech lab was Gideon's pride, the nerve center of the Order's operation. It was where they'd assembled and strategized before every night's mission. It took no effort at all for Lucan to see his brethren's faces, a fine group of honorable, courageous Breed males, gathered around the lab's conference table, each one ready to give his life for the other. Some of them had. And some likely would in the time still to come.

As the soft percussion of explosives continued to rumble belowground, Lucan felt a weight settle on his shoulder. He glanced beside him, to where Tegan stood, the warrior's big hand remaining a steady presence, his cool green eyes holding Lucan's gaze in an unexpected show of solidarity, as the last of the thunder faded into silence.

"That's it," Gideon announced. "That was the last one. It's over now."

For a long while, none of them spoke. There were no words. Nothing to be said in the dark shadow of the now-vacant mansion and its ruined compound below.

Finally, Lucan stepped forward. His fangs bit into the edges of his tongue as he took one last look at the place that had been his headquarters—his family's home—for so many years. Amber light filled his vision as his eyes transformed in his simmering fury.

He pivoted to face his two brethren, and when he at last found the words to speak, his voice was harsh and raw with determination. "We may be done here, but this night doesn't mark the end of anything. It's only the beginning. Dragos wants a war with the Order? Then, by God, he's damn well got it."

CHAPTER
Two

The holding cell at the Suffolk County Sheriff's Department reeked of mildew and urine and the pungent stench of human sweat, anxiety, and disease. Sterling Chase's acute senses recoiled as he cast a hooded glance at the trio of lowlifes currently handcuffed and parked along with him in the holding tank inside the Boston jail. Across the six-by-eight windowless room, the meth-head seated on the bench opposite him bounced his boot heels nervously on the scuffed white linoleum floor. His arms were restrained behind him, thin shoulders hunched forward under the wrinkled folds of a lumberjack-plaid flannel shirt. The junkie's dark-ringed eyes were sunk deep into the hollowed sockets of his strung-out face, his gaze darting back and forth, wall to wall, ceiling to floor, and back again. Yet all the while he was careful to avoid looking directly at Chase, like a trapped and terrified rodent with the instinctive understanding that a dangerous predator was nearby.

On the other end of the long bench, a balding middle-age man sat as still as stone, sweating profusely, a pitifully sparse comb-over drooping onto his greasy forehead as he quietly murmured under his breath. He was praying in a barely audible whisper that Chase heard word for word, a plea to his God for absolution of his sins and bargaining for mercy with the fervor of a man facing the gallows. Not an hour earlier, this same man had been wailing about his innocence, swearing to the cops who'd arrested him that he had no idea how hundreds of pictures of him posed with naked children had ended up on his computer. Chase could hardly stand to breathe the same air as the pedophile, let alone look at him.

But it was the third man in the holding tank, the heavy-browed bruiser who'd arrived ten minutes ago, fresh off an arrest for domestic battery, that had Chase's molars clamped together as tight as a vise. Loose jeans sagged under the pregnant swell of a beer gut cloaked in a Patriots sweatshirt from a few Super Bowls past. The gray shirt was torn at the shoulder seam, its red-white-and-blue logo on the front stained with the smeared remnants of a pot roast and mashed potatoes meal. Judging from the knot riding the bridge of the guy's busted-up nose and the bleeding fingernail tracks skating down the left side of his face, it looked like his female victim hadn't gone down without a fight. Chase's nostrils flared, throat tickled, as his eyes rooted on the four long, bloodied gashes raking the human's cheek.

"Bitch fuckin' broke my nose," Man of the Year complained as he leaned back against the white-glazed brick wall of the holding cell. "You believe that shit? I give her a little smack for dropping my dinner in my lap, tell her to watch where the fuck she's goin', for crissake, and she hauls off and cold-cocks me. Big mistake." He grunted, mouth curling in a sneer. "She won't be stupid enough to try a stunt like that again, though. And the friggin' cops, man! Shoulda known they'd take that bitch's word over mine. Just like last time. I'm supposed ta let a judge wave a piece of paper at me sayin' I gotta stay away from my own wife? I gotta stay outta my own damn house? Fuck that. And fuck her too. I've sent her to the hospital more 'an once. Next time I see her, I'm gonna fix that bitch so good, she'll never be able to sic the cops on me again."

Chase said nothing, merely listening in silence and trying not to fixate too intensely on the bright red rivulets that were making a liquid slide down onto the wife-beater's jaw. The sight and scent of fresh blood was enough to wake the predator in any member of the Breed, but all the worse for Chase.

Head tipped down toward his chest, he drew in a shallow breath and caught a whiff of something even more disturbing beneath the stale foulness of the room and the coppery tang of coagulating red cells—something raw and feral, verging on rabid.

Him.

The realization made his mouth quirk, but it was hard to appreciate the irony when his gums were throbbing with the need to feed.

Thanks to the fierce thirst that had been his constant companion for longer than he cared to admit, his sensory inputs were locked in overdrive. He felt every minute shift in the air around him. Saw every twitch and tic in the movements of his restless cellmates. He heard every anxious breath taken and expelled, every rhythmic heartbeat, every rush of blood pulsing through the veins of all three humans, who were little more than arm's reach from him inside the room.

His mouth watered feverishly at the thought. Behind his flattened upper lip, the points of his fangs pressed like twin daggers into the cushion of his tongue. His vision started to tighten, burning amber as his pupils narrowed to thin slits under his closed lids.

Fuck. This was a bad place for him to be, especially in his condition.

Bad place, bad idea. Bad damned odds of walking away from this whole situation in any way, shape, or form.

Not that he'd given a shit about bad ideas and doomed outcomes when he'd offered himself up to the police on the front lawn of the Order's estate earlier that day. His only concern had been protecting his friends. Giving them the opportunity—very likely their only prayer of a chance—to avoid discovery by human law enforcement and, he hoped, find a way to clear out of the compound and get to someplace safe.

And so he hadn't resisted when the cops clamped handcuffs on him and hauled him into the station. He'd cooperated during the seven hours of interrogation, doling out just enough information to the local boys and the feds to satisfy their endless questioning and keep them focused solely on him as the kingpin and mastermind of the violence that had taken place in the city over the last couple of days. Violence that had begun a few nights ago with a holiday party shooting at an up-and-coming young politician's swank North Shore home.

The botched assassination attempt had been Chase's doing, but the intended target wasn't the golden-boy senator or even his high-profile guest of honor, the United States vice president, as the cops and federal agents were inclined to believe. Chase had been gun-

ning for a vampire named Dragos that night. The Order
had been hunting Dragos for more than a year, and suddenly Chase had found the bastard rubbing elbows with
influential, well-connected humans, passing himself off
as one of them. To what end, Chase could only imagine,
and none of it was good. Which is why, when he saw the
opportunity to act, he didn't hesitate to pull the trigger
on the son of a bitch.

But he'd failed.

Not only had Dragos apparently walked away from
the assault, but Chase found himself the focus of every
media outlet in the country in the hours that followed.
He'd been spotted at the senator's party, and the eyewitness had given law enforcement a nearly photographic description of him.

Couple that with a bombing the next day at Boston's
United Nations and a police pursuit of the suspects—a
carload of heavily armed backwoods malcontents who
led the cops right to the Order's front door—and Boston's finest were sure they had uncovered a major domestic terrorist cell.

A misconception Chase was happy to indulge, at least
for the time being.

He'd spent the daylight hours inside the station, content to let the cops believe he was cooperative and under
their control. The longer he sat there, pretending that
the blame for all that had gone down lately rested
squarely on him, telling them all the things they wanted
to hear, the less impatient law enforcement was to stake
out the mansion or raid the place. He'd done all he
could to deflect attention from his friends at the compound. If they hadn't used the time wisely and evacu-
ated by now, there wasn't much he could do to fix that.

As for him, he had to get moving too.

He had payback to deliver on Dragos—payback and then some. The bastard had stepped up his game in the past few weeks, and after this latest strike, which had nearly exposed the Order to humankind, Chase dreaded to think what Dragos might be willing to do next. For what wasn't the first time, Chase considered the senator Dragos had been currying favor from lately. The man was in danger purely by association, if Dragos hadn't already recruited him into service since Chase had last seen him.

And if Dragos had turned a United States senator into one of his Minions—particularly a senator with Robert Clarence's personal access to the White House via his friendship with his university mentor, the vice president? The ramifications were unthinkable. The fallout from a move like that would be irreparable.

All the more reason to get the hell out of this place ASAP. He had to make sure Senator Robert Clarence wasn't already under Dragos's control. Better still, he had to find Dragos. He had to take him out once and for all, even if he had to do it single-handed.

The metal handcuffs at his back couldn't hold him any longer than he allowed. Neither could this locked room, nor any of the cops who'd strayed by the hallway and paused to glower in at him through the small glass pane in the holding cell's door.

Night had fallen. Chase knew that without the benefit of a clock on the bare walls or a window looking onto the city street outside the building. He could feel it in his bones, all the way to his weak and starving marrow. And with the night came the reminder of his hunger, the wild thirst that owned him now.

He shoved it down deep inside him and rallied his thoughts around his unfinished business with Dragos.

Hard to do when Man of the Year and his oozing cat scratches were making a slow swagger toward Chase's seat in the corner of the small room.

"Fuckin' cops, eh? Think they can leave us sitting in here without food or water, shackle us up together like a bunch of animals." He scoffed and planted his ass down next to Chase on the bench. "What'd they bust you for?"

Chase didn't answer. It took enough effort just to contain the low growl that was curling up from the back of his parched throat. He kept his head down, eyes averted so the human wouldn't catch the hungered glow radiating out of them.

"Whatta ya, too good to make conversation or sumthin'?"

He felt the guy sizing him up, checking out the sweats and T-shirt Chase had been wearing when the cops brought him in—the same clothes he'd had on in the compound's subterranean infirmary in the moments before he'd broken loose and ran topside in the effort to spare his friends. He'd been barefoot then too, but now he sported a pair of black plastic shower shoes, courtesy of the Suffolk County jail.

Even with his short blond hair raked down over his brow, his gaze averted, Chase could sense the human's eyes fixed on him. "Looks like somebody banged you up pretty good too, sport. Ya leg is bleedin' through ya pants."

So it was. Chase glanced at the small red bloom that was seeping through the gray fabric covering his right thigh. Bad sign, his wounds from the other night still not healing up. He needed blood for that.

"Cops do that to you, or what, man?"

"Or what," Chase muttered, his voice rough like

gravel. He slid a low glance at the human and let his upper lip curl back from just the tips of his fangs.

"Motherfu—" The big man's eyes flew wide. "What the fuck!"

He scrambled away from Chase in a clumsy back-pedal that had him knocking into the holding cell door just as a pair of uniformed officers were opening it.

"Time to take a walk, fellas," the first cop said. He looked around the room, from the pedophile and the junkie, both oblivious to anything but their own misery, to the bruiser who now had his spine plastered against the opposite wall, jaw slack, sucking in air like he'd just run a marathon. "We got a problem in here?"

Chase lifted his chin only high enough to send a narrow glare at the wheezing human across the room. This time, he kept his lips closed and schooled the amber glow of his irises into a dull glimmer. But the threat was there, and the big, tough wife-beater seemed unwilling to test him.

"N-naw," he stammered, and gave a quick shake of his head. "No problem in here, Officer. Everything's cool."

"Good." The cop strode farther into the holding cell while his partner held the door open. "Everybody up. Follow me." He paused in front of Chase and jerked his chin in the direction of the hallway outside. "You first, asshole."

Chase rose from the bench. At six-and-a-half-feet tall, he towered over the officer and the other humans in the cell with him. Although he'd never worked out a minute in his life, thanks to Breed genetics and a metabolism that ran like a high-performance vehicle, the muscular bulk of his body dwarfed the gym-rat cop. As if to assert his authority over Chase, the human drew up his chest and pointed him toward the door, letting his other hand settle on the butt of his holstered pistol.

Chase walked ahead of him, but only because it would be less hassle to make his escape from the hallway than from inside the holding cell.

Behind him, the pedophile's voice was oily, overly polite. "Would it be all right to ask where you're taking us, Officer?"

"This way," the other cop said, directing the group of them past the desk clerk in the hall and toward a length of corridor that stretched out in a long track toward the back of the station.

Chase stalked along the worn industrial-grade linoleum, gauging the opportune moment for him to make his break and speed out of the station before any of the humans could realize he was gone. It was a risky move, one certain to leave a hell of a lot of questions in its wake, but unfortunately he didn't see much choice.

As he prepared to take that first step toward freedom, a metal door opened at the far end of the corridor. Cold night air swept in, fine December snowflakes dancing around the tall, slender form of a young woman. She was bundled in a hooded, long wool coat. Waves of caramel-brown hair clung to her chill-reddened cheeks and drooped down toward calm, intelligent eyes.

Chase froze, watching as she stomped some of the fresh snow from her glossy leather boots and turned to say something to the police officer who accompanied her into the station.

Holy hell. It was the witness from the senator's party.

The cop escorting her inside caught Chase's gaze and his face went tight. With a scowl at the officers leading the poorly timed perp parade, he steered Senator Clarence's attractive personal assistant into a room off the corridor and out of view.

"Keep moving," said the cop at the rear of the group.

If Chase wanted to reach the senator, he figured there was a good chance Bobby Clarence might be in the police station tonight along with his pretty aide.

Curious enough to find out, Chase reconsidered his plan to bolt. Instead he fell in line and let the cops march him farther down the corridor toward the room where his eyewitness had gone.

CHAPTER
Three

"Please make yourself comfortable, Ms. Fairchild. This shouldn't take long." The police detective who met her at the station opened the door to the witness viewing room and waited as she walked in ahead of him. Several grim-faced men in dark suits and a handful of uniformed officers were already waiting inside.

Tavia recognized the federal agents, men she'd first been introduced to in the hours following the recent shooting at the senator's party. She nodded to the group in greeting as she stepped farther into the room.

It was movie-theater dark inside, the only light coming from the oversized pane of glass that looked into the empty lineup area on the other side. Overhead fluorescent panels bathed the room in a stark white glow that didn't make the place any more inviting. A height measurement chart traveled the length of the back wall, with the numbers 1 through 5 stenciled in evenly placed intervals above the seven-foot mark.

The detective gestured to one of several vinyl-upholstered chairs positioned in front of the large window. "We'll be starting soon, Ms. Fairchild. Have a seat, if you like."

"I'd prefer to stand," she replied. "And please, Detective Avery, call me Tavia."

He nodded, then strode over to a watercooler and countertop coffeemaker in the far corner. "I'd offer you coffee, but it's nasty even when it's freshly made. End of the day like this, it's worse than crude oil." He put a paper cup under the watercooler dispenser and pushed the lever. The clear jug belched a few big bubbles as the cup filled. "House white," he said, turning to hold the water out to her. "Yours, if you'd like it."

"No, thank you." Although she appreciated his efforts to make her feel at ease, she wasn't interested in pleasantries or delays. She had a job to do here, and a laptop full of schedules, spreadsheets, and presentations to be reviewed once she got home. Normally she didn't mind long hours of work that spilled into long nights of the same. God knew, she didn't have to worry about a social life getting in the way.

But she was on edge tonight, feeling the strange mix of mental hyperintensity and physical exhaustion that always dogged her after a round of treatments and examinations at her doctor's private clinic. She'd been under her specialist's care for most of the day, and while she wasn't thrilled about having to make an evening pit stop at the police station, part of her was anxious to see firsthand that the man who'd opened fire on a crowded room of people a few nights ago and then went on to orchestrate a bombing in the heart of the city this morning was, in fact, behind bars where he belonged.

Tavia walked closer to the viewing window and gave

it an experimental tap with her fingernail. "This glass must be fairly thick."

"Yep. Quarter-inch safety." Avery met her there and took a sip of water. "It's one-way glass, looks like a mirror on the other side. We can see them, but they can't see us. Same goes for audio; our room is soundproof, but we have speakers tuned in to monitor their side. So when the bad guys are standing against that wall out there, you don't have to worry about any of them being able to ID you or hear anything you say."

"I'm not worried." Tavia felt nothing but resolve as she met the middle-age man's eyes over the rim of the Dixie cup. She glanced at the other officers and agents. "I'm ready to do this. I want to do this."

"Okay. Now, in just a minute, a couple of officers are going to bring a group of four or five men into that room. All you have to do is have a good look at those men and tell me if any of them could be the man you saw at the senator's party the other night." The detective chuckled a little and shot a wink at his fellow officers. "After the detailed description you gave law enforcement following the shooting, I got a feeling you're gonna ace this exercise here tonight."

"Whatever I can do to help," she replied.

He swallowed the rest of his water and crushed the paper cup in his fist. "Normally we wouldn't disclose facts about our investigation, but since the guy confessed to everything and waived his rights to legal counsel, tonight's lineup is just a formality."

"He confessed?"

Avery nodded. "He knows we got him nailed on the trespassing and attempted murder charges. No way he could weasel out of that one when the sketch details you provided were a dead ringer for him and he's sporting fresh gunshot wounds from his escape."

"And the bombing downtown today?" Tavia prompted, looking to the federal agents for confirmation. "He's admitting responsibility for that too?"

One of the suits tipped his chin in acknowledgment. "Didn't even try to deny it. Says he orchestrated the whole thing."

"But I thought there were others involved. The news stations ran coverage of the police pursuit all day. I heard officers killed all three bombers at some local private estate."

"That's right," Avery cut in. "He stated he enlisted the three backwoods malcontents to rig the explosion at the city's UN building. Obviously not the sharpest tools in the shed, seeing how they led us right to him. Not that he put up any kind of fight. He came out of the house and surrendered to police right after they arrived on the property."

"You mean he lives there?" Tavia asked. She'd seen images of the mansion and its expansive grounds on the news. It was palatial. The pale limestone construction with its soaring four-story walls, black-lacquered doors, and high, arched windows seemed more suited to old-money, New England elite than a violent maniac with apparent terrorist leanings.

"We haven't been able to substantiate who actually owns the property," the detective told her. "The estate has been held in private trust for more than a hundred years. Got about ten layers of lawyers and legalese wrapped around the title to the place. Our perp claims he's been renting it for a few months, but he doesn't know anything about the owner. Says it came furnished, no contract, and he pays the rent in cash to one of the top law firms downtown."

"Has he said why he did all of this?" Tavia asked. "If he confessed to the shooting and the bombing, is he offering any excuse for what he's done?"

Detective Avery gave a loose shrug. "Why does any lunatic do these things? He didn't have a concrete answer for that. In fact, the guy is almost as much of an enigma as the place he's been living."

"How so?"

"We're not even sure what his real name is. The one he gave us doesn't have a social security number or any record of employment. No driver's license, no automobile registration, no credit report, voter card, nothing. It's like the guy's a ghost. The only thing we did turn up was a donation given to a Harvard University Alumni association made in his name. The trail dead-ends there."

"Well, that's a start, at least," Tavia replied.

The detective exhaled a grunt of a laugh. "It would be, I suppose. If the record didn't date back to the 1920s. Obviously it's not our bad guy. I may not be the best judge of age, but I feel pretty certain he's nowhere near ninety years old."

"No," Tavia murmured. Thinking back on the night of Senator Clarence's holiday party and the man she'd witnessed firing from the second-floor gallery of the house, she would have placed him somewhere around her age, mid-thirties at most. "A relative, maybe?"

"Maybe," the detective said. He glanced up as the door in the other room opened and a uniformed officer stepped in ahead of the line of men behind him. "Okay, here we go, Tavia. Showtime."

She nodded, then found herself taking a step back

from the one-way glass as the first of the suspects entered the lineup room.

It was him—the one she'd come to the station to identify.

She knew him on sight, instantly recognizing the chiseled, knife-edge cheekbones and the rigid, unforgiving jut of his squared jawline. His short golden-brown hair was disheveled, some of it drooping over his brow, but not enough to conceal the piercing color of his steel-blue eyes. And he was immense—every bit as tall and muscular as she remembered. His biceps bulged beneath the short sleeves of a white T-shirt. Loose-fitting heathered gray sweats hung from his slim hips and hinted at powerfully muscled thighs.

He prowled into the space with an air of defiance—of unapologetic arrogance—that made the fact that he was in a jail with his hands cuffed behind his back seem inconsequential. He walked ahead of the others, all long limbs and a loose gait that felt more animal than human. There was a slight limp in the otherwise smooth movement of his legs, she noticed. A spot of blood rode on his right thigh, a deep red splotch that soaked into the lighter fabric of his sweats. Tavia watched the stain grow a little with each long stride that carried him across the length of the lineup area. She shuddered a bit inside the warmth of her winter coat, feeling queasy. God, she never had been able to stand the sight of blood.

Over the speakers, one of the police officers instructed the man to stop at the number 4 position and face forward. He did, and when he was standing facing the glass, his eyes fixed squarely on her. Unerringly so.

A jolt of awareness arrowed through her. "Are you sure they can't—"

"I promise, you're perfectly safe and protected in here," Avery assured her.

And yet that scathing blue gaze stayed rooted on her, even after the last of the three other men was led into the lineup and made to face forward. Those other men slouched and shifted, anxious eyes held low beneath inclined heads or darting around and seeing nothing but their own reflection in the large pane of one-way glass.

"If you're ready," prompted the detective from beside her.

She nodded, letting her eyes travel down the line to the remaining three men even though there was no need. The others looked nothing like him. They were a rangy mix of shapes and sizes and ages. One man was rail-thin, with stringy brown hair hanging limply around his shoulders. Another was the size of a bull, broad shoulders and a big belly. He had a mean face framed by thick, dark waves and small eyes that glared out over the swollen red beak of his nose. The third was a balding lump of a man, probably in the neighborhood of fifty, who was sweating profusely under the bright glare of the spotlight.

And then there was *him* . . . the intense, almost cruelly handsome menace who still hadn't taken his eyes off her. Tavia wasn't the sort to let things rattle her, but she could hardly stand the weight of that stare—even if she was safely concealed in the darkened viewing area behind quarter-inch safety glass and surrounded by half a dozen armed law enforcement officers.

"That's him," she blurted, pointing toward position 4. Although it had to be impossible, she could have sworn she saw his mouth lift into a half smile as she raised her hand to single him out. "That's him, Detective Avery. He's the man I saw at the party that night."

Avery gave her shoulder a light pat as the cops in the other room began instructing the men to step forward one at a time. "I know I said this is just a formality, but we still need you to be sure, Tavia—"

"I'm absolutely certain of it," she replied, her tone crisp as the blood in her veins began to buzz with some kind of innate alarm. She glanced back into the other room just as Number 4 took his two steps forward. "There's no need to continue here. That man is the shooter. I would know his face anywhere."

"Okay, then. That's fine, Tavia." He chuckled. "What'd I tell ya? Done in no time. You did great."

She dismissed the praise as unnecessary, giving the officer a mild shake of her head. "Will there be anything else?"

"Ah, nope. It'll just take a few minutes for us to wrap things up here, and we can get you on your way. If you'd like me to see you home—"

"No, thank you. I'm sure I'll be fine." As she spoke, her eyes clashed once more with the man who might have killed someone at Senator Clarence's party. If he truly was the mastermind of the bombing downtown this morning too, then he had the lives of several innocent people on his hands. Tavia held that penetrating stare, hoping that he could see through the glass to the depth of contempt she held for him in her eyes. After a long moment, she pivoted away from the viewing window. "If that will be all, Detective, the senator has a big presentation tomorrow morning, and I have a lot of logistics and other work to catch up on yet tonight."

"Tavia Fairchild."

The deep growl—the unexpected sound of her name on a stranger's lips—made her freeze for a moment where she stood. She didn't have to wonder who spoke.

The low rumble of his voice went through her with the same cold certainty of the bullets he'd rained down on the crowd of party attendees the other night.

Still, shocked by what was happening, Tavia swiveled a questioning look on the detective and the other agents and officers. "This room . . . I thought you said—"

Avery sputtered an apology and grabbed for a wall-mounted phone next to the viewing window. As he spoke into the receiver, the man standing in the number 4 spot kept talking to her. He kept looking at her, as though there were nothing standing between her and his deadly focus.

He took a step forward. "Your boss is in a lot of trouble, Tavia. He's in danger. You could be too."

"Damn it! Get that son of a bitch under control right now," demanded one of the federal agents to the detective on the phone.

The officers in the lineup room snapped into action. "Number 4, shut up and get back in line!"

He ignored the order. Took another step forward, even as the second cop moved in from the other side of the room. "I need to find him, Tavia. He needs to know that Dragos will kill him—or worse. It might already be too late."

Mute, she shook her head. What he was saying made no sense. Senator Clarence was alive and well; she'd seen him at the office that morning, before he'd left for a full day of meetings and business engagements downtown.

"I don't know what you're talking about," she murmured, even though he shouldn't be able to hear her. He shouldn't be able to see her either, but he did. "I don't know anyone named Dragos."

Both cops moved in on him now. One on each restrained arm, they tried to haul him back toward the wall. He shook them off like they were nothing, all of his focus zeroed in on Tavia. "Listen to me. He was there that night. He was a guest at the party."

"No," she said, certain he was wrong now. She personally handwrote and addressed each of the 148 invitations. Her memory for things like that was infallible. If pressed, she could recite every name and recount every face on the guest list. There was no one there by that name that night.

"Dragos was there, Tavia." The cops in the lineup room made another grab for him. "He was there. I shot him. I only wish I would have killed the bastard."

She felt her head slowly moving side to side, her brows pinched as the lunacy of what he was saying sank in. There was only one casualty at the party. The only person wounded by the violence that night had been one of Senator Clarence's most generous campaign contributors, a successful local businessman and philanthropist named Drake Masters.

"You're crazy," she whispered. Yet even as she spoke the words, she didn't fully believe them herself. The man holding her gaze so improbably—so impossibly—through the glass didn't seem crazy. He seemed dangerous and intense, utterly certain of what he was saying. He seemed lethal, even with his hands cuffed behind his back.

He kept an unblinking lock on her eyes. Dismissing him as insane would have been easier to accept than the cold knot of dread that was forming in her stomach under the weight of his clear stare. No, whatever his intent the night of the senator's party, she doubted very much that it had been motivated by insanity.

Still, none of what he was saying made sense.

"This guy is deranged," said one of the feds. "Let's wrap this up and get the witness out of here."

Detective Avery nodded. "I apologize for this, Tavia. You don't need to be here any longer." He moved around in front of her. His face was drawn taut with a mix of bewilderment and annoyance as he held his arm out to indicate a path toward the hallway door. The other officers and federal agents slowly regrouped as well and started to fall in behind them.

In the lineup room, Tavia heard the shuffle and grunts of a physical struggle under way. She tried to peer around the detective, but he was already guiding her away from the window.

As they reached the viewing room door, there was a short knock on the other side before it opened ahead of them. Senator Clarence stood in the hallway, snowflakes clinging to his neatly combed hair and navy wool peacoat. "I'm sorry I couldn't be here sooner. My meeting with the mayor ran late, as usual." He glanced at Tavia and his friendly expression went a bit dark. "Is something wrong? Tavia, I've never seen you look so pale. What's going on in there?"

Before she could brush off his concern, the senator strode into the viewing room. "Gentlemen," he murmured, greeting the other law enforcement officials as he walked farther inside.

At his approach to the viewing window, a low growl erupted from inside the lineup area.

It was an inhuman sound. An otherworldly snarl that made the blood go cold in Tavia's veins. Alarm shot through her in an instant, every instinct clanging with warning. Something terrible was about to happen. She pivoted back into the room. "Senator Clarence, be careful—"

Too late.

The viewing window exploded.

Glass broke and shattered, spitting tiny pebbles in all directions as something huge came crashing through the opening and landed in a heap in the middle of the viewing room.

It was one of the men from the lineup—the dark-haired bull in the Patriots shirt. He was howling in pain, limbs twisted unnaturally. The skin on his face and neck and hands was torn open and bleeding from the impact.

Tavia shot a startled look behind her.

The large pane of one-way safety glass was nothing but air now.

Nothing but air . . . and, standing in front of its broken frame, a towering menace of hard muscle and deadly intent.

The handcuffs that had restrained him in the lineup dangled useless, one at each wrist. He'd somehow broken free of them. Good lord, how strong must he be if he was able to do not only that but also throw a full-grown man through a plate of safety glass? And how fast must he have moved to have done all of this before any of the officers in the lineup room could stop him?

Cold blue eyes looked past her, rooted like lasers onto Senator Clarence. "Goddamn Dragos," the man seethed, fury simmering in his gaze and in the low hiss of his voice. "He already got to you, didn't he? He already fucking owns you."

His right arm shot forward, reaching through the open space of the window. As swift as a cobra strike, he had the sleeve of Senator Clarence's coat in his fist. He yanked backward, pulling the senator off his feet. He hauled the man's entire weight with one hand, dragging him in mere instants through the broken glass and debris.

Oh, God. This man was going to kill Senator Clarence, right here and now.

"No." Tavia was moving before she realized it. She took hold of the metal handcuff that ringed his wrist and pulled with all she had. "No!"

Her paltry attempt to stop him hardly made him pause. But in that split-second moment, his gaze broke to hers. There was something unearthly in those eyes . . . something that seemed to crackle with unholy fire. Something that cleaved straight into the center of her being like the sharp edge of a blade, even as it stirred a dark curiosity that beckoned her closer.

Her heart was racing in her chest. Her pulse hammered, as loud as a drumbeat in her ears. For the first time in her life, Tavia Fairchild knew true terror. She stared into those strangely hypnotic blue eyes, and she screamed.

CHAPTER
Four

She didn't let go of him, even while her scream tore past her lips. Slender but deceptively strong fingers held on to the metal cuff at his wrist, as though her reflexes were ready for a fight regardless of the fear and panic that vibrated from all around the chaos-stricken room.

Tavia Fairchild was tenacious; Chase had to give her that.

She hadn't been afraid of him the night of the senator's party or a few minutes ago, when she'd looked him in the eyes through the one-way glass and condemned him to the cops and feds camped out in the viewing room.

He couldn't blame her for that. She and law enforcement both believed they were doing the right thing, trying to keep a dangerous man—a confessed killer—off the streets. Their human minds could not comprehend the kind of evil Chase and the rest of the Order were up against.

Nor did Tavia Fairchild have any idea that her boss was a dead man.

Senator Robert Clarence might look unchanged to mortal eyes, but Chase's Breed senses sniffed out the Minion the instant he walked into the viewing room. The man belonged to Dragos now, obedient to none but his Master. Chase saw the truth of it in the dull glint of the politician's gaze and in the utter lack of concern for himself or any other life in the room. Dragos had sent him to the police station. Chase meant to send the Minion back to the son of a bitch in pieces.

He swung his gaze away from Tavia Fairchild and ripped loose from her distracting grasp. "Where is Dragos?" He tightened his fist around the senator's arm and squeezed until he felt bones crack and pop against his palm. "Tell me now."

The Minion only howled in agony.

"Stand down!" shouted one of the cops from behind him in the lineup room. There was a scuffle of foot movement, a blur of motion in the viewing room as federal agents and the officers inside hustled to get Tavia clear of the struggle.

Chase squeezed the senator harder, shattering his forearm in a bruising grip. "I'm gonna find him. And you're gonna tell me where, you goddamn waste of—"

Something sharp slammed into his shoulder from behind. Not a bullet, but the piercing bite of fine twin barbs. Like fishhooks, sunk deep into his flesh. His ears filled with the rapid *clickety-clickety* staccato report of a Taser being discharged. At the same time, his body was pumped with fifty thousand volts of electricity. The current went through him in a violent jolt. The juice lit him up from scalp to heel, making his muscles scream in protest.

Chase roared, more from fury than pain. The hit was about as debilitating as a bee sting to one of his kind. He took a step forward, one hand still fastened on Senator Clarence, the other swinging around to find a better hold.

"For fuck's sake," someone in the viewing room gasped. "Did anyone check this guy for drugs? What the hell is he on?"

One of the feds in a dark suit had his semiauto out of its holster. "Hit this bastard again!" he commanded. "Take him down, damn it, or I'll make it permanent right here and now!"

Another Taser shot found its mark. The barbs latched on to the center of his spine this time, and he took another round of fifty thousand volts. The double whammy did the job well enough. Chase lost his grip on his prey. The instant Clarence was freed, several cops and feds rushed him and Tavia out of the room.

Chase swung his left arm around to rip away the electrodes that were stuck in the meat of his other shoulder. With the current from the second shot still riding his central nervous system, he charged the broken windowsill and made a clumsy leap onto the cracked metal frame.

The federal agent opened fire. So did one of the uniformed officers in the viewing room beside him.

Bullets chewed into Chase's chest and torso. Round after round, knocking him backward onto his heels. He staggered, looking down at the mess of red that was blooming all over him.

Not good. Not fucking good at all, but he was Breed. He could survive it.

And there was still a chance that he could get his

hands on Dragos's Minion before the cops whisked him out of the station . . .

While the fed reloaded his empty weapon, one of the straggler cops in the nearly empty viewing room edged forward, service pistol trained on Chase. "Stay where you are!" The cop was young, and his voice cracked a little, but his aim was steady. "Don't you fucking move, asshole."

Chase was dripping blood like water through a sieve. It pooled around his feet and in the broken glass that littered the floor. He took a step back, reaching inward for the speed and agility that was part of who—and what—he was. But the power wouldn't respond to his call.

His body was already compromised from the Bloodlust that had been nipping at his heels for so many months.

And he was losing blood. Too much, too fast.

But he could still smell Dragos's Minion somewhere in the building. He knew the mind slave was still within his reach, and there was another part of him—a tarnished bit of chivalry in him—that bristled at the thought of letting an innocent woman get within ten feet of one of Dragos's soulless servants.

He would see the Minion dead before he'd willingly allow Tavia Fairchild anywhere near that kind of evil.

Chase pivoted around, his fading vision seeking the door that would lead him to the corridor outside. He took a sluggish step, his feet dragging beneath him.

"Ah, shit," muttered one of the anxious cops.

A gun clicked hard behind him. The fed's voice again, all business. "One more step, and it's your funeral, asshole."

Chase couldn't have kept his legs from moving if he'd been shackled to an army tank.

He walked forward another pace.

The only shot he felt was the first one. The others hammered into him one after the other, until the floor went out from under him. He smelled gunpowder and a burst of spent human adrenaline. And as his legs crumpled, and his body came to a hard rest on the floor of the lineup room, he smelled the dark scent of his own blood pumping onto the field of filthy white linoleum in all directions around him.

The Breed male took his time making the short stroll from his chauffeured limousine standing at the curb and the private club tucked into the back of a narrow Chinatown alley. He took no bodyguards with him, made no cautionary glances into the surrounding gloom of the wintry streets or night-cloaked shadows of the buildings rising up on all sides of him.

Not tonight.

Tonight, he strode into the heart of Boston—into the heart of the Order's domain—without a single care. In place of guards, he'd opted for more amusing, more serviceable, companions. The pair of delectable human females hurried to keep pace with him, their high heels clicking rapidly on the ice-crusted pavement. He didn't know their names, didn't care. They were merely playthings, the leggy redhead and the fresh-faced blonde selected by him a few minutes ago, as he'd noticed the underage young women waiting on line to get into LaNotte, the city's current hot spot.

They trotted along after him, giggling and eager, as he approached the large bulk of a Breed male posted as sentry near the arched vestibule and metal door of the private club. The guard, an Enforcement Agency brute named Taggart who'd done the odd job for him during his tenure in the highest ranks of that impotent organization, glowered as he took up a forbidding stance in front of the door. But then the beady eyes under the heavy brow widened in surprise and recognition.

"Sir," Taggart murmured, offering a bow of his head as he reached for the door, opened it, and stepped aside to permit the trio into the club.

The respect was welcome, as was the feeling of freedom that he wore around his shoulders like a king's mantle as he cut through the crowded room of Breed males and scantily clad human men and women who provided the club's specialized entertainment. On the central stage, a dark-skinned beauty wrapped her naked body around a Lucite pole with the boneless grace of a serpent. At the tables and banquettes below the raised platform of the stage, dozens of Breed males watched in rapt attention. Still others reclined in their booths and private alcoves, enjoying more personalized services from the humans employed by this Agency-run sip-and-strip.

Yet despite the various sex acts and blood-drinking taking place on the floor of the club, there was an air of restraint about the place. Breed law prohibited the killing of humans, and for most members of the Enforcement Agency in particular, that law was inviolable. It was as sacrosanct as the tenet of secrecy, the vow that had allowed the Breed to live alongside mankind—to feed upon them—undetected and unchallenged for centuries.

For some, like him and the other male now making

his way through the club to greet him, that shackle had long begun to chafe.

Dragos watched as his lieutenant approached. He was one of a handful of like-minded, loyal members of Dragos's inner circle—a dwindling handful, thanks to a number of fuck-ups and failures along the way that had forced him to cull the weakest members from the herd. But that was behind him now. He was looking ahead, toward victory. It was so near, he could practically taste it on his tongue. "Good evening, Deputy Director Pike."

"Sir." The Enforcement Agent cast a furtive look around him before he met Dragos's gaze. "This is a . . . well, sir, it's an unexpected pleasure to see you here in the city."

"Then why do you look as though you're about to piss yourself?" Dragos replied, baring his teeth in a brief smile. Usually an unannounced, personal appearance from him meant a head was about to roll. "Relax, Pike. I'm here on pleasure tonight, not business."

"So, nothing is wrong, sir?"

"Not at all," Dragos replied.

His lieutenant still didn't look comfortable. He kept his voice lowered, no doubt afraid of being seen speaking too familiarly with him in such a public place. "But, sir, do you really think it's wise coming into the city like this—or coming here, of all places? It was only last week that the Order sent two of their warriors into this club asking questions about you."

Dragos gave a mild shake of his head. "I'm not concerned about the Order. They have their hands full right now. I saw to that personally today."

Pike stared for a moment. "The rumors are true? The Order's compound was uncovered by the hu—" Looking at Dragos's two mortal companions, Pike abruptly cleared his throat. "They were found out by local police?"

Dragos grinned. "Let's just say Boston's finest had a little help in that area."

The Breed male returned the smile, but his eyes kept straying uncertainly from Dragos to the pair of human females latched on to him from both sides. Dragos shrugged idly at the question in his cautious lieutenant's eyes. "Speak freely, Pike. I fed them so much liquor and cocaine on the way over, they won't remember their names in the morning. If I let them survive that long," he drawled, leering at the young women he could hardly wait to sample.

"Are you saying that the bombing downtown this morning and the police chase of the suspects that followed—"

"That's precisely what I'm saying, Pike." Dragos watched the impressed expression of his lieutenant deepen. "From the orchestration of the explosion by the Minions I recruited to do the job, to the pursuit that led law enforcement right to Lucan Thorne's front door. All of it was my doing."

"I hear one of the warriors is in police custody. Did they really arrest Sterling Chase?"

Dragos nodded. The warrior's apparent voluntary surrender was the one detail he hadn't arranged or foreseen in this entire offensive strike against the Order. He still wasn't quite sure what to make of that, but he'd sent his newest Minion servants to look in on the situation at the jail downtown. In fact, he should be hearing from the senator with a full report anytime now.

"Word on the street says Chase is nearly Rogue," Pike said. "Doesn't surprise me to hear that, I suppose. After the way he came in here looking for you last week with that other warrior—the reports I saw about how many Agents he injured and the way he fought like a rabid dog—doesn't sound like he's got far to fall before Bloodlust claims him for good. Hard to believe he's the same Sterling Chase of just a few years ago. Back then, it was accepted fact that he was headed straight for the top ranks of the Agency."

Dragos exhaled a sigh, instantly bored with Agent Pike's pointless meander down memory lane. "Let the son of a bitch go Rogue or die in human custody—I could give a flying fuck. One less warrior to contend with is all that matters to me."

"Of course, sir," Pike responded crisply. "I couldn't agree more."

Dragos dismissed the fawning obeisance with a curt wave. "I need a table, Pike." As he spoke, he reached out to pet the silky blond hair of one of his female companions. Not to neglect the redhead, he turned to her and stroked the long, slender column of her throat. "I'll take that one, near the stage."

It was the best in the house, a large half-moon leather banquette and table, centrally located, with a view both of the dancers onstage and the rest of the club. And it was also currently occupied by no fewer than eight Breed males, most of them of equal or higher rank than Deputy Director Arno Pike.

Although his lieutenant hardly looked comfortable with the command, he jogged off to do Dragos's bidding. There were a few turned heads from the Agents at the table, a couple of affronted stares and disgruntled scowls, but Pike cleared the men out, then hurried back to see Dragos to his seat.

Dragos prowled through the Agency club like he owned it.

Hell, it wouldn't be long before he did, in fact, own this club, the city, and everyone in it—Breed and human alike.

He wouldn't be satisfied until the whole goddamn world was kneeling at his feet.

Soon, he assured himself. His plan had been long in the making—several centuries of laying the foundation and setting each building block into its proper place. It was all coming together now, and not even the Order would be able to interfere with his goals.

He slid onto the sumptuous leather seat at his newly acquired table, the pretty redhead on one side of him, the wide-eyed blonde on the other. "Join us, Pike. Everyone here has already seen that your allegiance is to me. Besides, there's no need to pretend anymore. The game has changed as of this morning. Now *I* make the rules."

As Pike settled in next to the blonde, Dragos turned an appreciative eye on the other woman. The skin of her throat and generously exposed cleavage was as pale as cream, almost translucent. Fine blue veins ticked near her collarbone, tempting his fangs from his gums. The sharp canines swelled in his mouth. He descended on her in a single, punching strike—too swiftly for her to do anything more than gasp as he pierced her carotid and drew a long, hard swallow from the pulsing wound.

After a couple of greedy pulls, he pivoted to sample her friend on the other side of him. He was even less gentle with her, digging his fingers into her arms when she whimpered, trying to squirm out of his hold as he bit her. He could have calmed her with a light trance, a consideration most of his kind offered freely to their blood Hosts. But where was the fun in that?

Dragos fed openly from both women, his eyes on

Arno Pike, who was fighting like hell to keep the savage part of himself in check amid so much fresh, flowing blood. His eyes glowed as bright as embers, pupils narrowed to thin vertical slits. Even though his lips were clamped tightly closed, Dragos knew Pike's mouth would be full with the extended length of his fangs.

Dragos laughed. He reached over and grabbed a fistful of the male's Enforcement Agency standard issue black suit and white shirt, hauling him closer. "Why do you deny yourself? What are you afraid of—the Order?" He shook his head. "This is what we've been working toward. This freedom. It is the birthright of all the Breed."

Pike released a gust of air from his lungs. With the exhalation, his lips curled away from his teeth and fangs, baring them on a hungered growl as the scent of fresh blood wreathed the banquette. Pike swiveled his amber gaze onto the blonde, who now drooped in the booth between them, narcotics and blood loss leaving her dazed and unaware of what was happening.

"Take her," Dragos told his lieutenant. "She's yours."

With a snarl, Pike swung the woman onto the table and tore her dress open down the front. He fell upon her like an animal, feeding in a public spectacle that drew every pair of Breed eyes in the place.

Dragos watched with voyeuristic pleasure, not only for the unleashed, frenzied lust of his lieutenant but for the avid interest of the other males who slowly closed in from all sides, fangs gleaming, amber stares smoldering, in the relentless pound of the strobe lights ricocheting out from the stage.

How good it felt to know this sense of relaxation, of pure, predatory power. It had been too long since he'd been able to move about in public this freely, without the Order forever breathing down his neck, disrupting him at nearly every turn. He was finished running from Lucan Thorne and his warriors. The blow he delivered to them today should have been signal enough of that. Now it was their turn to go to ground. Their turn to wonder where he might strike next, and how deeply.

Right now, he was in charge.

He owned this moment and everything that would take place within it.

And he wasn't satisfied, not yet.

He sent the redhead up on the table with a command whispered into her ear. She disrobed as he'd instructed her, gyrating in time to the hard bass thumping from the club's sound system and trailing her slender fingers through the twin rivulets of blood that streaked down from the open bite wound in her neck.

The ranks tightened, sharks gathering for the kill. Only a few seconds passed before the first vampire broke from the crowd to leap up onto the table with her.

As he took her throat in his teeth, Dragos nodded his approval. "Drink," he said, then stood to address the crowd. "Take as much as you want, all of you! There are no laws here tonight. No one to stop us from being what we truly are."

With an assenting roar, another male vaulted up onto the table to drink from the redhead's wrist. Then another, fastening his mouth around her other one.

In a far corner of the club, a woman's scream ripped loose then fell abruptly silent as someone else took his fill in the shadows. More and more feedings began, punctuated here and there by the shrieked alarm of the humans who were being savaged by the suddenly ravenous pack of thirsting Breed vampires.

Dragos observed it all with the satisfaction of a barbarian king at home in his arena.

The coppery fragrance of spilling human blood rose up from everywhere, turning the club into an orgy of sex and savagery and unchecked madness.

Dragos savored the raw, violent energy vibrating all around him. This was power. This was freedom, at last.

And in this moment—this perfect, terrible moment—not even the Order could take it from him.

Let them learn what he'd done here and seethe that they hadn't been there to stop him. Let them tear apart the Enforcement Agency in a furious quest to find his secret allies. They could dismantle the entire organization for all he cared. His operation would only benefit from any distraction on the Order's part. And soon enough, nothing they did would matter anymore.

He would own them, the same way he would own the rest of the peasants of this insignificant, unsuspecting world.

With triumph surging through his veins, Dragos threw his head back and roared like the beast he'd been born to be.

CHAPTER
Five

"Do you think they killed him?"

"Hmm?" Senator Clarence grunted from his seat beside Tavia in the back of the FBI's fast-moving black Suburban. He hadn't spoken for most of the drive out of the city, except to insist that he and the federal agents personally ensured she'd make it home safely. Now he glanced over at her, his expression oddly bland, considering what had happened back at the police station.

Maybe it was shock. God knew, she was still in a state of disbelief herself. "There was so much gunfire as they took us out of that room . . . I just wondered if you think the police shot and killed that man."

"I wouldn't be surprised if they did." The senator gave a casual shrug. "I wouldn't care either. Nor should you, Tavia. There's no room in our world for someone like him. If it had been up to me, I would have pumped the bastard's brain full of lead myself."

The coldness of the remark disturbed her. She had known Bobby Clarence for nearly three years, first as an intern for him when he was assistant district attorney, then as his personal assistant from the time he decided to run for a seat in the Senate. She knew he drew a hard line when it came to national security and fighting terrorism; he'd built his entire campaign on his commitment to that platform. But she'd never heard him speak so callously about the life—or the presumed death—of another person.

Tavia turned away, watching the snowy landscape zoom past the dark-tinted window as the vehicle raced north along the highway, leaving the city proper miles behind them. "Who is Dragos?"

Because he was so quiet, at first she thought the senator hadn't heard her. But when she glanced back at him once more, he was staring right at her. Right *through* her, it seemed. A strange prickle edged its way up the back of her neck, there and gone, as her boss's handsome face relaxed into a look of mild confusion. "I don't know what you mean, Tavia. Should I know the name?"

"He seemed to think you did—that man back at the station." She searched the senator's face for some sign of recognition but saw none there. "Before you came into the room, he told me you were in danger from someone called Dragos. He said we both could be in danger. He wanted to warn you—"

Senator Clarence's eyes narrowed. "He said all of this to you? You spoke to this man? When?"

"I didn't speak to him. Not exactly." She was still trying to make sense of everything that had occurred tonight. "He saw me through the window in the viewing room. He started talking, saying a lot of strange things."

The senator slowly shook his head. "Paranoid, crazy things from the sound of it, Tavia."

"Yes, except he didn't seem crazy to me. He seemed disturbed and volatile, but not crazy." She stared at her boss, watching as he rubbed idly at his wrist—the same wrist that had been crushed in the punishing hold of the man who'd broken free of his handcuffs and breached a supposedly secure witness room before half a dozen police officers and federal agents could contain the situation. All so he could get his hands on Senator Clarence. "When he saw you, he said he was already too late. He said this person, Dragos, owned you. What did he mean by that? Why did he think you know this person, or where to find him?"

A tendon ticked in the lean, chiseled jaw. "I'm sure I don't know, Tavia. Politicians make a lot of enemies—some of them harmless crackpots, others destructive sociopaths who crave attention and think that violence and terror are the best ways to get it. Who knows what sins this lunatic thinks I'm guilty of. All I know is, he came to my house to commit murder, and when he failed in that, he and his militant pals decided to blow up a government building and take several innocent lives in the process. The only clear danger any of us seemed to be in tonight was coming from him and him alone."

Tavia acknowledged those sober facts with a grim nod. She couldn't argue with any of it, and she didn't know why she felt compelled to dissect and examine any of what she had heard in the police station viewing room. She didn't know why she couldn't get the man and every bizarre word he said out of her mind.

And his eyes . . .

She could still see their steely blue color, and the intensity with which he held her in his unflinching—undeniably sane—stare.

She could still feel the peculiar heat that seemed to radiate out from those stormy irises in that instant when their gazes clashed and held, mere seconds before the Tasers' probes bit into him and the bullets began to fly.

She was so deep in her thoughts, she jumped a little when the senator lightly smacked his palm against his knee. "Ah, damn. I knew I was forgetting something."

"What is it?" she asked, turning to look at him as the SUV exited the highway to begin the couple-mile stretch of rural blacktop that would lead to her house.

He gave her a sheepish look, the one he usually reserved for those times when he was about to ask her to work the entire weekend or help him find a last-minute gift for some society function hostess whom it was crucial he impress. "Tomorrow morning is the charity breakfast for the children's hospital."

Tavia nodded. "Eight o'clock at Copley Place. I sent your dry cleaning to your house and emailed your speech to both your mobile and your home computer before I left the office for the police station tonight."

She'd covered all the bases for him, as usual, but he didn't look satisfied. He winced a bit. "I was thinking of making some changes to the speech. Actually I was hoping you might help me rewrite it completely. With everything that's been going on lately, I haven't had a chance to talk to you about it. I'm sorry, Tavia. And I know you're probably exhausted, but can you spare me an hour or so tonight yet? We can work at my house, since we're halfway to Marblehead already—"

"I can't," she replied, the words tumbling out even before she realized she was going to say them. She'd never refused any task he gave her, but something about tonight—something about Bobby Clarence himself—made her instincts stir with an odd wariness. She shook her head, even as his look of surprise turned to one of disappointment, then cool disapproval. "I wish I could help, but my aunt is very sick. I have her medicine right here." She reached into her purse and pulled out a prescription bottle full of white pills. "I'm afraid if I'm not there to make sure she takes it and has a proper meal . . ."

"Of course. I understand," the senator replied. He was aware of her general living situation—the fact that her aunt Sarah had raised her alone for most of Tavia's life. She was the only family Tavia had ever known, and the fact that Tavia would drop everything to take care of the older woman was no stretch. At least that much was true.

The Suburban slowed, crunching ice and snow under its tires, as they approached the little gray Cape with its neat black shutters, Christmas wreath on the front door, and cheery yellow light glowing from nearly every window. Tavia met the senator's watchful gaze from across the wide bench seat. "I'm sorry I can't help this time. I'm sure your changes will be just fine."

He nodded. "Give your aunt Sarah my best. Tell her I hope she feels better soon." His mouth curved into a smile that might have looked sympathetic if not for the dark gleam of doubt in his eyes. "I'll see you in the morning, Tavia. We can talk more then."

She opened the SUV door and started to climb out.

Perhaps she should have bitten her tongue, but a question had been riding the tip of it since the moment they left the police station—a question that disturbed her almost as much as the ones now swirling in her head about the senator himself. In fact, it was something that had been nagging at her even longer than that . . . from sometime last week, and the instant she first laid eyes on one of Bobby Clarence's most generous supporters.

She paused outside the vehicle, pivoting to peer in at the senator. "How well do you know Drake Masters?"

She saw it then. The slip in an otherwise careful facade.

"Drake Masters," he said, less a question than a demand. The senator cleared his throat and attempted to school his features into a mask of mild befuddlement, but Tavia had already seen past it. "What does Drake Masters have to do with anything?"

She let the question linger and stretch out. She didn't have an answer for it. Not yet.

But she fully intended to find out.

"I have to go now," she said, and turned to make the short walk up to the house.

Aunt Sarah met her at the door, dressed in a red velour track suit with a green Christmas-themed apron tied around her hips. Holiday music poured out into the night, along with the aroma of fresh-baked bread and cinnamon and something meaty simmering on the stove. "There you are, at last," the older woman exclaimed. "Why haven't you been answering your cell phone? I've been trying to reach you all evening."

"I'm sorry. I must have the ringer turned off." Tavia stepped inside the house and watched as the black SUV slowly rolled away from the curb. "It's been a long day, Aunt Sarah. I should have called. I hope you didn't worry."

"Of course I worried. I love you." Her brown eyes crinkled at the corners as she looked Tavia over. "How was your visit with Dr. Lewis? Did you tell him about the night terrors and headaches you've been having lately? Did you pick up your medicine?"

"The appointment went fine, same as the last ten thousand of them. Got my new drug supply right here." Tavia shook her purse, making the pill bottle rattle as she met her aunt's welcoming gaze. She smiled at the older woman and all her questions and worry. It was the first real sense of comfort, of normalcy, she'd had all day. "I love you too, Aunt Sarah. What's for dinner?"

At first, Chase thought he was in hell. In addition to feeling as though he'd been run over by a truck—repeatedly—his mouth was cotton-dry and his head was ringing with the relentless beep and hiss of electronic machinery somewhere nearby.

He lay there for a moment, eyes closed, senses still attempting to come back online after a long, smothering sleep. Someone was in the room with him. Two people. Humans, a male and a female. They were speaking softly from both sides of him, the woman covering his bare legs with a thin sheet and blanket while the man reached over Chase's head to press buttons on one of the complaining monitors.

"BP's still wicked high," said the man, his booming Boston-roughened voice coming out of what sounded like a deep barrel chest. "Heart rate ain't come down much in the last hour either. This fella's body idles as fast as a damn race car."

"He's just lucky to be alive," replied the woman. "With all those bullet holes in him, his vitals should be flatlining, not clocking off the charts." She sounded middle age and tired, a wad of minty gum snapping as she chewed it noisily while she spoke. "I hear the lab screwed up his blood work again, so they're rerunning everything for the third time. Buncha clowns down there tonight or something, I swear to God. Meantime, looks like I'm going to have to start another bag of O negative before the next shift change."

Holy shit.

He wasn't dead, wasn't in hell either. He was in a human medical facility. Judging from the cold metal handcuff that secured his right wrist to the rail of the wheeled bed, Chase guessed he was still technically in the county lockup.

He had to get the fuck out of there.

His immediate instinct was to leap up and haul ass away from the place, before his strange lab results and unusual blood work started raising questions that no human being would be eager to learn the answers to. And as if that wasn't enough reason, there was also the fact that Dragos had recruited another Minion. Fury kindled below the thick fog of his injuries when he recalled the soulless glimmer of Senator Clarence's gaze. It burned even hotter when he thought of Tavia Fairchild, an innocent woman unaware of the evil looming close enough to touch her.

Chase had to do something. But he didn't have the strength to get up or get out. He couldn't even summon the wherewithal to lift his heavy eyelids.

He needed blood.

Not the packaged kind Nurse Doublemint was talking about, but fresh red cells, taken from an open human vein. The transfusions had probably kept his organs functioning in the time following the shooting, but in order for him to truly heal and regain all of his Breed strength and power, he needed to feed.

A lot.

And soon.

Moving beside him near the bed, the male nurse rearranged some of the tubes and tethers attached to Chase's free arm. "You hear about the other guy they brought back here from the situation in lockup tonight—the one this fella tried to use as a wrecking ball? He's busted up real bad."

The female exhaled a sharp grunt. "Oh, I heard about him all right. Severed spinal column, total paralysis from the neck down. Poetic justice, if you ask me."

"What do you mean?"

More gum-snapping and a whiff of peppermint as she leaned in to inspect one of Chase's chest wounds. "Before I came here, I used to work midnights over at Mass General. Admitted his wife to the ER more than once after he worked her over, then had an apparent attack of conscience and brought her in to be patched up. He always had some kind of excuse, like she ran into a wall or split her head open while she was cleaning. You won't see me crying that a guy like him is gonna spend the rest of his life flat on his ass, eating baby food and pissing in a bag."

"No shit." The male nurse blew out a low chuckle. "They don't say karma's a bitch for nothing."

"And so am I when I haven't had a cigarette in more than two hours," she said, chomping even harder on her gum. "Can you finish up here while I run down and have a quick smoke?"

"Yeah, sure. I'm almost done. Just need to prep a little nightcap for Mr., ah . . ." A pause as he looked up the name. "For Mr. Chase here. Something to take the edge off, after that suicide-by-lead-poisoning attempt he made tonight in the lineup room."

Nurse Doublemint stripped off her latex gloves with a violent snap that felt like a thunderclap in Chase's head.

"You're a doll, Mike. Be sure to turn the lights off when you're done in here, okay?"

"Yeah, yeah. Get outta here already. I got you covered."

Chase listened to the padding of the nurse's crepe-soled shoes as she left the room. The door settled closed with a whispered *snick*. Chase's senses began to bang with the impulse to act, to seize this chance and feed.

He peered through the slit of his parted eyelids. The male nurse was turned away, unwrapping a thin clear tube from a small plastic IV bag. He was a sizable man, as his voice had indicated—tall and strong, with thick shoulders bulking underneath his sky blue scrubs.

"All right, Mr. Chase. Got a bag of nighty-night for you here." He hung the bag on one of the hooked IV poles next to the bed, then leaned over Chase to pick up his left arm and attach the end of the tube to a readied line. "I promise you, this is some real good shit . . ."

Chase's eyes were fully open now.

"Jesus Christ!" The man's body jerked in alarm as he tried to leap back from the bed.

He didn't get far. Chase clamped his hand around the back of the human's neck and brought him down in a sudden burst of coiled power. It was all he had in him, but it was enough.

With the man's hoarse shouts muffled against the blanket at his chest, Chase sank his fangs into the human's neck.

He drank quickly, deeply, gulp after gulp. The coppery blood hit his parched tongue like fire, igniting his body's depleted cells and fueling his senses. It was an instantaneous flood of strength and power—the very thing that made it so addictive. He couldn't think about that now. Only one thing mattered, and that was getting out of this place.

The temptation to gorge himself was as powerful as it would be to any junkie, but as soon as Chase felt his power peak, he swept his tongue over the punctures and sealed the wound closed. The man was limp now, dazed from the feeding. To be safe, Chase placed the flat of his palm against the human's forehead, trancing him into a swift, heavy drowse. Chase pushed his heavy bulk off him with his free arm. The cuff on his other broke loose under a combination of mental command and sheer Breed strength.

Naked but for his many bandages, Chase sat up and began pulling the tubes and lines out of his arms. He freed himself of the tangle of medical apparatus, then hurried to strip the male nurse of his blue scrubs. He put them on, scowling when he got to the white Crocs that were easily two sizes too small for him.

Barefoot, Chase hefted the big human onto the bed in his place, clamping the heart rate monitor onto the nurse's finger before the machine had a chance to bleat in alarm. To be sure the human didn't wake up screaming the word "vampire," Chase made quick work of his memory, scrubbing the attack clean from his sleeping mind. After pulling the sheet and blanket up around the man's chin, Chase pivoted to head for the door.

Just as Nurse Doublemint was pushing it open ahead of her.

"I'm not sure, Darcy. I just got back from break," she called over her shoulder, her head turned back toward the nurses' station as she started to enter the room.

Chase drew back against the wall behind the door. His body was still riding the powerful high of its feeding, every muscle coiled and waiting for his command.

He didn't want to harm the woman, but if she saw him . . .

She lingered in the doorway and stared toward the bed where the big male nurse lay unmoving, still in a deep drowse. "Mike? You still in here?" she asked, speaking in a hushed tone so as not to wake the patient.

As she took a quiet step into the room, Chase pushed deeper into the shadows behind the open door. He gathered those shadows around him, calling on one of his personal abilities that was sometimes even more effective than the strength and brute power of his kind. He held the shadows close, bending them to his will as the woman peered around the room looking for her colleague.

"Michael?" She frowned, shivering a little in the cold of Chase's illusion. She pulled the fabric of her white cardigan tighter around her. "So much for remembering to turn off the lights when you were done."

With that, she pivoted on her heel and left, hitting the light switch on her way out.

The room went dark, and Chase released the curtain of gloom that had shielded him from her notice.

He glanced out the window of the door as she returned to the station up the hall and fell into a chatty conversation with the pair of young nurses manning it. Chase slipped out of the room in his stolen scrubs, his bare feet silent as he took the first step into the corridor toward escape.

They didn't see him.

Nor could any human eyes follow as he flashed with preternatural speed down the opposite length of the long hallway, as silent and stealthy as a ghost.

Once outside, Chase hit the street on foot. To the few

humans he passed, he was nothing but a cold gust amid the midnight flurries that fell from the dark sky. He knew exactly where he would go now. With predatory senses guiding him, he headed for a specific residence on the North Shore, as swift and certain as death itself.

CHAPTER
Six

Five hundred and thirty-two emails in his in-box since the afternoon—including the one Tavia Fairchild told him she'd sent containing his speech file for the morning fund-raiser.

Ever the efficient assistant, she'd gone to the trouble of including a separate file that provided anecdotal remarks about some of the people who'd be attending the charity breakfast. A social cheat sheet to assist him in maintaining his reputation for personality and effortless charm. He barely glanced at the document, finding it hard to care about the pet philanthropic ventures and causes du jour of a bunch of Back Bay socialites or the alma mater team standings of every deep-pocketed corporate executive on the guest list.

Under the low light of the desk lamp in his study, he flipped open his calendar and cast a disinterested eye over the sea of meetings and committees, public appearances and social engagements that filled the pages.

None of it mattered to him, not anymore.

Had it ever? He wasn't sure. He felt a cold sense of detachment from it all. Even from the sight of his own name, from his own being.

Oh, he still had a job to do. It was imperative that he continue his upwardly mobile career trajectory. But all of his old dreams and desires—the personal ambition that used to propel his every careful step—meant nothing to him now.

His life had a new purpose.

Drake Masters—Dragos, the only cause he served now—had shown him a truer path.

He'd made everything clear the last time they'd met. Was it only last night? He couldn't remember exactly how long it had been. Time, like everything else connected to the shell of who he'd once been, had somehow, somewhere, ceased to exist.

To him, it felt as though he'd belonged to his Master forever. There was nothing before or after him. Nothing beyond the purpose to serve at his pleasure and to protect him above all else.

Which is why the first thing he'd done upon returning to his North Shore residence was to contact his Master and inform him of what occurred at the police station with the Breed warrior in law enforcement custody.

He'd told his Master about Tavia Fairchild and all her questions—her careless suspicions—too. He'd hoped his Master would not be displeased that he had let the woman out of his sight, but there was no reprimand. In fact, his Master had seemed almost amused by the report.

"Leave the woman to me," he'd instructed. "I will deal with the inquisitive Tavia Fairchild personally. You have your orders, Minion. See that you complete them without delay."

And so he had.

The private audience was already in place for tomorrow evening, a personal favor impressed upon a longtime friend who had risen to one of the highest seats in the nation. His Master would be pleased. And by this time tomorrow, he would have another loyal servant added to his ranks.

The Minion smiled, eager to know his Master's approval.

He powered down his computer and was about to rise to go to bed when he heard a muffled noise in the hallway outside his study. He got up and walked to the closed door, then cautiously peered out.

One of his security detail lay motionless on the runner in the hall. His blood soaked the light-colored rug, leaking out swiftly from his slashed throat. The Minion cocked his head, listening to the unnatural quiet of his surroundings. There were no other guards in sight. No raised alarm from anywhere within the large house.

He'd had other men on armed watch tonight. Whoever was inside now had likely killed them all.

Breed.

The Minion's veins jangled with the warning. He drew back quickly into the study and pivoted to shut the door before the danger could reach him.

But it was too late for that.

Death was already in the room with him, manifesting from out of the shadows behind him. The Minion blinked and saw that the illusionary gloom had cleared. Standing in its place was the enemy of his Master. The warrior who should have been dead at the hands of the police tonight.

He was barefoot, water dripping from his snow-dampened hair and the sodden blue hospital scrubs that stretched tight and wet around his body. Blood splattered the front of him, though whether from the gunshot wounds he'd sustained at the police station or the spent lives of the men he'd killed on his way inside here, the Minion couldn't tell.

The Breed warrior took a step toward him, eyes throwing off vicious amber light. His fangs were huge, lethal daggers that could shred a body into pieces.

But the Minion wasn't afraid.

He was resolved.

This vampire had come to wring information from him, information he would never get, not even under the worst torture.

He knew that's what awaited him here tonight. Torture, and death.

"You will never defeat him," the Minion stated, devout in his faith of his Master's power. "You can't win."

But there was no uncertainty in the searing glower that leveled on him, only a wild fury that promised a hellish end.

His feet started moving beneath him, old instincts urging his body to flee this threat. He spun around and watched as a sudden stream of blood slashed in an arc across the wall and door in front of him.

His blood.

His hellish end, just beginning.

She was burning up.

Tavia shifted in her bed, suspended in that thick veil separating sleep from wakefulness. The sheets and comforter were too heavy, her body too warm beneath them in her cotton camisole and panties. In the daze of her fitful slumber, she pushed the covers away, but the heat stayed with her.

It was inside her, not the rash of sudden fire that sometimes swept across her skin and nerve endings when she went too long without her medicines, but another kind of heat. Something slow building and fluid, a hot unfurling from deep within her.

Sensation tingled at her breasts, a sweet ache that traveled over each nipple and swell, then down toward her belly. Eyes closed, sleep still holding her in its web, she arched into the pleasure, wanting the feeling to linger in one place yet hungry to feel it all over her too. Deep inside, her senses were coming alive, reaching, the same way her body roused to its erotic demand.

The heat licked a trail that plunged lower now, playing at the flare of her hip bone. Then down onto the tender flesh of her naked thigh. Her blood rushed through her veins and arteries. She could feel it surging with each rising beat of her heart.

Anticipation simmered as the hot, wet heat stirred the small nest of curls between her legs.

Yes. The silent plea echoed in the heavy pound of her pulse. *Yesss . . .*

She knew it was only a dream. Her semiconscious mind understood that this phantom lover seducing her now couldn't be real. She'd never been with a man. Had never felt a questing, hungered mouth on her body. Not even on her lips. She couldn't. Her reality was too fragile, too constricted by fear and shame.

But not now.

Not like this, when she was dizzy with arousal from a dream she couldn't bear to leave.

With sleep and pleasure enticing her to stay, she reached down to touch the part of her that was melting, alive with sensation. Her fingertips were his tongue, silky and relentless, kissing and stroking her in all the right places.

She pictured broad shoulders between her legs. Smooth skin and lean, hard muscle rubbing against her nakedness.

Surrender, let it all go. The low voice spoke inside her mind, the encouragements he murmured being so seductive she could feel his hot breath skating against her enlivened flesh. *I want to see you, taste you, all of you. I want to make you scream my name.*

But she didn't know his name, logic that tangled in the gossamer threads of the dream. She pushed away the intrusion of her conscience and sank further into her fantasy. She had no choice but to surrender, because the pleasure was coiling tighter now, her skin tingling, every inch of her on fire . . . on the verge of disintegration. She writhed on the bed, unable to take much more.

And then his voice was beside her ear. His mouth was wet and warm against her neck, his voice a deep vibration she felt all the way to her bones. *Let me taste you, Tavia . . .*

"Yes," she whispered into the darkness of her bedroom. "Oh, God. Yes."

She felt his mouth open on her neck, his tongue and teeth pressing down onto the tender flesh, piercing it. She cried out at the pain of his sharp bite, shock and pleasure exploding at once and sending the flood within her crashing over its banks.

She was drowning in the dream now, helplessly adrift as her phantom lover rose up to look at her where she lay beneath him.

It was *him.*

The man from the police lineup. The shooter from the

senator's party. The steely-eyed, deadly menace whose face had haunted her from the moment she first laid eyes on him.

Poised above her now in her dream, his gaze was no less cruel, still unflinching, devoid of mercy. His lips were parted, and his broad, sensual mouth—the mouth that had given her such pleasure—was slick and dark with blood.

Her blood.

The realization raked through her as startling as a blade against her skin.

He smiled then, beautiful and terrifying, baring the pearly tips of razor-sharp fangs . . .

"No!" Tavia jolted to full wakefulness at the sight of them, her horrified scream raw in her throat. She sat up, panting and shaken, even while her body still thrummed from release.

A knock on her bedroom door had her scrambling to cover herself.

"Tavia, are you all right?" the older woman's voice called through the closed door. "Is anything wrong?"

"I'm fine, Aunt Sarah. Nothing's wrong."

There was a hesitation, but only for a moment. "I heard you cry out in your sleep. Not another night terror, was it?"

No, something even worse, she thought. The night terrors had never started out so pleasantly, only to turn so hideous in the end. "It was nothing, really." She somehow managed to keep the distress from her voice. "I'm okay. Please don't worry. Go back to bed."

"You're sure? Can I get you anything?"

"No, thank you." Tavia closed her eyes in the darkness of her room, trying to forget the disturbing dream that was still ripe in her mind, still alive on her skin and in the pounding rhythm of her pulse. "Good night, Aunt Sarah. See you in the morning."

More silence as her worried aunt and caretaker waited outside her room. Then, finally, "All right. If you say so. Good night, sweetheart."

Tavia sat there for a long moment, listening to the sound of retreating footsteps and the soft creak of her aunt's bedroom door down the hall.

She swung her feet to the floor. Padded across the carpet to the cold tiles of her bathroom. Her face was pale and stricken in the medicine cabinet mirror. She slid the glass panel open and took out one of the monstrous pill bottles—the one Dr. Lewis prescribed to combat the anxiety attacks that had plagued her most of her life.

Tavia shook out one of the big white capsules and tossed it into her mouth, washing it down with a quick swig of water from the bathroom tap. Better make it a double. She'd never had a better reason to take the maximum dose. She swallowed the medicine and another mouthful of water, then headed back to bed.

Twenty minutes and she'd be under a heavy, medicated drowse. She climbed under the covers and waited for the powerful meds to obliterate all thought of the man who'd invaded her dreams like the dangerous criminal he'd proven himself to be.

CHAPTER
Seven

The enforcement agency hangout in Chinatown looked like the aftermath of a war zone.

Mathias Rowan, current director of the region for the Agency, struggled to ignore the dull throb of his emerging fangs as he stepped farther inside the private club to survey the carnage. Blood covered everything, from the floors and walls, seats and tabletops, to the raised platform of the stage—even the damn ceiling was foul with the stuff.

"Hell of an hour to call you down here like this, Director Rowan, but I thought you needed to see for yourself," said the Agent beside him.

It would be dawn soon, no time for any of their kind to be away from their Darkhavens with the sun about to rise. But a thing like this could not wait. A thing like this—such reckless, unspeakably savage anarchy—jeopardized all of their kind.

"I contacted you as soon as my team and I arrived to discover the situation, sir." The Agent's polished shoes crunched in broken glass and scattered debris as he came to a pause beside Rowan in the silent, corpse-littered establishment. "The humans were all dead and the place was already vacated when we got here. By the look and smell of the place, I'm guessing it's been over for several hours now."

Rowan's glance traveled over the evidence of the violence and death that had gone on unchecked in the club earlier that night. That it was perpetrated by members of the Breed was obvious, but never in his hundred-plus years of life had he seen such brutal disregard for human life. The fact that the slayings had almost certainly been carried out by his fellow Enforcement Agents sickened him to his soul.

"And no one has come forward as a witness to what went on here?" he confirmed. "What about Taggart; isn't he usually manning the door most nights? He had to have seen something. Or any one of the other dozen Agents who frequent this place like it's going out of style?"

"I don't know, sir."

Furious over all of it, Rowan wheeled on the Agent. "You don't know if they were here tonight, or you don't know if they're responsible for slaughtering these humans in the middle of goddamn Boston?"

"Um, neither, sir." The Agent's face blanched a bit under his superior's glare. "I wasn't sure where to begin with a situation like this. You were the first call I made."

Rowan blew out a frustrated sigh. The Agent was young, new to his post. Freshly promoted from the general ranks, he was afraid to step out of line or make a mistake. And he was devoted to justice, a rarity within the Agency these days, Rowan had to admit. He wondered how long the kid would maintain his sheen.

"It's okay, Ethan." He clapped the youth lightly on the shoulder. "You did the right thing here. Let's call in your team and start cleaning this mess up."

The Agent gave a brisk nod. "Yes, sir."

As he strode out to summon the others, Mathias Rowan took another long look at the bloodshed and death that surrounded him. It was heinous, what happened here. It was inexcusable. And he couldn't help feeling that the carnage bore the stamp of a villain he was coming to know all too well.

Dragos.

During the several months that Rowan had been covertly allying himself with the Order, he'd learned firsthand what Dragos was capable of—from the abduction and abuse of scores of innocent Breedmate females, to the recent attack on a local Darkhaven that took the lives of nearly everyone in that prominent Breed family.

And then there was the breach of the Order's secret headquarters by human law enforcement less than twenty-four hours ago.

More havoc instigated by Dragos.

Now this.

Rowan was certain Dragos was at the root of what went on here tonight. What better time for the devil to come out to play than when the Order had their hands full with a forced relocation of their compound and the surrender of one of their own to police custody? Rowan should have expected something like this. He should have been prepared to step in for Lucan and his warriors tonight, with half the Agency behind him.

Of course, that assumed half the Agency was still loyal to their oath of service. Rowan really wasn't sure about that, definitely not anymore. The Agency had not been without its share of problems over the many long decades of its existence. Bureaucratic, slow to move, far too political at times, it was the bloated, impotent cousin to the Order's lean, surgically precise efficacy as protectors of the Breed and humankind alike.

Corruption among the ranks was rampant, if festering below the surface. More and more, it was growing impossible to know who could be trusted. Good men did remain, but there were others—more than Rowan cared to admit—who hid their malfeasance behind a mask of Agency duty and authority. Dragos himself had been one of them, rising to one of the highest positions in the organization, and no doubt garnering a league of loyal followers, before the Order exposed him and sent him scurrying into deep hiding roughly a year ago.

No, Rowan thought grimly. There was no question that the mass slaughter tonight on Enforcement Agency turf was Dragos's way of pissing on both the Order and the Agency at the same time.

"Son of a bitch," he snarled into the tomblike silence of the club.

There was nothing to be done now, with morning about to break and the Order setting up temporary camp some five-plus hours north of Boston, but Lucan had to be informed of the situation.

Rowan pivoted away from the carnage and headed outside, passing the incoming team of Agents armed with body bags and cleanup equipment on his way to his vehicle. Once seated inside the sedan, he dialed a scrambled access line given to him by the Order. It rang through.

"Gideon, it's Mathias Rowan," he said when the line connected on the other end. "We have a situation down here. Lucan isn't going to like it. Bad news, my friend, and it's got Dragos's name written all over it."

* * *

"Shit, shit, shit." Tavia checked her watch again, impatiently waiting for the snarl of early morning commuters in front of her to step off the train at Boston's Government Center Station.

It was almost 8:00 A.M., and she was late to work.

Definitely a first for her, although it wasn't as if she didn't have a good excuse. The stress of the past few days apparently was getting to her. She was still tense from the incident at the police station and Senator Clarence's odd behavior afterward.

The troubling dream hadn't done anything for her nerves either. While doubling down on her antianxiety meds had allowed her to sleep, it had also made her hit the snooze button on her alarm one too many times this morning.

She saw an opening in the slow-moving throng and dashed through it. Walking briskly, she crossed the snow-spattered bricks outside the terminal, rushing past a florist stand bursting with red and white poinsettias and evergreen wreaths. On the street, a brisk, cold wind blew, carrying the repetitive jingle of a Salvation Army bell from somewhere nearby and the smoky aroma of coffee beans and baked goods from the Starbucks on the corner. Tavia's stomach growled in response, but she headed in the opposite direction.

She tried the senator's cell phone, but it went straight to voicemail, just as it had the two other times she'd called on her way into the city. He would be at the charity breakfast by now. Normally she would have double-checked with him first thing to make sure he had everything he needed for the event. Normally she would have been in the office for at least an hour already, getting a jump-start on the day's tasks while he was out courting his public.

Normally . . .

Nothing about the past few days seemed normal.

Not even close.

Tavia walked along the City Hall plaza toward the senator's offices, her head down, face dipped into the folds of her knit scarf as another wintry gust rolled up. She cut between the pair of towers and the squat government building next to them, hearing the cacophony of a gathered crowd even before she rounded the corner and saw the commotion.

News vans and camera crews from every local network and a couple of national cable channels lined New Sudbury Street like vultures. Police vehicles, not an unusual sight at the government offices when a large precinct sat directly across the street, were blocking the entrance and exit, shadowed by black federal-issued SUVs parked in front of the building doors and all along the arched fire lane at the curb.

Dread squeezed her stomach, turning it into an icy fist in her gut.

"Excuse me." Tavia approached a reporter from Channel Five who was fluffing her unmoving helmet of blond hair and performing a sound check. "What's happening here?"

"Get in line, honey," the woman replied. "That's what we're all waiting to find out. The police commissioner just called a press conference for eight o'clock."

Tavia stepped through the groups of hovering reporters and the gawkers who'd been drawn from around the neighboring streets by all the noise and activity. She weaved between the sea of bodies, trying to make her way closer to the building entrance where most of the police and federal agents had clustered.

Someone took sharp hold of her arm. "Ms. Fairchild."

"Detective Avery," she said, the kick in her chest relaxing a bit as she met the older man's sober gaze. "What's all this about?"

"Come with me, please." He walked her through the crowds and into the front entrance of the building. The lobby was busy with more uniformed officers and armed men in SWAT gear. The detective paused with her, his face fatigued, aging him even more. "When did you last speak to or see Senator Clarence, Tavia?"

The cold knot in her stomach got even harder. "Last night, when he dropped me off at home."

"Do you remember what time that was?"

She shook her head. "I'm not sure. It was right after we left the police station. Has something happened to him? Is that what all this is about?"

Detective Avery braced his fists on his hips and exhaled a heavy sigh. "There's no easy way to say it, I'm afraid. Someone broke into his house overnight and . . . attacked him. He was killed, Tavia. He and a couple of his security guards as well."

"What?" She struggled to process the news, even though her instincts had already been warning her that something terrible had occurred. Shock crept over her—shock and disbelief. "This can't be happening. Senator Clarence can't be dead. He was supposed to give a speech today at a hospital charity breakfast . . ."

Avery laid his hand consolingly on her shoulder. "We're gonna catch this guy. Don't you worry about that, all right?"

She mutely shook her head, trying to make some sense

out of the awful news. Looking for explanations, answers. "The man last night at the station—he warned that the senator was in danger. You heard what he said, didn't you? He said someone wanted to kill Senator Clarence. Someone called Dragos."

A harsh scoff sounded from beside her. Tavia looked over and met the hard gaze of a uniformed policeman who had drifted over while she and Detective Avery were talking. A scar split the dark slash of his left eyebrow, making his scowl look even more severe. "Nothing but bullshit out of that bastard. Shoulda pumped his skull full of bullets. Maybe that woulda kept him down."

At Tavia's confused look, Avery said, "The man we had in custody . . . he escaped last night from the infirmary."

"Escaped," she murmured. "I don't understand. How is that possible?"

"We're trying to figure that out ourselves. I saw the guy when he was brought out of the lineup room. He was in bad shape. Somehow he managed to overcome a two-hundred-pound male nurse, knocking him unconscious before slipping out of the building unnoticed. I mean, the guy shouldn't have been able to walk out of there on his own motor, let alone find his way to Marblehead to go after the senator like he did. I've never seen anything so brutal. So goddamn bloody."

Tavia swallowed past the lump of sadness and horror that had lodged in her throat.

"I'm sorry," Detective Avery said, looking at her in concern. "I realize you probably don't need to hear the ugly details. You've been through quite a bit yourself lately."

"It's all right." She drew in a quick breath, regaining her composure. "I'll be fine."

"We'd like you to come into the station, if you feel up to it. We have some more questions for you, and the feds will want to talk to you as well—"

"Of course."

He gestured toward the door of the building, to where the reporters had seemed to multiply in the time since she'd been inside. "We can go now, before this place really turns into a zoo."

Tavia nodded, falling in behind him as he and a small group of uniformed officers escorted her out to a waiting police sedan.

For a moment, as she stepped outside into the cold morning, she felt as though she were walking through a different world, one that didn't belong to her. There was an unreal quality to everything, as though she were peering through the gauze of a veil, unable to see anything clearly.

Or maybe it was simply that she didn't want to see.

She was unable to imagine the kind of man—the kind of inhuman lethality—it would take to do to Senator Clarence what Detective Avery had implied. She didn't want to think about the senator's final moments. She'd worked for him for years, knew he was a good man who believed he could make a difference. Sure, he'd seemed to be acting a bit odd lately. Detached somehow. Distracted. Who wouldn't be, after the shooting at his house just a few nights ago? A bullet that could have easily struck him but had instead hit one of his VIP guests.

Drake Masters.

The name played through her head, and she returned again to what the man in the jailhouse lineup had said—that at the party he'd shot the person he knew as Dragos. The person he seemed convinced meant to harm or kill Senator Clarence. Someone who probably didn't exist except in his imagination.

It sounded crazy to her now, even in her thoughts.

All the more so when she considered how violently that same man in police custody had leapt at Senator Clarence the moment he saw him in the viewing room.

And today Bobby Clarence was dead.

A confessed killer, clearly deranged, was on the loose.

Suddenly the troubling dream that had woken her last night felt even more disturbing in the chilling light of day.

As the police sedan rolled away from the curb, Tavia could only hope that the scorching blue eyes and merciless face that she could still see so vividly in her mind stayed relegated to her nightmares.

CHAPTER
Eight

Lucan's shitty night was turning into an even shittier morning.

It had started with the phone call from Mathias Rowan a few hours ago, around daybreak, reporting the mass slaughter of nearly a dozen humans in an Agency-run nightclub. Fortunately, Rowan had the situation cleaned up before the slayings could draw the attention of the public, but that was little comfort amid the hell storm of bad news and trouble the Order was facing.

And Lucan was sure things would only get worse before they got better.

Fuck, *if* they got better.

Now, while mankind was heading into their A.M. rush hour commutes elsewhere—the same hour that most of the night-dwelling Breed would be hunkered down in their Darkhavens to sleep and wait out the day—Lucan and the rest of the former Boston compound's residents were still settling into their new surroundings.

Lucan hadn't slept in more than thirty-six hours, not that any of the other warriors had either. Gathered in the makeshift war room of the sprawling Darkhaven retreat in the woods of northern Maine, which was now their base of operations, Lucan and Gideon had been going over facility inventories and systems status checks for the past several hours. They'd since been joined by some of the others, and the talk around the large hand-hewn timber table of the former dining room had turned toward mission strategies and the need to retaliate against Dragos for his continued—and escalating—offenses.

"You know," Dante said, "there is a bright side in all of this." He sat on the edge of the big table, dark brows quirking over whiskey-colored eyes. "If we've ever needed a license to kick some Enforcement Agency ass, we've sure as hell got it now."

"Damn right." Standing nearby, Rio gave a tilt of his scarred face and lifted his fist to knock knuckles with Dante. "Tonight we'll hit every sip-and-strip in the city with some heavy-duty payback," he added, his Spanish accent rolling with his anger. "Nothing sweeter than a chance to bring down Dragos and the Agency together."

Dante grinned. "Icing, meet cake."

"How many of these private clubs does the Enforcement Agency have?" This time it was Lazaro Archer who spoke. The Breed elder was the lone civilian in the room and, under normal circumstances, wouldn't have been permitted to sit in on Order business. But he was also the owner of the northern Maine property the warriors had commandeered as their temporary headquarters, and these were far from normal circumstances.

"According to Mathias Rowan," Gideon replied, "there are five known clubs around Boston, the one in Chinatown being the primary location."

"So, what are the odds Dragos will make another appearance at one of these places?" Archer asked.

Lucan grunted. "Slim to none."

At the opposite end of the table from him, Tegan, leaning back in his chair and contemplative for most of the impromptu meeting, nodded in agreement. "He had a point to make last night and he made it in about as public a way as he could. We won't find Dragos shooting the shit and slumming it with the Agency rank-and-file again anytime soon. Don't think he's gonna make it that easy for us."

Dante frowned, considering. "I still say it can't hurt to rustle the bushes with the Agency and see what we turn up. We might not flush out Dragos, but netting a few dirty Agents would be worth the effort. Especially if we can get one of them to talk." His thumb flicked idly at the leather blade sheath belted around his hips. A fraction of a second later, one of his twin curved blades was in his hand, titanium glinting as he made the weapon dance through his fingers. "If Harvard were here right now, I know he'd say the same thing."

Lucan couldn't disagree that Dante had a point. As for Sterling Chase—Harvard, as he'd been wryly christened by Dante from just about the moment the former Enforcement Agent had first set foot in the Order's compound a year and a half ago—he'd spent decades in the Breed's law enforcement organization. Long enough to have seen some of its ineffectiveness and corruption. It was because of him that the Order had found an ally in Mathias Rowan a few months ago. Rowan was one of

Chase's trusted colleagues during his time in the Agency and was proving to be a valuable asset as well as a friend to Lucan and the rest of the warriors.

There was a time Lucan would have said that about Chase too. Hell, he still felt that way, in spite of Harvard's faults and failures of late. Lucan hated that he'd been forced to draw a hard line in the sand with him. He understood all too well the beast Chase was fighting. He'd walked that same path, had seen it take down his family and long-ago friends, and, very nearly, himself.

Because he'd tasted the destructive power of Bloodlust and had seen what it could do to even the strongest of his kind, Lucan was all the less forgiving when it came to protecting his kith and kin from its harm. Chase's inability—or unwillingness—to right himself from his downward spiral had put everyone in the compound at risk.

Yet Lucan wouldn't hesitate to admit that the Order was a lot better for having had Chase in its fold. And working without him now—especially after what he'd done to buy them the much-needed opportunity to vacate the Boston compound—felt as though the Order had lost a limb.

For what hadn't been the first time, Lucan considered the viability of heading back into the city to retrieve Chase from police custody. It went against the grain to leave a comrade alone and exposed in the field. The Order had always taken great care with its fallen, and even though Chase was still alive—for all they knew, that is—it had been one of the damned hardest decisions Lucan had ever made to depart Boston with the rest of the compound and leave Chase behind.

It didn't help that there had been no word on him

since he'd been hauled into custody yesterday morning. Gideon was keeping an ear to the ground, monitoring news stations and cable sources for any updates, but there'd been nothing to report.

The radio silence was the thing that bugged Lucan the most. He didn't expect for a minute that Chase would stay put inside a human lockdown for any longer than he wanted. And it wouldn't have taken much time before his blood thirst drove him to feed. God forbid he lost his shit and attacked anyone inside the station.

Just thinking of it made Lucan blow out a low curse.

"All we'd need is one pair of loose lips," Rio was saying now, drawing him back to the topic at hand. "One Agent to tell us something we don't know about Dragos and we'll be that much closer to killing the bastard at last."

"I won't argue any of that," Lucan said. "The Order—hell, all of the Breed nation—would be better off if the Agency underwent some serious housecleaning. But we can't take our sights off Dragos as our primary target. As much as I'd like to storm down those hallowed Agency halls and start making heads roll, we've got our hands full enough without declaring all-out war on the Enforcement Agency as a whole."

Tegan met his gaze with a thoughtful narrowing of his green eyes. "That might be exactly what Dragos was hoping we'd do. Toss a little distraction our way while he's busy making other plans."

Gideon grunted. "Divide and conquer. He'd hardly be the first megalomaniac to draw that weapon."

And in another place, another time, Lucan might have been arrogant enough to fall into such a tactical trap, believing himself above failure. He'd been infallible once, for a long time undefeatable.

The Order had been founded on the edge of his sword and the mettle of his convictions. Back then he'd feared nothing, bowed to no one. He'd ridden into every battle alongside his fellow warriors, determined to defy death yet willing to accept it, should that moment come.

Nearly seven hundred years had passed since that time. But it was only recently—a matter of months, a blink of time compared to the centuries he'd been living—that he'd begun to make decisions not based solely on his confidence as a leader and the battle prowess of his men.

He'd never concerned himself with the well-being of anyone but himself. There'd been no need. But now?

Hell . . .

Now he felt the responsibility for the lives of everyone under his roof, and it was a weight that had gotten even heavier since the abrupt evacuation from Boston.

He heard the source of some of his angst—the bright laughter and delighted squeal of a little girl—drifting in from another room. "Oh, my gosh! Oh, my gosh, Rennie! He said he would do it and he really did!"

At Lucan's confused scowl, Gideon explained. "Apparently Mira's just discovered the Christmas tree Niko brought in for her from the woods before daybreak this morning."

"Christmas tree," Lucan echoed with mild annoyance. He vaguely recalled Nikolai saying something about the eight-year-old girl's want of holiday decorations at the new headquarters, but there had been no mention of bringing in a damn tree.

Lucan got up and stalked out of the meeting room to confront the foolery going on in the vaulted great room at the center of the large stone-and-timber house. By the time he got there, half the compound was already gathered to admire the seven-foot pine. Nikolai and his mate, Renata, stood with Rio's mate, Dylan, helping to position the tree while warriors Kade and Brock looked on with their respective mates, Alexandra and Jenna, both recent arrivals from Alaska.

Lazaro Archer's teenage grandson, Kellan, brooded on the periphery. At just fourteen, the lanky kid had already been through hell and back, thanks to Dragos. His only remaining kin was his grandfather, and even though the youth tried to insist he was all right about everything that had happened, Lucan guessed it was only going to be a matter of time before Kellan Archer either detonated like an atom bomb or imploded into himself.

The Breed youth stood at the back of the room like a bored spectator, his arms crossed over his chest, a hank of overlong ginger bangs drooping over his brow as he tried not to look too impressed with the whole production going on in front of him now. Lucan could relate.

Mira had no such restraint. She bounced in her purple pajamas and fleece-trimmed suede slippers, ebullient in her joy. "Rennie, isn't it the most wonderful tree you've ever seen?"

"It's pretty awesome, Mouse." Niko and Renata had for all intents and purposes adopted Mira as their own after the warrior had brought them both home to Boston with him from a mission in Montreal last summer. Dark-haired Renata was as lethal as any one of the Order's warriors, but her cool jade eyes softened as they lit on Nikolai's crooked smile on the other side of the tree as they tried to balance it on its stand. "It's perfect, babe."

"Wait—not there," Mira abruptly directed. "You're gonna put it too close to the fireplace, you guys!"

Niko shot the girl a wry look over his shoulder. "Of course. We don't want to block Santa from coming down the chimney with all your presents."

Kellan Archer scoffed from his post near the back of the room. "Santa Claus is a myth. Only babies believe in him."

"Kellan!" Renata gasped.

"It's okay, Rennie." Wispy blond hair swinging, Mira turned toward the boy, looking greatly offended. "I haven't believed in Santa since I was five years old. I just didn't want the tree to catch on fire if it was too close to the hearth." She rolled her eyes. "Kellan thinks I'm a baby."

"How should we decorate the tree, Mira?" This time it was Alex, Kade's Breedmate, who spoke. "Did you bring the ornaments you made?"

Mira's mouth pressed into a sullen line. "I only had time to pack up a few. I had to leave the rest back in Boston at the compound."

Ah, Christ. Lucan groaned inwardly. So much for clamping down on the merriment out here. He'd done that even before he entered the room.

Feeling awkward and out of place, he was about to turn around and leave the room when Niko threw him under the bus. "Hey, Mira, make sure you thank Lucan too. Bringing this tree in from the forest was all his idea."

"No," Lucan denied sharply. "I had nothing to do with—"

But the little girl had already launched herself in his direction. She caught him in a tight hug around the waist, her sweetly innocent face turned up to meet his glower. "Thanks, Lucan. This is gonna be the best Christmas ever."

For fuck's sake.

He stood there unmoving, helpless in the child's embrace.

"Maybe we can make popcorn garlands?" Mira wondered aloud, releasing him in that next instant to skip back over to continue her supervision of the tree setup. "Do you think so, Rennie?"

"Sure," Renata answered.

Brock's mate, Jenna, strode over to ruffle Mira's bed-head hair. "We could gather some pinecones from the woods today. They'd make pretty ornaments, don't you think?"

The girl nodded enthusiastically. "It's gonna be great!"

"What do you think?" Lucan asked the sulking Breed youth as he drew up next to him.

Kellan shrugged. "The tree looks kinda short and scraggly to me."

"Short and scraggly?" Niko replied. "The hell you say."

With the tree in place to Mira's satisfaction now, the Breed warrior put his hands into the brushy boughs and held them there. He was quiet for a long moment, and Lucan knew the Russian-born vampire was summoning the extrasensory ability that was unique to him. Every Breed male inherited some type of power from his Breedmate mother, be it a blessing or a curse. In Lucan's case, through hypnotic suggestion he could manipulate a human mind into seeing and believing whatever he willed.

As for Nikolai's ability, Lucan found an amusing irony in the fact that the gear-head weapons expert with a penchant for making things blow up was gifted with a talent rivaled only by Mother Nature herself. In

Niko's silence and concentration, something started to happen deep within the center of the pine. There was a soft rustling sound, then, as though flooded with new life, the tree's branches and needles began to flourish and stretch. It grew fuller, taller, inching another two feet toward the vaulted rafters of the great room's ceiling.

Mira giggled over the hush that had come over everyone else in the room. "Awesome!" she exclaimed, clapping excitedly as the tree soared even higher.

Kellan Archer, meanwhile, gaped, slack-jawed. "What the . . ."

Niko brought his hands out from within the tree's core and blew at the tips of his fingers like an Old West gunfighter. Beneath his crown of blond hair, Niko's icy Siberian eyes crinkled at the corners as he shot an arch look at the teen. "Now the only thing kind of short and scraggly in here is you, kid."

Everyone chuckled at the teen's ribbing, even Lucan. He watched Kellan's cheeks redden briefly before his color returned to the sallow paleness that had been its norm for more than a few days. Lucan cast an assessing eye over the Breed youth's thin frame and lean, almost wan, face. "Have you fed lately?"

Kellan gave a noncommittal shrug.

"He hasn't," Mira volunteered. "Not even one time since he was first brought to the compound in Boston."

The glare he sent the girl was nothing short of murderous.

"Is that true?" Lucan asked.

Another shrug, head down, refusing to meet Lucan's eyes. "I guess so."

No wonder he looked so anemic. It had been nearly two weeks since the teen had been abducted on Dragos's command. Only days less than that since he'd been rescued by the Order and brought, along with his grandfather, into the Order's protection at the Boston headquarters, the pair of them being the sole survivors of Dragos's attack on their family Darkhaven.

It was one thing for an adult of the Breed to go a week or more without blood; even that was pushing it. But an adolescent needed regular sustenance to feed his developing body and hone his preternatural strengths to their maximum potential. For those of Lucan's kind with blood-bonded Breedmates, feeding was an act of intimacy, as sacred as it was primal. For unmated males and children of hunting age, feeding required a human Host.

Kellan had spent his first few days in the infirmary at the compound recovering from his ordeal, but he'd been on his feet for a while now and his body was in serious need of nourishment.

Lucan stared at the teen. "It's been too long since you fed. You need to take care of that, Kellan. Sooner than later."

"I will," he replied, eyes remaining downcast.

Lucan reached out and lifted the youth's chin until he had no choice but to meet his gaze. "You will tonight. That's an order, son."

Kellan frowned. His body threw off a palpable mental recoil, like an animal suddenly getting backed into a corner. "My grandfather said he'd go with me. I've been waiting for him to have the time, but he's been so busy helping Jenna . . ."

Lucan shook his head, dismissing the comment as the excuse he was certain it was. "I'll take you myself if I have to. Tonight, Kellan. We clear?"

Finally, a nod, accompanied by another hard look in Mira's direction. "Yeah. We're clear."

With that issue resolved, Lucan glanced over at Jenna. The former Alaska State Trooper was the most recent addition to the Order's female population. Unlike the rest of the warriors' women and little Mira as well, Jenna was not a Breedmate but came from basic *Homo sapiens* stock. The other females had been gifted with unique DNA and blood properties that allowed them to share a life-extending blood bond with Breed males and to carry their offspring. Breedmates, a rarity among their mortal sisters, were identifiable by their unique ESP talents and personal blood scent, as well as a small scarlet birthmark somewhere on their bodies in the shape of a teardrop falling into the cradle of a crescent moon.

Although Jenna had been born human, to call her mortal now would not be quite accurate.

"Gideon tells me your latest blood work looks good. A few fluctuations in cell counts, but no more big surprises."

The tall brunette gave a sardonic laugh. "Nothing too unusual. Still a cyborg freak in progress."

"Freakin' hot, if you ask me," added her mate, Brock. The huge black warrior flashed her a broad smile that held a hint of fangs. "I kinda dig having my own personal RoboCop."

"Oh, yeah," she replied, smiling along with him. "I'll remind you of that the day I'm strong enough to kick your vampire butt."

Brock exhaled an exaggerated sigh. "Damn, woman. You already have me on my knees where you're concerned. Now you want me on my ass?"

Across the room, Nikolai laughed. "Hey, welcome to my world, man."

The jibe earned him a playful cuff in the shoulder

from Renata. She reached over to Mira and covered the girl's ears before adding quietly "On their ass or on their back, it's all good. Right, Jen?"

At Jenna's chuckling agreement, Brock drew her close and planted a kiss on her mouth. He wrapped his palm around the back of her neck, possessive but tender as he gazed into his mate's brown eyes. "She knows she's got me, any way she wants me. Forever, if I have anything to say about it."

Where his fingers rested at Jenna's nape was a rice-size bit of alien biotech matter embedded beneath her skin. An unwanted souvenir she'd woken up with following a recent, prolonged attack by an Ancient, the last of the eight vampiric otherworlders who'd fathered the first generation of the Breed on Earth. Jenna emerged from that ordeal miraculously alive, but changed in many ways. She was *still* changing, evolving both physically and genetically.

Her body was able to heal itself from injury, something Gideon described as adaptive regeneration—similar to the way the Breed healed, except in Jenna's case, she didn't require ingested blood to aid the process. She didn't have fangs or blood thirst, but she was stronger and faster than any human, as supernaturally agile as any of the Breed. Gideon wasn't entirely certain, but early tests seemed to indicate that some of the Ancient's DNA contained within the biotech chip was integrating with Jenna's genetic structure. Overtaking it, on several levels.

Part of that was obvious, even to the casual observer.

Curling around to her shoulders from the back of her neck, where the implant resided, were the swirling arcs and flourishes of a growing *dermaglyph*. The skin markings were unique to Lucan's kind and the otherworlders who fathered them, yet this human woman now bore her own. Jenna's *glyph* had never changed colors or pulsed as Lucan and his Breed brethren's did in moments of extreme emotion or hunger. Her *glyph*'s color remained static, just a shade darker than her fair skin.

And then there was the matter of Jenna's tendency to speak in the Ancients' language while she was asleep. The nightmares were a new development, having come on strong in just the last couple of days. Violent dreams of combat and catastrophe.

The Order was still trying to make sense of everything Jenna was becoming, and it seemed that one key to solving that question might be found in deciphering the alien words and images that plagued her unconscious mind. Lazaro Archer had enlisted himself to assist on that front. At somewhere near a thousand years old and a first-generation Breed like Lucan and Tegan, Archer also brought the useful experience of having spent more time than most in the company of his Ancient sire. Relying on his memory of the otherworlders' language, Archer was helping Jenna to journal all that she could in the hopes that the writings would offer some answers.

Lucan was about to ask for a quick update when the sound of his own mate's voice behind him snagged his full attention. "I hope you weren't planning on decorating that Christmas tree without us."

Gabrielle snaked her arm around his waist and smiled up at him as he wrapped her in the shelter of his arm. Just the feel of her close to him, her soft brown eyes like melted chocolate, made his pulse kick into a harder rhythm.

"Ohh, it's beautiful," said Dante's mate, Tess, who'd

come into the room as well now. She held their three-day-old infant son in her arms, a pink-skinned, swaddled bundle that cooed and gurgled within the pale blue blanket that surrounded his tiny form. She lowered her voice to a tender whisper as she dipped her face toward her child. "Look at this, Xander. Your very first Christmas tree."

As she spoke, Gideon's longtime mate, Savannah, and Elise, who'd been mated to Tegan for only the past year, entered the great room too. It didn't take more than a moment for all of the women, Mira included, to cluster around Tess and the baby. Not even Gabrielle was immune. She ditched Lucan without a word, apparently drawn like the others by some invisible, female-mesmerizing beacon to the presence of such a little package of innocent life.

Lucan spared the baby and his admirers only a passing notice, and begrudging at that. He'd long felt that the Order's base of operations was no place for children, let alone helpless infants. Then again, until he'd met and fallen in love with Gabrielle, he hadn't been too keen on females underfoot at the compound either.

Not that this was a compound, exactly. Or anything close to a viable command base, least of all now, when the Order needed every tactical advantage it could get in this war with Dragos.

He looked around him, at the borrowed Darkhaven in the middle of a secluded forest, the cozy great room with its fireplace and soaring rafters and the enormous pine that stretched up toward them, fragrant with the evergreen scent of the outdoors. He looked at the people who stood around him there, most of his brothers in arms and their beloved mates. The family he'd never wanted but had somehow ended up having anyway.

And then he looked at Gabrielle.

She was his irresistible beacon. His greatest strength, and his most vulnerable weakness. She was his heart. And it was there that he felt a tightness growing as he watched her stroke the velvety cheek of the baby in Tess's arms. She leaned her face down and kissed the infant's delicately rounded brow, and the pure beauty in that single instant made the fist around Lucan's heart squeeze even tighter.

He didn't want to acknowledge this thing that was infiltrating his body. This queer ache deep inside him that could mean no good, especially now.

It was a relief to hear the sudden, long stride of boots pounding in the hallway. The urgent beat thrust him into battle mode in an instant, even before Tegan appeared, trouble written across the warrior's stern face. "More bad news out of Boston."

"Chase?" Lucan asked, dreading the answer as the rest of the room fell into an equally grave silence.

Tegan nodded. "Gideon just got wind of it on an Internet newsfeed. Senator Clarence is dead, Lucan. Brutally attacked and killed in his home, along with several of his security detail. And guess who vanished without a trace from the police station last night?"

Lucan's veins erupted with fury. "Son of a bitch. What the fuck is wrong with Harvard?"

But he didn't really need to ask that, and Tegan didn't bother to answer. They'd both brushed shoulders with the addiction that Chase was suffering from now. And if it turned out that Bloodlust had driven him to kill— especially so blatantly, and such a highly visible individual whose death could have irrevocable consequences for all of the Breed nation—then Chase had effectively just signed his own death warrant.

CHAPTER
Nine

Chase flicked up the collar of his coat as he rounded a corner off a dark side street in the city and headed deeper into the evening crush of pedestrians and rush-hour commuters. His gunshot wounds were bleeding again. He could feel the liquid heat of his own blood seeping through the fabric of the baggy jeans and lumberjack flannel shirt he'd pinched from a church thrift shop box overflowing with holiday donations. His tan construction boots were too tight by a full size and the dark wool-blend coat carried the faint smell of mothballs, but he was warm. Too warm, in fact. His skin felt fiery, stretched too tight around him.

He knew it was the hunger calling him.

It had started as a prickling annoyance about an hour ago, his body's way of telling him that night was falling and it was time to feed.

Head pounding, veins jangling more insistently than an alarm clock, he'd woken up in an abandoned mill in Malden, where he'd gone after paying his unannounced visit to the Minion senator's house. He'd been lucky to find the shelter last night. Luckier still that his exhaustion had overwhelmed his addiction's greed. He wouldn't be the first of his kind to get stupid from Bloodlust and end up ashing himself in the morning.

But he hadn't fallen into that abyss yet.

The way his stomach was twisting on itself, he had to wonder if the plunge into blood madness wasn't actually a relief in the end. God knew, fighting it off every waking second was its own brand of hell.

The blood he'd taken from the nurse had given him the boost he needed to escape the infirmary and take care of Dragos's mind slave, but he was paying the price for it now. Like a neglected lover suddenly shown a brief but passing interest, his blood thirst demanded all of his undivided attention. It sent him prowling the street, back into the bustle of the city more out of selfish, slavish need than out of any sense of righteous purpose or duty.

His hooded gaze slid from one human to another, temptation everywhere as he strode among them like a wraith. Without intending to, he found himself falling in behind a group of young women toting shopping bags and long rolls of wrapping paper. He casually followed them as they made their way up the street, chattering and laughing with one another. While his hunger urged them to head for the poorly lit parking lot at the end of the block, the women instead hung an abrupt right and entered the din of an Irish pub.

As they disappeared into the crowded establishment, Chase slowed his pace outside. His fangs were sharp against his tongue, and under the low tilt of his head, he could see the faint glow from twin points of amber reflecting his gaze back at him in the pub's garland-draped, light-festooned window.

Shit.

He had to get a grip, get this thing under control. He knew where it was leading him, of course. He'd seen it happen to better men than he. Had seen it all too recently in his own family, in a promising young kid with the whole world ahead of him. Lost to Bloodlust and taken for good in a single, damning action that had haunted Chase ever since.

Camden.

Jesus, had it really been more than a year since his nephew's death?

It felt like a matter of days sometimes. Other times, like now, with his own feral reflection staring back at him, it felt like centuries had passed.

Ancient fucking history.

And he could hardly afford to stand around rehashing the past. Keep moving; that's the best thing he could do. And if he wanted a snowball's chance of beating back his hunger tonight, he'd better get his ass away from the general human population and find someplace to sweat it out alone. The way he was hurting—and the way his wounds were lingering, his body's healing in need of fresh red cells—it wasn't wise for him to be anywhere public.

Chase started to turn away, but through the pub windows, a flash of movement on one of the wall-mounted TV screens caught his eye. Behind a yammering blond news reporter covering a story from earlier that day, he caught a glimpse of silky caramel brown hair and a pretty face he recognized instantly.

Tavia Fairchild, being escorted out of a Boston office

building by several police officers and federal agents sometime that morning.

Chase stared at her image on the screen. Her cheeks were slack, gaze stricken with shock and grief as law enforcement hurried her toward a waiting vehicle outside the government building. A ticker at the bottom of the news video confirmed the senator's killing and a suspect still at large. The video went split screen to show his mug shot, but Chase only glanced at it. His attention was fixed on something else—something that made his blood run cold in his veins.

He peered closer at one of the cops who was taking Tavia out of the building. Not the detective from the station but another man—a uniformed officer with dark hair and the flat gaze of a mind slave. Holy hell. Just how deep did Dragos's reach go?

And what did it mean for Tavia Fairchild if his Minions were keeping her close in their sights?

It couldn't be good.

Chase's fury spiked as he watched the Minion cop put his hands on her to assist her into the vehicle—the same way it had spiked when he'd seen her stand next to Senator Clarence in the police station viewing room. Although he was far from being anyone's hero, Chase felt the tarnished inklings of his old sense of honor grind to life inside him when he thought of her being anywhere near Dragos or his legion of soulless servants.

The morning news report was easily eight hours old. Potentially eight hours that Tavia had been breathing the same air as the Minion cop who climbed into the car with her and the police detective and drove off. If Dragos had wanted to harm the woman, he'd had plenty of time to get it done. Not that Chase should be the one to save her. Hell, when it came right down to it, he doubted he could even save himself.

But that didn't keep his blood from surging with new purpose.

It didn't keep his feet from moving, stepping away from the pub and heading across the street for the shadows. He vanished into the gloom, all of his predatory focus rooted to a single goal: finding Tavia Fairchild.

Fifteen minutes later, Chase was crouched like a gargoyle at the edge of the Suffolk County Sheriff's Department rooftop, his eye trained on the employee parking lot below. After an end-of-shift parade of uniformed officers and shuffling office types trickled down to nil, his patience was strained and he was about two seconds away from storming the place to find the cop he was looking for. But then, at last, pay dirt. He recognized the middle-age police detective as soon as the human exited the building.

This was the man who'd been in the witness viewing room with Tavia Fairchild. The same man who'd accompanied her past the television news camera crews at the press conference that morning. Chase watched the human make his way across the lot toward his car. He aimed the little keyless remote in his hand and a rust-speckled silver Toyota sedan chirped halfway up the row.

Chase dropped down from the roof, his church donation box boots landing on the cold asphalt without a sound.

"Got time for a chat, Detective?" Chase was already in the passenger seat of the vehicle by the time the human had opened the driver's door and plopped down behind the wheel.

"Jesus Christ!" He jumped, panic flooding his jowly face. His cop instincts kicked in at the same time, sending his hands scrambling to the service revolver holstered at his hip.

"I wouldn't do that if I were you," Chase cautioned.

Apparently thinking better of it, the officer lunged for the door handle beside him. As if he stood any chance of escape. He hauled on the lever but it didn't release, even after repeated tries to work the electronic locks with his other hand. "Damn it!"

Chase stared at him, unfazed. "That'll do you no good either."

Nevertheless, Avery went another round on the locks and door handle, unaware that Chase was holding them closed by force of his Breed will. Then the aging cop suddenly got desperate and dropped his elbow on the horn. The cheery Japanese bleat shot loose like a scream before Chase seized the human's arm and wrenched him to full attention. "That was unwise."

"What're you gonna do? Fucking kill me right here in the parking lot?"

"If I wanted you dead, you wouldn't be sitting here about to piss yourself, Detective."

"Oh, Jesus," Avery moaned. "What the hell is going on? What the hell is wrong with your face?"

In the reflection shining back at him from the glass of the driver's side window, Chase saw the twin coals of his eyes glowing fiery amber in the dark of the vehicle. He looked monstrous, feral. Unhinged. Nothing close to human. He ground his jaws together, feeling the tips of his fangs graze sharply against his tongue.

The glimpse of his reflection sent his mind careening

back to another, similar moment from his recent past. Back then, little more than a year ago, Chase had been sitting in a darkened vehicle, eyes glowing and fangs drawn for the kill, as he stared into the terrified face of a human drug peddler who'd sent his nephew Camden into a narcotic-induced, tailspin addiction for blood.

Chase had been so self-righteous then, so certain he could be the one—perhaps the only one—able to save Camden. Instead he'd been the one who destroyed him. His mind echoed with the blast of gunfire that had opened up the boy's chest that night. He could still feel the unforgiving chill of metal in his hand, the reverberation of his biceps in the sudden silence that followed. The stench of spent bullets and spilling blood rank in the air as the raw, grief-stricken scream of a woman he'd once wanted for his own split the night.

And now it was Chase who was the afflicted, the doomed. Not because of a reckless taste of Crimson—the substance that had ruined the lives of young Cam and some of his friends the autumn before last—but because of his own negligence and weakness. The culmination of a lifetime of failings. His selfish, insatiable, damning need to fill a void that gaped deep inside him was finally swallowing him whole.

He felt sick with it as the police detective gaped at his transformed face in abject terror. The human's eyes were wide as saucers, mouth hanging open in mute stupor before a choked groan erupted from his throat. "My God, what *are* you? What the hell do you want from me?"

Chase blew out a harsh curse. This wasn't how he'd intended it to go down here, letting the human cop see him for what he truly was, but it was too late for that. He'd deal with it after he got the information he sought.

"Where is she?" Chase leaned in close, the beast in him snapping at the scent of raw fear. "I need to find Tavia Fairchild."

Despite the fear and confusion swamping the detective's gaze, a spark of protectiveness flared. "You think I'll tell you that so you can kill her too? Fuck you."

Chase had to respect the man for that. Cop or not, there weren't many of his species who'd show that kind of allegiance to someone they hardly knew. Especially when they were staring into the face of a walking nightmare. In Chase's experience, only Minions could be counted on for that depth of loyalty, and theirs came at the price of their own souls. Detective Avery here was very much alive and very afraid, yet he was glaring back at Chase with what he could only assume was some inviolable sense of honor.

Chase had known that feeling once himself. So long ago he barely recognized it anymore.

Didn't really matter now. The man he truly was was the one sending this decent human being into a cower before him. "I saw you with her this morning," Chase said. "You were with another cop—a uniform. Dark hair, nasty scar running into one of his eyebrows. What's his name? I need to find him too. Start talking, Detective."

"I'm not gonna tell you anything. Least of all where Murphy took her."

Holy hell. So she was still with the Minion. "Where is she, goddamn it?"

"Someplace safe." Avery practically spat the words.

Chase bore down on the man. "Safe from what?"

"From you, ya son of a bitch!" The detective started shaking, clutching at the collar of his rumpled white dress shirt and half-unhitched tie. "God almighty . . .

you can't be real. You can't be human. That's how you survived all those gunshots. That's how you were able to walk out of the infirmary last night . . ."

Chase felt the terror rolling off the man as comprehension finally, fully, took root in the human's stricken face. He gaped now, as if he expected to be torn to pieces any second by the beast that Chase was.

This was the reason the Breed had protected the secret of their existence all this time. This bone-deep fear, fueled by myth and grim folklore—not all of it completely untrue—was the reason the Breed could never expect any kind of peaceful cohabitation with man. Humankind's fear of things that went bump in the night was too ingrained. Too dangerous to be trusted.

Chase wasn't above using that terror to his advantage now. Nor would he hesitate to hurt this man in order to get the answers he came for. If Avery knew the kind of evil that was keeping company with Tavia Fairchild now, he'd need no coercion.

Then again, if this human or any other understood even half of the threat that Dragos and his followers presented to mankind's way of life, there might be no reasoning with any of them.

Still, Chase opted for the unvarnished truth.

In frank, unsparing terms, he told Detective Avery everything.

When he was through, and after the aging officer wearily divulged Tavia Fairchild's location, Chase spared him the burden of carrying his awful knowledge beyond that moment.

He scrubbed the man's memory clean of it all and left him sitting alone, mentally numb but unharmed, in the dark cockpit of his Toyota.

* * *

Tavia lingered in the hotel suite shower, unwilling to let go of the decadent, undisturbed solitude. It didn't bother her too much that she wasn't exactly alone. The pair of federal agents and the uniformed officer who'd brought her there that day were down the short hallway, in the living room of the spacious quarters.

Separated from her by two closed doors—her private bathroom and bedroom—the men were currently engrossed in a basketball game they'd turned on a few minutes before she'd excused herself to have a shower and take a nap until room service arrived with dinner. Under the warm spray of the water, she heard the tinny chatter of the television in the living room, accompanied by an occasional shout of dismay or a triumphant whoop from the men watching the game.

She'd been surprised when Officer Murphy informed her she'd be spending the night at the hotel—possibly more than one—under armed watch. The hard-eyed cop with the sinister scar across his eyebrow had been her close companion all day, since the moment he and Detective Avery had taken her away from Senator Clarence's office that morning. God, it was all so surreal. She had no experience being an eyewitness to a crime, let alone one in need of police protection at an undisclosed location.

In truth, though, it didn't seem much different from her usual home life: never left totally on her own, someone forever checking on her well-being, encroaching on her privacy whenever they liked, with the reasoning that it was all simply for her own good. She'd never felt particularly helpless or infirm, regardless of what Dr. Lewis and Aunt Sarah seemed to think. Admittedly, her body rebelled on her from time to time, whether in reaction to new treatments for her mystifying condition or in situations of heightened stress. Tavia had never quite figured out how to predict the onslaught of her "spells," as Aunt Sarah referred to them. Dr. Lewis said she had an unusual form of epilepsy, complicated by a host of other strange ailments that had required her to be in his specialized care from the time she was a baby.

The silver-haired physician had been as much a father figure to her as Aunt Sarah had been the only mother she'd ever known. Tavia hadn't seen so much as a photograph of her birth parents, having lost both of them in a vicious house fire that had somehow, miraculously, spared her.

All she had to remind her of the past she'd lost were the scars that covered nearly all of her body.

Tavia lathered the small bar of hotel soap and ran it along her arms and torso, then down the length of her legs. The scars tracked nearly everywhere she touched, even up onto her neck, painless for as long as she could remember. Based on how much of her body they covered, the scars should have looked more severe than they did. Dr. Lewis's treatments had worked some kind of magic on them, apparently.

They were still hideous to her, of course, a relentless webwork of pinkish tan skin that could be hidden only beneath turtleneck collars, long sleeves, and slacks.

The conservative dress code of her job with the senator had been a blessing; not even he had known of her extensive flaws or her complicated medical conditions. To him and to everyone else she came in contact with, Tavia was reserved, professional, and exacting. Her work life was the only thing she felt truly in control of, and she'd made it her mission to be perfect in every way possible.

God knew, she had no personal life to worry about.

Only Aunt Sarah, who had given up her own personal life to devote herself to looking after her dead brother's child. The older woman never spoke of her past or the dreams she might have held as a young woman. She'd never married, never regretted the fact that she'd gone without a family or children of her own.

Tavia often wondered why her aunt had made the choice to appoint herself lifelong guardian and caretaker of her niece. Not that she hadn't posed that question, more than once. Aunt Sarah would merely smile placidly whenever asked about those things and dismiss all questions with a kindly pat on Tavia's hand. "Don't you fret about me, dear. You're what's important. And I'm exactly where I'm supposed to be."

Too bad Aunt Sarah didn't feel the same about dissecting every action and thought of Tavia's. She wanted to know everything, always. But she never got angry or impatient—not in all the time Tavia had known her. She never complained, which made Tavia feel a bit guilty to be enjoying a few hours away from Aunt Sarah's constant attention now.

In twenty-seven years, she'd spent less than an accumulated month away from home, counting business trips with the senator and the occasional emergency overnight observation and treatment at Dr. Lewis's private care clinic. Aunt Sarah was never unconcerned on any of those occasions, but when Tavia spoke with her on the phone earlier tonight, after the news and cable networks had been broadcasting the report of Senator Clarence's murder on practically every station for most of the day, the woman was as upset as Tavia had ever heard her.

It had taken fifteen minutes just to convince her that Tavia was safe, particularly when the federal agents and officers had forbade her from disclosing to anyone where she was staying. Tavia was sure that if Aunt Sarah was given the hotel name or address, she would have been knocking on the door as soon as she could get there. She had fretted that Tavia wasn't telling her everything, which she wasn't.

"I don't understand, dear. Are you in some kind of trouble? Why would the police need you to stay somewhere overnight?"

"They have a lot of questions for me yet, Aunt Sarah. The detective in charge of the investigation thought it would be more convenient if I stayed in the city so we can talk some more tonight, then start again early in the morning."

"But they don't know about your condition. You're not well, Tavia. You should be home, not stuck somewhere for their convenience."

"I'm perfectly fine," she'd insisted, but it had been clear that Aunt Sarah hadn't totally believed it.

Ten more minutes had been spent assuring her that Tavia did, indeed, have her medicines—all of them, including the small stash she kept on hand in case of an emergency such as this that might delay her from getting home as expected—in her pocketbook.

Tavia didn't have the energy to explain she might be gone for more than one night. Nor did she divulge the fact that she'd convinced Detective Avery to send an unmarked squad car to Aunt Sarah's neighborhood to make sure none of the danger Tavia might be in spilled over onto her only living relative.

"Don't worry about me, Aunt Sarah," she'd told the old woman as gently as she could. "I'm going to be all right. I really will."

The conversation had left her feeling more stifled than protected. She hated begrudging Aunt Sarah's concern, but there were times when Tavia couldn't picture a future without her aunt in her life. Under the same roof. She felt trapped, suffocating with it, at the same time shamed by even this small resentment for a woman who clearly wanted only what was best for her.

Tavia put her head under the warm spray and worked a dollop of shampoo into her long hair. She scrubbed her scalp, feeling the nearly imperceptible outlines of the curved tangle of old scars that tracked up the back of her nape and into her hairline. She rinsed away the soap, then squirted some of the conditioner into her palms and smoothed it on.

In the other room of the suite, a game horn sounded on the television, marking the end of a shot clock. The men's voices carried as they argued the last play and made cutting remarks about the out-of-town team.

Tavia took her time rinsing off, dousing her hair and body, reluctant to let go of the warm, wet peace she was enjoying. But with her stomach starting to growl and the men waiting to order dinner for themselves until she was ready to eat too, she finally reached out to crank the lever on the tub and shower's water supply. It cut off with a squeak.

And then . . . silence.

An unnatural, ominous silence.

Naked and dripping, she peeked out from behind the plastic curtain. Listened for a long moment.

Nothing but quiet—not even the sound of the television running now.

"Hello?" she called anxiously. "Officer Murphy?"

She stepped out onto the bath mat. No time to bother with a towel, she grabbed the terry hotel robe from its hook on the back of the door and wrapped it around herself. Wet strands of hair drooped into her face as she hastily tied the belt at her waist and crept forward to put her hand on the doorknob.

Something was wrong. Very wrong. She could feel it in every fiber of her being, nerve endings jolting with sudden, certain alarm.

She slipped out to the empty bedroom and padded silently toward the closed door that led to the suite's living quarters just down the hall.

As she neared, a muffled groan cut short in the other room, followed by a hard thump that vibrated the floor beneath her bare soles.

Tavia froze.

She didn't need to open the door to know that death waited on the other side, but she couldn't keep her hand from quietly turning the knob. She peered out through the smallest wedge of space she dared. Her eyes met the unseeing gaze of Officer Murphy, lying motionless at the other end of the hallway. A big man, yet his neck was twisted and broken like a doll's, his head turned at a morbid angle on the floor.

Tavia's heart slammed hard against her rib cage.

Had the intruder killed them all?

It was *him,* she knew it with a visceral certainty that throbbed in her veins.

Her instincts screamed for her to get out of there now. She spun on her heel and hurried to the curtained slider on the far side of the bed. Fumbling with the lever lock on the handle, she finally wrenched the glass door and screen open. A wintry gust swept inside, blowing fine icy snowflakes into her eyes. Two steps out onto the frigid concrete balcony, she stopped short and exhaled a hissed curse.

The room was ten stories above the street.

No way out, not from here. Whatever was going on in the suite outside her bedroom, she was trapped in the middle of it.

"Shit." Tavia backed away from the open slider. She turned around . . . and came up short with a gasp.

The man from her nightmares—the deranged psychopath who'd murdered Senator Clarence in cold blood and undoubtedly now wanted to finish her off too—stood less than two inches from her face.

She opened her mouth to scream but didn't manage even the smallest sound before he clamped one hand around the back of her neck and the other came down swiftly across her lips. His grip was strong, unbreakable. Wild-eyed, terrified, she reached up to grab at his fingers, but they resisted like iron.

"Be still," he rasped, a curt command. His voice was rough and deep, far more powerful up close than it had been last night at the police station. There was something fuller about the grim set of his mouth too, and something not quite right at all about his eyes.

At first she dismissed their odd emberlike glow as a trick of her panicked mind. The pupils seemed distorted somehow, stretched thin and narrow in the center of his burning irises. Impossible that it could be anything but imagined.

But no . . . it wasn't distress that made her see it. This was real. As real as the unrelenting heat of his hands on her, fingers searing her nape and pressing hotly against her mouth.

As real as the sharp, elongated white tips of his teeth,

which glinted as he parted his lips to speak once more. "I'm not going to hurt you, Tavia."

Oh, God.

Here was her nightmare, standing before her in real life.

He wasn't human; he couldn't be. Her mind rejected the word that leapt at her from out of the horror stories and dark fiction Aunt Sarah had chided her for reading when she was a child.

Tavia wasn't sure what he was, but she didn't believe even for a second that he wasn't going to kill her in that next instant like he had the senator and the men in the other room. She struggled against him with all she had now, attempting to twist and fight her way free. But she couldn't budge him off her.

He was strong—as strong as any monster should be.

And with the sudden surge of adrenaline into her bloodstream, Tavia felt her body begin to rebel beneath the forced calm that her medicines provided. Her heart rate jackhammered, sending her pulse throbbing in her temples. She groaned against the fingers that held her mouth closed, all the while trying to will herself out of an anxiety tailspin.

He maneuvered her around and pushed her down onto the bed.

"No!" her mind screamed, the physical cry snuffed in her throat.

She was on her back and struggling uselessly, his hand still flat on her lips. The other had come around swiftly from behind her neck, only to rest across her brow. Here he touched her lightly, the warmth of his broad palm barely skimming the surface of her skin.

"Relax, Tavia," he said, that low, graveled growl not so much menacing now as coaxing. "Close your eyes."

She bucked, thrashing her head beneath the odd comfort of his words. He seemed confused that she wouldn't comply. Those inhuman eyes narrowed, pinning her in a scathing amber glow.

"Sleep." It was a command this time, his hand still held to her forehead.

She glared up at him in defiance, letting him read her fury in her own seething gaze. Fighting with her legs, slamming her fists futilely against the rock-solid muscles of his back and shoulders, she made another desperate attempt to break free.

As she shifted and fought, she felt cool air hit the naked skin of her chest. Her hotel robe gaped open in a wide downward V, baring her to his gaze from throat to navel. Baring the worst of her skin's flaws.

He stared.

Then he swore. "Holy hell . . ."

Tavia moaned, humiliation making her fright compound into something even more terrible. It was awful enough to be assaulted and in fear of her life. Now this astonishingly inhuman being gaped at her as though *she* were the freak.

The press of his palm against her mouth fell away on another, more vivid curse. Head cocked in an animalistic angle, his wild amber eyes came back up to her face in obvious disbelief. "What the fuck is this?"

CHAPTER
Ten

He was hallucinating.

Had to be.

Chase knew what Bloodlust could do to one of his kind. He understood how the disease could corrode logic, rob the senses and reason until nothing remained of even the soundest mind. He'd sure as hell felt it nipping at his own sanity in recent days.

Bloodlust had been raking him hard after he left the detective back at the police station parking lot. The hand-to-hand combat with the two unconscious feds and the dead Minion lying in the other room had made it even worse. He was in a bad way, he knew, but never had his affliction manifested in such a crazed mental trick as it did now.

Because what he thought he was seeing on Tavia Fairchild's bared skin was impossible.

A pattern of dense but delicate markings tracked her body from neck to torso. They were light-colored, a faint mauve barely darker than her fair skin tone. To his impaired vision, swamped in the amber light of his hunger, the webwork of interconnecting flourishes and twining swirls looked like something he was intimately familiar with.

The markings looked very much like Breed *dermaglyphs*.

"Impossible," he said, hearing his own confusion in the feral growl of his voice.

Skin designs like these occurred only on his kind. And courtesy of a genetic anomaly of the race, beginning when the Ancients sired their young on Breedmates and created the Breed, all of Chase's kind—for all the thousands of years they'd existed on this planet—were born male.

Through the fog of his questionable reason, he was reminded of Jenna Darrow, the woman who'd recently come to the Order from Alaska following an assault by the last of the Ancients. Brock's human mate had marks like these now, but they were minor in comparison and caused by the alien DNA contained in the rice-size bit of biotechnology the Ancient had implanted in her during her ordeal.

This was something altogether different.

Where the thick terry robe was still loosely fastened at Tavia's waist, the intricate skin pattern disappeared beneath the folds of the fabric. He caught a glimpse of more on her hip as she tried to scramble away from him on the bed.

Jesus, how far did they extend?

He reached for the belted tie, about to yank it open.

"No!" she cried, eyes fixed on him in abject horror as she drew the edges closed in trembling fists. "Get away! Don't touch me!"

Her fear jolted him from the insane tack his mind was

taking. He hadn't come there to terrify her. His objective had been to see her safe, to make certain the Minion cop accompanying her didn't harm her. At the same time, he'd been damned curious why Dragos would enlist one of his mind slaves to act as her guard.

That question burned more fiercely as he stared down at her white-knuckled hands that gripped the robe closed over her body like her life depended on it.

Chase laid his palm to her forehead once more, another attempt to trance her, but she had a strong mind that didn't want to go down easy. She fought the lull that should have put her under in just a few moments and would have made it easier for him to decide what to do with her next. She pushed and fought, refusing to surrender despite the fear that he could feel rolling off her tall, deceptively athletic body in waves.

And he had other problems stirring now.

In the room outside, one of the federal agents Chase'd knocked unconscious was starting to rouse. If either of them woke and saw him there, eyes throwing off amber sparks and fangs extended to razor-sharp points, his mind scrub on them a few minutes ago would have been for nothing. And he didn't have time for a do-over.

"Stand up," he growled at Tavia Fairchild. He took off his stolen coat and covered her with it, robe and all. Then he fisted his hand in the woolen lapels and hauled her up off the bed. "Come with me."

He gave her little choice. Pulling her along the short hallway to the living room of the hotel suite, he ignored her choked gasp as she saw the signs of the struggle and the three large law enforcement personnel lying in crumpled heaps on the floor. Her breath was coming fast and hard now, on the verge of hyperventilation.

"You killed them," she cried. "Oh, God . . . let me go!"

"I only killed the one who needed killing," he said as he dragged her through the room, past the dead Minion. One of the feds moaned, started to move where he lay on the floor nearby. It would only be seconds before he came to, and Chase needed to be gone before that happened.

"Please," Tavia choked. "Please, don't do this. Tell me what you want from me!"

God help him, he wasn't sure how to answer that now. All he knew was he had to get out of there and he couldn't leave her behind. So she was coming with him.

When she sucked in a breath and he felt her prepare to let it loose in a scream, he brought the Minion cop's gun around from the back waistband of his pants where he'd stashed it after the scuffle. All it took was one look at the weapon and she got quiet. He never would have used it on her; he was Breed, and that gave him about a dozen other ways he could have threatened her into silence. But the pistol spoke the most convincingly to her mortal sensibilities.

"This way," he ordered her. "Quickly."

Shocked and confused, she didn't resist. Chase pushed her into the empty hotel corridor outside the suite, then hustled her toward the back stairwell.

Fresh from a shower, Lucan stepped out the French doors of his and Gabrielle's private bedroom at the Maine compound and stood alone on the timber deck. He was naked, beads of water still clinging to his skin, which steamed in tendrils all around him as he walked into the brittle night air. It was cold this far north and this deep into winter, punishingly so. He breathed it in, let it clear his mind and crystallize his thoughts around mission goals and duty. The things he knew best—the burdens he had elected to carry on his shoulders alone when he founded the Order all those centuries ago.

He'd never resented that choice, and he'd be damned if he let himself start doing so now.

On a muttered curse, he inhaled another lungful of bracing cold and pushed it deep down, determined to smother the strange ache that had been troubling him all day. It had plagued him longer than that, he had to admit, although it had taken seeing Gabrielle with Dante and Tess's baby before the disturbing ache—the unwanted void—had given itself a name.

It was longing.

Bone-deep, and undeniable.

Christ, he was sick with it.

He saw his beloved mate near the small Breed infant and knew an instant, intense yearning to see her swell with his own sons. Everything male in him had roared with the need to claim her in that most primal, basic way. In that moment earlier today, he had wanted it more than anything he'd ever known.

And that was something he could not afford to feel right now.

Not when their world was in the midst of war with Dragos and everyone was looking to Lucan to lead. Bad enough he worried for Gabrielle every time he left her behind to walk into combat. He couldn't bear to think of possibly leaving her to raise his child alone.

That was why he'd always frowned on warriors taking a mate, had all but forbidden any of them from starting a family while serving the Order. It was just two summers ago when his point had proven out tragically in the Boston compound when Conlan, a member of the Order for more than a hundred years, took a fatal blast of bomb shrapnel and C-4 explosives while on patrol pursuing a Minion. Conlan's grieving widow, Danika, had been forced to release her dead mate to the sun while pregnant with their firstborn. She'd decided to leave Boston soon afterward, devastated and bereft.

Not that the painful lesson had been warning enough to any of the other warriors to avoid emotional entanglements. Somehow, within the space of less than two years, they'd nearly all taken Breedmates—Lucan himself included. Things had only gotten more complicated when Niko and Renata brought eight-year-old Mira in with them as their own child when they'd paired up some six months ago, and now Dante and Tess had newborn Xander Raphael.

Lucan tilted his face up to glower at the pale gray wedge of a waning crescent moon peeking through the canopy of soaring pines overhead. He'd have to be a fool to think about adding another innocent life to the potential casualty list, should this situation with Dragos escalate into the catastrophe Lucan dreaded was coming.

He raked a hand through his damp hair and exhaled a curse into the frigid, dark night.

"I didn't realize you'd come back already."

Gabrielle's warm voice jolted him to attention. He turned to face her and was struck, as always, by how beautiful she was. Tonight her long auburn hair was swept up off her delicate nape in a loose twist, curling tendrils framing her pretty face and soothing brown eyes. She was dressed all in black—not the soft colors and easy lines she normally wore, but a low-cut silk blouse unbuttoned to just between her breasts. The fabric was filmy, skating over her alabaster skin and lacy black bra. Her skirt was fitted and clinging to her every curve, hinting at the flare of her hips and her long, lean legs. Sharp-toed, glossy leather boots lifted her a good five inches on thin stiletto heels.

Damn, she was hot.

No wonder he'd been doomed from the moment he first laid eyes on her.

Lucan cleared his throat. "I got back about an hour ago. You look amazing."

She smiled and walked out to meet him, crossing her arms around herself to rub at the cold. Her breath puffed in a light cloud as she spoke. "You've been home for an hour? What are you doing out here?"

Lucan shrugged and brought her under the warmth of his sheltering arm. "Just getting some air."

"It's freezing," she pointed out. "And you're naked."

He put his mouth to her temple. "Suddenly I wish you were too."

Her quiet laugh didn't seem as light as it sounded. "How did it go with Kellan tonight?"

"He hunted," Lucan replied. "He fed."

"That's good news."

Lucan grunted. "It'll be good news when he doesn't need to be told to do it or require an escort to make sure it happens."

"He's been through a lot," Gabrielle reminded him. "And he's just a boy. Give him time."

Lucan nodded, guessing she had a point. Kellan had been none too pleased to discover Lucan had been serious about taking him out personally to find a blood Host that night if Lazaro hadn't already made firm plans to see the task done. At nightfall, Lucan had found the youth in the Order's makeshift weapons room, engaged in solo mock combat, wielding a pair of long daggers. He wasn't very good—all gangly arms and lanky, uncooperative legs—but he wouldn't have had much practice at battle while living in the Darkhavens. He'd almost cut off his foot with a fumbled blade when Lucan announced they were going hunting right then, just the two of them, together.

Lazaro Archer would have been perfectly capable and ready to take the boy himself, but Lucan had been curious. He'd taken Kellan to Bangor, the nearest city with a decent population and enough public gathering places to select from without being noticed as anything more than tourists from "away."

Kellan had chosen an old drunk sleeping off a bender in the downtown park—easy prey, but the exercise tonight hadn't been about challenge or technique. Lucan had stood back while the boy quickly fed, then left his blood Host in a peaceful, trance-induced drowse. Kellan didn't say two words to him on the drive back to headquarters, but his eyes had lost their dark circles and his skin color was flushed a ruddy, healthy pink from the feeding.

Gabrielle turned a questioning look on him. "You've been back all this time, but you didn't come to find me and let me know? That's not like you."

He kissed her furrowed brow. "You were with Tess. I didn't want to disturb, in case they were resting. Besides, I'd asked Gideon for a systems check earlier today and he'd been waiting for me to return."

Gabrielle's inquisitiveness took on a suspicious edge. "If I didn't know better, I might think you were trying to avoid me."

He scoffed at the idea, but part of him wondered if she could be right. He cast a dark glance up at the night sky and that damned sliver of a moon suspended within it. This was the fertile time for Gabrielle, and for every

Breedmate who shared a blood bond with one of Lucan's kind.

It took blood and seed given together, a mutual feeding at the moment of release—during the cycle of a crescent moon—to create the spark of new Breed life.

The act was sacred, not to be entered into with any trace of doubt.

Gabrielle stared at him in his silence. She took a small step forward, moving out from under his arm to gaze up at the black velvet sky herself. She released a small sigh, wordless but rife with understanding. She gave her back to the moon and faced him, leaning against the waist-high railing of the deck. "I hear there's been word from Hunter tonight. He and Corinne are on their way north?"

Lucan nodded, more than willing to take her offered detour in the conversation. "Had to wait out the daylight in Pennsylvania, but they're on the road again tonight. They expect to make New England before daybreak, arriving here tomorrow night."

It still seemed strange sometimes to think of Hunter as part of the Order, but the lethal Gen One who'd once served as assassin for Dragos had proven himself to be a vital asset in the short time he'd been with the warriors. Now he was returning from a mission in New Orleans—one that had netted the Order valuable intel from a key area of Dragos's operation. Hunter was bringing that intel with him.

He was bringing something else too: Corinne, his new mate, and the boy she'd given birth to some thirteen years ago, while she'd been held captive in one of Dragos's genetics labs.

"I can't say I'm surprised that Hunter and Corinne are together," Gabrielle remarked, as if she were tuned into Lucan's thoughts as much as her blood bond to him had connected them emotionally. "They're both survivors of Dragos's evil. Now they have a fresh start, together. Nathan too, that poor child."

Lucan considered Corinne's Breed son, one of many sired on scores of imprisoned Breedmates whom Dragos had used to create his own private army of first generation Breed assassins. Those Gen One offspring all shared the same paternal DNA—taken from the Ancient that Dragos had kept hidden and secret for centuries, enslaved to do his bidding until the otherworlder escaped to the wilds of Alaska. That Ancient was dead now, killed by the Order after cutting a bloody swath through a number of settlements up there before the attack on Jenna that had left her changed forever.

But his laboratory-bred progeny lived on, raised in solitude by Minions and schooled by Dragos in the art of killing. They were called Hunters, stripped of their identities and all humanity from the time they were born. Boys like Corinne's son, Nathan. And the Order's own Hunter, whose imprisoned Breedmate mother hadn't lived long enough to see freedom from her captivity or been given the opportunity to search for her lost child the way Corinne recently had. Thanks to the dogged efforts of Gabrielle and the other women of the Order, Corinne and the few remaining Breedmate survivors had been located in their secret prison and set free to try to begin their lives again.

"How many boys like Nathan do you think there are?" Gabrielle asked.

Lucan shook his head. "Too many. Dragos has been breeding his assassins for decades, beginning with Hunter, fifty-odd years ago."

"And I suppose we shouldn't expect that Dragos's experiments were limited to his breeding labs," she added, her tone grave. "God only knows the extent of his sick work."

"With any luck," Lucan said, "the lab intel that Hunter's bringing back with him from New Orleans will give us some idea about that."

Gabrielle's mouth curved. "I'm sure Gideon can't wait to get his hands on the computer files. Not to mention the genetic samples Dragos had been keeping in cold storage."

Lucan nodded. "I've been hearing about it from Gideon ever since Hunter first contacted us, saying he had the cryo tanks and lab records and would soon be heading our way."

The recovery of the laboratory intel was only the latest blow the Order had dealt Dragos's operation. It was also very likely the thing that had pushed him to the edge, made him desperate enough to pull the trigger on the bombing of the building in Boston and deliver human law enforcement right to the Order's front door.

"This thing with Dragos is far from over," Lucan said, sharing his troubling thoughts with Gabrielle. "He's not finished, not by a long shot. He's going to do something that can't be fixed. I can feel it in my bones. We're never going to be able to go back to the way things were."

Gabrielle stepped toward him. She wrapped her arms around his naked waist, her cheek coming to rest warmly against his chest. "You're doing all you can. We all are, Lucan. Put Dragos out of your head for now."

He ground his molars together, ready to tell her there was no way to put the bastard out of his mind. Dragos lived inside him like a ghost now, mocking and foul, oily with menace.

Gabrielle reached up and took his tense jaw in her tender hands. She brought his mouth down to hers, pressing a slow kiss to his lips. "Try to forget him for a little while," she said. Her eyes shone up at him with a hint of mischief. "It is your birthday, after all. Or did you forget?"

He grunted, surprised at the reminder. "I never give the day much thought," he said as he stroked his fingertips along the graceful line of her throat.

"Well, I do," she said. "And I have something for you."

She drew out of his arms and walked back into their bedroom. He followed behind her, unable to take his eyes from the sway of her perfect ass that looked even more incredible with every long stride she took in those spiked black heels. She pulled something from out of a bureau drawer on the other side of the room and held it behind her as she turned to face him. "It's not much, just something I thought you'd like to have."

"You didn't have to get me anything," he replied, voice a bit thick now that his fangs were erupting out of his gums in desire for his woman. He wanted to peel her out of that clingy skirt and lick her from the toe of her glossy boots to the peachy tips of the nipples that were pressing through the lacy black bra and gauzy silk of her blouse. "I already have everything I could possibly want."

She brought the gift around, a large, folded square of fabric tied with a red satin ribbon. Gabrielle placed it in his hands. "Open it."

He tugged the bow loose and untied the ribbon. As he began to unfold the embroidered swatch, he realized at once what it was. The tapestry was old—centuries old, a medieval depiction of a dark knight on horseback, a hilltop castle smoldering in the distance behind him. Lucan remembered that moment very well; he'd lived it. He had commissioned the tapestry not long after he'd founded the Order, never suspecting the secrets it would hold within its design, or for how long it would keep them.

The tapestry was important to him for many reasons, but mostly now because his Breedmate had seen to it that the piece made it safely out of Boston.

"You were so busy gathering up combat gear and equipment, I decided to bring a few things of yours from before."

Lucan glanced up to meet his beloved's gaze. "Thank you. I've never had a nicer gift."

He put the tapestry down on the bed nearby and pulled Gabrielle into his arms. Their mouths met in a deep kiss, unhurried, sensual. Lucan soaked her in, felt the heat of her body pressed against his naked skin, silk sliding between them as he drew her close and ran his tongue along the wet softness of her lips, desire stirring like a flame meeting gasoline inside him.

His breath escaped on a rough growl as he skated his hands along the elegant line of her spine, then down to the strong curve of her backside. She moaned as he caressed and kissed her, the slick tip of her tongue pushing past his teeth and fangs to enter his mouth. Her fingers found his cock and took him in a firm grasp. He was already hard as granite, but her touch sent his blood surging southward, building toward an impossible ache. Mouth locked with his, she toyed with him, lightly stroking his shaft, teasing his balls with just the tips of her fingers.

Lucan brought his hand up between them and palmed her breast, flicking his thumb over the pebbled bead of a nipple that strained against the lace and silk that confined it. He made quick work of the tiny buttons on her blouse, then eased it off her shoulders and let it fall to the floor at their feet. When he started to reach for the front closure on the skimpy bra, Gabrielle took his hand and guided him to her hips.

"Touch me," she whispered around heady kisses. "Feel how much I want you."

He obeyed at once, lifting the long drape of her skirt until he could slide his hand beneath. Her firm thighs were encased in silk stockings that rasped against his roughened fingertips as he stroked up the length of them. The silk ended abruptly, topped off by a band of grippy lace. Her hips and ass were bare.

No panties.

Ah, Christ.

She let go of a shuddery sigh as he let his hands roam over her smooth, naked skin. When he slipped his fingers between the wet satin of her sex, he felt her answering moan vibrate deep inside his own throat. His arousal throbbed with the need to be in her. His blood went molten, desire hot and possessive in his veins. He found the zipper on the side of her skirt and tugged it down. His hands were clumsy and rough as he pushed it over her hips and watched as his woman was revealed to him, in nothing but a black lacy bra, thigh-highs, and gleaming leather boots.

"Holy hell," he murmured, feasting his gaze on her.

She smiled, a catlike curve of her kiss-swollen mouth. "The tapestry might not be the best gift you've ever gotten."

Lucan could only stand there at full attention as she slowly sank down onto those slender heels before him and took his stiff cock in her hands. Her eyes on his, she stroked his shaft and palmed his balls, her thumb working the underside, fingers slick with his arousal. God help him, when her mouth closed around the head of him, he nearly lost it, right on the spot.

She sucked him until he could hardly stand it anymore, until all he could do was lift her up to her feet and bury himself to the hilt where they were standing. He didn't know how they made it over to the wall near the open French doors a moment later, didn't have control enough to pause this fevered fucking and bring her to the bed, where he could make love to her properly.

Not that this didn't feel proper. He'd never felt anything more proper in his life than the heat of Gabrielle engulfing him completely, her body caught in his arms, her mouth hungry and demanding on his.

"Feed me," she whispered against his lips now, nipping at him with her blunt little teeth. "Let me drink from you, Lucan."

He couldn't refuse her. There was nothing more intimate than the bond they shared. There was nothing more precious he could offer his mate than the lifeblood that gave her immortality with him and bound her to him for as long as they both drew breath. And drinking from him would heighten her pleasure now like nothing else could.

Gathering her weight in one arm as he continued to thrust into her welcoming body, Lucan brought his other wrist to his mouth and sank his fangs into the veins that pulsed there. Gabrielle drew him to her and latched on hard. She moaned with ecstasy as the first drops of his blood hit her tongue.

He could feel her climax building. His own was right behind her, gaining power as she suckled at his wrist and wrapped herself more tightly around him. He could see her pulse ticking strongly in the veins of her pretty throat. That rhythmic drum pounded inside him too, driving him toward release and beckoning him to take the pleasure that waited just beneath the delicate flesh of his beautiful Breedmate's neck.

Gabrielle's eyes were open, watching him, imploring him. She angled her head, presenting herself to him like an offering atop an altar.

Lucan snarled with the force of the temptation. But his release was too close. And there was a crescent moon out tonight. His gaze flicked toward it through the open French doors and he couldn't bite back his growl.

Gabrielle's mouth drew away from the small wounds on his wrist. She reached up to touch his face, her eyes tender with understanding. "Would it be so bad, Lucan? I want this too."

He couldn't speak. He looked into her loving gaze, torn with longing and fear, dread for what kind of future their sons would have if he failed in his mission now. Could he risk that?

Could he risk knowing that the sons he shared with Gabrielle might be born into this war of his making—or, worse, become casualties of it?

Gabrielle showed him no mercy. Her lips fastened once more to the open vein at his wrist, as her legs wrapped tighter at his hips, spiked boot heels digging into him like spurs as she held him against her and cried out with the first tremors of her orgasm. Lucan roared as pleasure rocked her body, the sheath of her sex clutching hard around him, tiny muscles coaxing him toward the point of no return.

"Do it," she whispered harshly, lips stained red with his blood as she reached up to take his nape in her palm.

She guided his face down to her vulnerable throat. Pressed his mouth against her throbbing carotid as her slender body began to crest beneath him in release. "Oh, God, Lucan. Please . . . do it now. I can feel how much you want this too."

Lucan's orgasm coiled hard at the base of his shaft. He couldn't stop his hips from moving, couldn't stop his seed from its want to boil over, his release on the verge of exploding.

One nick of his fangs against her skin. That's all it would take. One taste of her blood on the tip of his tongue and he would be unable to keep from taking her in full. She'd be pregnant with his child by the end of the night.

Ah, fuck . . .

"No," he snarled, more to himself than in rejection of what she'd asked of him. His cock shuddered as he drove in deeper, his control beginning to snap its leash. "I can't . . . I won't do this to you."

He'd barely gotten the words out before his body detonated inside her. His release shot through him, a rushing, endless stream. Lucan turned his face away from the temptation of Gabrielle's fast-ticking vein as his seed flooded her and she went very still against him.

"I'm sorry," he murmured when he was finally able to summon his voice again. He gently pulled his wrist out of her slack grasp and sealed the punctures with a sweep of his tongue. "Gabrielle . . . I'm sorry."

Feeling like a coward and a bastard, he bowed his head to hers and held her in a prolonged and awful silence.

CHAPTER
Eleven

She didn't know where he'd taken her. The room was dark, windows shuttered with louvered steel sandwiched between twin panes of glass. There was no light coming in from the street outside, but in the hours that had passed since she'd been brought there, Tavia could hear the muffled din of traffic increasing with the rise of dawn. The late-night hush was gone, punctuated now by the ruckus of the morning commute, the occasional blare of a car horn or the hiss of a slowing mass transit bus interrupting the rhythmic hum of tires speeding over frozen asphalt.

She was in a house of some sort. Probably still within Boston, perhaps even in the heart of the city.

She'd expected to be dead by now. After being forced from the hotel at gunpoint, having witnessed what she had inside the suite—three fully armed law enforcement officials disabled and left unmoving at the hands of one clearly unhinged, lethal man—Tavia hadn't been given any logical reason to think she'd be spared, never mind her abductor's word that he wasn't going to hurt her. She'd been alert and waiting for death to come at any moment, listening to the quiet inside the strange place he'd brought her, wondering if he merely slept outside the locked door of the bedroom or was deciding how best to dispose of her.

Even now, after the night had passed into dawn and she was still breathing, she wasn't at all convinced she was going to make it out of this situation alive. She sat on the edge of a bare king-size mattress in a room that was vacant except for its few pieces of shrouded furniture, dreading that the next time she saw him would likely be the last.

He hadn't told her where they were going, had simply rushed her down the back stairwell of the hotel to the parking garage below street level, tossed her into the trunk of the federal agents' sedan, and sped away with her. Although it had seemed like they'd driven for more than an hour, Tavia could have sworn they'd never left the city. The sounds and smells, the bumps and turns of the tight network of streets, the general crackle of activity—her senses had known all of it as though she could almost picture the city from inside the cramped darkness of the trunk.

It was familiar to her. It was freedom out there, if only she could find her way out of this locked room.

Away from this lifeless, shrouded phantom of a house.

Wrapping the robe tighter around herself, Tavia got off the bed and padded over to the window once more. There was nothing to see, no means of opening the shutters. They appeared to be electronically controlled and as secure as a bank vault. The glass panes were thick, stationary panels. The only way through them would be to smash her way out, assuming the glass could be broken. And assuming she could find any kind of tool to use on it.

Her eyes having long since adjusted to the lightless gloom, Tavia glanced at the furniture that stood draped in pale sheets around the bedroom. Sturdy, masculine shapes hinted at a tall bureau and mirrored dresser across the floor from the four-poster bed. She walked over and lifted the shroud to make a quick perusal of the drawers. To her surprise she found them neatly packed with folded socks and underwear, organized with military precision into grouped color ranges and fabric styles.

The walk-in closet yielded the same unexpected discovery: a full wardrobe of men's clothing, from scores of expensive-looking tailored suits and tuxedos, to easily tens of thousands of dollars' worth of conservative casual wear. A collection of size-fourteen shoes, all black, and all meticulously polished and maintained, lined the bottom row of the enormous closet. Whoever had lived here enjoyed a privileged life surrounded by very fine things.

And they'd apparently left it all behind.

The entire bedroom screamed of old money and long-established roots. Tavia glanced up at the crown molding that framed the ten-foot ceilings, the wainscoted walls that weren't painted or papered but covered in delicate ivory silk. She drifted to the other side of the large room, her bare feet cushioned by a dark-patterned Oriental rug that spread out over nearly the entire span of the floor.

A wide desk ate up most of the wall space across from the bed. She pulled off its linen drape and sat down in the sumptuous leather chair. The top of the desk had been swept clean, but its drawers, like those of the bureau and dresser, held the neatly ordered contents of a life interrupted and abandoned.

Tavia sifted through the pens and office implements, looking for something she might wield as a weapon against her abductor or a tool to break out of her confinement. As she dug toward the back of the drawer, her fingertips disrupted a stack of printed snapshots collected with an assortment of other memorabilia in a shallow silver tray.

She pulled the tray out and set it atop the polished wood surface of the desk. It was engraved with a distinguished-sounding name: Sterling Chase. His? she wondered.

A small metal vial about the size of her thumb rolled back and forth on top of the photos. Tavia picked it up and examined it, but she couldn't tell what, if anything, was inside. It felt light in her hand, and made no sound when she shook it, but its corked stopper had been carefully sealed with red wax. She set it aside as her gaze lit on the photographs.

There were about a dozen in all. Random events and subjects documenting what seemed to be a decade of time: A formal reception inside a posh country club. Some award presentation attended by a crowd of immense men dressed in the same kind of dark suits she'd found in the bedroom closet. A young boy's birthday party, resplendent with bright balloons and streamers and a mound of gift-wrapped presents, the celebration held in what appeared to be this very house.

And one final snapshot, buried at the bottom of the stack.

Tavia stared at it and felt some of the blood rush out of her head . . .

It was her captor.

The deranged menace—the man whom her instincts warned was something more than human. He stood behind a pricey-looking sofa, his muscled arms spread along its back to form a protective arch around the slender shoulders of a petite blond woman and the young boy from the birthday party picture. The boy had gotten older, no longer the towheaded, grinning child holding a giant box with a bow on top of it but a handsome teen wearing a Harvard University sweatshirt and a cocky smile that seemed to say he had the world by the tail.

The woman was stunning. Delicate and beautiful, her perfect oval face was as flawless as the ivory silk on the walls that surrounded her, her long blond hair the color of corn silk, her wide lavender eyes fringed in dark lashes. She beamed at the young man like a proud mother, even though she looked to be only a few years older than he.

Tavia's abductor was smiling too, a subtle, practiced curve of his broad mouth that made him look at once charming and devastating. Attractive didn't even come close to describing the lean angles of his face and the determined, square cut of his jaw.

But where his smile seemed rehearsed and posed, his gaze was disarmingly naked. It smoldered with a pained kind of desire.

All of it aimed at the pretty young woman held loosely in the shelter of his arm.

Tavia sifted back through the rest of the photos once more. He was in most of them, attending important-looking gatherings, dressed in his impeccable suits, surrounded by wealth and privilege and gentility.

My God.

Whoever he was—whatever he had become—this was the life he'd come from.

This was his family.

This place he'd brought her to?

It had once been his home.

Chase awoke to a fierce banging in his head.

He came to on a guttural snarl, blood thirst shredding him with sharp talons that had barely loosened their grip from the night before. His skull was throbbing, mouth as dry as cotton. Every particle of his being felt raw, strung out. Starving for a fix.

Without opening his eyes, he pushed himself up from the floor where he'd slumped a few hours ago, weakened from exertion and injury, in desperate need of a feeding. A feeding he could not afford to take, when his addiction would only crave it more and more the next time.

He sensed it was dawn outside. Hours had passed since he'd arrived in this place with the woman from the hotel.

Tavia Fairchild.

Her name seemed less like a stranger's now than a puzzle that needed solving. She was a mystery that didn't make sense to him but was one he could not ignore.

That was why he'd brought her here, to this place he'd never expected to return to again.

He'd needed time to think, time to observe her. In the urgent moments following his breach of her cop-secured hotel suite and the precious time he'd wasted driving around Boston in search of viable shelter, he'd finally come to accept there was only one place he could go now. His former Darkhaven, where he'd been leader of his family's enclave following the death of his older brother in service to the Breed's Enforcement Agency.

Chase had walked away from it when he'd joined up with the Order a year and a half ago, never looking back. The near-dozen kin he'd been responsible for then, the young cousins, family friends, and distant relations, had since moved on to other Darkhavens in the area. Now his former home was nothing but a vacant tomb housing the memories of his past sins and failures.

This brownstone mansion in Boston's Back Bay was the last place he wanted to be, but he could think of nowhere else that would be safe enough for Tavia and far enough off-grid for him. As far as human law enforcement knew, his sole place of residence had been the Order's mansion. They didn't know anything about him except what he'd been willing to give them.

All of it amounting to little more than lies and half-truths.

Chase groaned, unwilling to drag his eyelids open as another bout of hammering crashed behind his temples. His whole body recoiled under the relentless *bang!* . . . *bang!* . . . *bang!* . . . that seemed to echo from all around him and within him.

Then, the sudden crash of breaking glass.

Chase was on his feet and at the locked door of his bedroom in an instant.

He threw it open and found Tavia standing in her white hotel robe in front of the shuttered window, breath sawing as she paused to lift his heavy desk chair and slam it against the glass again. A piercingly bright nimbus of sunlight arrowed in through the splintered glass, blinding him as soon as he entered.

Chase hissed at the solar onslaught, his fangs punching out of his gums in his rage. He raised his arm to his forehead to shield his eyes and charged in to take hold of her arm before she could level another blow. "What the fuck do you think you're doing?"

"Let go of me!" She shrieked as he ripped the chair out of her hands. "I'm getting out of here!"

Chase grabbed her by the arm and pulled her out of the room with him, slamming the door closed behind them. He pushed her into the adjacent study where he'd spent the night. "Are you out of your goddamn mind?"

He thrust her away from him none too gently, barely able to control the feral part of him that was snapping at its tether, looking for any reason to get loose. She was half down on the floor near the fireplace, her robe gaping enough to bare the better part of one perfect breast. Chase swore. His vision was bathed in fiery amber, his skin prickling with the churning of his livid *dermaglyphs*.

Normally, he would have tried to glance away, attempted to hide himself from curious human eyes, but she stared at him unblinking, unflinching, her intelligent gaze locked unerringly on his transformation from man to monster.

"What are you? What's wrong with your eyes? I saw your teeth last night in the hotel. You have—" She choked a bit on the word. "I saw your fangs. I can see them now too. So tell me the truth. What the hell are you?"

"I think you know, Tavia," he answered flatly.

"No," she said. She let out a short bark of a laugh. "No, I promise you, I don't know. I'm not even sure I want to know."

She was trembling now, legs shaking beneath her as she started to get to her feet. He cocked his head, watching her. Studying her for a reaction that would tell him more about who—and what—she was. "You're afraid."

Her face went a bit paler. "I'm terrified, you sick son of a bitch! You killed my boss. You killed several cops and federal agents—"

"I told you, the agents were mostly unharmed," he interrupted to remind her.

"I don't care what you say. I don't believe you," she replied hotly. "You're a cold-blooded psychopath. At best, that's what you are. At worst, I don't even want to think about what you might be. You're a monster!"

Chase took a step toward her, watching her chest heave beneath the loose terry-cloth robe that barely covered her the more she struggled to stay on her feet. "Now you're angry."

"Stay away from me," she said as he came closer.

He looked at her exposed skin. The plunging V of her robe showed him an ample slice of the markings that covered her chest and torso. Those markings were still the same dusty mauve they'd been when he'd first spotted them last night in the hotel suite.

They couldn't be *glyphs*, he realized now. His own were pulsing and alive with color—a visceral reaction to his heightened emotional state—and yet hers, despite her fear and rage right now, remained static, wholly unchanging. "These markings of yours . . . how the hell can you have them?"

"Haven't you ever seen burn scars?" She tugged the robe closed to hide them as color rose into her cheeks. "Not that it's any business of yours, but when I was a baby, there was an accident. I was burned all over my body."

Although the story seemed plausible, and she certainly seemed to believe it herself, Chase wasn't convinced. "I've seen burn scars before and they don't look like that."

"Well, mine do," she said. "And I think you should know that I also have a serious medical condition. I'm not well. I need my medications."

He scoffed, unmoved by the obvious line of bullshit. "You don't look sick to me."

"I'm telling you the truth," she insisted. "My meds are in my pocketbook, back at the hotel. I can't go more than eight hours without taking them. It could be deadly for me."

He took another step toward her, close enough to see the desperation in her citrusy green eyes. She glanced down toward the fireplace tools, then made a hasty grab for an iron poker. She wielded the thing like a blade in front of her, about to make a hard jab at him with it.

Chase flung the length of metal out of her hands and across the room with the power of his mind alone. Her jaw dropped, eyes going wide as the poker went airborne. It hit the hardwood floor with a jarring clatter before skidding to a stop twenty feet away.

"You're not very strong, Tavia." Chase closed in on her before she could even realize he was moving. She blinked up at him in alarm as he brought his hands down on her shoulders in a subtle but firm hold. "Not very fast either."

She struggled against him, but he held her easily. Even if her mortal brain worked to process what it was witnessing, her instincts were immediately ready to take him on. Eyes blazing, her chin hiked up in challenge. "Is that what this is about for you? You want someone to put up a fight for you before you finally kill them?"

This close, it was impossible not to notice how beautiful she was. Her caramel-brown hair fell in glossy waves that broke at her shoulders, framing high cheekbones, a gracefully curved jaw and elegant throat. Her bright green gaze, even swamped with anger and fear, radiated keen intelligence. Inky black lashes fringed those eyes, softening the sharp wit with a doelike innocence. Her mouth was generous, dusky pink, full lips made for kissing. Among other things.

Chase drank her in, his earlier suspicion of her morphing into interest of another kind, no less powerful. An unbidden, unwelcome desire needled him in that moment, intensifying and darkening now that he was holding her just a breath away from his mouth.

No delicate waif, this was a lean, athletically built woman who stood only a few inches less than his six-and-a-half-foot height. She had a swimmer's body, perfectly proportioned muscle, toned and strong and agile. She seemed naturally fit, not shaped by the rigors of a personal trainer and strict diet. Each curve and angle was a flawless construction of female anatomy— scantily covered by one large scrap of draping terry cloth—and his male body responded in rising approval.

He could feel her anxiety spike as he studied her. His nostrils tingled with the scent of her fear and outrage, something more than simple *Homo sapiens* adrenaline shooting through her veins. Scowling, he tried to process what his senses were telling him.

He bent his head toward her, face moving in close to the side of her neck. She went utterly still as he dragged in a long breath against her skin, sniffing her hard. "You don't smell human."

"Oh, God," she moaned, her voice vibrating through him. "Please don't do this."

Hunger lashed him for the mistake of getting this

close to her throbbing carotid. It was far too easy to imagine penetrating the soft flesh. Drinking from her open vein.

He wondered what she would taste like. Would her blood be tangy, mundane copper, or something more exotic?

Taking her vein was probably the fastest way to determine if she was, in fact, human or something other. But he knew one sip would be too much. He needed to starve this thirst out of himself, not feed the addiction. And Tavia Fairchild was off limits completely until he got to the bottom of who, and what, she truly was.

Chase searched her gaze. "Tell me the truth, Tavia. You know you're not what you're pretending to be."

"I don't know what you're talking about," she insisted. "You're crazy."

"No," he said, giving a rough, humorless laugh. "Not quite crazy, not yet. I'm sane enough to see that you're keeping a secret. So tell me what it is. Tell me what you are. Did Dragos do this to you?"

She made another futile attempt to break out of his hold. "You're a lunatic! I've never even heard the name Dragos until you said it at the police station."

When she turned away from him, Chase reached out and lifted her face back to his. He watched, waited, expecting to see her pupils start to narrow into thin vertical slits the way his were now. But there was no change in the rounded pools of black that stared back at him. She couldn't be Breed—no matter how certain his instincts were that nothing else could explain her.

Impulsively, he put his finger to her lips and forced his way into her soft, wet mouth to check her teeth for the presence of fangs. There were none, of course. Only a straight row of blunt human pearly whites.

She clamped down on his finger with them, biting him hard enough to draw blood.

Chase yanked his hand back with a sharp curse.

She stared at the small wound, her eyes locked on to it and full of rage. Her body was shuddering now, quaking all over as though she were about to break. A droplet of Chase's blood beaded on her bottom lip.

"Christ," he murmured, recognizing only now how far he was pushing her. Some part of him felt shame for the terror he was inflicting on her, but the other part of him, the one that was still throbbing and wild with hunger, dug its claws into his backside, demanding to be let loose from its leash.

Everything Breed in Chase urged him to take this female and slake his thirst on her. Desire and suspicion and raw blood need was a dangerous combination, one he wasn't certain how long he could withstand. It rose up on him in a black wave, almost too powerful to resist. He had to put some distance between himself and this female, before the Bloodlust took hold of him completely.

With a growl, he spun Tavia around and pulled her hands behind her.

"What are you doing?" she demanded.

He didn't answer. He had no voice, now that his hunger was roaring to life again inside him. A mental command sent a braided silk drapery tie snaking into his palm from the nearby shuttered window. He secured it around her wrists, then set her down on a covered chair beside the fireplace.

"Please," she said, her tone gone from fear and outrage to one of desperate bargaining. "Please, I won't tell anyone what I've seen. I promise. Just let me go."

He crouched down in front of her, their faces level.

She was shivering and shaking, a sheen of perspiration breaking out on her tense brow. Looking at her now, he had to wonder if she'd been telling him the truth about her medical condition. She looked ill and pale since she'd bitten him, on the verge of fainting.

Chase didn't feel so well himself. It was easily eight hours before nightfall. Eight hours before he could even entertain the idea of getting out of there to work off some of his aggression. Eight hours of being trapped in close quarters with a woman who tempted him on more levels than he wanted to consider.

His fingers shook with the force of his mounting blood hunger as he reached out to wipe away the scarlet stain from her lips. Her eyes implored him for mercy, but the beast raging to life inside him now had none.

He stood and strode away from her without a word.

CHAPTER
Twelve

"Police today had no comment when asked whether the incident that occurred last night at the Hyatt Regency downtown was in any way connected to the recent killing of Senator Robert Clarence. Channel 5 has unconfirmed reports that at least one body was recovered from the scene. However, law enforcement officials are not willing to disclose any further details pending a complete invest—"

Dragos silenced the large flat-screen TV and tossed the remote behind him onto the bed. Naked, his *glyph*-covered skin still glistening with sweat and spilled human blood, he retrieved his pants from where they'd hit the floor a few hours ago and stepped into them.

"Get dressed," he told the pair of females who'd serviced his recent needs, basic and carnal both. The two humans were young and stupid, plucked from local stock on the mainland last night and brought the handful of miles offshore to his hidden island lair. They'd taken one look at his chauffeured car as it waited at a stoplight in their sorry little town and had climbed inside as soon as he curled his finger at them in invitation.

It would be their last mistake; as with all of his playthings, he didn't intend that either one of them would live to make it out of his lair in one piece.

Dismissing the thought of them already, he strode out of the room. Since relocating to the remote fortress off the coast of Maine more than a month ago, he'd managed to get most of his operation back online and functional. Systems had been in place on a contingency basis for years, and his Minion staff of technology and laboratory experts worked around the clock to see that everything continued to run smoothly.

He had other Minions as well, embedded around Boston and elsewhere, a veritable legion of human mind slaves whose eyes and ears—and sometimes their killing hands—were loyal solely to him. It was those Minions who'd reported last night's hotel break-in to him, hours before the newshounds at the local television station started sniffing around the incident.

Dragos knew the cop who'd been killed inside the suite belonged to him. He also knew it was the work of the Order—specifically, Sterling Chase, who'd done the killing. The warrior's escape from police custody had cost Dragos several Minion pawns already, not the least of whom was Senator Robert Clarence himself.

Not that Dragos hadn't been making quick and prudent use of the upwardly mobile human's political connections from the moment he'd written his first contribution check to the senator's election campaign. In fact, the senator might prove even more useful in death than he had while he was breathing.

A pity to have to forfeit Tavia Fairchild this early in the game, however.

The news that she'd gone missing overnight hadn't come as a complete surprise. She'd been under the watch of his Minion and the two federal agents at the hotel. With the raid of the suite by Sterling Chase, it seemed almost certain that the female was in the Order's hands now.

Would they kill her when they realized what she was? he wondered idly.

No matter. She wasn't the first of her kind, nor the last. And once the Order figured that out, it would be too late for them to act on the knowledge anyway.

Dragos was smiling as he entered his command center. Ignoring the lowered heads of his Minion staff on his approach, he strode to the heart of the operations room and sat down in the seat hastily vacated by one of the technicians. He called up an encrypted file directory on one of the computers and watched with pride as the monitor filled with building schematics and security clearance codes for numerous government and infrastructure facilities. More intel loaded on-screen: layouts of power plants, military operations, and transportation control rooms both in the United States and abroad. Political and corporate organizational structures.

Top-secret documents that only a mole of consummate ability and years of dedicated effort could provide.

Dragos was looking at the means to topple mankind from the inside out. All that was left for him to do was open the door.

As he paused to admire the fruits of his own genius, his cell phone began to ring in his pants pocket. It was the line he used only for specific business—had, in fact, given the private number out to just two people. With Senator Clarence slaughtered two nights ago, that left just one other possible option.

"Drake Masters," he announced as he answered, giving the name his caller would be expecting to hear.

The United States' second in command cleared his throat. "Good morning, Mr. Masters. I hope I'm not calling at a bad time."

"Not at all," Dragos replied smoothly. Although his voice was calm and professional, his pulse spiked with the promise of a baited snare about to spring tight on unsuspecting prey. "And please, sir, call me Drake."

"Well, thank you, Drake," said the former university professor who was currently just one heartbeat away from arguably the highest seat of power in the world. He had also been a longtime friend and mentor to Robert Clarence, and the weight of his grief was evident in the faint rasp of the aging human's voice. "A terrible, terrible thing, what happened to Bobby. Our country lost a true patriot, one of the best. And I think you should know that he spoke very highly of you."

Dragos gave a mild chuckle before effecting a suitably sober tone as he spoke of his Minion. "The senator and I had a meeting of the minds, if you will. We shared a common dream for this country. Indeed, for all the world."

"I don't doubt that," the vice president agreed. "I realize you didn't know Bobby for very long, but you made quite an impression on him, Drake. You were practically all he talked about lately, especially in the last few days. He felt it was very important that you and I have the chance to sit down together and discuss how our interests for the country might mesh. Hell, the kid pretty much insisted that I make room for you on my calendar, so who was I to refuse?"

"Bobby could be quite persuasive when it came to

campaigning for what he believed in," Dragos said. "But then, wasn't that part of his charm?"

The human chuckled. "Right you are, Drake. Right you are. Listen, I wanted to apologize that we weren't able to connect last night as Bobby had arranged for us to do before he was . . ." The voice trailed off for a moment. "Obviously, a lot has changed over the past couple of days."

"Of course. No need to apologize." But Dragos wasn't about to let the face-to-face meeting with the important politician slip through his fingers. "I wouldn't think of imposing on your time, sir, especially after you've just lost a close friend." He paused as if to compose himself. "You and I both have lost a good friend. Business can wait for another time."

"Actually," the human hedged, "I'm planning to be in Boston tomorrow afternoon for Bobby's funeral. Perhaps you and I could find some time to talk following the service."

"Certainly," Dragos said, working to keep the eagerness from his voice. All he needed was a few minutes alone with the human and he would own him completely. Dragos's lips parted with his growing smile, fangs filling his mouth in anticipation of the triumph soon to come. "Until tomorrow, sir."

Chase stood in front of the bathroom sink in the Darkhaven's master suite, sewing up the last of his gunshot wounds from the other night. Spent cotton balls and gauze littered the deep black basin of the sink, all of it soaked and reeking of antiseptic and blood. It had been roughly seventy-two hours since he'd been injured at the police station. The wounds should be healed by now. That they still lingered wasn't a good sign at all.

Nor was the gnawing ache that rattled deep in his marrow, compelling him to hunt. To feed. To fill the void that would soon be endless, unquenchable.

His fingers shook around the drugstore sewing kit needle. His vision blurred at the edges of his sight, making it hard as hell to focus under the yellow glare of the bathroom lights. He blinked away the annoying jangle of his senses, gritting his teeth as he pushed the needle and quadrupled mending thread through the frayed skin above his left pectoral muscle. He tugged the last stitch tight, then made a rudimentary knot to tie the sutures off.

As he bit the tail of the thread free, he caught his reflection in the mirror. Haggard, dark-ringed eyes stared back at him in the glass. Sallow skin and gaunt cheeks aged him—not quite to the hundred-plus years of his true age, but easily a decade beyond the vibrant thirty that was his normal appearance as an adult member of the Breed. He looked tired and worn, on the verge of defeat.

Hell, he felt it too.

With a muttered curse, he tossed the needle into the sink with the rest of the rubbish. His breath was ragged as he pulled in a long breath, then pushed it out on a low growl. What the fuck was he doing, holing up in this godforsaken place, keeping a woman against her will in the other room? Even if she did prove to be something more than she seemed—even if she proved to be connected in some way to Dragos himself—who was he to be her judge and jury? He wasn't a part of the Order anymore. He hadn't been part of the Enforcement Agency in a long time either.

From where he stood now, it wasn't that difficult to see himself through Tavia's frightened eyes. He was deranged, dangerous . . . a monster.

For what wasn't the first time, his eyes strayed to the small silver vial that rested on the edge of the black granite countertop. He'd found it in the bedroom, lying on top of his old desk with a handful of printed snapshots from the time when he'd called this Darkhaven home. He'd been unable to resist picking up the slender container with its damnable contents sealed inside.

Even now his hand moved toward it as though drawn by an invisible tether.

Chase palmed the vial, the metal cold against his skin. The red wax that sealed the cork stopper felt smooth under the pad of his thumb. Inside the silver capsule was all that remained of a manufactured substance that had destroyed many lives the autumn before last—including that of his nephew, Camden.

The lab and the human who'd created the drug were long gone, but Chase had saved this last dose as a reminder to himself of the evil he'd helped destroy. And looking at it now, he had to acknowledge that he'd saved the poisonous sample for another reason too. It was his final out. His guarantee that if his struggle to resist Bloodlust became too much for him to bear, he could end it in a single moment.

A taste of Crimson was enough to turn him into a mindless, blood-crazed Rogue in an instant. Just as it had Camden and too many of the Breed youth's innocent friends last year. But inside the innocuous, polished silver vial was a deadly dose of the drug. More than enough to kill.

Chase rolled the slim cylinder in his palm, seeing it for what it truly was: his suicide pill.

He was halfway gone, all on his own. How much worse would he have to get before Crimson looked like his best option?

A stirring in the other room pulled his thoughts back to more immediate problems. Tavia was waking. She'd finally fallen asleep just before sundown, exhausted, slumped in the chair where he'd left her. Now it was deep night, and Chase had already been out for supplies and back while she'd slept. He set the Crimson down on the bathroom counter and walked out to the study.

She was sitting up now, the hotel robe wrapped around her like a blanket, her hands still restrained behind her. Her head lifted slowly as he entered the room, her movements heavy and listless. She groaned with the effort. Her tongue came out to wet her dry lips. "What time is it?"

Chase shrugged as he approached her. "Around ten, I guess."

She groaned again, gave a miserable shake of her head. "Too long. I've never gone this long without my medicines."

"You'll feel better after you eat." Chase gestured to the end table beside her, where a paper deli bag and bottle of water sat. "I brought you a sandwich."

She winced as if the mere idea repulsed her. "I'm not hungry. I feel light-headed. I need to get out of here. My body aches everywhere and my skin . . . it feels too tight all over."

Chase grunted. She was practically describing how he felt right now, his body barely out of the racking wave of blood thirst that had ridden him most of the day and into the night. The suffering had been intense. The temptation to hunt and feed while he was out earlier tonight had nearly beaten him.

"Lean forward," he told Tavia as he hunkered down in front of her at the chair. Despite the look of mistrust in her eyes, she drooped against him as he reached around her to untie the drapery cord that bound her wrists at her back.

He didn't want to notice how good she smelled this close to his face, how her skin and hair still carried the faint fragrance of hotel soap and shampoo and the more intriguing scent that was hers alone. He tried to ignore the weight of her forehead on his bare shoulder and the fact that everywhere her body touched him, his senses smoldered with instant awareness. Her soft exhalation scorched him like fire as the restraints fell away from her hands and she sagged further into his arms.

Chase cupped his palm around her nape and drew back to look at her face. He searched for signs of illness in her flushed cheeks and glittering green eyes. Although he could see she was tired, taxed physically and emotionally, there was still a strength about her, a quiet defiance that seemed more instinct than conscious power. She was lovely, beauty and intelligence in her delicate but proud features.

And she was studying him now too.

Her gaze roamed his face, lingering on his mouth before lifting to meet and hold his eyes. "You look normal now," she murmured. "Different from before. Right now, you look human . . . but you're not, are you?"

"No," he said simply, deciding it was pointless to deny it when she'd already seen him at his worst.

She swallowed but didn't shrink away or dissolve into hysterics. She was calm and cool-headed, processing his admission in a cautious silence. "Did your family know? Is that why they left you?"

He scowled, confused now. "My family. What are you talking about?"

"This house," she said. "And the photos . . . I found them in the desk in the other room. There was a silver tray inside the drawer. It has a name engraved on it. Your name, right? Your name is Sterling Chase."

"The less you know about me, the better, Tavia."

"But Sterling is your name," she insisted, refusing to let it go.

"Chase," he muttered. "Nobody calls me Sterling. Not anymore."

She watched him now, studying him too closely for his liking. "What happened to your family, Chase? I saw the picture of you with a young woman and a boy. I just wondered if your wife—"

Chase cut her off with a curse hissed under his breath. "She was my brother's mate. Not mine."

"Oh." Tavia's eyes left him then, a quick downward glance that made him feel more awkward than he should have. "From the way you were looking at her in the picture, I thought—"

"You thought wrong," he replied, knowingly curt. He wasn't about to dredge up his past sins, let alone bare them for her judgment. Bad enough he had the burden of his own conscience when it came to this Darkhaven and the memories it held. "This was my home once," he told her. "But I was the one who left. I never wanted to see this place again."

"How long have you been gone?"

Her question caught him off guard, such a simple thing to ask. Although he didn't want to relive it, he found the answer slipping easily off his tongue. "It was a year ago this past fall. Just after Halloween."

He could still hear the percussion of the gunshot ringing in his ears. The devastated scream of his brother's mate, Elise, echoing into the night as her son—her only child—dropped lifeless to the ground. A beautiful teenage boy, turned Rogue on Crimson and shot dead by titanium rounds fired from Chase's pistol.

"Were you in love with her?"

Chase jolted out of his bleak recollections, a scowl bunching between his eyes. "I told you, she belonged to my brother."

"I heard you," Tavia said evenly. "But that's not what I asked."

"I'm not sure I've ever loved anyone," he murmured. "Christ, I'm not even sure I'm capable."

It wasn't a sullen remark but the plain truth. He'd never thought about it before. Never said the words out loud until now.

He held Tavia's gaze, realizing just then that his palm was still wrapped around the back of her neck. Her pulse kicked against his fingertips, the fine tendons of her throat going taut as he held her in a loose but unrelenting grasp. He watched her lips part with her indrawn breath and felt a sudden, fierce urge to kiss her. A crazy impulse, but then he wasn't exactly operating on full sanity lately. He swallowed past the unwanted desire, his throat as dry as ash. "You should eat now," he said, releasing her to rise abruptly to his feet. "I brought you some clothes too. You can change into them after you've had some food."

"I told you, I'm not hungry," she said, pushing the sandwich away.

Chase shrugged. "Suit yourself."

He put as much distance between them as he could, moving to the far side of the study to pace an agitated track near the tall windows. The electronic shutters were closed and had been since the Darkhaven's residents moved away last year. But Chase's body knew it was night on the other side of the steel and glass. His veins throbbed with the knowledge, each hard beat of his pulse a reminder of the thirst he was trying so hard to deny.

"You're not well either," Tavia said, watching him pace and prowl from across the room. "Even if you're not . . . no matter what you truly are, I can see that you need medical attention. So do I."

He scoffed, a raw-sounding snarl low in his throat. "You don't need to worry about me. As for yourself, you don't seem as sick as you want me to believe."

"But I am," she insisted. "Whether or not you believe me, you're playing with my life by keeping me here like this. You've already killed several innocent people. Do you really want another life staining your hands?"

"None of them was innocent," he replied harshly. "They were Dragos's Minions, all of them. Soulless. Mindless. They were as good as dead long before I got to any of them."

"Minions," she said, watching him cautiously. "What do you mean, they were Dragos's Minions? At the police station, you tried to warn me that the senator was in danger. But then when you saw him, you said it was too late, that Dragos already owned him. What did you mean by that?"

She was genuinely confused, which only made his suspicion of her deepen. Either she truly was oblivious to Dragos and his machinations, or she was a stellar actor. Chase dismissed her with a curt flick of his hand. "Never mind. I've said too much as it is."

But she wouldn't let it go. "Tell me what this is really about. I'm just trying to understand—"

"It might be better for you if you don't."

"Maybe you should have thought of that before you put me in the middle of it."

Her tone held no venom, just a bold frankness he had to respect. Chase looked at her, realizing she had a point. She was in deep now, all thanks to him. And while he couldn't be certain she would still be alive if he hadn't intervened with the senator and the Minion cop who'd been with her at the hotel, he had to admit he'd all but ensured her life would never return to its status quo of before.

Even if that status quo had been a lie.

There was still a part of him convinced she wasn't who she claimed to be, whether or not she knew it herself. He couldn't dismiss the feeling that she was something more than human. Something *other*. But what?

Could Dragos have that answer?

The thought had crossed his mind before, but now it nagged at him. It chilled him to think she might somehow be connected to Dragos, unwitting or otherwise. And deep down, in the part of him that was still committed to the Order's cause—still determined to see Dragos annihilated—Chase wondered if Tavia Fairchild might be useful in helping him get close to the enemy he meant to destroy.

His own life was already forfeit. He was fully prepared to go down in flames along with Dragos, if that's what it took to defeat him once and for all. After all, he had nothing left to lose.

Had he stooped so low that he would be willing to gamble this woman's life as well? He wasn't sure he wanted to know the answer to that question.

On the other side of the study, Tavia moaned quietly and took her head in her hands. "Oh, God . . . it's getting worse. I really need to have my medicines. I need to get out of here . . ." She glanced at him then, and it was impossible to ignore the true suffering in her eyes. "Please," she said. "Won't you please . . . just let me go?"

Chase stared, trying to see through her game. But there was no guile in play here, only misery and fear and confusion. He knew the right thing would be to do as she asked and release her.

And if he were a better man, he might have.

CHAPTER
Thirteen

Tavia woke up screaming in the dark.

Her skin felt shredded and raw, on fire one second, the next chilled to the bone. She thrashed and bucked—only to realize she was flat on her back in a large bed, restrained at her wrists and ankles by the thick, braided ropes of the drapery cords from the other room. She dimly recalled being brought back into the bedroom after she'd refused the food and drink, too ill to stomach either one. She'd tried to tell her captor that she wouldn't attempt escape—that she couldn't attempt it, the worse her body began to rebel.

She'd begged him to let her go, pleaded for his mercy. He'd shown her none.

Tavia tried to fight the ties that held her down on the mattress now, but she had no strength. Her limbs were heavy, her head woozy, stomach pitching and roiling.

Oh, God . . . what was happening to her?

She was so sick now, sicker than she'd ever been before. She ached all over, racked with a full-body tremble that seemed to originate deep down in her marrow. Her senses seemed at war with themselves, swinging from drained and weak to hyperalert. She felt her pulse drumming in her temples and in the sides of her neck. Her heart banged against her rib cage, beating so fast and hard it was a wonder the organ didn't explode.

Eyes squeezed shut, she made another futile attempt to wrest her hands free of the cord that secured them to the headboard. She yanked and pulled, moaning sharply as the tender skin at her wrists began to chafe.

"Easy now." Warm, strong fingers clamped around both her wrists. Her captor, Chase. She hadn't even heard him come into the room, but there he was, enveloped in the gloomy shadows. His touch was firm but gentle, his voice a rough whisper that skated over her brow. "Be still, Tavia. You're okay."

His eyes searched hers, flecks of amber fire smoldering in his scowling gaze. She didn't want his deep voice to soothe her, any more than she wanted his large palm to ease some of the burn from the restraints he had placed on her.

Yet she did find some comfort in his low-murmured words. His thumb idly stroking her wrists calmed her jagged pulse. Against her will, she stilled, her senses responding to him like the tide stretching to meet the moon.

"Let me go," she said, still wanting to deny what she was feeling. Her body wasn't her own right now, but she hadn't completely lost hold of her mind. Not yet, anyway.

At least she was dressed now. Before he'd returned her to the bedroom that had apparently become her prison, Chase had given her a shopping bag from a Back Bay clothing store and allowed her to use the bathroom to freshen up and change out of the hotel bathrobe into a black track suit. He'd bought her a bra and panties as well, and she didn't want to know how closely he'd had to look at her while she'd slept earlier that day in order to size her up so perfectly.

But despite his reassurances, she wasn't okay. She felt something slipping loose inside of her, a part of her breaking away, drifting out of her reach. She struggled against the feeling of helplessness, panic rising, shortening her breath.

"Let me go," she panted. She couldn't bite back her moan or the desperate whimper that leaked from between her lips. The tide of her illness was dragging her under again. She didn't know how long she could fight it. "Please . . . I think I'm dying. I have to . . . get out of here . . ."

As her voice faded into the haze that swamped her senses, she felt Chase's gentle touch on her brow. With tender care that didn't seem possible, coming from the monster she'd seen him to be, he swept aside some of the damp hair that clung to her forehead. His touch lingered, tracing a light trail along the curve of her cheek, then the line of her rigidly held jaw.

"Please," she whispered, but her voice was nearly gone now. Consciousness was dimming behind her heavy eyelids, pulling her back toward an inescapable sleep.

As her mind began to slide into darkness, she thought she saw a glimpse of humanity in his eyes, a note of regret in the faint twist of his mouth as he gazed down at her.

But he said nothing.

And then she was drifting further away from her reality, darkness rising up to take her. She turned her head from him, her cheeks wetting with hot tears as he slowly withdrew from her side and disappeared back into the shadows.

Hunter arrived at the Order's new location that night, just ahead of a blustery winter storm. Lucan and the other warriors had hurried to help him unload the box truck he'd commandeered back in New Orleans, which carried a wealth of intel taken from one of Dragos's fallen lieutenants.

A fireproof safe held printed laboratory records and multiple storage drives of encrypted computer data. There was a pair of large, stainless steel drums, heavy bastards, crowned with polished metal, hydraulically sealed caps that looked like steering wheels. Only one of the cryogenic containers housed viable genetic specimens; the other sported a huge dent and a compromised lid, dried blood spattered down the tank's side.

No need for Lucan to guess how the damage was done. Hunter had also brought the shattered pieces of an ultraviolet-charged polymer obedience collar that had broken off its wearer in combat. Dragos's homegrown assassin had been sent to protect the laboratory haul with his life. Thanks to Hunter's deadly skills, the assassin had failed. And now the boon of that confiscated lab intel belonged to the Order.

Hunter had delivered the shards of another broken UV collar too—this one freed from the neck of a thirteen-year-old boy. Corinne's son, Nathan. Like all of the Breed, the youth took his eye and hair color from his mother. This boy's ebony hair was only a shadow on his skull, shaven clean in the typical assassin way. Just one of many methods Dragos used—and by far the least cruel of them all—to strip away individuality and raise his assassins to be emotionless tools of destruction from the time they were little children.

Lucan eyed the deadly youth with sober reservation, noting how Nathan hung back from the rest of the group that had gathered inside the new headquarters to greet Hunter and Corinne. The boy watched stone-faced as his mother was quickly ensconced in warm hugs by the other Breedmates of the Order. His seawater gaze was flat and unreadable, moving in detached observation from Tess and the baby and the rest of the chattering females, to Gideon and Rio and Kade, who had crowded around the cryo containers to inspect the newly arrived intel along with Nikolai, Brock, Dante, and Tegan.

"The boy could be a problem," Lucan remarked, turning his attention toward Hunter, who stood beside him in the great room. He too was watching Nathan in silent consideration. "I don't like the idea of bringing one of Dragos's foot soldiers into my home, no matter how young the little killer might be."

Hunter cocked his head almost imperceptibly. "You had similar reservations about me, if I recall. I haven't murdered anyone in their sleep so far. Not even Chase."

Lucan stared at the typically stoic former assassin. "Humor—from you? Well, I'll be goddamned." He exhaled a chuckle that managed to take away some of the weight on his shoulders. Some, not all. "It just concerns me that the boy has been plucked out of one bad situation and dropped into another. We're not exactly equipped to help a fucked-up kid like that get back in touch with his feelings."

Hunter nodded. "I take full personal responsibility

for him. Nathan will be my problem to manage, not the Order's."

"He means that much to you?"

Hunter nodded again, more solemnly this time. "He does. Because he means so much to her."

Lucan followed the warrior's golden gaze to petite, beautiful Corinne. The pair's eyes met and held, and Lucan could practically feel the electricity thrumming in the air between them. "What about the rest of the assassins still carrying out Dragos's commands?" It was a grim reminder, but a fact none of them could afford to ignore. "Part of your mission with the Order is to help us hunt down and neutralize all assets where Dragos is concerned. Even the youngest assassins he commands pose a very real, very lethal threat."

When Hunter's attention swung back to Lucan, it was cold with conviction. "My mission to see his operation dismantled hasn't changed, nor has my vow to you and the rest of the Order. What I'm doing now, I do for Corinne. And for her boy."

Lucan grunted. "And you think he's different from the others like him?"

Hunter was thoughtful, and it took him a moment to answer. "Nathan has something none of us ever knew. Or not for very long. He is loved. That's possibly the only thing strong enough to undo the worst of Dragos's training."

The observation—the very human comprehension of the miraculous power of love—came as a shock to Lucan, especially espoused from this male's lips. But hell, he could hardly argue. Without Gabrielle's love, he could only imagine where he'd be. Heading swiftly down the same dark path toward Bloodlust that Chase was currently on, he had no doubt.

Lucan put his hand on Hunter's massive shoulder. "I hope to hell you're not mistaken about this, my man. For her sake, and the boy's."

"I do not make mistakes," he replied, the level, almost robotic statement showing a glimpse of the flawless soldier he'd been born and bred to be. But when he met Lucan's gaze, his eyes held a determination that was nothing if not personal. "I stake my own life on this decision, Lucan. I will not let you down. Neither will Nathan."

A tendon ticked in Lucan's jaw as he considered the myriad potential risks, and the trust Hunter was asking from him. Finally, he gave a firm nod. "Bring the boy over."

In moments, Hunter had ushered him forward, his large hand resting on the lean, athletic shoulder of the young killer to steer him toward where Lucan waited, apart from the activity still going on around them in the room.

"Nathan. This is Lucan. He is leader and founder of the Order."

The boy's eyes were blank, unblinking as he stood there mutely. Lucan offered his hand. "Nathan," he said, tipping his head in greeting as he waited for the boy to respond. He thought his hand would go unaccepted, but then, at the last second, Nathan extended his as well. There was uncertainty in the move, the boy's gesture more a mimic of Lucan's than understanding of what was expected of him. But it was a start. Lucan briefly clasped the cool, startlingly strong fingers in his grasp. "You are safe here, son. You are welcome here."

Eyes seeming to stare right through him, Nathan retracted his hand and fisted it at his side.

"Hunter!" squealed a little girl's voice amid a chaotic clamber as she burst into the room, her fine blond hair bouncing. "Hunter, you finally made it back!"

Mira tore into the middle of the gathering like a mini-cyclone, energetic and loud, totally uninhibited in her joy. She threw herself into the big Gen One's arms, giggling as he hoisted her up and held Mira so her face was level with his own. His smile was affectionate, more patient than most might give the lethal male credit for.

Then again, it had been Mira who'd been instrumental in bringing Hunter into the Order's fold. Since that time, the two had become genuine, if unlikely, friends.

"Do you realize you almost missed Christmas?" she informed him, part scold, part girlish incredulity. Her attention diverted just as quickly as it had arrived, her petite face swiveled around to study the newcomer in their midst. "Who's that?"

"Corinne's son," Hunter replied. Then, with a meaningful pause: "His name is Nathan."

She scrambled out of Hunter's arms and went right up to the teenage assassin. "Hi, Nathan. I'm Mira."

He didn't say anything, just stared at her as though she were some strange new species he'd never encountered before. Lucan wondered if the boy had ever been that close to a female besides his mother, even a pint-size one like Mira. The poor kid wasn't going to know what hit him if she decided to make him one of her personal projects as she seemed to have done with Kellan Archer.

Leaving the kids to their awkward introductions, Lucan motioned for Hunter to follow him as he strode over to join the conversation taking place around the recovered lab intel. "Let's get some juice on these cryo tanks before their backup batteries die. Hunter, there're a couple of unclaimed bedrooms, so if you and Corinne want to take your pick and settle in, go ahead."

He glanced over to where Nathan was currently being shown the huge evergreen near the fireplace, Mira excitedly explaining that she was making decorations for it and would enjoy his help when the time came to hang them. Lucan shook his head and exhaled a sympathetic chuckle. To Hunter he added, "Have Mira show Nathan to Kellan's room. The two boys can bunk together."

CHAPTER
Fourteen

Morning hit him like a hammer cracking into the top of his skull.

Chase's eyelids blinked open, every fiber of his body on instant, full alarm.

Something wasn't right in the house.

It was too damned quiet. As quiet as a tomb.

Fuck. How long had he been out? Bloodlust had ridden him during the night, but he'd resisted the urge to leave the Darkhaven and hunt. The last thing he remembered was fighting off that hunger, a battle he'd only narrowly won. Now he got to his feet in the study, mentally shaking off the niggling twitch of his blood thirst and the dull ache of his bones from having crashed on the bare floor. Every blood-starved muscle screamed in protest as he made a swift but heavy-footed trek toward the closed door of the bedroom.

Not a sound on the other side of that locked slab of hundred-year-old wood.

She'd been in bad shape last night. When he'd gone in

to check on her, easily several hours ago now, she told him she thought she was dying. He'd doubted it, but she seemed so miserable he had almost taken her out of there as she'd begged him. Her pain appealed to him on a level he wasn't prepared to acknowledge, let alone submit to.

But now he wondered if he'd been wrong about how ill she'd been.

Jesus, if he'd been dead wrong—

"Tavia?" His voice was gravel in his dry throat. He didn't bother knocking, just willed the lock open and pushed the door wide. He stepped into the room.

It was empty.

The drapery cords he'd used to restrain her lay in a frayed tangle on the bed. Tavia was nowhere to be seen.

"Holy hell." Chase flicked a glance at the window, still boarded up with pieces of the desk he'd smashed apart to bar the cracked window and prevent her escape. He stalked farther inside.

And then he heard her.

A soft, rapid panting, like that of a small, frightened animal, coming from the other side of the big bed.

"Tavia." She was hunched on her heels in a tight ball, head drooped low. She didn't respond to his voice, just sat there breathing in a shallow, fast tempo. Her body trembled all over. Sweat dampened her limp hair and made the fabric of her black track suit cling to the curved arch of her spine. "Christ . . . Tavia, are you all right?"

He reached out, placing his hand lightly on her back. She flinched away on contact, a violent lunge that put two feet between them. Her head swung around, hair drooping in a thick curtain over her face . . . though not enough to hide the bright amber glow of her eyes.

Ah, fuck. The reality of what Chase was seeing made his blood chill in his veins. *This couldn't be.*

He could only stare as her lips curled back on a wild snarl. She drew in a ragged breath, then gave a fierce hiss through her teeth and the sharp lengths of her gleaming fangs.

Even though he had suspected she was something more than what she seemed, seeing it for a fact now took him totally aback.

Tavia Fairchild was somehow—impossibly—Breed.

Little wonder the restraints didn't hold her. They were no more effective than thread on one of his kind. Which this female clearly was.

Crouched low and seething, she held him in a glower that was at once startling and amazing in its fury. Her narrowed pupils were thinnest slits, swamped by the fiery embers of her irises. She growled at him, head cocked slightly, a deadly she-beast sizing up her prey.

It was the only warning he had before she sprang off her heels and took him down in a swift, vicious strike.

They landed hard, Chase's spine crashing onto the floor under their combined weight. His breath went out of him in a gust and a groan, Tavia's banshee cry echoing in his skull. She started fighting as soon as they hit the hardwood. Fast and strong, she clawed at him, shrieking and growling as he tried to ward off her frenzied assault.

The zippered front of her track suit hoodie was open just enough to give him a decent look at the web of *dermaglyphs* that spread in a flourish across her chest and up onto her throat. He had no doubt now that that's what they were: The Breed skin markings were flooded with color, variegating hues of deep purple, blood wine, and black. She was furious and pained from starvation, her *glyphs* told him that much on sight.

How had the genetic markings lain dormant until now?

What the hell had been done to her to keep her true nature suppressed?

Chase didn't have long to wonder about it. Tavia pulled her arm back and swung a fist toward his face. He dodged the blow, faster than her only because of experience and training. She was unschooled and out of control, a raw, natural power unleashed for what was clearly the first time. She was ferocious Breed might in a sleek, feminine form.

And goddamn if Chase had ever known anything hotter in his whole life.

She struggled against him some more, grunting as he deflected her every strike, roaring and snarling when he finally grabbed hold of her by the wrists and splayed her arms above him. Her pulse beat hard and steady in the sides of her slender neck. He could feel it banging against his fingertips where he held her strong wrists. And he could feel that solid, thumping throb along the insides of her thighs too, which gripped him like iron bands around his waist, pinning him beneath her with astonishing force.

She panted and heaved, those bright amber eyes and bared fangs telling him the fight wasn't drained out of her yet.

Not even close.

"Tavia, listen to me." Her muscles twitched with a warning that she was about to strike. Chase spat a curse, teeth gritted with the effort to keep his hold on her tense arms. "Tavia, for fuck's sake, you need to calm—"

She roared over his attempt to reason with her, but she didn't try to break free of his hold.

No, she bit him.

Chase spewed a wordless shout as her fangs sank deep into the flesh and tendons of his left wrist. It wasn't the pain of the bite that shook him but the sudden, alarming realization that his blood was gushing freely into her mouth.

He tried to speak her name—warn her to stop—but the only thing that came out of his mouth was a strangled moan. The pleasure and pain of her bite speared through him, like a jolt of current shot into every fiber of his being.

Christ, it felt good.

Too good, especially when he wasn't even sure what his blood would do to her. She was somehow Breed; he understood that now. But how would her body react to his red cells pouring into her?

He had that answer not even a second later.

Tavia released him on a guttural cry. Her eyes burned brighter now, throwing off amber light as hot as smoldering coals. Her fangs dripped blood—his blood—down onto her chin and the heaving swell of her chest. Her *glyphs* pulsed, alive and changeable, sexy as hell against the smooth cream of her skin.

As he brought his punctured wrist to his mouth to seal the wounds, Tavia avidly watched him. She licked her lips, her dark pink tongue lapping up every drop of his spilled blood that lingered on her mouth. Tipping her head back for a moment, her hands moved absently up to her neck, then over the top of her zippered hoodie to caress the curve of her breasts. It was a sensual move, unconsciously so, an instinctual reaction to the blood that was now feeding her cells. When she looked at him again, her smoldering gaze rooted on his throat. Her breathing was still hard and frenzied, her body still vibrating with coiled aggression.

And she was hot. Chase could feel her body radiating into his where they connected, her nylon-clad hips straddling his naked abdomen. His own pants felt too confining, his erection rising where her backside rubbed too pleasantly against his groin.

God, she was magnificent. Beyond beautiful.

And everything male in him was responding with swift, unwanted—quite obvious—interest.

He didn't have the chance to summon the will to push her away before she fell on him again, swifter than before, moving so fast he could hardly track her. Her bite was harder this time. A dead-aim strike at his carotid.

Chase's body arced violently, every muscle and tendon going taut as cables when her fangs pierced his neck and sank deep. She suckled him hard, drawing in a long pull at his vein that made his cock surge so tight, he thought he would explode on the spot.

He didn't want to acknowledge the pleasure he was experiencing, but he was damned if he could deny it. His raging hard-on was evidence enough, but already he could feel his *glyphs* lighting up with approval as Tavia sucked in another mouthful of his blood.

"Christ," he hissed, unable to do anything but comply with the demand of her mouth on his throat. The sensation was unlike anything he'd ever known.

Unmated, he'd fed exclusively on humans all his life. And never had he permitted a blood Host to drink from him. Not that blunt little teeth could compare to the razor-sharp pleasure of Tavia's fangs, holding him tight against her mouth as she greedily fed from his vein.

With every beat of his heart, he felt his energy being

drawn from within him, from limbs and core and senses, flowing into her. Nourishing her. He could feel her power growing. Her hunger deepened with every hard tug at his wounds. She moaned against his skin as she drank some more, the hum of her pleasure ratcheting his own desire ever tighter.

Tavia's hips began to move, grinding against him. He knew she was feeling the same arousal he was. He could see it in the liquid churn of her body. Could taste the fragrance of her desire in every hard breath he sucked into his lungs.

His cock was hard as stone beneath her undulating hips. The ache of his want was brutal, a pure, delicious agony.

And if his need was unbearable, hers could only be worse.

Genetically enhanced with qualities meant to make a Host more pliable when bitten, Breed blood was even more potent when ingested. To a female born a Breedmate, it was arousal in its most primal form.

To Tavia?

He couldn't know. His only answer came in the form of her hips grinding more demandingly on his. He brought his hands up to rest along her back, on the verge of madness as she slid herself lower on his body, aligning the heat of her core to the hard ridge of his groin.

He knew he should stop this before it went any further. But any thought of denying her was losing ground quickly under the sensual assault being waged on his already tarnished honor.

"Tavia," he muttered thickly, feeling the jab of his own fangs pressing into the soft flesh of his tongue as his body gave itself over to the dark nature of what he truly was. "Ah, fuck . . ."

More.

It was all she knew in that moment, the only thing that mattered.

More.

More of the quenching fluid that cooled the desert that was her throat. More of the power that was surging into every particle of her being, soothing the ache of her racked bones and muscles, calming the fury—the violent tempest of animal rage—that had first awakened her from her sleep overnight and left her shivering and confused, huddled on the floor of the room.

She wanted more of the pleasure that had started with her first taste of the spicy dark elixir that flowed over her tongue like liquid velvet from some exotic other world. It was blood. She knew this in the part of her mind that was still tethered to reality.

It was his blood. Sterling Chase. The man she should fear and probably despise. The man who was no man at all, but something dangerous and wild.

She wanted more of *him*.

Her pulse spiked at the thought, drumming harder in her veins. She felt her blood pumping, hot and alive, into every organ and muscle. Could practically hear the suck of her body's cells, drinking in his dark strength, claiming it as their own.

And oh, he felt good.

Everywhere they made contact, her skin buzzed with arousal. She couldn't deny the pleasure, any more than she could deny the need to slake the thirst that felt as though it had been building inside her all her life.

She'd felt so ill before—dying, she was sure. But now she felt no sickness. No quivering weakness, or the anxiety that so often had her scrambling for medicinal relief. She felt alive now. Infinitely, powerfully alive.

She drank urgently at his open vein, unable to be gentle. Nor could she curb the other craving that was lashing itself around her, a smoldering need that licked across her skin and into her heightened senses.

Everything seemed more vivid now. Her head filled with the dark scent of his skin and the blood that pulsed so forcefully against her tongue. She breathed him in, savored the wild taste of him. Indulged in the hard power of his body beneath her, the muscled planes of his bare chest warm and satin smooth under her fingertips.

His heart was hammering as hard as hers, a beat she could feel, somehow, throbbing in her own veins too. She could feel the power of his desire, a need that made the molten pool in the core of her burn even more intensely.

Tavia moaned, losing her hold on what little control she had left.

"More," she murmured against his skin. Her hips were moving of their own accord, wanton despite her inexperience. All she knew was the yearning, the ache that swelled to consume her as she moved her virgin body against the large, unyielding bulge that nestled between her spread thighs. Pleasure burst inside her with the delicious friction, but it wasn't enough to sate her. Not nearly enough.

She was panting as she finally tore her mouth away from the twin punctures she'd made in his throat. She rose up on top of him and stared down into his tormented face. His eyes glowed like hot coals. Behind his parted lips, his fangs gleamed snowy white and sharp as daggers.

"Please," she whispered, lost to everything but the demands of her new consciousness. To make her point clear, she rocked her pelvis over him, hissing with the hungered need that yearned to be filled. "Please . . . make this ache go away."

His answering groan sounded raw in his throat, on the verge of refusal.

But then he reached up and cupped his big hand around her nape. With a feral-sounding growl, he pulled her down to his mouth and claimed her in a ferocious kiss.

CHAPTER
Fifteen

Tavia's mouth was hot on his, responsive and eager as he pushed his tongue past her parted lips in a deep, unforgiving kiss. She took him in, kissing him back with equal ferocity, even though her mouth was a little clumsy, her tongue a little untrained, clashing against the long points of his fangs. But she was a damn quick learner; he had to give her that.

Still seated on top of him, she moved her hips in time with the aggressive thrusts of his tongue, then soon she was matching the boldness of his mouth, grinding her body against him in a demanding rhythm. Her feminine fangs grazing his larger ones was an erotic sensation unlike anything he'd ever known. The sharp points abraded his lips as she pressed deeper into his kiss, nipping and prodding, driving him wild.

He broke contact on a growl, his lungs sawing, breath rushing as fast as his heart rate. He released his hold on her nape only to reach for the zippered front of her top. Tugged it open to bare her skin to his appreciative gaze.

Her *glyphs* were livid with dark colors. Beautiful swirls and arcs played across her clavicle and down onto her chest, disappearing under the modest black bra he'd bought with her clothes. He'd chosen the thing in haste, grabbing a simple cotton one that looked like it would fit her. The bra couldn't have been sexier on her if it was made out of lace and satin. Her pert, buoyant little breasts filled it out perfectly.

Chase flicked open the front clasp with his finger and thumb, then peeled away the fabric. Pretty flourishes pulsing with deep wine and indigo hues tracked around her dark, rosy nipples. The colors of desire, written all over her creamy skin as if rendered by an artist's hand. He drank in the sight of her, and the breath that had been racing in and out of him now left on a ragged sigh.

"So lovely," he whispered, the words gruff, his voice thick and parched. Then he raised his shoulders up off the floor so he could take one of those exquisite buds into his mouth. He suckled her with as much care as he could manage, loath to graze the delicate skin with his fangs. He didn't want to hurt her, nor did he want to accidentally nick her and make her bleed. He was already too far gone with this erotic hunger to deal with even the slightest drop of her spilled blood.

Even if the mere idea made his hard-on kick with avid interest.

Tavia made a sound of torment as he swirled his tongue around the pebbled knot of her nipple. He could feel her need vibrating through her. The heat swamped him through their clothing, and every slow grind of her hips sent his dubious self-control hurtling further out of reach.

Eyes closed, she threw her head back on a low moan as he suckled her some more, trading one sweet nipple for the other. He watched the passion play over her skin, the jewel-dark shades of her *glyphs* muting and flooding, a living dance of color that spread across her breasts and down onto her flat belly. Her waist tapered so perfectly, he could probably span its circumference with his hands.

He did just that a moment later, using the leverage to roll her off him as he followed, moving with her until he was the one on top, his pelvis wedged just right between her thighs. He gave an ungentle thrust, a taste of what was soon to come. She groaned as he made a slow retreat. When her eyelids lifted, her gaze blasted him with amber fire. She grabbed his head in her hands and hauled him down to her in a kiss that was ripe with primal demand.

"More," she rasped into his open mouth. And then she bit him again, a hard, prodding nip that sent a delicious sting straight down to his cock.

With a growl, he broke away and reared up onto his knees above her. His hands shook as he grabbed the waistband of her track pants and yanked them down her thighs, underwear too, in one fierce tug.

And, ah, Christ. There were more artful *glyphs* here, caressing the curves of her hips and accentuating the delicate nest of dark curls on the mound of her sex. He slipped his fingers between her legs and found her wet and hot and tight. So damn tight.

He groaned, breathing in the fragrance of her, a scent that was both earthy and exotic, innocent and wild. He couldn't resist a taste. With his eyes locked on hers, he drew his fingers up to his mouth and licked her sweetness into his mouth.

She was writhing beneath him, panting and grabbing for him, her gaze smoldering. Face twisted in anguish.

Her scent intensified, spurring his own need to a fever pitch.

He undid his pants and shoved them down off his hips, hissing as the first rush of cool air hit his naked cock. He couldn't get it inside her fast enough. No time to undress properly, his need was rampant.

Tavia grabbed on to his shoulders as he slid the head of his sex along the slick cleft of her body. Her blunt fingernails scored his flesh as he nudged into position, then sank inside her in one deep thrust. She cried out then, her grip on his shoulders clenching harder.

Dimly he registered just how tight she truly was. An alarming thought flickered in his desire-drenched brain: She couldn't possibly be a virgin, could she?

But then her scream quieted into a low moan, a sound of mingled pleasure and pain. And now that he was inside her, he couldn't keep from moving, driving in and out of the warm, wet fist of her core.

Her lids dragged open slowly as he thrust deeper with every stroke. Her amber eyes fixed on him, piercing and feverish, as he increased his tempo to meet the racing beat of her heart. Her lips parted on a shivery sigh, her fangs gleaming.

He felt her climax rising. The soft undulations of the fine muscles along her sheath clutched at him as the first tiny spasm raced through her. She gasped sharply, tensing beneath him while he drove deeper, pushing her harder. "That's it," he muttered hoarsely. "You wanted it. Now take it."

She let loose a strangled cry as her body shuddered, her hands still clenched like twin vises on his shoulders. Her throat went taut with the eruption of her scream, a savage shout of release. He kept moving within her, lost to the erotic tension of her core wrapped so tightly around him, the tiny spasms of her orgasm milking him, dragging a raw curse from between his teeth and fangs.

His own need had no mercy either. He drove himself deeper and harder into her heat, lost to a primal, urgent drive. Intense sensation slammed over him, and smoldering beneath the surface of his pleasure, he felt the rousing of that darker yearning he'd been slowly failing to outrun. The hunger reached for him now, a predator sensing him at his weakest. His most distracted.

Against his will, Chase's eyes rooted on the vulnerable length of Tavia's throat. He wrenched his face away, an effort that took such force his whole body shook with it.

Or maybe it was the sex that had him trembling.

It hadn't been that long since he'd fucked someone, but the human females he'd banged when it suited him had never given him pleasure. Release, sure. But he got the same decompression out of a good fight. The pain he could handle. He courted it, in fact, the more brutal the better. That's how he'd coped these past few months that his addiction had been its worst. He'd held off Bloodlust through aggression and combat, hoping to trade one wicked high for another. A dangerous dance, but the only one he knew.

Pleasure wasn't something he'd indulged in for a long time. Pain and brutality was a much safer option for him. Kept him clear and grounded. Not like now.

Now he could hardly think straight as the pleasure of Tavia's body and the daggers of his blood thirst did battle for his soul.

He risked another look at her and found her watching him intently. Her climax had ebbed, but he could feel her balanced on the edge of another. He knew he should end this—before the punishing lash of his rising blood thirst proved too much for him to bear. But his libido had other ideas. His hips rocked forward, a powerful thrust that seated him to the hilt.

He pressed deeper, staring down at her, his voice little better than ash in the back of his throat. "More?"

Tavia's reply was a rapt hiss through bared teeth and gleaming fangs. "Yes."

Her permission was its own kind of torment. Because Chase didn't think he had control enough to stop now. Not even if she begged him to.

Tavia clung to his thick shoulders as a tide of bright ecstasy crashed over her once again. Wave after wave, flooding all her senses, whisking her out of her own skin with the intensity of all she was feeling. She couldn't speak. Couldn't breathe, except to close her eyes and let go of the pleasured sigh that seemed to originate from the very core of her being.

She felt electrified, every nerve ending exploded and ragged, tingling with sensation.

There was a dull pain between her legs, but she was only dimly aware of it, too swept up in the overwhelming transformation of her entire person. Her whole existence was tangled up in a vortex of pain and pleasure, clarity and confusion.

She opened her eyes and saw the source of it all.

Chase. Unearthly, demonically handsome, he hovered above her as her body absorbed the battering impact of his thrusts. She couldn't tear her gaze away from him, the slender thread of her conscious mind mesmerized by the unholy beauty of his fiery eyes and the skin markings that fanned over his pecs and onto his thick arms braced on either side of her.

Skin markings that were surging with dark colors, just like her own.

It all seemed like some kind of dark dream, yet she was living it. Feeling it, in every awakened cell and fiber of her body. She rocked beneath him, helpless to his urgent rhythm. The tension spread from his wild features, into the hard bulk of his shoulders and down along the rigid line of his big body.

With a low growl, his tempo intensified, and the daggerlike lengths of his fangs stretched even longer behind his parted lips. His cat's-eye pupils thinned to barest slits as his gaze drifted lower, settling on her throat. Heat radiated from that feral gaze, like a hot blade pressed against her neck. His mouth grew taut, full lips peeling back as he drove into her with relentless, mounting aggression.

She knew she should be afraid. She knew that none of this should be happening—not in any kind of reality she could comprehend.

But she knew no fear now. Only an instinctual anticipation as her body cushioned his, her head tilting to the side as though drawn on unseen strings, giving him full access to her neck.

"Yes," she heard herself whisper as his strokes became more frenzied. His eyes were fixed on her throat, unblinking, ravenous. Tavia swallowed, feeling an overwhelming need for his fangs to penetrate the tender flesh. She licked her parched lips, hungry for him again too.

When she reached up and took hold of the back of his head, he went rigid, hissing as if she'd burned him. He grunted an angered sound, his face contorting in a pained grimace as his pace quickened even more. His gaze grew hotter, searing her exposed throat with a heat she felt running all through her now.

The pressure mounted, building toward something immense and glorious. Tavia rode it with him, awash in amazement and the sudden, swelling bloom of yet another shattering release. He dropped his head beside hers, breath gusting over her enlivened skin and the exposed column of her neck. For the smallest moment, his mouth brushed against the sensitive curve of her shoulder. She waited to feel his lips close over her flesh. Held her breath as her pleasure began to crest its banks and the need to feel his fangs sink into her flesh became a deafening pound in her veins.

"No," he rasped sharply. "Goddamn it. *No*."

And with a dark curse huffed against her ear, everything ended.

He withdrew, rolling away from her so abruptly she felt his absence strike her like a slap. His broad back flexed and rippled as he pivoted to his feet, unmistakable anger in his haste. He pulled up his pants in one ungentle tug and stalked away from where she lay, breathless and confused, oddly bereft. Not to mention humiliated.

Her cheeks flushed with a new kind of heat as she watched him enter the adjacent bathroom without so much as a backward glance. As though he couldn't get away from her fast enough. The door banged closed in his wake, not loud enough to muffle the low roar that erupted from behind the shut panel.

Tavia rose up from the floor in a mute, dazed silence.

Her body was still thrumming with sensation, slower to react to the rejection than the rest of her. Her veins still throbbed, her pulse hammering in a steady, strong beat that was now beginning to make her temples ache. And deep inside her, the power that had awakened within her had yet to ebb.

The burn scars that had covered her for as long as she could remember were pulsing and vibrant. Not the dusky color she was accustomed to seeing but the florid, changeable hues that defied all logic of what she'd been raised to believe about herself. They weren't scars. They couldn't be. Nothing about them—nothing about her body and this power coursing through her—was normal. She knew that now.

She herself wasn't normal.

A miserable groan leaked from between her lips when she felt the sharp pressure of her teeth resting against her tongue. No, she corrected herself. Not her teeth—her fangs.

"Oh, God." She looked down at the blood smeared across her breasts and abdomen. His blood, dark and sticky from when she'd bitten him.

Between her legs was more blood, but those faint pink stains on her thighs didn't belong to him. Tavia moaned, feeling a twinge of panic beginning to creep up the back of her throat as the weight of what she'd done here—the stunning reality of all that had happened in the last couple of days—bore down on her.

The sex wasn't the worst part. God, not even close. She would likely spend the rest of her life trying to convince herself it was the stupidest thing she'd ever done—better yet, that it never happened at all. But right now, with her nerve endings crackling and the rest of her lifted in a floating, pleasant kind of bonelessness, she couldn't pretend the sex was anything less than incredible.

And unprotected.

Oh, God.

"Stupid, stupid, stupid," she chided herself under her breath as she scrambled to put her clothes back on, keeping her eyes on the closed bathroom door as she pulled on her pants and righted her bra and zippered hoodie.

No, far more disturbing than throwing her virginity away with total, reckless abandon was biting the neck of a stranger in some fevered daze that had her convinced they both were . . . Jesus, the word wouldn't even form in her mind, it seemed so ridiculous.

And yet, it wasn't ridiculous.

She tugged up her sleeve to stare at the scars that weren't scars, their colors still livid and churning, changing from the inky shades of violet and burgundy to a deep russet bronze before her eyes. In her mouth, the sharp points of her canines were still elongated, though not the same fierce presence they'd been before. Her vision was still tinged with amber, but that too was beginning to subside.

No, she thought, stricken and dismayed. Not ridiculous at all.

Her body knew that, even if logic and reason refused to accept it.

She tried to dismiss it all, but try as she might, she could not shake the feeling that she'd never been more aware or present in her entire life. Her body felt— finally—as if it belonged to her.

As if a shroud had been lifted from her consciousness, she felt alive for the very first time.

"No," she moaned softly, struggling to push the astonishing truth away.

None of this could be happening. She'd been very sick just hours ago. Maybe this was all an enormous hallucination. After all, Dr. Lewis had warned her time and again that a break in her medication—even as much as one skipped dose—could result in unpredictable, but very serious, complications.

Maybe that's what this was. Maybe none of it was real at all. Maybe her mind and body had conspired against her as soon as she missed those first pills. Maybe she was dying as she'd feared, had been dying from the moment he locked her in this room after grabbing her from the hotel. Better that than the disturbing alternative. Her mind and body were dying, working through some terrible fantasy that began with the nightmare that had awakened her in her bedroom at home with visions of blood and sex and a man who was no man at all.

She clung to that rationale with desperate need as she went to grab the pair of sneakers from the shoe box that sat next to the bed.

Not real, she told herself, tearing through tissue paper to retrieve the brand-new Nikes from the box. *Not real. Just an uncannily tactile, detailed trick of her unmedicated, probably dying, mind.*

"What are you doing?" He came out of the bathroom without her realizing it.

Not real, she reminded herself. There was no need to answer him, or even acknowledge his presence. Focusing wholly on untangling the laces from the pair of sneakers, she made a desperate attempt to ignore him.

It wasn't working.

He was no hallucination. He was flesh and bone, six-and-a-half feet of muscled, nearly naked male. He seemed calmer now, but there was no escaping the ember-bright glow of his eyes. Not to mention the razor-sharp tips of his fangs. Rising panic formed a bubble in the back of her throat.

"Tavia, we need to talk."

"No, we don't. We've done enough, I think." She slipped on the first shoe and quickly laced it up.

He came over to her, his tawny brows low over those inhuman eyes. "There are some things you need to understand. Jesus, there are things about you that I need to understand—"

"Shut up," she snapped, worry starting to burn even hotter than any embarrassment or confusion over his sudden departure a few moments ago. She rammed her foot into the other shoe and yanked the laces tight. "And if I were you? I'd plan on staying far away from me, or I promise you, I'll press charges. I can have every cop in the Commonwealth at your door in five minutes. A fleet of federal agents too."

He actually had the audacity to chuckle, although it held little humor. "Press charges? Call the cops on me? Sweetheart, I'm a problem that no human law enforcement officer is going to solve for you. After what just happened between us, it should be pretty obvious to you that we've both got big problems."

She stood up and met his grave look. "Don't try to find me. Don't come near me ever again. I just want to forget that any of this happened. I just want to go home."

She took a step to move around him, but he caught her by the arm. His fingers held her firmly, not letting go even when she tried to wrench loose. "Let go of me, damn it."

He shook his head, his eyes grim. "You have nowhere to go."

"I'm going home!" She pulled out of his grasp, outrage spiking like acid in her veins. It was building inside her, making her skin tingle with heat. She didn't have to see her scars—rather, the inexplicable marks on her chest and arms—to know that they were surging with more color now. Reacting to her temper like some kind of emotional barometer. She sidestepped him and headed for the open bedroom door. "Leave me the hell alone."

He stood in the threshold before she even reached it herself.

Tavia gaped, came up short mere inches away from his bare chest. "Get out of my way."

"You're not going anywhere." His face had become more than serious now. There was a threat in his other-worldly eyes, a warning that he would have no qualms about physically forcing her to stay for as long as he deemed necessary.

Tavia bristled at that threat. "I said move. I need to see my aunt. I need to call my doctor—why can't you understand that I'm not well?"

"Whatever you are," he murmured, his deep voice level, "it's not unwell. You're scared and confused. Hell, I'm not standing on totally firm ground myself at the moment. Whatever you've been through—whatever you are—we need answers, Tavia. I'm going to help you get them."

She shook her head, unwilling to hear him. Still not able to reconcile any of what she was experiencing. "All I need is to go home. Right now."

When she tried to step past him again, he braced both arms up on the doorjambs, caging her inside the room with his body. "As soon as night falls, I'm going to take you somewhere safe. There are people I know who can help you make sense of everything. People far more suited to looking after you than I am."

"I don't need anyone looking after me. Least of all you or anyone you know."

He exhaled a scoff, dropped his arms, and started moving forward. Pushing her into a retreat with just his encroaching presence. "You don't trust me."

"No, I don't."

"That's probably smart, considering what nearly happened in here."

Nearly? She was concerned enough about what *had* happened. Tavia took a pace backward on her heels, less afraid of him than outraged. Her fury coiled in her belly, mingling with the remnants of the thrumming power that was still alive and racing through her veins. "I don't trust you because of everything you've done. Because of everything I've seen here. I'm not even sure I can trust myself anymore. None of this makes any sense to me."

"It does," he said evenly. "You just wish it didn't."

"Shut up." She shook her head vigorously, anger and fear pushing into her throat. "I don't want to hear any more. I just want to get the hell out of here."

"That's not going to happen, Tavia."

When he started to reach for her again, something exploded inside her. It was her fury and panic, erupting out of her in a physical reflex. Before she could think about it—before she was even aware that her arm was moving—she shoved him with all her might. He flew backward as if yanked on a tether, but a second later he had regained his footing.

In less than a blink he was back in her face, looming over her with nostrils flaring, eyes blazing. "Goddamn it, I'm not going to hurt you."

She didn't dare believe him. Nor did she wait to find out if she could. The instant she felt his fingers come to rest on her arm, she pulled back her other one and let her fist fly—connecting with a bone-jarring *crack* on the underside of his jaw.

To her complete amazement, he went down with the impact. His harsh curse as he staggered onto his knees rattled the broken glass of the crudely barred window behind them.

Tavia didn't hang around to go another round with him. As he tried to shake off the blow, she leapt around him. She tore out of the bedroom and through the large brownstone, across the inlaid marble foyer and out the front door to the morning bustle of the Back Bay residential area.

She heard him bellow behind her, but only dared a fleeting glance in his direction as her feet flew over the snow-dusted sidewalk. He stood in the open doorway, his arm raised up to shield his eyes.

He stayed there, hanging back, watching her from within the shadowed shelter as she dashed into the street and frantically hailed a passing taxi. The yellow cab slowed to a halt and she climbed in, giving the driver her address in a breathless rush.

The car lurched back into traffic, belching a cloud of opaque steam and exhaust that billowed up like a veil, blotting out the brownstone and the man Tavia hoped to never see again.

CHAPTER
Sixteen

Senator Bobby Clarence had been a good Catholic apparently, but an even better politician. The church he'd shrewdly joined fresh off the bus from Bangor as a first-year law student at Harvard was only the largest, most prestigious in Boston. Some fifty years ago, this same church had mourned a parishioner who was more famously a beloved fallen human president, a fact that Dragos guessed had played a role in the ambitious young Clarence's decision to join its flock.

Although the bachelor senator had no immediate family, outside the Cathedral of the Holy Cross that cold early afternoon, police were directing traffic to accommodate the crowd of funeral attendees waiting to get one of the two thousand seats at his service. The line of mourners stretched from the pair of red double doors at the entrance, out to the bricked sidewalk and around the large corner lot on which the massive neo-Gothic cathedral sat.

Dragos sat inside his idling, chauffeured sedan about

a block down the street, impatient for the service to begin. He was risking a great deal, venturing out during daylight hours. Even with the precautions he'd taken—UV-blocking wraparound sunglasses, a brimmed hat made of dense, boiled wool, and a generous length of knit scarf to shield his neck and head—his nearly pure Breed genes were a liability here. Being second generation of his kind, he could withstand less than a half hour in direct sunlight before his solar-sensitive skin began to cook.

But some risks were to be expected.

Some things, he supposed, were worth a little pain.

He'd endured his share already, thanks to the Order. The killing of his Minion senator so soon after Dragos had turned him had been inconvenient to say the least. It still grated to have lost the human before his full potential could have been realized. But then again, Dragos's plans wouldn't have waited the handful of years it might have taken Bobby Clarence's political star to complete its natural, some might say inevitable, ascent to the White House.

Dragos certainly had intended to help clear the way by any means necessary.

But fuck that. Bobby Clarence would soon be dust, and Dragos had better options to pursue. Assuming those options played into his hands as he expected.

"What time do you have?" Dragos asked his Minion driver for what hadn't been the first time.

"Ten minutes before two, Master."

Dragos hissed a curse against the dark-tinted glass of his backseat window. "He's late. The service will be starting soon. Any sign of a Secret Service motorcade up ahead? Any federal vehicles anywhere at all yet?"

"No, Master. Shall I drive around the cathedral to have a better look?"

Dragos dismissed the suggestion with a curt wave of his gloved hand. "Forget it. He may already be inside. I need to go in before it gets any later. Drive toward the rear of the place, away from all the commotion and prying eyes. I'll find a way in through the back."

"Of course, Master."

The Minion eased the sedan around the corner to inspect the perimeter of the cathedral. As Dragos had hoped, there was an unimportant little nook that provided service and staff access to the monstrous building. The waist-high wrought-iron gate stood open, nothing but a couple of small Dumpsters and a parked car sitting on the poorly patched asphalt. Two red doors provided a couple of choices in terms of entry.

"Over there." Dragos pointed to the one farthest back, where the afternoon shadows and a peaked eave provided a pocket of shade amid the glare of the afternoon sun. The Minion brought him in front of the door. Organ music vibrated from all around the building, a holy place unaware it was about to usher in the launch of Dragos's unholy war. He stepped out of the car. "Wait at the curb until I summon you. This shouldn't take long."

The Minion gave him an obedient nod. "Yes, Master."

Tavia raced into the house, leaving Aunt Sarah out at the curb taking care of the cab fare, since her own money—like her medicine—was left behind in her pocketbook the other night at the hotel. She felt on the verge of relieved collapse as the familiarity of home greeted her. All of Aunt Sarah's soft, ruffle-edged furniture and assorted knickknacks on every available surface, the very things that had long ago begun to make Tavia yearn for a place of her own, with her own belongings arranged to her own taste, now felt as comfortable and welcome as the cocooning warmth of a fleece blanket.

The house felt normal.

It felt solid and real, when just a short while ago, she'd been sure she was trapped in some kind of harrowing, inescapable dream.

As she took a seat at the kitchen table, a gust of wintry air blew across the floor from behind her as Aunt Sarah came back into the house. "Where have you been all this time, Tavia? Don't you know I've been worried sick about you?"

Tavia pivoted on the chair to face the older woman, feeling nothing but glad for the concern that radiated in from her wringing hands and wide, desperate brown eyes.

"The police were here yesterday," she informed Tavia in a questioning voice, her hands fisted on her hips. "They told me if I heard from you, I needed to call them right away. Of course, I thought you were with them. Isn't that what you told me? When we spoke last, you said you were staying at a hotel downtown to help the police with their investigation."

God. The police-arranged hotel suite seemed like a hundred years ago now. Everything that happened since that night seemed like it had occurred over the span of a lifetime. All she wanted was to put it behind her and get on with the life she knew. This life, the only one she wanted.

"You've never lied to me before, Tavia. It's going to

break my heart if you're keeping something from me now, after all these years . . ."

"No." Tavia took her aunt's nervous hands in a light grasp and guided her to the chair next to her at the little table. "I wouldn't lie to you, but a lot of very strange things have been happening lately. Terrible things, Aunt Sarah. The gunman from the senator's holiday party—he broke out of police custody and killed Senator Clarence."

"I know," the older woman murmured. "It was all over the news. There's a manhunt under way for him all across New England."

Tavia shook her head at the futility of that notion. "They'll never get him. Even if the police find him and take him in, they won't be able to keep him behind bars. He'll just break out again. He's more dangerous than anyone can possibly imagine."

Aunt Sarah was frowning now, her gaze searching. "Where did you get these clothes? And where's your pocketbook? I was so relieved to see you, I didn't even think to ask why you didn't have money to pay the taxi driver . . ."

Tavia kept talking, even as her aunt's voice trailed off. "He can't be dealt with like a normal criminal. He can't be dealt with like a human, because he's not. He's not human."

"You look positively peaked, dear." Aunt Sarah reached out and touched her fingertips to Tavia's forehead, then clucked her tongue as she picked up one of her hands and clasped it between her smooth, cool palms. Her skin felt like wax against Tavia's significantly warmer touch. "Are you feeling queasy right now? When was the last time you took your medications?"

"Goddamn it, will you please stop fussing and listen to me!"

The older woman went immediately silent, her eyes fixed on Tavia now. Guarded and uncertain.

"That man, he broke into the hotel suite just a little while after I called you, Aunt Sarah. He killed a police officer and he incapacitated two federal agents. Then he came into the room where I was, and he took me away."

Aunt Sarah seemed somehow stony now, not breaking into the hysterical fretting that was her usual reaction to everything where Tavia was concerned. Her brown eyes unblinking, scrutinizing, she was serious and contemplative in her calm. "Did he touch you, Tavia? Did he do . . . anything to you? Did he hurt you?"

Tavia had a hard time answering that. He didn't physically harm her, even though the threat had seemed very real when it was happening. "He brought me someplace—to where he used to live, I guess. He tied me up. He kept asking me questions about who I was. He didn't seem to believe anything I told him."

There was a long silence as her aunt watched her speak, absorbing the weight of her words. Then: "What did you tell him, Tavia?"

She shrugged, gave a slow shake of her head. "I told him I was no one, that I just wanted to go home. I told him I was very sick and that I left my medicines back at the hotel—"

Aunt Sarah drew a sharp breath over that bit of news. "You haven't taken them since two full nights ago?" She stood up. "I have to call Dr. Lewis right now. He'll need to come here to the house and give you an emergency treatment."

Tavia grabbed her hand and held her in place. "Aunt

Sarah, something very strange happened to me today. I can't begin to make sense of it . . ."

She pulled up the long sleeve of her hoodie, baring her forearm. The markings there were back to their normal color now, just faintly darker than her own skin tone.

"What is it?" her aunt asked, peering at her uncovered arm. "Tell me what to look for. Are your scars giving you pain? Because Dr. Lewis can prescribe something for that, I'm sure—"

"They're not scars," Tavia murmured. She ran her fingers over the webwork of swirls and arcs, feeling nothing unusual. "I don't know what they are, but just a little while ago, these markings were all different colors. They were . . . I don't know how to explain it. They were . . . *alive* somehow."

Aunt Sarah was staring at her, not at the markings on her arm but deep into her eyes. "They look perfectly ordinary to me, sweetheart. I don't see anything wrong."

"No," Tavia said. "Neither do I. Not anymore." Which made her wonder once again—made her hope desperately—that the transformation she thought she'd experienced had just been a bizarre hallucination. "What about my eyes, Aunt Sarah? How do they look to you?"

"The same pretty green as always," she answered gently. "But those dark circles under them concern me very much. You need rest and you need your medication."

"And my teeth?" she pressed. "Nothing strange there?"

As Aunt Sarah's look turned pitying, Tavia ran her tongue over the line of her teeth, finding only her usual slight overbite. Her canines were in alignment with the rest of her mouth, no fangs jutting down from her gums.

"I'm going to call Dr. Lewis now, okay?" the older woman said, speaking to her like she was a moron. And really, that shouldn't come as a surprise, given the outlandish things that had just come out of her mouth. "I have more of your medicines in the hall closet. You stay right here, and I'll get you some to take while we're waiting for the doctor. Does that sound all right to you, Tavia honey?"

She nodded as she was left alone in the kitchen, weary of all that had happened, whether it was some jarring new reality or manufactured completely in her mind.

She wasn't about to bring up the sex. That, she was sure, had happened. And she thought better about mentioning the blood on her body too, even if some of it might help substantiate her ordeal. Telling Aunt Sarah about that would only prompt a full body scan—or worse, an examination of her person by Dr. Lewis and his icy hands and implements.

"Here you are now." Aunt Sarah hurried back in with a handful of brown prescription bottles. She set them down in front of Tavia then went to the sink to fill a glass with water. "Go on, take them. You'll feel better; you know that."

Tavia shook out the various tablets and capsules that made up her thrice-daily meds regimen. She washed them down with a big gulp of water, shuddering as the knot of pills and the cold liquid cascaded into her body. "I need a shower," she murmured, winding down quickly now that she was back on familiar ground. "I'm so thirsty and tired."

"Of course you are." Aunt Sarah helped her get to her feet. "You freshen up and get some rest. I'm calling the doctor right now. I'm sure he'll be here within the hour."

* * *

Chase cleaned the bloodstains from the bedroom floor as best he could, although he didn't know why he bothered. The Darkhaven hadn't been lived in for more than a year, and he sure as hell had no reason to step foot in it ever again. Nothing but bad memories and shame within these walls.

And today, with what happened between Tavia and him, he'd added the cherry on top.

Figuratively, if not literally.

"Jesus, way to fuck things up." He bunched up the wad of wet paper towels, taken from a yellowing roll he'd found in the kitchen, and pitched them into the bathroom trash with the bandage wrappers and bent needle from his earlier self-stitchery.

As he passed the sink, his gaze snagged on the silver vial of Crimson. He picked it up, held it for a moment. Rolled the slender container in his palm. Considered ripping out the wax-sealed cork and flushing the poisonous contents down the toilet.

But his hand refused to give the damn thing up.

Less a lifeline than a swift means to a certain end, this last existing dose of Crimson was a crutch he dreaded he might need—maybe sooner than later.

Still midafternoon and his blood thirst was clawing at him already again, if it had ever truly left him. He wasn't sure anymore. The cold, constant ache was becoming a part of him. How long before it owned him completely?

Considering how close he'd come to taking a bite out of Tavia's neck today, his descent into Bloodlust was getting slipperier all the time.

Just the thought—and the reminder of how incredible

it had felt to be inside her—made him hard all over again, his blood surging through his veins like lava in its rush to head south. All the worse when he was still torqued from the release he'd interrupted in order to prevent himself from sinking his fangs into her throat as his orgasm had begun to crest.

The urge to free himself into his hand now and work her out of his system was one he didn't even attempt to resist. The vial of Crimson fisted in the hand he braced against the black granite countertop, he took his shaft in the other and furiously pumped it off into the sink. He came on a rough shout that was more about relief than pleasure.

With his release went some of the edge that was riding him, but the greater need still lingered. And now that he'd had a small taste of Tavia Fairchild, he knew better than to think he could be trusted anywhere near the female.

There had been a time—a million years ago, it seemed—when he'd been all about restraint and honor. He'd held himself to exacting standards and high ideals, dismissive of anything less than perfection. Like his father and brother before him, he'd been an impeccable enforcer of Breed law, merciless when it came to those who could not keep themselves or their own selfish needs in check.

What he'd been in truth was a self-righteous prick who'd considered himself leagues above the rest of the unwashed masses, his own kind and human alike.

What a fucking joke.

He had somehow become the thing he'd despised the most. And even worse, he'd dragged an innocent, frightened young woman into the mess along with him.

She was probably spilling everything to the cops by now. Maybe the news outlets as well. Just another mess he'd made that would have to be cleaned up quickly. He shouldn't have let her run out like she had. There was too much that needed explaining. Too many things that she needed to know in order to understand what she truly was.

A Breed female.

Not only that, but a Breed female with Gen One *dermaglyphs* and the inexplicable ability to walk unharmed in broad daylight.

Holy. Hell.

The thought hadn't lost any of its impact on him. If anything, it was more astonishing to think that she actually existed. Deeply disturbing to imagine the only way that could be possible.

Dragos had made her.

The bastard had to have created her in one of his labs, playing God with genetics—something the Breed had long decried as the worst kind of blasphemy within the race. Babies were sacred, not science. Everyone knew that. Everyone within the Breed subscribed to that simple tenet.

But not Dragos.

His secret breeding labs had produced a Gen One army of homegrown assassins, so why not this?

But what was his intention with her? It seemed obvious now that Tavia had been unaware that she was anything other than human. Her true nature, and its physical manifestations, had been somehow suppressed. By medications? Was her professed "sickness" actually her body struggling to deny the part of her that was Breed?

"Jesus Christ," he hissed, making a quick cleanup of himself and the basin.

The Order needed to be informed ASAP.

The problem there was he didn't even know where they were, or how to reach them. He'd made himself persona non grata with Lucan and the rest of the warriors. Worn out his welcome, possibly for good.

But he did know someone who might be willing to intervene. Someone who might be willing to take Tavia Fairchild under his protection as well. God knew Chase was a poor candidate for that duty.

Which meant he was going to have to call in a big favor—possibly the last he had coming to him—from his former Enforcement Agency colleague Mathias Rowan.

CHAPTER
Seventeen

She couldn't sleep.

After a long, hot shower, Tavia dressed in her own clothes, then lay on her bed staring up at the ceiling in a state of quiet anticipation. Of what, she couldn't say. But no matter how she tried to close her eyes and take a much-needed rest, her body seemed to be running at a strange new calibration.

Her blood rushed in her ears and through her veins. Her muscles were tense with power, everything prickly and twitching with idle, unspent energy. She was about to sit up and work off the feeling with a brisk pace around her room when she heard the front door open.

Voices in the foyer: Aunt Sarah bringing Dr. Lewis inside and giving him a quick summary of why she'd called him to the house. The two of them spoke in hushed tones, from all the way up the hallway and around through the living room, but Tavia caught the basics of their conversation.

"Two full nights since she last took her medications," Aunt Sarah informed him, stress in her quiet voice.

Dr. Lewis's usual baritone was subdued, little more than a rumble that carried through the walls and into Tavia's room. "Any outward indication of systemic distress?"

"No. But she said she noticed . . . *changes*." This last word was whispered, yet heavy with significance.

Tavia sat up on the bed, concentrating on catching everything that was said.

"These changes occurred while she was with him?" Dr. Lewis asked.

"That was my assumption, yes."

A pause. "Was there contact with him, physical or . . . intimate in nature?"

Oh, God. Tavia winced, hating how every aspect of her life was open for discussion and dissection by everyone around her. She hated her prolonged medical condition the most for that reason alone. True privacy was something she'd never known.

"I don't know precisely what occurred between them," Aunt Sarah replied. "She said she was physically restrained. He asked a lot of questions. She mentioned nothing more than that."

"Mmm-hmm. And how did she present to you when she arrived back here today? Anything peculiar?"

Floorboards creaked softly as the pair began to move through the house, farther inside, still careful to keep their voices low. They stood near the head of the hallway, if Tavia could trust her hearing.

"She was warm to the touch but not fevered. And flushed in the face. As for the rest, I noted nothing unusual."

"Nothing else?" Dr. Lewis grunted. "That in itself *is*

unusual. Forty-eight hours without medical suppression of the condition should have produced some kind of marked reaction. We've seen it in all the others."

All the others? Tavia held her breath as a jolt of alarm went through her, as cold as ice. *What is he talking about? What others?*

"She complained of being tired," Aunt Sarah added. "I sent her to take a shower and rest a while."

"Is she still asleep?"

"Yes. In her bedroom down the hall."

"Good," Dr. Lewis said. "I'll go in and have a quick look before we wake her to assess her for in-clinic treatment."

Every tendon and nerve ending in her body was firing off like small explosions inside her as the footsteps neared her closed bedroom door. Her senses were hyperacute now, skin tingling as though rained upon by thousands of tiny needles. She jumped as the knob twisted and Dr. Lewis appeared in the slowly widening wedge of space behind the door.

"Oh. Tavia, you're awake." He smiled, a faint curve of his mouth, which was partially hidden within the whiskers of his graying beard. "Your aunt told me you had gone to take a little nap. I hope I didn't disturb your sleep."

She was too uptight to bother with being polite. "What's wrong with me, Dr. Lewis?"

"Don't you worry. That's why I'm here," he said, stepping inside. He carried the big leather case that held his house-call medical supplies. Tavia had seen that bag of cold instruments and bitter medicines more often over the course of her lifetime than she cared to recall.

"No, no. Sit," he said when she started to get up from the bed. "No need to trouble yourself with a thing. It's all under control now. You'll see, I'm going to fix you right up."

Tavia eyed him warily. "Something's happening to me."

"I know," he said, nodding soberly. "But there's no cause for alarm, I assure you. I'm going to administer a small booster treatment that's going to make you feel good as new. Even better than a week at the spa. How does that sound?"

Tavia barely resisted the urge to tell him she'd never stepped foot in a spa. Things like that were off limits to her on account of her delicate physiology and her extensive skin issues—a fact he well knew, having been her sole care provider since she was an orphaned infant. He was trying to be light and humorous, but there was a flatness to his voice. A dull gravity to his gaze. It made her shudder a little, deep in her bones.

He came over to where she sat on the edge of the bed. "Lift your sleeve, if you would, please?" She hesitated, then complied, slowly inching up the long sleeve of her sweater. "Everything looks all right with your skin," he told her. "That's marvelous, Tavia. Very encouraging."

He ripped open a sterile alcohol packet and dabbed the cold pad over her bared biceps. "How many others have you treated like me, Dr. Lewis?"

He looked up, clearly startled. "Excuse me?"

"Are there a lot with my condition?" she asked. "Who are they? Where do they live?"

He didn't answer. Crushing the used alcohol wipe and foil packet in his fist, he pivoted away and tossed it into the nearby trash bin.

"I thought I was the only one," she said, unsure why this revelation was making her breath come so rapidly, her pulse kicking with a note of apprehension. With dread for an answer she suddenly wasn't all that certain she wanted to hear. "Why didn't you tell me there were others?"

He chuckled lightly. "Somebody's been listening through the door. You always did have an overly inquisitive mind, Tavia. From the time you were a child."

He busied himself in his medical bag now, his voice coy, mildly patronizing. And frankly, it was pissing her off. "How many, Dr. Lewis? Have any of them died from this . . . illness I have?"

"Let's concentrate on making you better, okay? We can talk about everything once you're fully recovered."

"I don't feel sick."

"But you are, Tavia." He heaved a sigh as he withdrew several instruments from his bag. "You are a very sick young woman, and you were lucky this time. Next time, it might be another story."

Her instincts spiked toward alarm as she watched him fill a large syringe from a vial of clear liquid medicine he'd taken out of his case. He turned around then and came toward her with it, a chilling smile on his lips. "You'll feel a lot better in just a few moments."

Oh, hell no. Tavia flinched away, acting on pure survival impulse. She didn't know where it came from, nor did she know how she'd managed to move her body so quickly.

She was suddenly up and on the other side of her bed in the amount of time it took for the thought to form in her mind.

Dr. Lewis gaped. He cleared his throat, hardly missing a beat. "Now, let's not make this difficult, Tavia. I'm not here to hurt you. I only want to help."

He gently closed the door and walked toward her, syringe held fast in his hand. His smile had gone from chilling to menacing. Tavia's skin began to crawl, getting warm and tight. Her teeth ached, and she could feel her vision sharpening, narrowing in on him as if he were prey caught in her sights.

Dr. Lewis cocked his head and gave a soft cluck of his tongue. "Bad girl. Someone hasn't told the whole truth about where she's been or what she's been doing."

Tavia moved opposite him as he came around the foot of the bed. "The one who hasn't been telling the truth is you." As she spoke, she felt the scrape of her fangs against her tongue. "What the hell have you been giving me all these years? What have you done to me?"

"Tavia? Dr. Lewis?" Aunt Sarah's voice sounded on the other side of the closed door. "Is everything all right in there?"

"Aunt Sarah, stay out!" Tavia screamed. "Please don't come in!"

Her concern for her aunt was genuine, but there was a part of her that couldn't bear to let the older woman see her in this state. She didn't want to lose her aunt's love if she were to discover the girl she'd raised was, in fact, a monster.

"Tavia, what's going on—"

"It's not safe," she shouted. "Call for help, but don't come in. Dr. Lewis—"

"The girl has been compromised," he interrupted, speaking over her with unnerving calm. "The process has been activated."

The process? What the hell did that mean? Just what had Dr. Lewis been doing to her all these years? Tavia didn't get much chance to guess about it.

Dr. Lewis lunged for her. The long needle of the syringe started to come down toward her face in a swift, deadly arc. Tavia leapt out of its path, muscles and

limbs moving in perfect concert, as effortless as breathing. One instant she was in front of her attacker, the
next she was behind him, crouched and ready to spring.

No time to wonder if he realized he couldn't win
against her. He came at her again, and she looked at
him as though seeing him for the first time now. How
had she missed the dull glint of his eyes before? Like a
shark's eyes. Dead and cold. Soulless.

It was her new, clearer vision that let her see this, and
she knew that her irises were amber bright by the faint
glow that bathed Dr. Lewis's murderous face as he
charged toward her, wielding his syringe like a weapon.

Tavia came up off the balls of her feet and took him
down to the floor. As he fell, his head knocked into the
edge of the bed frame. A bloodied gash opened up on
his grayed scalp, spilling bitter copper red cells. Even
with her newly attuned senses, she could smell a foul
taint on him. He was human, and yet . . . not.

And he wasn't about to give up easily. He tried to
stick her with the needle, but Tavia grabbed his wrist.
Wrenched it until it snapped. He only grunted, even
though the pain must have been excruciating. With a
snarl boiling up her throat, Tavia twisted his broken
limb and jammed the syringe into the old man's chest,
plunging the contents.

Immediately he started to wheeze and cough. He
sputtered a thick foam, eyes nearly popping out of his
skull as his jaw went slack and spittle crept down onto
his chin. The medicine was poison, at least to him. He
convulsed into death, his last breath leaving on a choked
rattle.

Tavia leapt up and bolted for the hallway, frantic. She
had to find Aunt Sarah and get them both out of there.

The older woman was on the phone in the kitchen.

She spoke in a rush, her voice lowered to a careful whisper, unaware of Tavia's approach or the fact that Tavia could hear her as plainly as anything in this powerful new form that had overtaken her.

"—process has been activated. Yes, Master. Lewis is in with her now. Of course. I understand, Master."

Tavia's legs felt a bit unstable beneath her as she listened to her aunt speak. Strange words. An odd, flat intonation. Servile and unfeeling. Tavia had to work to find her voice. "Aunt Sarah?"

She abruptly hung up and wheeled around. "Tavia! Are you all right? What on Earth was going on in there? Where is Dr. Lewis?"

Tavia didn't even blink. Aunt Sarah's concern felt altogether false now. As false as Dr. Lewis's had proven to be. Sad with a sick, dawning comprehension, she said, "I killed him."

"You—you what?"

"Aunt Sarah, who was that on the phone?"

She busied her hand over her cheery Christmas apron, brushing at nonexistent wrinkles. "It was, ah, Dr. Lewis's office. The way things sounded in there a moment ago, I thought I'd better call . . . to see about . . . having them . . . send . . ."

The lie died on her lips. Her face relaxed into a strange kind of calm. Emotionless.

Tavia shook her head, noting that Sarah's eyes had taken on the same flat luster that Dr. Lewis's had. She could see it now, her vision clearer than it had ever been. No more medicines to mute this preternaturally powerful part of her that had been living inside her, probably all her life.

Sarah moved back into the kitchen, away from Tavia. She pivoted to return the phone to its cradle.

"You betrayed me," Tavia said to the rounded bulk of her grandmotherly back. "All this time. You and Dr. Lewis both. You've lied to me."

"It wasn't you that we served."

The admission opened a cold pit in Tavia's chest. "What are you talking about? Who do you serve?"

"Our Master." Sarah turned to face her again. She had a butcher knife in her hand.

Dread and sorrow crept up Tavia's spine. "You would actually kill me?"

Sarah gave a small shake of her head. "Whether you live is up to him to decide. He owns you too. He's owned you from the very beginning, child."

"Him, who?" Tavia asked, but already a sickening thought was cleaving into her brain, as cutting as the edge of Sarah's knife. "Dragos."

She thought about Senator Clarence and what Sterling Chase had said about him. That Dragos already owned him. Now Aunt Sarah and Dr. Lewis too?

"Tell me what's going on," she demanded of the old woman. She moved forward, prepared to rattle the truth out of her if she had to.

"I have my instructions," Sarah replied evenly. And with that, with not even the slightest hesitation, she sliced the blade across her own throat.

Her body dropped to the creamy linoleum floor in a lifeless heap, blood pooling in a dark red slick beneath it.

Tavia stood there, numb and shaking, staring down at the corpse of the woman she'd never really known in truth. She felt bereft anyway. She'd just lost the only family she'd ever had.

She also knew her house was no longer safe for her.

Dr. Lewis and Aunt Sarah were dead, but there had to be others. Others who served this evil named Dragos.

He owns you too.

He's owned you from the very beginning, child.

Tavia shook off the debilitating feeling that rose on the wake of that thought.

She ran out of the house without looking back.

Everything had changed now, and she could never go back. Not to this house that had been the only home she'd ever had, nor to the life she'd been living for all of her twenty-seven years.

A life that had been nothing but a terrible, monstrous lie.

CHAPTER
Eighteen

Mathias Rowan was late.

The Enforcement Agency director had been shocked to hear from Chase earlier that afternoon when he'd called Rowan from the long-unused landline in Chase's empty Darkhaven. Nevertheless, to his credit, Rowan had agreed to make the trip over to the Back Bay as soon as the sun set. But now it was dusk and no sign of him yet.

Chase was dressed for battle, having pulled out black jeans, lug-soled boots, and a black long-sleeved knit shirt from the back of his old wardrobe. His holstered Agency-issued pistol felt insubstantial compared to the pair of 9-mm semiautos he was used to carrying as a member of the Order.

He didn't care to admit just how much it stung to realize he would likely never ride out on another patrol with Dante or the other warriors. He'd let that honor slip through his fingers, too busy grasping at selfish indulgences to realize what he stood to lose. Now it was too late to call it all back, no matter how much he wanted to prove himself worthy of their trust. Assuming he wasn't already too far gone to try.

With darkness settling outside, Chase's veins were lit up with the urge to hunt, and it was taking a hell of a lot of effort to resist the feral pull of his hunger. Instead he began a tight prowl of his vacant quarters, pacing the study and trying to ignore the insidious whisper of his blood thirst, tempting him to step outside and let the cool wash of wintry night air soothe some of the fever from his senses.

It was a siren's call and he knew it. A beckon toward disaster.

If his blood thirst didn't seize him the moment he stepped outside into the dark, there was a damn good chance human law enforcement would. Chase didn't want to risk either scenario, least of all letting his current notoriety inadvertently lead the cops or feds to Mathias Rowan's Darkhaven across town.

God knew his careless actions had jeopardized enough people he cared about lately. He wasn't about to add Rowan and his kin to that list.

Tavia Fairchild either.

She'd been the whole reason for calling in this favor with Rowan. He would know what to do with her. He, better than Chase, would be the best one to retrieve her and bring her to the Order where she'd be protected from Dragos and his servants and allies.

Safe from Chase himself too.

"Christ," he muttered, raking a hand over his head as he made another circuit of the study. She hadn't left his mind since the moment she'd run out, and even now he couldn't help wondering where she was, whom she was with . . . whether she was safe.

Part of him wanted to go after her, even more than he wanted to feed.

Part of him simply wanted her, and that was not good news at all.

Not in the dangerous shape he was in. Not when Dragos was still out there, making his Minions and plotting his next strike against the Order.

Maybe against the world as a whole.

That thought alone was enough to wrench his head back on track. Chase had no business worrying about the safety of one female—even a female as extraordinary as Tavia Fairchild. His life was already near to forfeit. Hell, he'd been willing to throw it away numerous times in the past few months. If he could get close enough to Dragos to take the bastard out, he'd gladly spend his last breath to make it happen.

But first he needed to be sure that Tavia wouldn't get caught in the crossfire. And that meant getting her under the Order's protection.

Where the fuck was Rowan?

When the rap of the brass knocker on the brownstone's front door sounded a moment later, Chase opened the heavy oak panel on a growled curse. "About damn time you—"

It wasn't Mathias Rowan standing there. It was Tavia. She waited on the stoop in the dark, shivering in just a turtleneck sweater, loose jeans, and leather flats. "I've been walking for hours. I . . . didn't know where to go." She took a breath. It was a ragged, shaky inhalation. She blew it out on a steaming gust that sounded very close to a sob. "I killed someone today."

"Jesus Christ." Everything else fell away as he stared at Tavia's stricken expression. Chase stepped out and wrapped his arm around her trembling shoulders. "Come inside."

She felt wooden as he guided her into the foyer, moving with robotic stiffness. Shock, he guessed, looking at her unfocused gaze and the slack lines of her face. "Are you all right? Are you hurt anywhere?"

She gave a weak shake of her head. "He tried to kill me. I think he was going to poison me with something. He said it would make me feel better, but I knew he was lying. There was something very wrong about him. I just sensed it, even before he attacked me. I killed him. I killed Dr. Lewis." She took another hitching breath as a shudder ran through her from head to foot. "I didn't know what to do. I didn't know where to go or whom I could trust. Somehow, I ended up here."

"It's okay," he said. "Come on, let's get you warm."

He brought her into the study and sat her down on the shrouded chair. He crouched in front of her and took her hands between his to rub some heat into them. When he looked up at her, there were tears welling in her eyes. "My aunt Sarah," she murmured. "She's dead too. She cut her own throat, right in front of me."

"I'm sorry," Chase said, hearing the pain and confusion in her broken voice.

"I don't understand how they could both lie to me. All my life, they'd been lying to me." She frowned, gave a slow shake of her head. "And their eyes. I never noticed how cold their eyes were. Dr. Lewis and Aunt Sarah—they'd changed somehow."

"No, Tavia. It was you who changed." He held her confused gaze. "You wouldn't have noticed anything unusual because until today you were living as a human. Your true nature was being suppressed, no doubt by the same medicines you thought were helping you. I don't think you were ever sick."

She listened in silence for a long moment, absorbing his words. "They betrayed me. They never cared about me, did they? I saw that today, when each of them looked at me. There was such a terrible emptiness in their eyes. Like a shark's eyes."

Chase grunted, knowing that look well. "They were Minions. All of them have that same dead glint in their eyes. You'll know it right away when you see them."

"Minions?"

He nodded. "Humans bled to the brink of death and turned mind slaves by a powerful member of my kind." He traced his thumb over the tangled pattern of *dermaglyphs* that swept along the underside of her wrist. "Our kind."

She drew her hands out of his grasp. "Vampires." She swallowed, fine brows knit together. "Is that what I am—a vampire? I know that's what you are. Isn't it?"

"Not exactly."

"Then what, exactly?" she demanded, shooting up from the chair, her voice climbing toward panic. "What the hell is happening to me? Tell me what's going on!"

He stood along with her. "I'm not sure what you are, Tavia. Or how you can be what you seem to be. I've never seen anything like you. No one has. What you are is . . . impossible."

"Great." She made a strangled sound in the back of her throat. "So, I'm a monster. Even by your standards."

Ah, Christ. He was not the person to explain all of this to her. His days of diplomacy and gentle conversation were long gone. Better that she learn what she needed to know from Mathias Rowan, someone still a part of Darkhaven culture who could ease her into the truth. But even as he thought it, Chase bristled a bit at the idea of Tavia being schooled by someone else. Particularly someone as noble and charming and smoothly mannered as Mathias Rowan.

Not that Tavia Fairchild seemed like a woman who needed handling with kid gloves.

And for better or worse, at the moment, Chase was all she had.

"What you are, Tavia, is Breed. Human folklore would call us vampires, but those stories exaggerate the truth. Like me, like the rest of the Breed, you are a living, breathing, very powerful being. Those of our kind live for a long time, centuries at least. Some of us have lived for more than a thousand years. And yes, we subsist by drinking human blood from an open vein."

"No," she interjected. "That's not right. Not me. For twenty-seven years, I've eaten normal food. I drink normal things, like any other human being. I've never even tasted a drop of blood, let alone drank it from someone's vein. Until . . ."

He watched her face go a little red. "Until you fed from me earlier today. And that was after your body had a chance to purge some of the drugs that were keeping the part of you that isn't human—the part of you that's Breed—on some kind of medically induced leash."

"I'm not like you. I can't be." She moved away from him, taking several paces across the room and giving him her back. "I don't want to be part of this . . . this nightmare."

"It's reality, Tavia." He walked up behind her and brought his hands down lightly on her shoulders. She didn't resist when he turned her around to face him.

"You don't have the choice to be part of this or not. Like it or not, you're living it now."

"Well, I don't like it." He could see her struggling to accept all that she was hearing. Her bright green eyes were still moist from unshed tears, but not a single one fell. She radiated a steely strength, chin held rigid and high, staring at him with a stubborn, unbreakable look that was more Breed than she would care to admit. "I don't like it at all, but if this is the truth, then I'm not going to run from it."

He nodded once, acknowledgment of her courage. "I won't lie to you. That much I can promise."

He didn't tell her there was little else of worth he had to give. If she spent any more time near him, she'd figure that out soon enough on her own.

"Tell me about Dragos." Her gaze was unflinching as it held his. "At the police station that night, you said Senator Clarence belonged to him. That Dragos owned him."

"Yes," Chase said. "The senator was one of Dragos's Minions. The cop in your hotel suite was also Minion. As were your aunt and doctor. They all belonged to Dragos. We can't be sure how many more mind slaves he has under his command. After all the years he's been at it, there could be thousands."

Tavia frowned. "So, where do I fit into this? Aunt Sarah said he owns me too. That he's owned me from the beginning—that's how she phrased it. I'm not one of his Minions."

"No," Chase said. "But based on what you are, there's no question that Dragos is involved. Until you, Tavia, there has never been a female Breed. Not one, not ever. Our race began thousands of years ago, when a ship carrying a group of biologically advanced otherworlders crash-landed on this planet. They killed and they raped, and sometimes they left certain females—genetically unique females known as Breedmates—pregnant with their young."

He couldn't read her expression now. It seemed one part quiet understanding, one part bald skepticism. "You're telling me that aliens and humans mated thousands of years ago and produced vampire babies?" She scoffed. "That's ridiculous. Do you know how crazy that makes you sound?"

"You should know by now that I'm not crazy." When she tried to look away from him, he steered her gaze back with his fingertips under her stubborn chin. He told her he wouldn't lie to her, so he decided to give her the unvarnished truth. "Our Ancient forefathers were not of this world, that's true. They were blood-drinking warrior savages who slaughtered entire civilizations at a time. The Ancients are all dead now, but until just a few weeks ago, one remained. Dragos kept him contained in his labs for decades, until the Ancient escaped to Alaska and the Order eventually killed him. But until then, Dragos used this captive Ancient for various genetic experimentations and to create an army of Breed assassins, the most powerful army this planet will ever know. If Dragos decides to unleash them, there's no telling how much havoc he can wreak."

"And me?" Tavia asked now. "I don't understand what any of this has to do with me."

"Don't you?" Chase paused, letting her sharp mind consider the possibilities.

"Dragos created me," she said after a moment. "I was one of his genetic experiments."

Chase's answering nod was grim. "There's no other way to explain the fact that you exist, Tavia. You're obviously Breed, but you're female—something we've never seen. And you can walk in daylight without burning. That's been an impossibility for our kind too. Until now. Until you."

"So, if I was fathered by a creature in Dragos's laboratory, what about my mother?"

"A Breedmate, I'm sure," Chase said. "Dragos kept dozens imprisoned in his labs over decades of time. If I'm right, you probably have a small red birthmark somewhere on your body. It would be in the shape of a teardrop and crescent moon."

Tavia stared at him in stunned silence. "On my lower back. I've always believed it was just part of my scars. Nothing I believed before was true, was it? It was all lies." She backed away, clutching her arms over her midsection as though she might be sick. She wheeled a stricken look on him, her green eyes throwing off amber sparks. "Why would he do this to me? What could Dragos possibly stand to gain by creating me like some kind of Frankenstein's monster?"

"You're not a monster," Chase assured her.

"I'm a fucking abomination!" she cried. The *glyphs* peeking over the edge of her high-collared sweater were alive with color and churning from one dark hue to another in her mounting distress. The sharp points of her fangs were just visible beneath the dusky edge of her upper lip.

She was so beautiful like this, he could hardly think straight. But she didn't see that. With a rough snarl, she tugged at the long sleeves of her top, exposing her forearms. Then she began rubbing at the *dermaglyphs* that tracked up her arms, scrubbing her palms over them in a ruthless frenzy, as though she wanted to scrape them off her skin.

Chase stilled her hands, taking them in his. "You're not a monster, Tavia. What you are is a miracle."

He reached up between them and smoothed some of her loose hair away from her flushed face. The urge to kiss her was nearly overwhelming, but he held back, unwilling to take advantage of her distress and confusion. Too bad he didn't have the same restraint earlier that day.

As much as it shamed him to think about the feel of her strong, lithe body wrapped around him, he couldn't deny that if she let him kiss her now, they'd end up naked all over again. And now that he was thinking about getting Tavia naked, his own body started to react in obvious interest.

He stroked the velvety slope of her cheek. Through emerging fangs, he said, "Jesus Christ . . . you are the most incredible thing I've ever seen. Possibly the only one of your kind."

"No." She gave a vague shake of her head but didn't pull away from his touch. "I'm not the only one. There are more like me."

Chase's hand paused where it rested against her beautiful face. "There are others? You're sure?"

"I heard Dr. Lewis say so. When Aunt Sarah told him I hadn't had my medication for a couple of days, he seemed alarmed. He said the others had never gone without treatment as long as me without severe reactions."

Holy hell. Chase's veins went cold with astonishment. "What else did he say? Did he mention how many there were? Where they might be?"

Tavia shook her head. "He tried to deny it when I asked him about it."

"Do you know where his office is?"

"Of course. I've been going there for exams and special medical trials since I was a child. He has a private clinic and treatment facility on an old farm property in Sherborn, southwest of Boston."

"That's where he keeps his patient records?"

"As far as I know, everything is kept on-site at the clinic."

While Chase was doing a mental calculation of how fast he could get to the rural farmland clinic, a knock sounded on the Darkhaven's front door. "It's okay," Chase told her. "I'm expecting someone."

He went to the foyer and opened the door for Mathias Rowan. "Sorry to keep you waiting, Chase. Things at the Agency have never been worse. I've got my hands full dealing with Agency traitors and a mass human slaughter that took place at the Chinatown sip-and-strip the other night. I came as soon as I could." As they made their way through the entry hall toward the study, Rowan looked around at the empty Darkhaven and exhaled a low breath. "Crissakes, I never thought you'd return to this place. Especially after what happened with Camden."

"Neither did I." Chase paused in front of his old Agency colleague. "And know that I wouldn't have called you for help unless I had no other choice. I hate dragging you into this shit—"

Rowan put his hand on Chase's shoulder. "In case you hadn't noticed, I'm already in it. You're in trouble, I know that. Hell, everyone in a hundred-mile radius knows that, human and Breed alike. You can't turn on the television without seeing your face on every news channel in the country. The dead last place you ought to be right now is Boston, my friend."

Chase nodded. "Yeah. But I need your help with something, Mathias. It's urgent, and it's important."

"I figured it had to be something big if you were calling me. What can I do?"

Chase stepped aside and let Rowan continue on into the study where Tavia stood. Her eyes lit on the Breed male, her thin pupils unwavering in the center of her amber-bright irises. The *glyphs* on her bared forearms were still alive with changing colors.

Mathias Rowan lost his normally polished demeanor and gaped outright at her. "What the . . ."

"Tavia Fairchild," Chase said. "Meet my old friend Mathias Rowan."

"Hello," she said, the tips of her fangs glinting bright as diamonds in her mouth.

"Is she—" Rowan began, then stopped short. He peered at her in disbelief, then shot a questioning look back at Chase. "She can't be . . ."

"She is," Chase said. "And I need you to look after her for me. Get her to the Order as soon as possible. She needs protection from Dragos."

"My God," Rowan gasped. He strode toward her cautiously, scrutinizing her as he might some new wonder of the world. Which wasn't far off the mark. "Remarkable. But . . . how can this be?"

"I'll explain it later." Chase checked his weapons belt and grabbed more rounds from the box sitting on the fireplace mantel of the study. "Just get her out of Boston. Take her personally to Lucan. He'll know what to do."

Rowan opened his mouth, but before he could protest or ask more questions, Tavia piped in. "I'm not going anywhere with anyone."

"You are," Chase replied. "It's not safe for you now.

Dragos will know his Minions are dead, and he'll come for you. Believe me when I tell you that nothing could be worse for you than falling into his hands."

That stubborn chin went up a notch. "I'll take my chances. But I'm not going anywhere until I know more about who I really am and what's going on."

"And I'll help you with that, if I can. You said your doctor's office is in Sherborn? That's where he keeps your patient records and all the others he's been treating under Dragos's command?"

"Yes, but the clinic property is gated. It's staffed around the clock with an armed security detail."

Chase shrugged. "Not a problem."

"Hold on here," Rowan interjected. "Let's slow down. Tell me what this is about, Chase. If this has something to do with Dragos, we should bring the Order in sooner rather than later."

"There's no time for that. Hell, it's probably too late to get much intel as it is. Dragos might have the place on lockdown already."

Rowan cursed darkly. "All the more reason to have Lucan and the Order here too. I'm going to call them—"

"Do whatever you have to," Chase replied, finding it hard to curb the bitterness from his voice, knowing Rowan had open access to the Order while he didn't even know where they'd gone. "I'm not going to wait around cooling my heels. I'm heading out to that goddamn clinic now."

Tavia was at his side before he took the first step. It was still a bit unnerving for a female to move with the same speed and agility as any other Breed. "I'm going with you," she said. "This is my life we're talking about. I'm not going to stand back and let anyone control me.

Not ever again. Besides, I'm the only one of us familiar with the clinic and its records. You need me."

As much as he wanted to deny her, Chase could see that arguing would be pointless. It would only waste precious time—something they didn't have, if they stood even the slightest chance of collecting any information of value from the dead doctor's clinic.

Tavia Fairchild might be untrained and untried, but in her blood and bones she was Breed—physically strong and powerful in her own right. She was also female, and Chase could see from her determined expression that she would not take his no for any kind of answer.

"All right, then," he said. "What are we waiting for? Let's go."

CHAPTER
Nineteen

Dr. Lewis's private clinic was nestled on a pastoral stretch of land that had once been a colonial farm in the rural town of Sherborn. Partway down the moonlit, one-lane track leading to the medical facility and clinic grounds stood a guard shack and automated arm that served as a gate.

The modern enhancements had always struck Tavia as sorely out of place beside the property's stout, rambling stone walls and rolling meadows. But Dr. Lewis had been meticulous about his special patients' privacy and security, which made it all the more peculiar when Tavia, Chase, and Mathias Rowan drove up to the darkened guard shack and found it empty.

"Something's not right," she said from the backseat of their dark SUV. "There's always security personnel on duty here, no matter what hour. Dr. Lewis had someone posted at the gate around the clock."

Chase glanced out the passenger window at the darkened landscape, then gave a grim look to his friend seated behind the wheel. "Dragos knows this facility has been compromised."

Rowan nodded, equally grave. "It could be a trap. Might not be worth the risk to go any farther."

"We have to." Tavia sat forward, her hands gripping the side of Chase's black leather seat. She wasn't about to come all this way only to turn around without trying. "My life is inside that clinic. This could be the only chance I have to learn who, and what, I really am. If there are others like me, they deserve the truth too."

She watched a tendon tick in Chase's rigid jaw. He said nothing, but she could see his doubt in the dark blue of his gaze as he looked at her. She could *feel* it, a cold indecision running through her own veins. "I need to know what he did to me and why. I need to know the whole truth, something I haven't had even once in my life. I can't let you deny me that. Not after everything I've been through already."

Chase's answering nod was a long time coming, just a faint tilt of his chin in Rowan's direction. On his cue, the vehicle swerved off the pavement and onto the snowy grounds, engine roaring as Rowan gunned the big SUV up and over the little stacked stone wall, sending the old rocks tumbling beneath the crush of the vehicle's large wheels. With a jostling bump and heave, they plowed through the fallen stones and rolled on toward the clinic building several hundred feet ahead.

Chase jumped out before they stopped. Moving almost faster than Tavia could track him, he ran to the building, breaking a reception area window and climbing inside ahead of them. It struck her, how easily he assumed the role of leader. It seemed to come naturally to him, leaping to the front lines, clearing the way for others to follow him. She caught a glimpse of something golden in him in that moment, something shining and heroic beneath the rough surface of the dangerous man he was now.

"We're clear," he said, reappearing in the open space as Tavia and Rowan ran up to meet him. He knocked aside some of the jagged shards of glass with his boot and offered Tavia his hand. "Watch your step."

She climbed inside the dark office and stood next to Chase, Rowan following right behind. The clinic looked different to her now, unlit and empty. No longer the place she came for healing, but a nest of deception. Its comfortably appointed waiting room, with its soft club chairs and pleasant watercolor paintings framed on the walls, now felt as falsely welcoming as a tranquil lagoon infested with piranhas.

"This way," she said, heading around the partitioned wall that separated the waiting room from the receptionist desk on the other side.

"Where are all the patient files?" Mathias Rowan asked, as he and Chase followed her into the area. Frowning, he quickly scanned their surroundings. "Every medical clinic I've ever seen has reams of paper records on hand."

Tavia shook her head. "Not Dr. Lewis. He is—he *was*—maniacal when it came to patient security. Everything in here is computerized and password-protected."

"Interesting," Chase remarked.

Rowan pulled one of his pistols out of the holster under his black parka. "If you two have things under control in here, I'm going to have a look around the rest of this place."

Chase nodded to his friend as Rowan ducked out to the hallway, but his eyes never left Tavia. He watched as she fired up one of the desktop computers and took a seat in the wheeled chair behind the workstation. When a password prompt appeared, she entered a complicated string of letters and numbers on the keyboard. The machine accepted the code, then resumed its start-up process.

When she glanced over at him, Chase was staring at her with a questioning look on his face. She gave him a mild shrug. "I was here a few months ago during a power outage. When the staff rebooted the computer, I couldn't help noticing what she typed in for the password."

Chase leaned down nearer to her, his big hands braced on the edge of the desk. "That sequence had to be about a dozen characters long."

"Thirteen, actually."

He grunted, eyebrows quirking. "And you remembered it perfectly all this time?"

"I only have to see something once to remember it. That's just how my mind works."

"Impressive." He gave her a devastating grin that made her pulse kick into a higher gear.

She wasn't used to having feelings of attraction, but it was impossible not to notice how close he stood to her now. How she could hear him breathing, could practically feel the steady, rhythmic pound of his heartbeat. Or how the thick bulk of his powerful biceps was brushing against her shoulder, each soft friction seeming to enter her bloodstream like an electrical current, as she brought up a login screen for the clinic's records program.

Another password prompt appeared, and this one she fumbled at first, too busy trying to ignore the warmth of Chase's body beside her and the heated weight of his attentive gaze. She tried the code again. "We're in. This is the patient database. I've seen it in use probably a thousand times."

Chase nodded. "Let's find your file."

She typed her name into the search field and held her breath as the screen began to fill with dates and records of her treatments. The data went back the full twenty-seven years of her life. Her entire existence, condensed into several thousands of line item entries stored as bits and bytes on a cold computer hard drive.

All the betrayals, waiting to be discovered with just a click of the mouse.

"Hey." His deep voice was quiet beside her. He rested his large palm over the top of her fisted hand in a gesture that made her feel both comforted and unsettled. "You gonna be okay with this?"

She swallowed. Gave him a shaky nod. "Yeah. I'm fine. I want to know."

Before she could think better of it and change her mind, Tavia clicked to open the most recent record. It was her visit from earlier that week. "I had an appointment with Dr. Lewis about recurring migraines. He treated me for a couple of hours here in the clinic and sent me home with new meds."

Chase eyed the record on the monitor. "Just a few days ago."

Tavia nodded. "And later that night, I was brought into the police station to identify you as the shooter from Senator Clarence's party." It seemed impossible that it was less than a week ago that her world was turned upside down. Less than a week ago that this man standing next to her had entered her life so abruptly. So strangely, darkly unexpected. "Nothing's been the same for me since that night. It won't be the same for me ever again."

Chase's stormy blue eyes fixed on her for a long moment, sober, remorseful. She realized only then that his hand was still resting on top of hers. His pulse beat in his fingertips, and in the heated center of his strong palm. "You wish you'd never met me. Trust me, I get it. I wish that for you too, Tavia."

"No, I don't wish that at all," she said, surprised by how deeply she meant it. True, her life had been thrown into chaos from the first moment she laid eyes on him—when he'd stood in the gallery balcony of the senator's house with a gun trained on a crowd of innocent party guests. She'd thought him unhinged and dangerous, and maybe he was both even now, but she couldn't blame him for any of the mess that was her life currently.

Because of him, she'd had to question her own reality. He'd opened her eyes, and just because she didn't want to see the things in front of her, didn't mean he was at fault. If anything, this deadly, terrifyingly brutal man had saved her life.

She looked at him, taking in the hard lines of his stark, handsome face and the world-weariness of his ruthless, beautiful eyes. "I'm glad I met you, Sterling Chase. Right now, you're the only friend I have."

He stared at her. Then he laughed, low and cynical. His hand withdrew from hers now, leaving a chill behind on her skin. "You should know something about me, Tavia. I don't have friends. What I do have is a bad habit of disappointing everyone around me. Better you hear that now than be fool enough to think you can count on me later."

There was no anger in his voice, only flat statement of fact. She felt sad for him somehow, watching the subtle way he distanced himself from her now. First his withdrawn touch, then his cool warning that felt as effective as a physical rebuff. Even his eyes were shuttered, no longer attentive and open but hooded and dark. Unreadable.

He stood up and paced to the far wall of the room to peer out between the closed metal blinds. "Let's get going," he said, his voice clipped and impersonal. "We don't have much time to take what we need and get the hell out of here."

Tavia went right to work, sending the full contents of her file to the printer in the corner of the office space. As the records displayed on the computer screen, she scanned the data, reading the details of her every visit to Dr. Lewis's clinic. Every medical trial and experimental treatment was documented. Each specialized medicinal serum and bitter pill was noted in the file, along with the results it produced for her condition.

And there were more records associated with her file.

Tavia paused on one of the entries, frowning as she recognized her own handwriting on a scan-captured page. Still another page followed the first. Several more too, all of them produced by her own hand, filled with names and codes and diagrams. She recognized them all, but she didn't remember writing any of it down.

Chase came over and looked at the screen from over her shoulder. "What is it?"

"A list of Senator Clarence's largest campaign contributors. Every name is here, along with the issuing banks and account numbers from the checks they wrote."

"Are you sure?"

Tavia nodded. "I was the one who processed the deposits. This is my handwriting."

"Why would you give that information to your doctor?"

"I didn't," she said. "I wouldn't. At least, not knowingly."

She paged down to a further document that showed a hand-drawn sketch of a federal judge's residence. Another diagram showed the floor plan sketch of a nuclear plant she'd toured with the senator last spring. Still more documents listed personal data and security-sensitive information on dozens of Senator Clarence's political allies and rivals.

"My God," she whispered, horrified at what she was seeing. "This collection of intelligence would be worth a fortune to enemies of the United States."

"Or to someone like Dragos," Chase said. He pointed to one of the earliest entries in her file. "Open that."

She clicked it, and data from her first in-clinic treatment filled the screen. By the date on the record, she'd been just six months old. Tavia read the page, feeling a mixture of fury and sorrow wash over her as the truth of her origins was spelled out to her in cold, clinical terms.

Ancient + Breedmate genetic splicing successful. Viable female specimen transferred to gestational surrogate. Laboratory live birth at full term. Subject 8 removed to Minion care, residing at 251 Pleasant Street, Saugus, Massachusetts. Admission to treatment program on this date as Patient "Octavia."

She scrolled to a later record and read the information in stunned, sickened silence. "There were others before me, but they died as infants in the medical trials. Dr. Lewis apparently discovered a combination of chemicals and synthetically engineered immunosuppressants that could inhibit blood thirst and halt genetic transformation. He tested it on us, knowing some would die."

Chase's mouth was pressed in a flat line as he read the record along with her. "Life means nothing to Dragos and his followers. Not even the most innocent."

Tavia paged to a different section of her file and quickly read the contents. "He's orchestrated every aspect of my life from the moment I was born. The medical trials and lies about who I was would've been bad enough, but that was only the start of it." She pointed to a notation about her photographic memory. There were references to detailed exercises the clinic had put her through in order to help build her innate ability and hone it like a weapon. There were other documents too, explaining hypnosis sessions that had gone on for hours and days at a stretch—time in which they'd pumped her unconscious mind for information, forcing her to document everything she'd seen and heard, page after page of details, written while her mind and body were under a narcotic spell. It had all been training for the real mission Dragos had in store for her.

Tavia pulled up another entry, no longer shocked by anything she read. The reality of it settled on her like a wet, cold blanket. It chilled her to the bone, made her ache inside with a void she thought might never be filled.

"He used me, Chase. He created me so he could use me. From the very beginning, just like Aunt Sarah—" She stopped herself, closing her eyes at the pang of hurt that welled inside her from the betrayal. "Just like the Minion who *pretended* to be my aunt had said. Dragos has owned me from day one. He made sure I had the right education, the right contacts, the right social skills and access. Then he cleared the path for me to get my job with an up-and-coming political star like Senator Clarence. All that time, I was nothing but a puppet for him."

"We're all puppets as far as Dragos is concerned. Every living being on this planet is either a tool for him to use or an obstacle that needs to be pushed out of his way."

There was a gravity to Chase's voice that made Tavia's stomach clench with dread. "Can he be stopped?"

The fact that it took Chase more than a few seconds to reply only made the knot in her gut coil a bit tighter, a bit colder. "I don't know," he said. "If you'd asked me that a year ago, I would've had a different answer. Back then, I believed that good always triumphs over evil. Everything was black or white, right or wrong, and the bad guys always lost in the end."

"And now?"

He exhaled a sharp sigh and shook his head. "Now there are moments when I can't even be sure which side I'm on."

Tavia held his haunted gaze. "You're one of the good guys. Maybe you don't know that. Or maybe you've just forgotten. Maybe someday you'll tell me about it."

For the longest time, he said nothing. Just stared at her in a way that made her heart ache a little for him. In that moment, she had the sudden urge to pull him close and reassure him that he wasn't alone. A crazy thought. One that would only earn her a swift, cutting rejection. If Sterling Chase was alone or adrift in his world, it was because he chose to be. He sure as hell didn't need her sympathy or friendship.

Maybe she was the one who needed reassuring.

Not that she'd find that in the stern face and merciless eyes locked on her right now.

To her relief, Mathias Rowan broke the awkward silence as he strode in from the adjacent hallway. "Damn, Chase, you have to see this place. It's more like a data center than a medical clinic. There's a server room at the other end of this corridor that must have thirty stacks of active drives in it. They must be warehousing millions of gigs here."

"Let's pull it all," Chase said. "Start yanking the drives. We'll take them with us. Maybe Gideon can take something useful off them."

"Right." Rowan nodded and pivoted to carry out the order. He froze an instant later, head cocked.

Tavia heard it too—a vague disturbance in the air outside the clinic building. Nearly indiscernible, yet unmistakable to her heightened senses.

"Shit." Chase swung a grim look at Rowan and her. He kept his voice low, barely above a whisper. "We've got company on the way. We need to clear out."

"What about the servers?" Rowan asked.

Chase shook his head. "May be too late for that."

"I think I can grab a few."

"Then make it fast."

When Rowan took off in a flash of movement, Chase grabbed the pistol from its shoulder holster. With his other hand, he took Tavia's arm and hauled her up from the chair at the desk. "You need to get out of here. Now."

She looked back at the printer, still churning out paper from her clinic records. "Wait! I don't have my files. And what if there are more like me still out there somewhere? I need to know. I have to search more of these files."

"Fuck the files. Fuck the others," Chase growled, taking her with him bodily into the hallway. "The only thing I care about right now is making sure you get out of here alive."

He brought her around to the waiting room where the broken window yawned open into the chill night. Chase stopped short. Tavia did too, her lungs freezing in the center of her chest.

A huge male form stood in front of them, garbed from head to toe in body-hugging black, like some kind of ninja on steroids. A knit skullcap covered the male's head and half his face, leaving only cold dark eyes visible.

He was Breed; Tavia knew it to the depths of her marrow.

And he was there to deliver death on Dragos's command.

CHAPTER
Twenty

In the scant seconds it took Mathias Rowan to reach the server room at the other end of the clinic, he realized he was too late.

Someone was already inside.

He crept toward the partially open door, making no sound at all as he drew his Agency pistol and peered into the dimly lit data center.

Crouched on the floor near the racks of servers was a human dressed in a security guard uniform and thick winter parka. A shoe box–size container lined in cushioned foam lay open near the man's boots. The rectangular center of the foam was hollowed out, emptied of its contents.

What the . . . ?

Rowan moved closer. The human had affixed a small digital keypad to the wall of servers and was entering a sequence of numbers. A fast *beep-beep-beep* followed an instant later, then a countdown clock appeared on the digital face of the device.

Cold comprehension washed through Rowan like a river of ice.

It was a bomb.

"Son of a bitch." Rowan was inside the server room now. He had his weapon raised, aimed at the back of the human's head. "Get up before I decorate this room with your gray matter."

The man came up slowly, hands raised in surrender. Rowan wasn't surprised at all to find himself staring into the dull gaze of a Minion.

Behind Dragos's mind slave, the countdown clock on the bomb's detonator was speeding in fractions of seconds. Not even ten minutes to go.

"Shut it off," Rowan snarled. He put the gun right up in the Minion's face, already feeling the points of his fangs emerging with his anger. "Do it now, asshole."

The Minion just stared, unblinking. Unmoving. Unfazed. "Pull the trigger now or watch this place erupt around us in less than nine minutes. It makes no difference to me, vampire. Either way, my Master's orders are fulfilled."

Rowan's lips peeled back from his fangs on a growl. He wanted nothing more than to waste this soulless bastard and wipe the smug look from his face with a whole lot of gunpowder and lead.

He wanted it so fiercely, he didn't hear the other Minion creep up behind him until it was too late to fend off the coming blow. Something hard and cold smashed across the side of his head.

Stunned, he felt his legs go out from under him.

Dropped on all fours, he turned his head and saw the length of steel pipe swinging down at him again, a direct hit aimed at the center of his face.

* * *

Mother of God, Chase thought as he stared at the massive Gen One male in front of them.

"Back the way we came," he ordered Tavia. "Find Rowan. Get out of here."

But before she took the first step, even as he told her to go, he knew it was too late for any of them to run and hope to get away. Too late to open fire on the Hunter, a highly specialized weapon, born and bred in Dragos's labs for a single purpose: to kill.

The assassin saw the gun in Chase's hand and sent it flying from his grasp with the power of his mind. It hurtled into a framed watercolor on the near wall, pistol and painting crashing to the reception area floor.

Not good.

Chase glanced past the bulk of the assassin in front of him, gauging the odds of getting Tavia out through the shattered window, their only viable exit. They'd never make it. And behind them in the clinic was nothing but silence. For all he knew, Mathias could already be dead, whether from more Hunters like this one or some other threat, Chase could only guess.

He knew one thing for certain: There would be no mercy here, only unfailing execution of Dragos's orders.

The assassin's dark gaze skimmed past Chase to settle and lock on Tavia. There was pure menace in those unfeeling eyes, clear and cold, unswerving. A sniper's sights trained on its target. Chase understood the message at once. It was Tavia this Hunter had come for; Chase was merely standing in the way.

The assassin took a bold step forward, broken glass crunching under his black combat boots. "Release the female."

Chase snorted at the command. "Like hell I will." He tightened his hold on Tavia's wrist, feeling her tendons go taut against his fingers as he wheeled her behind him. No way would this laboratory-raised killing machine get anywhere near her so long as Chase was breathing. He felt the feral stirrings of Bloodlust coming to life inside him, and instead of fighting the savage part of him, he welcomed it. "You want her," he growled at Dragos's homegrown killer, "then you're gonna have to come through me first."

The assassin didn't so much as blink at the threat. Nor did he reach for his own weapon. No, these killers were trained to disarm and end an opponent even more swiftly using bare hands and brute Gen One strength. Chase had seen more than one of them in action before, knowledge that made his own muscles twitch with instant battle-readiness as the Hunter lowered his chin and strode forward.

The assassin made a grab for Tavia, a long-armed swing that Chase blocked with a downward thrust of his elbow. As the Hunter's reach fell away—a moment's distraction that was all they could hope for—Chase turned a wild look on Tavia behind him.

"Run!" he shouted, his transformed irises gilding her stricken face in a fiery amber glow. "Get out of here, any way you can!"

The words were barely out of his mouth before the assassin's hands took hold of him. Suddenly he was airborne. He smashed into the sliding, opaque windows that separated the waiting room from the receptionist's workspace on the other side of the wall. Beaded safety glass exploded all around him with the impact.

As he dropped to the floor amid the raining debris, he saw the Hunter stalking toward Tavia. The punishing hands came down on her shoulders, yanking her into the killer's grasp.

"No!" Chase's rage poured out of him on a roar. He got to his feet and vaulted through the air in one furious leap.

The assassin staggered as Chase plowed into him. He lost his grasp on Tavia, snarling as she jumped out of his reach. But the Gen One bastard didn't go down. Chase slammed his fist into the side of the male's jaw, a repeated assault that cracked bone and teeth, yet hardly registered in the cold nonreaction of Dragos's trained Hunter.

And damn it, Tavia wasn't running as he'd ordered her. She had precious little chance of getting away as it was, and every second mattered. If this fight ended him here and now, she was finished too.

He started to bark another command at her to get the hell out of there, but her raised voice interrupted the thought.

"Chase, watch out!"

Her warning drew his attention to the assassin's free hand, which was coming up with a nasty-looking blade. He dodged the swift slice of the weapon, but the defensive move cost him. Still clinging to the Hunter, still landing blow after blow as the Gen One heaved beneath him like a wild horse, Chase didn't have time to react before the blade came at him again. This time it connected—a stunning blast of cold and pain stabbing into the side of his rib cage.

Agony exploded behind his eyelids. His punctured lung wheezed out a sharp gasp, the edges of his vision going gray and murky. The assassin threw him off like the dead weight he'd suddenly become, then pivoted around to finish him off.

"Chase!" Tavia screamed. She started running toward him, even as the Hunter raised his huge dagger over Chase's body, poised for the killing strike.

Ah, fuck.

No.

Chase's protective instincts warred with the pain and injury that had taken him down. He couldn't fail her like this. He couldn't let Tavia face the wrath of Dragos's killing machine all alone.

He bellowed past the anguish of his searing lungs and the dense fog of unconsciousness that was rising up to engulf him. In the split second the Hunter moved in above him for the kill, Chase rolled out of the blade's path and came up fast to his feet. The assassin swung toward him, dagger about to strike again, cold eyes narrowed in the open space of the Hunter's black head covering.

And there was Tavia too, standing behind the massive Gen One in the blink of an eye.

Her bright green irises glittered with flashes of amber now. The smooth angles of her face were drawn tight across her delicate bones. Chase saw the purpose in her transforming gaze and tried to dissuade her with a subtle shake of his head.

A command she flatly ignored.

Lips parted over the elongated tips of her fangs, she reached out with lightning-quick speed to grab the Hunter's upraised hand. She caught it in both of hers and wrenched it, a savage twist of motion. Bone and tendons gave up with an audible crack. As his blade tumbled to the floor, the assassin hissed, whirling on her like a viper.

His useless hand drooping at his side, the Hunter lashed out with the other and took hold of Tavia by the front of her throat. Only then did the cold assassin's training slip its tether. His fangs punched out from his gums as he bore down on Tavia, his fingers clamped ruthlessly around her neck.

Chase's own rage went nuclear. The sight of her gasping and sputtering, clawing at the punishing vise that was squeezing the life from her, put him in motion like nothing ever had before.

He lunged for his dropped pistol and came up firing, his arm steady despite the pain in his chest and the feral roar of his veins. Merciless, Chase plugged round after round into the Hunter's head. The skull splintered, spraying Tavia with blood and gore as the big Gen One staggered under the assault and, finally, dropped in a motionless heap at her feet.

Tavia stared at the dead Breed male, inhaling on shallow gasps, all she could manage after the bruising hold that would have crushed the life from her if not for Chase. She could taste blood on her lips, could smell it in her hair and on her skin and clothes. It turned her stomach, but at the same time it roused a dark power deep inside her.

If she had wanted to deny it before, now there was no room for doubt.

She was one of them—one of the Breed.

She felt that power living within her, a power that gave her strength to stand by without flinching as Chase stalked forward and chambered the last round in his pistol. He eyed the assassin with contempt, toeing the ruined head to expose a thick black collar that ringed the dead male's neck. Chase took aim on that collar and fired the final bullet at it, point blank.

A flash of light—impossibly bright—exploded all around them. Immediately Tavia felt Chase's body shielding her, his strong arms wrapped around her as the nimbus of pure white light shot out then vanished just as quickly. Chase's heat lingered only a moment longer than that, safe and comforting. Then it too was gone.

"Are you okay?" he asked, his voice rough, urgent.

She looked down at the head that was now severed from its body and smoldering. "I'm all right," she said, even though her throat felt raw, her voice a sandpaper growl when she tried to speak. "Wh-what about you?"

Her fangs throbbed at the scent of his spilling blood, which leaked from the stab wound in his side. Chase shrugged off his injury with little more than a grimace. "I'll survive." He grabbed her hand and steered her away from the carnage.

"That light," she said as she ran along beside him. "What did you do? What came out of that collar?"

"UV rays. Dragos makes his Hunters wear obedience devices around their necks. Any tampering or damage trips the ultraviolet detonator."

"Good to know," she said, still astonished and shaken by all she'd witnessed. She took one last glance behind them as Chase guided her into the corridor with him. "How many Hunters does Dragos have?"

Chase grunted. "Too damn many."

Gunfire sounded from somewhere near the back of the clinic, a rapid hail of shots that echoed all the way into Tavia's bones.

"Mathias." Chase swore under his breath. "I won't leave him behind."

Tavia nodded. "I'm coming with you."

He didn't argue this time. Together they raced down the long corridor of the clinic.

They found Mathias Rowan limping out from a back room, fresh blood smeared in a trail behind him. His head was bleeding profusely, and his left leg dragged stiffly as he hobbled toward them. "Get out! Get out now! There's a bomb in the server room," he shouted, waving them back. "I killed the two Minions who set it, but the timer is counting down fast. We have to get out of here now!"

They ran for the front window of the clinic and had barely cleared the building before a low rumble stirred deep underground. It expanded, in both vibration and roar, growing stronger as the three hurried across the snow-filled meadow.

The blast that followed was bone-rattling.

Fire lit the night sky as Dr. Lewis's clinic—and all its decades of secrets and lies—erupted in a ball of flames and smoke and flying debris.

CHAPTER
Twenty-one

The antique chair in Dragos's island lair had been in his possession for more than a century. An uncomfortable monstrosity, it was a throne carved of six-hundred-year-old Wallachian hardwood and acquired from an old church in the southwestern Transylvanian Alps. Legend had it that the polished seat and dragon's-head arms had once held the weight of a bloodthirsty medieval ruler whose name instilled fear in most humans even to this day.

Dragos normally found such folklore amusing at best. Tonight, he envied the mortal dread the chair's former owner had inspired in his subjects.

Tonight, Dragos longed to mete out that kind of raw, unholy terror—not only on those who served him but on the world as a whole.

His rage had started earlier that day, when the vice president had failed to show at Senator Clarence's memorial service. A last-minute security concern had forced the human government official to cancel his appearance in Boston. As for Dragos, the wasted daylight trip and an hour lost waiting among the throng of human mourners hadn't done anything to improve his mood. Nor did the fact that now his calls to the politician's office were being routed to lackeys who politely brushed him off with offers to check the vice president's calendar for availability to meet again sometime later in the year.

Dragos snarled just thinking on it.

His fingernails dug into the wooden arms of the Impaler's throne as he watched the news coverage of a fire raging out of control in a private stretch of land in the rural town of Sherborn. It wasn't the loss of Dr. Lewis's clinic that had Dragos's fury escalating; the destruction of the building and its collected data had been on his command, an order issued soon after he'd been made aware of his Minion doctor's demise.

It was the fact that his dispatched Hunter had not reported back with Tavia Fairchild that had his temper simmering toward a full boil. He'd sent the assassin to fetch her at nightfall, suspecting that she'd end up back at the clinic sooner than later, curiosity about her true past certain to carry her right back into her creator's hands. Dragos had been so looking forward to schooling beautiful Tavia in all the ways she could please him, now that the facade of her mortal existence had been stripped away.

But the Hunter had failed to bring Dragos his prize.

One more failure on top of a day filled with setbacks and annoyances.

He'd abide no more.

His patience had reached its end and there would be no more delaying his birthright.

Dragos launched himself out of the chair on a violent

curse, taking the priceless antique up in his hands as he rose to his feet. In a fit of rage, he flung the thing at the massive stone fireplace that filled one whole side of the room. The chair smashed to pieces as it hit the towering wall of immovable granite rock and mortar.

Six centuries of history reduced to splinters at his whim.

The totality of that loss—the irrevocable destruction—filled him with a satisfaction as real and visceral as the most explosive orgasm. Dragos savored the rush of power through his veins. He drank it in, let it feed him like life-giving, free-flowing blood.

He was seething, drunk on his own magnificence as he burst through the door of his private chambers and barked to one of his Minion servants.

"Summon my lieutenants," he snarled. "I want every last one of them dialed in to the secure video line within the hour. Have them ready and awaiting my command."

Rowan sucked his breath in through his teeth as Chase mopped the last of the blood from the back of his contused, split scalp. "Jesus, that knot hurts like a bitch. Your heavy hands aren't helping the situation either. You make a damned awful nurse."

Chase grunted. "Bedside manners were never my strong suit."

"No shit. You about finished back there?"

"Done." Chase had already dressed his own wounds from the battle at the clinic, he and Rowan having turned the latter's Darkhaven kitchen into a makeshift field medic station while Tavia had been shown to an upstairs guest room to clean up and rest. The mansion was quiet but for the occasional murmur of conversation as Rowan's civilian kin—a handful of younger brothers and nephews, a few of them with Breedmates of their own—went about their business elsewhere in the Darkhaven.

Chase tossed the mess from Rowan's injuries and eyed the wincing Enforcement Agent with a sidelong glance. "When's the last time you took a hit on duty, anyway?"

Rowan shrugged. "You mean, since I was promoted to director of the region? Hard to get hit when you're sitting behind a desk or pushing paperwork most of the time."

"Thought you knew what the job entailed when you campaigned for it."

"I only campaigned for it because you refused to," Rowan said. "You know the director's spot had your name on it. Hell, it was tradition that it should go to you. There'd been a Chase in that office for as long as the Agency's had a presence in Boston."

More than two hundred years, in fact.

First Chase's father, then Quentin, Chase's brother. It had been six years since Quent had been killed on the job. Everyone in the family and the Agency alike had assumed Chase would step in as director. Instead, after the shock of what had happened to Quent and the grief of his death had faded, Chase had thrown himself into fieldwork, taking the street patrols and other shit jobs that usually went to the new recruits and discipline cases. Work intended to get their hands dirty, make their balls sweat a little in action before any of them started jockeying for council attention or political favors within the Agency.

To those looking in from the outside, Chase's decision to avoid the director's office had been one of honor, of courage. A mourning brother, sole surviving son of one of the most respected names in Breed society, turning away from title and privilege to continue his family's legacy of selfless service in the trenches.

The truth of it had little to do with any of those things. Chase couldn't bear the thought of attempting to fill Quentin's or his father's shoes. His success never would have measured up to the impossible standards they'd set, and his failure by comparison would have been more than he could bear. The shame of just how deeply he understood this fact had dogged Chase even to today.

So he'd shunned the responsibility.

He'd run away from it, a disgrace that was only made worse for the way everyone concluded that he acted out of the same shining integrity that had guided his kin before him. And he'd let the facade stand, all those years. Even after he'd joined up with the Order, he'd continued to play his holier-than-thou role. But it hadn't lasted. No, they'd seen through him soon enough.

He'd been a fraud all his life. Golden and impeccable on the outside, yet festering and sick to death of himself within. All the worse after Quent was killed. Thanks to his rising affliction, this dangerous dance with Bloodlust, Chase no longer cared to hold up the mask he'd hidden behind for so long. The effort was too much.

Now he wore his sickness on the outside. Even his talent for bending shadows had all but deserted him. He was naked now, exposed. Nothing could conceal him anymore.

Rowan heaved a sigh, disrupting the dark path of Chase's thoughts. "There are days—many more than not, if you want to know the unvarnished truth—that I don't even know what the Agency stands for. I took my office because I thought I could make a difference. I haven't. The corruption has been there too long, and it goes too deep. It's a cancer whose tendrils have touched nearly everyone in the organization."

Chase understood. He'd felt the crush of that weight himself. "Things in the Agency have been on a downward slide for a long time. To clean it up? Christ." He shook his head, considering the breadth of changes it would require. "You'd have to turn the whole place inside out. Start all over, with a handpicked few and reconstruct from the inside. New philosophies, new measurables. Reform the Agency, piece by piece."

Rowan was watching him closely, nodding along in agreement. "Maybe one day you'll come back and help me do just that."

"Fuck." Chase scoffed. "Not me. I was glad for the chance to get out when I did. It never had been a good fit for me."

Rowan grunted, his dark brows coming together in a frown. "I thought maybe you left the Agency for a different reason. I guess I wondered if maybe you left to follow Elise. You know, to make sure she wasn't making a mistake, getting involved with one of the warriors of the Order," he added, when Chase snapped a hard look on him.

"She couldn't be in better hands," Chase said, meaning it too. "Tegan adores her, as well he should. He's a good man, worthy of her. And she loves him, maybe even more than she did Quent."

"Yes. I've seen that for myself too," Rowan replied. "But at the time . . ."

Chase picked up his old friend's trailing thought. "At the time I quit the Agency, I didn't know what I wanted.

I only knew that if I wanted to keep my sanity—keep my damned soul—I needed to get out."

He gave Rowan the truth now—as much as he was willing to share. There were some things he didn't divulge to anyone. Things he had never shared, shames from his past that he expected he would keep to himself forever.

"And now?" Rowan asked after a moment.

Chase exhaled a humorless chuckle. "I don't worry about those things anymore."

"Maybe you should." Rowan reached over and put his hand on Chase's shoulder. "You and I go back a long time, my friend. I've seen you at your best. Even at your worst, you're a hell of a lot better than most of the assholes calling themselves my friends inside the Agency. You ever need anything, I've got your back."

Chase frowned, reluctant to accept so undeserving a gift. "I wouldn't ask it of you, Mathias. Except—"

"The female upstairs," Rowan said with a grave nod. "Jesus Christ, Chase. I've seen her with my own eyes, but I still can hardly believe it. Dragos engineered a female Gen One in his labs?"

"More than one, according to the patient records we saw at the clinic tonight."

Rowan kept his voice low, so as not to be heard by any of the other civilian residents of his Darkhaven. "Do you realize what that means? What that means to the future of our entire race? That young woman up there changes everything."

"Yes," Chase said. "And that's why she needs to be protected. The safest place for her is with the Order. I'm hoping you'll make sure she gets there."

"You can do that yourself, Chase." Rowan's shoulder lifted in a vague shrug. "I told you I had to inform

Lucan about all of this. I called him as soon as we got back. He's sent Tegan and a few of the others down to collect the female. They're en route already, should be here within the hour."

Chase swore under his breath. When he walked out of the Order's mansion and into police custody with the humans a few mornings ago, he'd done it as an act of finality. His way of releasing his warrior brethren from the burden of his presence and all the failures he'd been at the center of since he'd begun to lose his battle with Bloodlust.

His walking out had been a last-ditch effort to scrape together a small bit of honor—a feeble grab at redemption—by sacrificing his own freedom for theirs. He didn't think he'd ever face Lucan or Dante or Tegan and the rest of the Order again. He sure as hell didn't want to see their rightful contempt now.

"You'll have to do the honors for me," he told Rowan. "I'm not planning to stick around that long."

"Where else do you have to go?"

The question wasn't posed with any challenge, but the concern wasn't welcome either. Chase got up and began a tight prowl around the kitchen. Above his head was the private guest room Tavia had been shown to on their arrival. The water from her shower was still running; he could hear the muffled whine of old copper pipes through the thick plaster walls. "She's been up there a long time. Do you think she's all right?"

"Considering everything she's gone through today alone, I'd say she's holding it together remarkably well."

"Yeah," Chase said. "Tavia is . . . remarkable."

He thought back on the past several days and nights. All the astonishing revelations. The unexpected concern— the unwanted caring—he felt for a woman who'd been a stranger to him not even a week before. And yes, there was the added complication of his desire for her.

All the more reason for him to cut and run now, before he let himself get entangled any further.

"Shit." Chase raked his splayed fingers over his scalp on a deep sigh. "I gotta go. It's better this way. Better for her. Hell, it's better for me too."

Rowan studied him now. The shrewd Agency director didn't need anything more to understand just how intimately Chase had fucked things up with Tavia already. "What am I supposed to tell her?"

Chase swore again, more vividly this time. "Just tell her I'm sorry. For everything."

CHAPTER
Twenty-two

"Do you think it's true?" Lucan stood just inside Gideon's makeshift computer command center, leaning one shoulder against the wall. "Could Dragos have created a female Breed in his labs?"

Gideon glanced up from his study at one of several workstations. His gaze was serious over the rims of the pale blue glasses resting low on his nose. "Based on what I've found in the cryo container Hunter brought back from New Orleans, I'd say it's more than possible."

He rolled his chair across the polished pine-plank floor, stopping in front of another busy computer. "See this here?" He pointed to the schematic displayed on the monitor. Lucan strode over to have a look. "This is just one of a dozen analyses I've been running on the genetic popsicles in that laboratory ice box. We're talking about countless specimens, Lucan, harvested from the Ancient, his lab-bred offspring, and upward of twenty Breedmates. Hell, I even found some human samples in that tank. Dragos has been collecting DNA, blood cells, stem cells, embryos—everything a lab full of Minion geneticists could possibly need to keep them busy for a generation."

"Jesus Christ," Lucan muttered.

"And those are just the viable specimens," Gideon added. "The second cryo container had more of the same, but damage to the tank had broken the seals and destroyed all its contents."

"What's going on over there?" Lucan asked, gesturing to still another computer with a monitor full of scrolling data. A program was running on it in split-screen mode, the bottom half ripping through line after line of rapid-fire code, the top displaying a string of thirteen-character fields.

Only three of the fields were filled in with a static number: 5, 0, and 5.

"That," Gideon said, "is a little deencryption routine I wrote the other night. I hacked through some of the lab data without any problems, but one of the files has an extra password lock on it. My usual bag of tricks didn't make a dent in the encryption, so I'm coming at it from another angle."

"And it's working?" Lucan asked, watching the dizzying code fill the monitor and keep on going.

"It's working," Gideon said. "But going a lot slower than I'd hoped. The program's been running for roughly twenty-four hours and that's all it's returned. At this rate, we're looking at another four or five days to crack the whole sequence. Assuming the program's results are accurate."

Lucan grunted. "And we have no way of knowing what's in the file even if we crack the encryption."

"Right," Gideon replied. "But since Dragos took the

extra step to lock it down with multiple safeties, I'm guessing whatever's inside is intel we're gonna want."

"Agreed, but another four or five days could be too late to make use of whatever we find in there. Tell me you have something more than this."

Gideon nodded. "I've been hacking into the GPS transmissions that Hunter sent us while he was down in New Orleans. Since that intel led us to Corinne's son, maybe we can get a bead on Dragos's other Hunter cells across the country. We locate those cells, we can start taking them out one by one. Disassemble Dragos's homegrown army from the ground up."

"Sounds like a plan. We need some wins, now that we're beginning to see all that Dragos has been doing in the years—hell, the decades—he's been running unchecked."

"A female Gen One," Gideon mused, getting busy on one of the keyboards in front of him. "How is it she's been living among the humans all this time? And what the hell did Dragos stand to gain from creating her in the first place?"

"Questions I have myself," Lucan replied. "We'll have the chance to debrief her once Tegan and the others collect her from Rowan's place."

Uncertain if Tavia Fairchild would be cooperative, Lucan had sent Hunter and Niko along with Tegan. Renata went too, not only because the presence of another female might offer some sense of comfort to Tavia, but also because of Renata's unique Breedmate ability. Niko's mate had the power to temporarily immobilize any of the Breed using the ESP strength of her mind. Unfortunately, the industrial-strength migraines she tended to suffer afterward meant Renata used her talent sparingly.

"What about Chase?" Gideon asked. "Did Rowan tell you anything about him when he called?"

"Only that he was there at Rowan's Darkhaven, and that he looks like hell." One more reason Lucan felt it was a good idea to send Renata down to Boston tonight with the rest of the crew.

"For better or worse," Gideon said, "I gotta say I'm relieved to know that Harvard is still breathing."

"Don't get your hopes up where he's concerned," Lucan replied, but the truth was, he too was relieved that Chase was still alive. And more than a little grateful that he'd brought Tavia Fairchild to the Order's attention. This, on top of the personal risk Chase had taken in surrendering himself to the humans the morning of the compound's raid. He'd likely saved more than one life that day, an act of sacrifice that still humbled Lucan to reflect on now.

Lucan was the Order's leader all this time because he knew when to draw the hard lines in the sand, but he also knew when those lines should be allowed to bend.

Sterling Chase was more tarnish than shine lately, but he wasn't a total lost cause.

Lucan ought to know. He'd been there himself not so long ago.

"What was it like?" Gideon had turned away from his computer keyboards and was watching Lucan from behind the icy lenses of his shades. The tech genius's usual jocularity was replaced with a sober quiet as he stared at Lucan now. "You've never said what it felt like to brush up against Bloodlust."

It didn't take much to recall. Lucan's struggle with his own feral nature had eased some since Gabrielle had come into his life a year and a half ago, but the memory of it wasn't far out of reach.

"It was hell," he admitted. "Unrelenting, all-consuming hell. Hunger and aggression were constant. It's a dangerous combination, self-destructive. The thirst fuels the compulsion toward violence, and violence intensifies the urge to hunt and feed." He bit off a curse. "As bad as I had it, Tegan endured something even worse."

Gideon gave a grim nod. He knew the basics of Tegan's history. "He lost his Breedmate and went Rogue. You saved him."

"Several long months of seclusion and near starvation saved Tegan, not me. Even then, there had been no guarantee that he'd come out better on the other side." But he had, in spite of everything, even the grief and rage that had owned the warrior. Lucan was glad that somehow Tegan still considered him a friend. A brother. "It was a long time ago, centuries for him, but I can tell you that the itch of Bloodlust never leaves you completely. Tegan came out of his tailspin over time. A great deal of time—something we can't offer Chase right now, with Dragos on the loose."

One of Gideon's brows quirked over his serious eyes. "The walls of the fallout shelter beneath this Darkhaven are made of steel and concrete, twenty inches thick. There's a triple-reinforced door built to withstand a nuclear blast. Ought to be strong enough to hold one pissed-off vampire until we do have time to deal with him properly."

Lucan held the warrior's gaze, feeling a spark of conspiracy tug at the corner of his mouth. "I've already been down to check out the situation myself. Took a look right after I spoke with Rowan tonight."

Gideon was nodding now, a smile breaking across his face. "And here I thought you'd written Harvard off."

"I might yet," he cautioned soberly. "It'll be up to him to persuade me one way or the other. Like I said, best we don't get our hopes up until we see him for our—"

The sudden thunder of footsteps pounding across the floor outside the room cut Lucan's warning short. He and Gideon both got up and hurried out to see what was going on.

Lazaro Archer nearly collided with them. "It's Jenna," he said, concern etched in hard lines on the Breed elder's stern face. "Come quickly!"

They followed him to the great room at the other end of the expansive residence. Brock was already there, crouched at his mate's side where she slumped in a boneless droop on the brown leather sofa.

"*Jenna.*" Brock's voice was soft but urgent, his dark hands roaming over her listless face. "Baby, can you hear me? Come on, Jenna. Open your eyes for me. Wake up now."

Lucan glanced to Archer. "What happened?"

"I'm not sure. We were reviewing the Ancient language journals, trying to work out translations for some of the more elusive alien phrases she's been speaking in her sleep the past few weeks. She asked if she could rest a while, so I went to look in on Kellan. When I came back, she was thrashing on the sofa, panting for breath."

"Another nightmare," Gideon suggested. He kept his voice low while Brock worked to bring Jenna around as only he could. "Yesterday she told me she's been having bad dreams. Dreams about being trapped in a small compartment in the dark, about being pierced repeatedly with needles and knives, her skin flayed from her body while all she can do is watch it happen."

"Jesus," Lucan hissed. "That can't be a coincidence."

"No," Gideon agreed. "My best guess is that along

with the bit of alien material the Ancient implanted in her, some of his memories came with it."

And that wasn't all the Ancient had given Jenna. Her body was still changing, cells and organs adapting toward something more than human. The *glyph* on her nape and shoulders grew a little bigger every day; there was no telling how much of her body it would cover in a year's time or a decade. The way her physiology was mutating, enhancing, Gideon was convinced that like her superhuman strength and stamina, Jenna's life span could no longer be measured in human terms.

"Jenna," Brock soothed, gathering her close as she began to rouse and murmur quietly in his arms. "That's it, baby. You're okay now. I've got you. I'll keep you safe."

"Brock?" Her eyelids fluttered as he continued to speak to her. She moaned, breath coming faster as the weight of sleep lifted and she started to regain consciousness. Her body stirred now, waking fully. She sucked in a shallow sob and clung to him, her eyes wide and welled with tears. "There was water everywhere. It kept rising and rising, and the people . . . there were people screaming all around me, drowning. Oh, God . . . it was so awful!"

Lucan slanted a questioning look at Gideon, who shook his head, equally confused.

Brock took her face in his hands, holding her still, soothing her with his touch. "What people, baby? What water? Who was drowning?"

"I don't know." She pressed her cheek against his chest and sucked in a ragged sob. "I don't know who they were, but they were dying. Men and women, children. Animals too. The wave roared over everything. It washed away the whole city."

Gideon's wary frown must have been a good match for Lucan's. Even Lazaro Archer looked a bit rattled by Jenna's description of chaos and mass destruction.

Brock whispered soothing words against her ear. "Just a bad dream, baby. You're safe. Nobody died. It was just a bad dream." The warrior lifted a dark, grim look on Lucan, Gideon, and Archer. "We're pushing her too hard. She's exhausted, physically and mentally. All these tests and journals and analyses. It's too damned much. It stops, right now."

"No." It wasn't Lucan or any of the others who spoke to refuse him but Jenna. She drew back from Brock's embrace, shaking her head. Her face was tearstained and flushed, but her soft brown eyes were steady with resolve. "No, Brock. I don't need to stop looking for answers. I don't want to stop."

"Look what it's doing to you," he pointed out. "You can hardly close your eyes without waking up screaming from a new nightmare—usually worse than the ones that came before."

She was still shaking her head as she caught his taut face in her palms. "I'm all right. Shaken up a little, but I'm fine. I want to do this. We're getting close to something big, I can feel it. I want to understand these dreams, even if they terrify me. They're a part of who I am now, Brock. I need to know what they mean."

"There may be someone who can help," Gideon put in. All heads turned to him. "Claire Reichen," he said. "Andreas Reichen's Breedmate is a dreamwalker. She might be able to help Jenna navigate these dreams and collect details we might miss otherwise."

"Yes," Jenna said. "Do you think she would be willing to do it?"

"Claire's in Rhode Island," Lucan reminded everyone. "With Reichen in Europe at the moment, running reconnaissance on the Agency for us over there, we can't ask Claire to abandon her Darkhaven and come north on a whim."

"Maybe she wouldn't have to," Gideon said. "She's dreamwalked remotely before. It's not the easiest thing for her to do, but it's not out of the question."

Brock rubbed his hand over the top of his skull-trimmed head. "I'm not feeling good about any of this. What if something happens?"

"What can happen?" Jenna asked him. "They're only dreams. Maybe they're the Ancient's memories, I don't know. But I *need* to know, Brock. He let me live for a reason. He made me choose, and then he put this living piece of himself under my skin. Why? What did he want from me? I can't rest until I have those answers. You can't ask me to run away from what I am becoming."

"I wouldn't," Brock told her gently. He lowered his voice to a rough whisper. "You know I love you more than anything, Jenna. I only want you to be safe."

"I am safe." She smiled at him as though no one else were in the room. "I'm safe with you, and I'm not afraid. Just promise you'll be here to catch me when I wake up."

"Forever." He kissed her, a brief meeting of their mouths that radiated as much heat as a furnace.

Jenna didn't take her eyes off her mate for a moment. "Make the call to Claire, will you please, Gideon?"

At Lucan's nod of agreement, Gideon pulled out his cell phone and speed-dialed Reichen's oceanfront Dark-haven in Newport, Rhode Island.

CHAPTER
Twenty-three

He'd had every intention of leaving.

After walking out of Mathias Rowan's kitchen, his mind had been made up. Avoid the certain contempt of his former brethren of the Order and simply disappear into the night; that was the extent of his plan. Yet, somehow, Chase instead found himself climbing the stairs to the Darkhaven's second floor.

The living quarters upstairs were quiet, most of the mansion's residents either in their own suites or out for the evening to hunt or play in the city.

The room where Tavia was stood at the far end of the broad hallway. Chase walked over the antique runner that spanned the floor from the top of the wide, curving stairwell, to either end of the living quarter wings of the regal old home. He stood motionless in front of the closed door, uncertain if he should disturb her.

From the other side of the thick panel of carved and polished mahogany, he heard the faint hiss of running water.

She was still in the shower?

She'd been up there for more than an hour.

Was she all right?

"Tavia." Chase rapped lightly on the door. No answer. He knocked again, harder this time. More of the same troubling silence. "Tavia, are you in there?"

He tried the faceted crystal knob and found it unlocked. His breath going shallow in his lungs, he pushed open the door and stepped into the unlit bedroom suite.

"Tavia? Why didn't you answer . . ."

His voice trailed off to nothingness as he rounded the corner of the bedroom and found her sitting quietly against the wall in the dark.

Weeping.

"Ah, Christ."

Still dressed in her clothes from the clinic, arms wrapped around her bent knees, she shook with the force of her tears. Head bowed, her hair drooped to conceal her face, the long caramel waves matted and tangled from the battle earlier that night. Although she was no waif, far from helpless or weak, she had never looked so small or vulnerable to Chase.

He crossed the room and crouched before her. She didn't even look up to acknowledge he was there. Her shoulders trembled as soft sobs racked her body. "Hey," he whispered, reaching a tentative hand out to gentle her.

He stroked her hunched back, slow caresses that only seemed to make her cry harder. She didn't speak, just sucked in air and wept it out again.

"Shh," he soothed, uncertain how to comfort her, knowing he was a poor choice for the job. If there was one thing he preferred to avoid more than disappointing those who depended on him, it was dealing with such a raw display of feminine emotion.

But he couldn't walk away from Tavia's sorrow, not even if she deserved the arms of someone better.

"It's okay," he murmured, sweeping aside the limp strands of her hair. He lifted her chin, bringing her red-rimmed eyes up to meet his gaze.

God, she was breathtaking. Even wrecked with distress, her face spattered with dried blood and grime from the clinic, eyes wet with tears and puffy from crying. Chase looked at her and realized he'd never heard her laugh. Had never seen her smile. Since she'd been with him, she'd gone from terrified to outraged, then anguished and confused to lost and alone. Now, utterly destroyed.

Yes, there had been passion between them too, but even that had been fierce and raw-edged. He'd taken something precious from her when he allowed things to go as far as he had. The sex and the blood—her first time knowing either one—and he the selfish bastard who'd greedily enjoyed the pleasure in both.

The guilt of that pressed down on him as he gathered Tavia into his embrace and rocked her as she cried against his chest. "None of my life before was true," she said, her voice thick and choked with tears. "I thought I could deal with it, but it hurts so much. Everyone I knew was lying to me. Using me. All my life, they were betraying me."

Chase caressed her head and back, smoothed his rough palm over the tangled silk of her hair. "You'll be okay," he told her. "You're strong, Tavia. You'll come through this, I have no doubt. And there are people among the Breed who can help you."

Not him, surely. He'd done enough damage where she

was concerned. And even though it felt good to hold her, felt somehow comforting to feel her arms wrapped around him as she wept, the embers of his hunger kindled just below the surface of his calm. It was a struggle to tamp it down, to curb the fevered glow of his irises as Tavia lifted her head to meet his gaze.

"You want to know the irony in all of this?" She bit off a strangled sigh. "I loved her—the Minion that Dragos assigned to be my family. I loved her like she was my mother. I even loved Dr. Lewis. They were the two people I trusted most in this world, the only people who really knew me. I thought they were protecting me, making me better." Another sob tore loose from her throat, raw with pain. "They would have killed me if Dragos wanted them to. I didn't mean a thing to either one of them. Not to anyone. That hurts even more than the shock of learning what I really am."

Seeing her in such anguish, Chase wanted to deal a little death of his own. The two Minions who'd betrayed her were already gone, but Dragos still had a brutal end coming to him. More than anything, Chase wanted to be the one to deliver it—prolonged and bloody, the more violent the better.

But he was careful to keep his hands tender as he brushed the pad of his thumb over a smear of soot that rode the delicate angle of her cheek. He swept the marks away and couldn't resist touching his lips to the furrowed center of her brow. The smoky tang of the clinic explosion clung to her skin and hair. Dried blood from the battle with Dragos's Hunter stained her clothes and dotted her face in dark, rusty speckles.

"Come here," he whispered, moving her out of his arms and helping her to her feet.

He took her hand and led her into the warmth of the

adjacent bathroom. Steam wafted over the top of the long glass panels of the running shower. The silvery mist wreathed Tavia as she stood before him, silent, unresisting, while he carefully peeled her soiled clothing from her body.

The *dermaglyphs* that painted her torso, from the base of her throat to the dusky tips of her breasts and lower, down along the smooth plane of her belly and onto her bare thighs, flickered with the faintest blush of color.

Color that darkened as his eyes roamed over her in undeniable admiration.

Her hand trembled only a little as she reached out to cup her palm along the side of his jaw. Eyes the color of new leaves grew stormy and heavy-lidded as she stepped toward him and pressed her parted lips to his mouth.

Chase kissed her, calling upon every ounce of self-control to keep his mouth tender on hers despite the flare of desire that arced through his veins like lightning. It took even more effort to raise his hands between them and ease her away from his hardening body.

But this wasn't about his own need. He'd come to her only out of concern; if he stayed here any longer, it would be only to offer comfort, not to take anything more from her than he already had.

He slid open the shower door and motioned for her to step inside. He followed a moment after her, stripping hastily out of his own clothes, then palming the glass panel shut behind him.

He washed her hair and body with tender, unhurried care. Soon the blood and ash of the violent hours earlier that night were sluiced away, leaving only Tavia's naked beauty before him. Her *glyphs* stirred with color, the dark indigo, wine, and gold a more delicate palette than the one playing out over Chase's own nude skin. His mouth was full of his elongated fangs and a need that made his throat feel desert dry. He clamped his jaw tight to keep her from seeing just how badly he hungered for her.

Not that she could overlook the thick upward jut of his cock. The painfully obvious evidence of his desire filled the scant space between them, growing harder by the moment each time Tavia's wet, satiny skin brushed against him.

Her palm rested lightly on his chest. He could feel the drum of her pulse beating in her fingertips. He could hear it pounding in his ears, a low throb running undercurrent to the soft, sibilant hiss of the shower.

She wanted him too.

Despite the anguish that had all but wrecked her, desire put an amber spark in her green eyes. Her pupils narrowed, intensifying the fiery heat of her irises. Her palm skated in a slick path down the front of him, over his many healing cuts and contusions, injuries he barely noticed under the warm touch of her hand. But she noticed them. He saw her wince as she found the worst of them, heard her soft intake of breath as she studied the most recent wound—the one he'd taken at the end of the Hunter's blade.

"Does it hurt?" Her voice was velvety rough, the pearly tips of her fangs glinting as she spoke.

Chase shook his head, unable to find his voice as she continued her tactile exploration of his body. He didn't know whether to will her away or pray she'd keep going. His cock answered for him, jerking with eager anticipation as her wet fingers trailed lower, toward his groin.

Her name was a curse grated through his teeth and fangs as she trailed her fingers down his shaft and stroked the length of him. His body tensed under the hot spray of the shower, blood racing molten through his veins. He watched her soft, pale hand skate lightly over his hard flesh, agonizing in the teasing pleasure of it. Dying for her to take him fully in hand. Knowing he should stop her before he let things go too far again.

If he'd had even a meager scrap of honor in him, he'd have done just that.

He had a hundred reasons to simply turn and walk away as he'd intended all along. A hundred more reasons why a female as rare and unique, as miraculous, as Tavia deserved a better male—hell, any other male—than him. She deserved someone good and true, someone worthy, to usher her into the life that awaited her as one of the Breed.

But God help him, as he looked at her now, as he felt her touch ignite a heat all the way into his marrow, Chase felt a surge of possessiveness so complete and powerful, it left him shaking.

He didn't want to crave her. Not on top of his other, hellish addictions. Blood and violence had nearly destroyed him. Looking at Tavia as she was now, naked and dripping under the shower, so lovely in her transformation from beautiful woman to glorious Breed female, Chase could hardly imagine a more consuming want than what he felt when he was near her.

But as fevered as that need was, he touched her with utmost tenderness. One hand slipping beneath the wet curtain of her hair, he cupped her nape and gently drew her close. He kissed her, only the barest, briefest brushing of his lips against hers.

"The way we came together before," he rasped thickly, then bit off a harsh curse. "It was your first time. You deserved something better. I had no right—"

She silenced him with another kiss, more demanding than his had been. When she lifted her head to look up at him, there was no regret in her fiery eyes. Only need. Open and honest, shameless need. "You gave me exactly what I wanted."

"Did I?" He touched her face and hair, marveling at how she could look so damned sure of herself and yet so heartbreakingly innocent at the same time. "What about now?"

Her eyes smoldered even brighter. Behind her parted lips, her fangs were even longer now, sharper. Exquisite white points that made the feral vampire in him snap at its feeble tether.

She stepped in close, the heat of her body touching his skin like an open flame. Her palm was between them, soft fingers trailing fire along his abdomen, then down toward his arousal. Her gaze on his, Tavia wrapped her hand around the girth of his shaft and stroked it from base to tip and back again.

Chase couldn't bite back the growl of approval that erupted from his throat.

He killed the water and opened the shower door.

Then he scooped Tavia up into his arms and carried her out to the bedroom in a few long strides.

CHAPTER
Twenty-four

Despite his body pulsing with obvious need, he placed her down on the bed as if he thought she were made of glass.

His transformed eyes were throwing off fire, heating her skin as he let his gaze roam over her face. When he spoke, his voice was barely more than a growl. "This time, we're taking it slow." He prowled up onto the mattress with her, crouched on all fours above her like a big cat. "This time, I want to give you what you want . . . but not until you're screaming for it."

Oh, God.

The anticipation of what he might mean was nearly enough to undo her. She lay back and let him touch her, his fingertips skating from her forehead, cheek, and chin, to the tender hollow at the base of her throat, where her pulse hammered in rapid beats. He took his time studying her, tracing the flaring, arching tangle of color on her skin.

"So beautiful," he murmured thickly. "How could

you be led to think you were anything less than perfect? I could kill Dragos for that reason alone."

She heard the restrained fury in his voice, felt it in the hard pound of his pulse, which all but filled her ears, filled her senses. But his touch was gentle, reverent. So very careful.

The first brush of his lips across hers was warm and indulgent, a lazy crawl that sucked all the breath from her lungs. His tongue slipped inside, sweeping between her teeth before testing the sharp tips of her fangs. True to his word, he took the kiss slowly, not breaking contact until she was melting beneath him, awash in the pleasure of his mouth on hers.

"You taste like heaven," he drawled against her parted lips. "So pure and clean and bright. God, what you do to me."

She couldn't speak, could only fist her hands in the quilted coverlet on the bed and hold on as his kiss traveled lower. His lips and tongue were moist and hot on her breasts, teeth and fangs grazing her pebbled nipples as he moved down her body in a maddening, pleasurable path.

He kissed her belly and tongued the indentation of her navel, and then his mouth was drifting over the flare of her hip bone and down onto the tender flesh of her inner thigh. She moaned as his warm breath fanned her sensitive skin. Gasped as his slick tongue traced the cleft of her body. Shuddered on an indrawn cry as he began to suckle the tight bud of her sex, kissing her with the same slow, sensual attention he'd lavished on her mouth.

"Feels so good," she whispered, her fangs sharp and cool, the long points filling her mouth.

Tavia arched into his kiss, her hips moving of their own accord, every inch of her alive and on fire, his to command. She couldn't fight the pleasure he stoked within her, could only let herself go as he brought her to the sheerest height of sensation, then tumbled her over the edge.

Her orgasm splintered at her core, spreading its light into her limbs like warm, sun-spangled rain. She let it carry her away, leaving all the hurt and ugliness of the past twenty-four hours long behind her as Chase's mouth continued its blissful assault on her senses.

She was still panting, her body still reverberating with pleasure, as he climbed onto her with hungry eyes. His lips were glossy with her juices, sweet with the taste of her own climax as he caught her mouth in a deep, bone-melting kiss. Their fangs tangled and clashed, the scrape of their razored tips an unexpectedly erotic sensation.

Tavia's body was molten, needful for more of him even before the thrumming heat of her release had yet to ebb. She clawed at his back and shoulders as he kissed her, feeling the swell of another climax building. Its deep ache made something animal rouse within her. She nipped at his lower lip, a bite nearly hard enough to draw blood. Her voice felt like ash in her throat, hardly recognizable to her own ears. "I want you inside me."

His answering growl was a rumble that vibrated in her bones. "Patience," he rasped, his glowing eyes flashing with dark amusement. "I haven't showed you all the other ways I can make you come."

He caught her lips in another long kiss. This time, his tongue went deep, filling her mouth as he reached down between them and inserted his fingers into the tight sheath of her sex. He probed her in rhythm with his kiss, pushing deep into her core while his hot mouth plundered her from above. Her body clenched around him, trying to hold him inside even as the friction of his movement made her thrust and mewl with pleasure.

"You're so wet," he murmured hotly. "You feel like silk. So hot and tight around my fingers. I could come just feeling you like this."

He moved his hips against the side of her thigh, the thick ridge of his erection as hard as steel but smooth as velvet. She wanted to feel him filling her, desire for him making everything female inside her coil with greedy hunger. She exhaled a wordless protest as he withdrew his touch, but then the slick pressure of his fingertips met her clitoris and her cry became a choked gasp, sensation jolting through her. He stroked and rubbed the sensitive little knot, swirling his thumb over it as his fingers delved back into her cleft. Her climax came swiftly, ripple after ripple, her sheath contracting in tiny waves. Her voice was ragged, torn from her on a shout of release that she tried to muffle in the strong curve of his neck.

With a primal-sounding snarl, he brought his hips down over hers and lowered himself until his thick shaft rested between her wet thighs. Without entering her, he began a slow melding of their bodies, his cock nestled in the cleft of her core. He moved against her, lifting his body weight, then easing it down again, teasing her with the hot, wet promise of penetration. She was already ripe with arousal; a few torturous strokes was all it took before she was catapulted into yet another shattering release.

"Christ, you are lovely like this, Tavia." He watched her come, his gaze searing and rapt, the amber glow of his eyes bathing her face and skin in delicious heat. His own desire flared in dark hues over the beautiful pattern of his *dermaglyphs,* a churning storm of color that painted his strong arms and torso in tempestuous burgundy, gold, and indigo. He shuddered with his next slow thrust, which set the head of his penis against the mouth of her womb. "Ah, fuck. I can't wait any longer. I have to be in you."

He pushed inside on a low growl, seating himself to the hilt.

With a hard grimace, he rocked into her, riding her hard. She couldn't stop the rising tide of sensation that washed over her with every deep thrust of his body. No more than she could stop the primal urge that made her rise up to take the hard bulk of his shoulder between her teeth. Release poured through her as she bit down on him, scoring his skin with her fangs.

He grunted through his teeth. His frenzied tempo became more fierce, more animal, with every stroke. She could feel him struggle against his own nature. She felt the ravenous thirst that lived inside him and the anguish it caused him to purposely deny it. He suffered in that denial, a brutal, soul-shredding ache.

In the hard, heavy drum of his pulse, she could sense the primal urge that compelled him to bite her in that moment—to drink from her and mark her as his own.

But he didn't do that.

Instead, he turned his head away from her, roaring with a mix of anger and relief as he plunged deep and came. His heat spilled into her, his big body shuddering, sheened in clean sweat. Tavia stroked his muscled back as he slowed above her. She studied his face, trying to understand what it was about him that made him seem so open and trustworthy yet so coolly remote. So haunted and detached. So shadowed and alone.

She felt somehow sad for him. Concerned for him.

Right. Ridiculous. As if he seemed in need of her sympathy or worry.

But that didn't stop her from wanting to figure him out, even a little. When nothing in her life made sense anymore, being with Chase somehow did. It wasn't just the sex, incredible as that was. It was the fact that he was the first person to ever be honest with her, even if she hadn't been prepared to hear it. For better or worse, he was her only safe mooring in a world blown so fast and far off course from what she'd known before. What she'd told him at the clinic earlier tonight had been the truth: He was the only friend she had now. And it troubled her to know that he endured a private pain.

They made slow love again on the bed, indulging in each other's bodies for what seemed like hours. After they had lain there for a long while, Chase's body draped across her, their legs still joined in a pleasant tangle, Tavia asked the question that echoed in her mind with every hard thump of his heartbeat.

"Why don't you allow yourself to feed?" An uncomfortable tension crept through him in reply, palpable in the flicker of his pulse and the subtle stillness of his body against hers. "I don't mean just me," she said. "You don't let yourself drink from anyone. How long has it been?"

He shrugged. "A few days, I guess."

The way his voice sounded, so gravelly and raw, he might have said he'd been starving himself for a year. "How long can you go without?"

"Normally one of my generation can go a week on a single feeding. Sometimes longer."

"But that's not normal for you, is it?" She hardly had to ask; his pulse was still pounding through him in a hollow beat, an ache that she felt reverberating in her own veins. "I can sense your hunger, Chase. I'm not sure how, but I can feel it inside me like it's my own."

He rolled away from her and swore, low and angry, under his breath. "It's the bond." His expression was grave, mouth flattened in a hard line. He raked a rough hand over the top of his head and cursed again, darker this time. "You drank my blood, Tavia. It's bonded you to me. If you were human, it wouldn't matter. But you're not. You're not only Breed either. The part of you that's Breedmate is linked to me through my blood, which lives inside you now."

Astonished, she smoothed a hand over her chest, where the dull ache of his hunger now burned with the bitter tang of his regret.

He nodded, a grim acknowledgment. "That's right. If I feel something strongly enough, whether it's pain or pleasure or grief or joy, you'll feel it too. The blood bond will draw you to me. You'll feel it like an echo in your veins."

She held his troubled stare. "For how long?"

"Until one of us dies."

Tavia swallowed, her eyes widening as she attempted to absorb what it might mean to always feel his presence as a part of her own being. The dark throb of his emotions was a powerful force, intense, but not exactly pleasant.

Watching her reaction, Chase scoffed quietly. "I should've made sure you understood what you were doing—what it would cost you—before you bit me."

"I don't know that you could have stopped me," she said, recalling all too vividly how ravenous she'd been that day in his keeping. In the moments after her fever had broken and Dr. Lewis's medications had worn off, a savage creature had torn loose for the first time. "I'd never felt hunger like that before. It owned me. If you think I blame you—"

"You should," he grated harshly. "It was up to me to be the one in control. There were any number of ways I could've kept the situation from getting so far out of hand. Regardless of how good it felt to have your pretty fangs sunk deep in my throat." His eyes scorched her. A bolt of desire shot through her—his or hers, she wasn't even sure in that moment. He reached for her, his fingers light on her chin, his thumb stroking her lips with tenderness. "You feel so fucking good. The sweetest thing I've ever known."

"But you regret it."

He gave a faint nod. "I'd take it all back in a second. The blood bond is sacred. It's unbreakable, and it's meant to be shared with someone you love, Tavia. With your mate."

And obviously, he wasn't volunteering for that role. That wounded pang she felt in response should have been relief. The way her life was going right now, getting involved with a semipsychotic, blood-starved vampire was the last thing she needed to be dealing with.

Except she *was* involved. Whether either of them chose it or not, they were very much involved now. Especially if she was going to be linked to him by some kind of inextricable psychic bond.

A one-sided bond, she realized, watching the remorse play across his harsh, handsome face.

"Have you ever been bonded to someone, Chase?"

"No."

"But you wanted to be," she said softly. "The woman in the photograph I found at your old house . . ."

"Elise?" He blew out a curse and shook his head.

Tavia thought back on how he'd told her that woman

was his dead brother's mate. Just the mention of her at the time had made Chase very defensive about what he might have felt for her. "You said you weren't in love with her, but that's not quite the truth, is it?"

He let out a long sigh and leaned back on the carved wood of the headboard, quietly contemplative. She waited to feel his emotional walls climb higher. She knew so little about him, but it wasn't hard to imagine that her prying would only make him slam the door in her face that much harder.

She cleared her throat and started to sit up, suddenly wanting a little space herself. "Never mind. You don't have to tell—"

"I did want her," he blurted. The words were rough, self-condemning. "She belonged to Quentin, had always belonged to him . . . but there was a part of me that wanted her anyway."

Tavia stilled beside him, pivoting around to face him. "Did you seduce her?"

"In my thoughts, many times. That was bad enough." He gave a vague shake of his head. "Elise was only part of my problem, but it took a while for me to realize that. I wanted everything my brother had. I wanted to be like him, everything he was. All the things that seemed to fit him so well. Things that came so easy to him yet were never within my reach. I tried to be the man I saw in him, even after I realized I was only pretending I could even come close."

There was such torment on his face, it made her chest squeeze. His eyes were haunted, filled with guilt and shame and a secret, inwardly directed contempt she could hardly fathom. Good lord, how long had he lived with this intense hatred for himself?

"Did your brother know how you felt?"

"No. God, no. Nor would he have suspected." He pursed his lips, eyes downcast. "We were both Chases, after all. It would have been beneath Quent to think I envied him, even a little. We'd been groomed to be morally pristine, nothing less than perfect in every way. Our venerable father would've accepted no less." His voice had taken on a brittle, caustic edge. "There were certain expectations that came with being born one of August Chase's sons. Quent had no problem exceeding our father's exacting standards."

"And you?" Tavia asked gently.

His mouth twisted sardonically. "Top of my class in every contest. Influential, respected. Well connected in my profession and among my social peers. The path ahead of me was golden, spread out before me as far as I wanted to take it."

"I don't doubt that," she replied. "But that's not what I was asking. I meant—"

"My father," he finished for her, no inflection in his tone. "The problem with having a brother like Quentin ahead of you is that he tends to cast a very long shadow. It's easy to get swallowed up by it, to become invisible." He shrugged. "I gave up trying to compete with my brother when I was still a boy and he was already a decade in the Agency, making good on the Chase family's centuries-long legacy of service."

"Then what happened?"

He grunted, nonchalant. "A lot of years of going through the motions. Decades of following every rule, doing whatever was expected of me and then some. Pointless time spent collecting Agency accolades and admiration from people who called themselves my friends only as long as it served their interests or their whims."

"But not your father." Tavia understood now.

"He already had the son he wanted. I was . . . redundant." He exhaled sharply, shaking his head. "You've told me how alone and empty you feel, after realizing your past was built on lies and that no one you knew ever really cared about you." At her nod, he went on. "Sometimes you can feel that way even when you're surrounded by family."

She reached over and unfolded the fist that rested at his side, twined her fingers with his. For some time, he remained silent, staring at their linked hands. When he spoke, there was an odd vulnerability to his deep voice. As if he were letting her peek inside one of the dark chambers of the heart he seemed so sure he didn't possess.

"My brother died six years ago. He was killed on duty for the Agency, by a Rogue who'd been brought in for rehabilitation."

"A Rogue?" She shook her head, uncertain.

"If a member of the Breed lets his hunger overtake him, addiction isn't far behind. It's called Bloodlust, and there's no turning back once it takes hold. You go Rogue—the worst kind of insanity. You thirst, and you hunt, and you kill. You destroy, until someone either takes you out or you do the world a favor and let the sun ash you."

She wasn't sure what sounded more terrible: the affliction itself, or the grim finality of its cure. "But the Agency is able to rehabilitate some?"

His mirthless chuckle didn't give her much hope. "For a long time, the Enforcement Agency has operated under the notion that there was reason to think so. Of course, the Agency is also in charge of the facilities that house these diseased members of the race all across

Europe and the United States. Many empire builders within the Agency's upper tiers would try to convince you that the system does have its successes."

"You don't think so."

"Not that I've ever seen or heard. If you ask me, those facilities are nothing more than cold storage for a population of locusts just waiting for the chance to swarm and devour everything in their path."

Tavia shuddered at the horrific image he painted. "Nothing can stop a Rogue?"

"Only a bullet or blade forged of titanium. The metal acts like poison on a Rogue's diseased blood system. Failing that, a long, hot sunbath will also do the job."

She studied him, seeing the anguish written in the tense lines of his face. "It must've been awful, losing your brother to one of those monsters."

"Yeah. It was." He nodded grimly, his expression distant and pensive, a thousand miles away. It seemed to take a moment for his focus to return. "I hardly remember the days and nights that followed. I had so much rage and grief inside me . . . it's all I knew for a long time afterward."

Shadows filled his eyes as he spoke, and Tavia sensed that he was holding something back, a secret he wasn't ready to share with her. Maybe not with anyone. And it was clear that the things he'd done at that time still haunted him now, despite his claims that he'd left the memories behind.

"It was unthinkable that Quent could be taken down so suddenly. Elise was destroyed, of course. So was their son, Camden. The boy was barely a teen. He'd already been making plans to attend private, specially arranged night classes at Harvard, the same as Quentin and I both did, and our father before us. Cam had been so excited. The whole world was ahead of him."

The photograph of Chase and Elise and the smiling boy came back to her in full detail. Even without her genetic gift of flawless memory, Tavia would have recalled the covetous look in Chase's eyes in that candid shot. "What happened to Elise and her son after your brother was killed?"

Chase's expression clouded again, shadows filling his eyes. "They lived under my care for a while. My father had been killed on patrol before Quent died, so that left me as the leader of my kin's Darkhaven. Elise and Cam moved in to my Back Bay brownstone immediately after Quent's death. To be honest, I thought I could just step in and pick up the pieces Quent's death had left behind. I thought maybe I could finally know what it was like to be him—just once. But I could still feel the chill of his shadow, even after he was gone."

"What about Elise?" Tavia asked, wishing she could deny the twinge of dread that was needling her already, expecting to hear that he might still feel something for the woman beyond familial bonds. "How was it for you, suddenly having her in your house, under your protection?"

"It was like living with two ghosts—my brother's and hers. She withdrew from everyone after Quent died. No one but Camden mattered to her." His exhaled sigh was deep, edged with a thick kind of remorse. "None of us could've known that soon he would be dead too, gone Rogue himself and shot to death in front of her like a rabid dog."

Tavia's hand came up to her mouth. She could feel the grief tearing through him like a fresh wound. "My God, Chase. That's awful."

"Yeah," he said, nodding in sober agreement. His silence stretched, cold and heavy. "She may never forgive me for pulling that trigger."

Tavia couldn't help it—she gaped at him, stricken speechless at his confession. But before she could ask him what could have brought him to do such a terrible thing, the sound of muffled voices carried up from the floor below.

Male voices, deep and rolling, filling the mansion's foyer. A female was down there too. Tavia heard Mathias Rowan greet them all like old friends.

"What's going on? Who is that downstairs?"

Beside her on the bed, Chase had gone tense and still. "The Order has arrived."

CHAPTER
Twenty-five

Chase closed Tavia's bedroom door behind him without making a sound. He'd gotten dressed as soon as he heard the warriors' voices, reassuring Tavia there was no cause for alarm and that she should wait upstairs until he or Rowan came to fetch her.

To his amazement, she didn't try to debate it with him. No doubt she had enough on her mind already, after he'd unloaded his whole inglorious past on her. Or most of it, that is. He hadn't gone so far as to divulge the worst of his shame. If he could help it, she'd never know how dubious his honor truly was.

Not that he let that stand in the way of seducing her here tonight, despite his good intentions.

He knew too well where good intentions usually led him, but damn if he could describe making love to Tavia as anything close to hell.

His pulse simmered at the thought of her, and it didn't help matters that he could still smell her on his skin and taste her on his tongue. He could still feel the heat of her body clenched around him. His cock responded with an eager twinge, already on notice and up to a repeat performance.

Ah, shit.

Maybe this was hell after all.

Chase tugged his dark shirt over the growing bulge in his black jeans and headed out to face his former brothers in arms. Downstairs in the Darkhaven's foyer entryway, Tegan's voice rumbled with its typical menacing cool.

"Appreciate the call, Mathias, and the interception of both the female and Chase. Wish we'd gotten here sooner to provide some backup tonight. I would've liked to get a look at those clinic records myself."

"That's right." Nikolai was down there with Tegan too. Chase knew the Siberian-born vampire by his quicksilver chuckle and his airless, icy growl. "Personally, I would've liked nothing more than to help you smoke a couple of brain-rotted Minions and one of Dragos's Terminator freaks of nature."

Chase walked the length of the second-floor hallway and paused at the top of the stairs. Down below, Niko had cocked a sidelong grin at the third warrior accompanying them on this retrieval mission to Boston. "No offense intended by the freak-of-nature crack, Hunter."

The former assassin didn't even blink. "None taken."

Standing with Rowan and the three members of the Order was Niko's Breedmate, Renata. The dark-haired beauty in head-to-toe black leather glanced up as Chase arrived. Pale jade-green eyes skewered him. "Guys," she murmured, alerting them to his presence with a subtle lift of her chin.

Chase started down the stairs without any acknowledgment.

Tegan was first to break the tense silence. "Speak of the devil. Gotta say, I'm surprised to find you waiting here for us, Harvard. Figured you for a quick cut and run. That's more your style these days."

Chase smirked, gave a sardonic grunt. "Now that you mention it, I was actually just on my way out."

He took a few more steps toward the crowded foyer and the Darkhaven door that stood just behind Tegan and the others. Only a few scant yards to freedom. Yet his gait slowed until he was practically standing still.

As much as he wanted to avoid this clash with Tegan, Niko, and the others, he could hardly stand the idea of abandoning Tavia without a word of explanation. Especially now. It would have been easier before, if he'd gone like he'd intended earlier tonight. Before he'd ended up back in her arms. Back inside her sweet, wet heat.

Fuck.

Who was he kidding?

Nothing about walking away from that female would be easy, now or before.

What would Tavia's reaction be when she found out these three warriors and the take-no-prisoners female who could debilitate even the most powerful of the Breed with a single zap of her mind-blasting power were there to take her into Order custody?

He should have explained a few things to her, but he'd been too busy undressing her and making sure her exquisite body would never forget him. Yeah, he should've done a lot of things differently where Tavia was concerned. Losing even more freedom, even more sense of control wasn't going to sit well with her. She was going to be pissed off and confused—pretty much status quo since she'd had the misfortune of crossing paths with him.

As for Chase, facing the disapproving gazes of his brethren was bad enough. He didn't want to see disappointment in Tavia's eyes too.

He took another step down and felt the tension in the warriors below ratchet up a notch. "Where the fuck do you think you're going?" Tegan asked, that deep voice even more lethal in its calm.

The feral part of Chase flared in response to the recognized threat. His blood scraped through his veins, raw and cold. "Don't let me interrupt important Order business," he snarled, more venom in his tone than he'd intended. But it was the affliction speaking for him now, sparking hot like a match to dry tinder and itching for a fight. One he didn't want to start with any of these people.

He'd left the Order on bad enough terms; it would kill him to bring any more disgrace or disappointment to the one group of individuals who'd ever truly known him and appreciated him. And the thought of raising a fist or weapon to any one of them now was enough to make him recoil with shame.

Hands clenched at his sides, he stepped off the last stair. "I've overstayed my welcome already. I'm outta here."

"I don't think so, Harvard." Tegan moved into his path. "You've made yourself Public Enemy Number One with the humans. Lucan wants you off the streets."

"So, what, then? You're here to conduct some kind of intervention?" Chase scoffed, aggression seething in him now. "Well, you can fucking spare me. I didn't ask for it."

"No, you didn't." The huge warrior glowered, tawny head tilted down like a bull preparing for the charge. His eyes pierced Chase, merciless in their assessment.

There was never any hiding when it came to the Order's second-longest-standing member. Even less of a chance for Chase, when all it would take was one touch of Tegan's emotion-reading hands for him to understand just how close Chase teetered at the edge of disaster. "Maybe you're not comprehending what I'm trying to tell you, Harvard. You're coming back with us. You and the female both."

The feral part of Chase bristled, pulling his lips back from his teeth and fangs in a sneer. "Last I knew, Lucan and the rest of you had written me off. Didn't need to be any clearer to me that I wasn't welcome anymore."

Ever the peacemaker, Rowan cleared his throat. "Chase, for God's sake. Dial it down."

Tegan shrugged off the plea, unfazed by the threat of confrontation. "You can either come freely, or we're prepared to take you by force."

When Chase barked out a caustic, humorless laugh, Renata moved in between Tegan and Niko, as graceful as she was dangerous. "I'd listen to him if I were you. We have our orders."

"Is that right," he challenged, bearing down on her with a look that had shriveled more than one Agency squad of fully armed Breed males into a knot of anxious, perspiring little girls. But not Renata. Nikolai's Breedmate braced her long legs in a battle-ready stance and stared him right back. Which only pissed him off more. "If you hit me with that mind-zapping talent of yours, better make damn sure you kill me fast. Or you won't even see me coming back at you."

Niko's growl was as deadly as Chase had ever heard it. The warrior took a hard step forward, his palm curled around the grip of a nasty-looking semiauto that was holstered under his arm. Chase knew the weapon

would be loaded with an arsenal of Rogue-killing titanium hollowpoints—Niko's handcrafted specialty.

The way his blood was raking him now, cold and
acidic, Chase had little doubt that one round would
probably be enough to smoke him on the spot. God help
him, he was half tempted to test the idea right then and
there.

Instead, with a curse, he started to lift his hands in a
show of surrender.

He barely twitched before he felt the sudden jolt of
lightning entering his skull. Renata. She'd opened up on
him before he even knew what hit him. It was brief and
only a warning shot; he knew that. Otherwise he
wouldn't have wits enough to question it. But holy hell,
did it feel like death. Chase let out a strangled roar as
the psychic energy ricocheted in his skull and sent him
down on one knee.

He didn't see Tavia coming.

None of them could have, she moved so fast and so
stealthily. Materializing as though out of nowhere, she
leapt over the second-floor rail of the hallway and
dropped, catlike, to the tiled foyer below.

One second Chase was stooped brokenly on the floor.
The next, he was pushed behind her sleek form, watching through pain-squeezed eyes as she faced off alone
against three heavily armed, lethal Breed warriors and
a Breedmate who could just as easily turn her staggering power away from Chase and blast it full force onto
Tavia.

God, no.

If she took a bullet or a jolt of Renata's fury because
of him—

"Don't hurt her!" he roared, the words tearing out of
his throat, wild and otherworldly. Commanding all his

strength to push past the pain of Renata's mental blast, he scrambled to his feet and took his place at Tavia's side. "Don't any of you fucking hurt her!"

But none of them made an untoward move.

They wouldn't have, he realized only then. They hadn't come here to hurt anyone, not even him, except he'd forced their hand. They all stared, Mathias Rowan included, gaping wide-eyed and slack-jawed at Tavia Fairchild in all her transformed magnificence.

Crouched low, her long, jeans-clad legs were bent, bare feet ready to spring. Her loose hair swung around her shoulders like a caramel-colored mane, untamed waves barely concealing the amber blaze of her eyes. She hissed, lips peeled back to expose the twin fangs that gleamed as bright as diamonds and sharp as daggers. Between the deep V of her black sweater, her *dermaglyphs* were alive with furious color, churning like a tempest written on her smooth, pale skin.

There could be no mistaking what this female was: dangerous, stealthy, utterly lethal Gen One Breed.

And hotter than hell itself.

The three warriors from the Order seemed to shake themselves back to their senses all at once. They spoke in nearly perfect unison, Tegan, Niko, then Hunter, one after the other.

"Holy—"

"Fucking—"

"Shit."

Renata was still staring, vaguely shaking her head in disbelief. Her fine jet brows lifted then and a smile began to twist the curve of her broad mouth. The sight of her relaxation—the wry humor in her shrewd gaze— diffused the tension in the room by huge degrees.

She glanced from Tavia to Chase, then back again to

Tavia in utter amazement. "Now, that's what I call making an entrance."

Dragos strolled into the video conference with his lieutenants more than forty-five minutes late.

His lack of punctuality accomplished a couple of things: First, it never hurt to remind his underlings that they served at his whim and convenience; more important was the fact that his tardiness gave each of the four remaining members of his original circle ample time to reflect on their slightest missteps and fret over whether one of their heads had landed on his chopping block.

That particular concern carried even more weight, considering the fact that each of his lieutenants on-screen was attended by one of Dragos's personally selected Hunters. If the lieutenants gave him reason to doubt, it would take less than a second for any one of the Gen One killers standing at their sides to dispatch the problem permanently.

But no one's head was in jeopardy here tonight.

Dragos's rage was centered wholly on the Order. It was because of them that he'd met one setback after another. Because of them that his operation was splintered and limping now, all his good work and promising experiments halted or destroyed. Because of them that he'd been forced to accelerate his plans where humankind was concerned.

Instead of waiting until he had all of his Minion players in position around the world—an objective that would only get more difficult with Lucan and his warriors breathing down his neck, driving him to ground at every opportunity—Dragos had decided the time for waiting was over.

He took his seat at the head of his long conference table, facing the wall of monitors mounted in front of him. Four screens showed the faces of his lieutenants: Arno Pike of the Enforcement Agency in Boston; Ruarke Louvell, longtime Agency director from Seattle; reporting in from Europe was Móric Kaszab of the Agency in Budapest; and, last, Nigel Traherne, a well-connected, well-heeled Darkhaven leader from London and the only one of Dragos's surviving circle not intimately associated with the Enforcement Agency.

There had been three others in this cadre at one time, ultimately unworthy males who'd met their ends in various violent ways. Dragos had personally seen to that. The names—Fabian, Roth, and Vachon—hardly registered to him now. They were dust under his boot heels, insignificant.

Gone and forgotten.

What the eight of them had shared in common, Dragos and his inner circle of seven loyal foot soldiers, was their second-generation bloodlines and, more crucially, the unshakable belief that it was the Breed—not humankind—that deserved to rule this orbiting clump of rock. For many long decades, they'd worked together, plotting and conspiring, secretly fueling the operation's vision with matériel, personnel and funding, intel and support. Everything Dragos asked for, including their unwavering allegiance.

The four standing by on video now still held to the belief that Dragos's vision for the future was the only acceptable one. They believed in him as their leader. Their eventual king. So long as they did, and until they proved to be ineffectual or a liability to his goals, Dragos would permit them to live. He might even make good on his promise that they would enjoy some of the spoils soon to come.

Very soon, he thought, hardly able to contain the excitement that coursed through him when he considered the chaos he was about to deliver on the world.

"Gentlemen," he said, giving them each a nod of greeting. "We have waited a long time for this moment. But no more. I've summoned you all tonight to let you know that our triumph is finally at hand."

Cold smiles and eager gazes met the comment. Dragos let the current of dark excitement settle in for a moment, reveling in his power. Although his decision earlier tonight had come on the heels of outrage and vengeful impulse, he'd had time enough to consider all the ramifications of the Armageddon he was about to enact. If it had seemed a fitting solution before, now, with a cooler, more calculating head, he was even more convinced it was time to throw down the gauntlet.

"Each of you in this meeting was brought into my trust because of a common resolve. A dream we all shared, to design a world around our own ideals. Our own liberties and laws. We are close, my comrades. Close enough that it would be unthinkable that our vision for our world—for the future of our very race—should be derailed by the Order or the fools who would ally with them." He scanned the faces of his lieutenants, pleased to see the rancor simmering in more than one pair of narrowed eyes. "With victory in our grasp, we cannot afford to let it slip through our fingers. Our time of hiding and planning and waiting is over." Dragos slammed his fist on the table in front of him as he rose out of his chair. "I'm sick to death with all of it! The time has come to make this goddamn world bleed!"

Three of the four Breed males staring back at him

gave assenting nods at this explosive declaration of war. Dragos's breath sawed in and out of his lungs, rekindled fury making his veins prickle with violent impulse. That smoldering aggression deepened when he looked to Nigel Traherne and found the Londoner frowning, his fair-haired head shaking slowly in quiet dissent.

"You have something to say, Mr. Traherne?"

Nigel cleared his throat, looking suddenly uncomfortable. As well he should. "If I am correct in assuming what you have in mind, sire . . ."

The words trailed off, unnecessary to complete. Everyone assembled in this room understood precisely what he was suggesting. It had been the operation's worst-case scenario option all along.

"An act of this magnitude cannot be undone," Traherne cautioned. "I have to wonder if, perhaps . . . sire, I fear that recent setbacks in your endeavors to acquire the American senator and clear the path into other areas of human governments may be pushing you into somewhat rash thinking."

"Rash thinking." Dragos grunted, his fists braced on the table, knuckles crushing the polished wood. He fumed over the challenge to his authority. The foolhardy dissent. But he refrained from lashing out. Barely. "Do I seem rash to the rest of you?"

One by one, the other three lieutenants weighed in with their support.

"I'm more than tired of waiting." Obedient, bloodthirsty Pike spoke out first. "I trust you to guide us, sire, as you've done all along. I am prepared to strike on your command."

"I'll be honest," added Louvell. "I've often feared it would come to this. But I'm on board, whatever is decided. I've come too far to turn back now. We all have."

Kaszab grinned a nasty smirk, his dark eyes gleaming. "Mankind has held the reins of power for long enough. I, for one, am more than ready to see the Breed rise up to rule the night as is our birthright."

Dragos looked back to Traherne's uneasy expression and shrugged. "Clearly, you are alone in your concerns, Nigel."

"Sire, I—"

Dragos held up his hand and gave a mild shake of his head. "I understand, of course. Decisions like this—like many of the ones necessary to have brought our operation to this pivotal moment and the victory that awaits on the other side—are not for the squeamish or the meek."

"Sire, I've gone along more than willingly on everything else thus far. I still believe in the cause—you must know that." Fear had crept into the vampire's voice now, and a note of something else. Sorrow, Dragos hazarded to guess, watching the proud male's face collapse into a hopeless sag. "Sire, my Breedmate is expecting our child any day now. My two older sons have given me more than a dozen grandchildren—fine boys who will come into adulthood in the world we create. I agree that the Breed should seize its place as the dominant race on this planet. I only hope there is a better way to ensure that happens."

Dragos crossed his arms over his chest, waiting for Traherne to exhaust his problematic, eleventh-hour attack of conscience. Behind the male, the assassin assigned to ensure his security kept his gaze fixed on Dragos. A leashed but lethal hound awaiting his master's command.

"I've long had my reservations about bringing a civilian into this circle," Dragos stated evenly. "But you've proven valuable, Nigel. You brought me Breedmates for the breeding and genetics programs. You located some of the brightest human scientific minds to become the Minion staff of the operation's laboratories. You poured in hundreds of millions of dollars over the decades to help outfit the facilities, and you provided valuable intel from both a social and political standpoint among the European branches of the Breed nation."

"Yes, sire," he agreed eagerly. "And I did all of that because I have faith in you, in your vision."

Dragos's anger hadn't ebbed a bit. But he smiled, his mouth feeling tight with the presence of his emerging fangs. "I've never doubted your faith, my good Mr. Traherne. You've had the heart and the means. You even had the malice, when it was called for. What you've always lacked, however, was balls." With the faintest flick of his eyes, Dragos signaled to the Hunter who stood behind Traherne. "End him."

The kill was swift and clean. On the video monitor, Traherne's eyes bulged as his head fell forward, twisted at an unnatural angle on his broken neck. His skull landed with a hard *thump* on the desk in front of him.

Dragos barely paid the death even a second's notice. He let the dead lieutenant remain on-screen as he turned his attention back to the three other members of his unholy alliance. "We have ventured where none before us has dared," he told them without missing a beat. "Now we begin preparations to take the ultimate step toward securing our rightful place in history."

CHAPTER
Twenty-six

They headed north in a large black Land Rover SUV, hours out of Boston and deep into the state of Maine.

Tavia hadn't wanted to go anywhere with anyone, least of all a group of three heavily armed Breed males and a leather-clad woman who seemed equally dangerous with or without the guns and blades that bristled from her weapons belt. But Chase's promise that she would be safe with them—safe at the Order's haven, which was where they headed now—was reassurance enough for her to accept.

He sat in the backseat of the vehicle, sandwiched between her and the apparent warrior in charge of their retrieval, a formidable male with unforgiving gem-green eyes and a mane of shaggy, tawny hair. His name was Tegan. Nikolai and Renata sat up front, the fast-talking, quick-witted blond warrior behind the wheel and his ebony-haired mate next to him in the passenger seat.

Riding in the jump seat behind Tavia, Chase, and Tegan was a stoic giant of a male with close-cropped, light brown hair and piercing golden eyes. Of all the vehicle's occupants, it was this one who put Tavia most on guard. Cool, detached—everything about the male called Hunter was measured and in control. All business and lethal efficiency, like the killing edge of a blade. Which wasn't surprising, considering his former profession.

Tavia wanted to know more about him, particularly considering the fact that they had been spawned from some of the same DNA in Dragos's labs. But there had been little time for questions or conversation at Mathias Rowan's house. The ride north hadn't exactly been filled with chatter so far either.

Chase hadn't said a word the whole time they'd been driving. His chin was dipped low toward his chest, but even under the tousled hank of hair drooping over his brow, the ember glow of his eyes was hard to miss. The *glyphs* on his bare forearms still seethed with dark hues. Her own body had resumed its normal state before they'd even left Boston, but Chase's seemed to be coming down a lot slower. His rage, which had exploded back at Mathias's place, still simmered like a poison under his skin.

The psychic pain Renata had dealt him also lingered. Tavia felt the echoes of it in the blood bond she was still trying to get accustomed to. God, she'd been so alarmed—bone-jarringly terrified—the moment that jolt of mental fury slammed into Chase's skull. She'd reacted on pure instinct, leaping over the banister railing without a thought for the human impossibility of the move and sailing down to the foyer below. All that had mattered to her in that instant was Chase. Her relief at finding him alive, seeing him come to his feet beside her, had been so deep and complete, it defied description.

As did the warmth that cocooned her when she heard the protective rage in his deep, booming voice as he'd bellowed for his friends not to harm her.

Now his brooding silence—his very presence in the close confines of the SUV—seemed to put everyone on guard. Pressed up against her, his rigid body radiated heat and banked aggression. Maybe she should have felt some of the same apprehension about him that his friends did, but the warmth of his thigh was a comfort against hers. His bulky shoulder was firm under her head as she rested lightly on him, her gaze trained on the dark landscape blurring past outside the vehicle's windows as the miles fell away behind them.

When she glanced up, she found Nikolai's wintry blue eyes looking at her in the rearview mirror. It wasn't the first time he'd flicked a curious, scrutinizing peek at her. This time, Renata reached over from the passenger seat and gave his shoulder a light cuff. "Stop gaping at the poor girl, Niko. She's not a sideshow, for crissake."

"Sorry," he said, and swore something in what sounded like Russian. "It's just gonna take me a while to get used to the idea."

Renata rolled her eyes at him, then swiveled around in her seat to face Tavia. "Forgive him. I think we're all trying really hard not to stare. I mean, Mathias told us about you, but actually seeing you for ourselves . . . and back at the Darkhaven? Well, wow." She sent a look to the others in the vehicle, then shook her head, making her chin-length black hair sift fluidly at her jawline. "Between Jenna and Tavia, things are going to get really interesting around here."

"Who's Jenna?" Tavia asked. "Is she . . . like me?"

She felt a prickle of hope at the thought, even though she wasn't sure she should wish her life—and all the betrayals that came with it—on anyone else.

"Jenna's human," Nikolai replied, glancing at her once more in the rearview. "Or she was, that is. Until a few weeks ago."

"Jenna's still human where it counts." Renata turned to her mate and tapped the center of her chest. "She may be changing physically and psychically, but inside she's still Jenna."

"What happened to her?"

Renata glanced briefly to Tegan as though asking permission before she explained. "Jenna was attacked a few weeks ago in Alaska, where she used to live. The creature that did it was an Ancient—"

"The one Dragos had been holding in his labs," Tavia finished, recalling what Chase had told her about the last of the Breed's alien forefathers. "I thought the Order killed him."

"Yes," Renata said. "But before they caught him, the Ancient had broken into Jenna's home. He terrorized her, held her hostage, and fed from her. And before it was all over, he embedded some kind of alien technology into her skin, at the top of her spinal cord. It also contained strands of his DNA."

Nikolai nodded. "After we brought Jenna to Boston with us, she was unconscious for days. When she woke up, things about her started changing."

"What kind of changes?"

"Inhuman strength, for one thing," Renata said. "Overnight, it seemed, she had incredible speed and agility. Her body started learning to heal itself from injuries. The kind of things you definitely don't see in your average human being."

"To say nothing of the *glyph* that's spreading like kudzu from the spot where the chip was implanted."

Tavia met Nikolai's eyes in the mirror. "So, did the Ancient turn her into one of you—one of the Breed?"

"She's not Breed," he replied. "But she's not exactly human now either. Gideon's been running all sorts of tests, and the best he's come up with is the Ancient's DNA is replicating faster than her own *Homo sapiens* DNA. It's taking over her nervous system and vital organs, even her blood."

"My God," Tavia murmured. "It must be terrifying for her."

"It's no picnic," Nikolai agreed. "But she's coping with it like the trouper she is. Not too bad of a deal, all things considered. She's stronger, faster, healthier than any human could hope to be. And from Gideon's findings, he's guessing her life expectancy has increased exponentially."

"Still," Tavia said, unable to keep from relating Jenna's sudden changes to her own unexpected revelations. "It's not easy finding out you're something other than you thought."

Renata's gaze was sympathetic. "How are you holding up?"

"I'm okay." She nodded, realizing it was true. "I was scared at first, but I'm glad to finally know the truth."

Nikolai went on. "I think the scariest part for Jenna now is the dreams. Gideon thinks the chip is projecting the Ancient's memories into her subconscious. She's been having wicked nightmares lately. A lot of violent, Armageddon-style dreams. It's really wreaking havoc on her."

"At least Jenna has Brock," Renata said, glancing lovingly at her own mate. "He'll help her get through whatever's still ahead of her. And she has the rest of us too."

Nikolai's returned glance was as heated as it was tender. He reached over and took Renata's hand, lifted it to his mouth, and pressed a kiss into the center of her palm.

"How much do you know about the Breed?" This time, it was Tegan who spoke. He didn't look at Tavia, but his low snarl of a voice drifted from around the other side of Chase.

"You mean, other than the fact that there's some kind of alien roots in your history?"

"Your history too," the warrior remarked tonelessly.

Right, she thought. It was the stuff of horror novels and science fiction movies, but she might as well start owning it. "Chase has told me a few things. It's a lot to absorb. He's been trying to help me make sense of it all."

Tegan's quiet scoff had a skeptical tone to it. "And here I thought he might've been too busy getting famous with the humans to have time for tutoring. I guess I don't need to ask what else you might have taught her, eh, Harvard?"

The mild jab sent a flare of white-hot anger shooting through her veins—not her anger, but Chase's. She felt his whole body go rigid beside her as Tegan turned a measuring look on him. The warrior watched, expressionless but assessing just the same. For one tensely uncertain moment, Tavia wondered if Chase was going to lash out at the other male for what had clearly been intended as provocation.

Everyone must have wondered that same thing, because they all kept utterly silent. Tentative. On notice for what Chase might do in that next instant.

But he didn't explode like the grenade they seemed to think he was.

Tavia felt him fighting to rein himself in. Even though it seemed dangerous—about as ill advised as petting a grizzly—she reached over to him in the dark cabin of the SUV. His big hand was splayed on his denim-clad thigh, fingers gripped there like a vise. Tavia stroked the tip of her index finger along the back of his hand, a silent reassurance. A signal of her trust in him, her faith.

That she knew he struggled with something powerful and dark, and that she cared.

He didn't look at her, but his fingertips relaxed. He let his hand move down toward hers—the barest skate of contact. It warmed her from deep within, this unspoken connection that had formed between them. It seemed less about blood bonds or the insane circumstances that had brought them together than it did about something deep and meaningful—something profound and precious—that was taking shape within both of them.

She cared about this man—this complicated and haunted, dangerous Breed male. And whether he would ever admit it, she could feel that he cared about her too.

On the other side of Chase, Tegan's face relaxed into nonchalance. He sat back with a slowly exhaled sigh. "We're almost there."

The vehicle had exited the turnpike some time ago and now began a bumping, twisting trek down a rural two-lane that cut between what appeared to be thick, virgin forest. They drove miles into the moonlit darkness before Nikolai eased onto a snow-packed trail that hardly seemed fit for anything more sophisticated than a horse and sleigh. When it seemed the desolate path might never end, the SUV's headlights knifed through the dense woods and swept across the front of a sprawling stone-and-timber fortress. It was rugged but beautiful. Like something out of a Gothic fairy tale.

Beside her, Chase sat up a bit straighter, peering out into the tree-choked parcel. "The Order's new headquarters?" he asked, his voice sounding as dry as ash.

"This is it." Nikolai slowed to a stop and killed the engine. "Home sweet home."

"Are you ready to begin, Jenna?"

She nodded to Gideon and squeezed Brock's hand a little tighter. His handsome face was drawn with concern, his fathomless brown eyes fixed on her. "You don't have to do this if you're not sure. You've already been through enough—"

"I'm sure," she replied, reaching up from where she lay on their bed to caress his strong jaw. "It's just a dream, after all. You don't have to worry about me."

His chuckle was a soft rasp, wry but not relaxed. "Telling me not to worry about you is like telling me to stop breathing. No can do, babe. You knew that when you signed on with me."

"Yeah, I did." Jenna smiled at her mate, wondering how it was possible that her love for him deepened every day. "And you know well enough that I'm as hard-headed as you are—"

"More," he cut in, arching a black brow.

She wouldn't argue that. Nor would she let her fear or his concern keep her from seizing this mission with both hands. Because that's what this quest for answers had become to her: a mission. Like any of the dozens of patrols she'd been on as a Statie in Alaska. She was going to give this one her all.

Even if she had to do it shaking in her boots.

"It's only a dream," she told Brock again, and maybe she needed the reassurance just as much as he did. Her nerves were still raw and jangling from the last time the nightmare had dragged her under. The massive wall of water, crashing in from all sides. The screams of the dying rising up on the night wind. So much terror and destruction, hundreds of lives being swept away in an instant. It had felt so real. Horrifically, vividly real. Even now it made her heart hammer in panic, made her palms go damp with anxiety. "It's not real, just a nightmare. I'll be fine, Brock. I can do this."

He frowned skeptically, and for the first time since she'd known her mate, Jenna was glad for the absence of a blood bond with him. She'd been born human, not a Breedmate, and the lack of that tiny red teardrop-and-crescent-moon birthmark had been an obstacle between them in the beginning. But only briefly. Love had been the glue that bonded them as one. Brock might not be able to read her deepest feelings through her blood, but their emotional connection was no weaker for it.

Which is why his frown only furrowed more as he stroked her hand and watched Gideon prepare the light sedative that would help her sleep now and, hopefully, submerge her even deeper into the dream. "I don't like this one damn bit. I don't care if it's only a dream or some kind of psychic echo of the Ancient's memories replaying in your subconscious. I don't want to let you go—"

"Then don't," she said, wrapping her fingers a little tighter around his. "Keep holding my hand. I can face anything if I know you're with me. And I'll have Claire inside to guide me this time too."

They had contacted Andreas Reichen's mate in Rhode Island several hours ago, after Jenna's last bout with the terrifying dream. Claire had agreed on the spot to help in whatever way she could and was currently standing by at her Darkhaven, awaiting Gideon's call. Once Jenna was sleeping, Claire would join her in the dreamscape. Together they hoped to come back with a clearer picture of what the nightmare—and its apocalyptic events—might possibly mean.

Jenna pressed a kiss to Brock's knuckles, then glanced over at Gideon. "Let's do this."

With an apologetic look at his fellow warrior, the Order's resident genius and part-time medic leaned in with the syringe of sedative. Jenna winced as the needle pricked her, then slowly exhaled the breath she hadn't been aware she was holding. After a moment, a pleasant warmth spread over her slowly, like a fluffy blanket being raised up from her feet to her chin.

"Feel okay so far, Jen?" Gideon's voice came at her in exaggerated slow motion, each syllable stretched out and warped.

It took great effort for her to manage even a faint nod. Her eyelids were beginning to droop, feeling as heavy as lead. "I think it's wor—"

She didn't get a chance to finish the thought.

A thick gray fog engulfed her, carried her away from her bed and the conscious weight of her body. She let it take her, too listless to resist. The dark cloud held her aloft as it drifted away from the Order's headquarters . . . away from everything she knew.

After a long time, eternity, it seemed, the fog began to thin and her feet touched ground.

Her eyelids lifted, showing her nothing but darkness. She was alone. No sign of anyone. Only her, standing under a cloud-choked night sky, her bare feet perched on a steep ledge of rock.

"Claire?" she called, but the cold wind blew her words into nothingness as soon as they left her tongue.

She tried not to be afraid, but she knew what was coming.

No sooner had she thought it, then the waves crashed in from all directions.

Beneath her perch on the soaring precipice, water swelled and roiled, devouring the valley below. It had been a city down there; she knew that. Knew its entire population was being swallowed up, drowned by the sudden, punishing flood.

"No!" The word exploded in her head, but her mouth made no sound at all. She watched through uncaring eyes as the catastrophe spread, destroying everything in its path. "No! Noo!"

Bereft, sick with horror, she hardly felt the soft, warm touch on her arm. The din of chaos and annihilation was deafening. The entire world around her had gone dark and bleak. Empty.

"Jenna."

She startled at the sound of the feminine voice—someone else alive with her in this hellish plane, someone who knew her name.

"Jenna, can you hear me?" Claire Reichen's voice, velvety and steady, coming from the left side of her. "Look away from the carnage, Jenna. See me. I'm here with you now."

She did as instructed, amazed to find she had the strength. The racket of the disaster and the death it was leaving in its wake still filled her head, but there was a peace now too. A tether reaching out to her from the dark.

Claire took her hand and nodded. "I found you. Do

you want to try to go back to the beginning with me now that I'm here?"

Jenna nodded, unable to command her voice—the voice of whomever she embodied in this dreamscape—to speak. She wanted to go back. She could do this. She had to.

A sudden jerk of motion yanked her backward through the darkness.

The waves retreated at hyperspeed, flood and destruction unwinding in an instant. Rolling her back to the moment she always entered the dream, teetering at the brink of coming destruction.

Then back even further.

She looked down from the tall crag, astonished. The moonlit city in the valley below was ancient. Columned white temples and bricked roads spread out in all directions. Massive gates and stone towers, protective moats and water-filled canals that ran like arteries through the heart of a pristine, thriving metropolis. Its beauty was mythical, breathtaking.

She swiveled her head to see if Claire was witnessing the same thing. But before she could glance her way, a sudden bright light flashed on the far horizon in front of her, illuminating the night sky like a newborn sun.

The earth rumbled beneath her feet. The tremor rocked with terrific force, so massive she staggered where she stood, nearly losing her purchase on the jagged mountain ledge. The entire planet trembled, as though about to crack open at its core.

And out over the sea beyond, a great cloud was forming. It billowed high and furious, ashes churning up from a stalklike funnel crowned with a roiling mushroom head. The cloud blew a gale of heat so intense, she had to lift her arm to shield her face from the burn.

Below her in the valley, some of the taller white temples began to shudder and break apart. People poured out of homes and taverns, spilling into the cobbled streets in a din of panic and confusion. Their screams went up on the dry night wind like banshee cries.

The wail and howl of a population experiencing its own sudden, wholesale demise.

As the waves rose up from all directions, Jenna tore her gaze away from the carnage about to take place. She searched for Claire beside her, but she was gone.

Now someone else stood next to her on the cliff.

An Ancient.

There were three others with him, all the same immense height, hairless heads and bared torsos covered in otherworldly *dermaglyphs*. Their thin-pupiled eyes were catlike in the darkness, raptly enthusiastic as they watched the destruction taking shape before them.

They were exultant.

And they had done this terrible thing, she was certain of it.

All at once, the reality of it hit her. Here, in this moment, this awful landscape, she wasn't Jenna. She was one of them. One of these Ancient marauders—the one who implanted his bit of alien material into her human body and made her into something else. A shadow of himself. A vessel to carry his history, no matter how cancerous and ugly it was.

This moment wasn't only a dream. It was memory. It was a past event playing out for her, frame by horrific frame.

In the city below, people screamed and wept. They tried to flee, but the ocean was swelling even more, crashing high onto land. There was nowhere for them to run. No hope for any of them to survive.

One of the Ancients at her side pivoted his unfeeling amber eyes on her. *The fools should have surrendered when they had the chance.*

Not a voice, but a thought sent deep into her brain.

Another glanced her way, equally unmoved. *She will never surrender.*

From a third: *And what of her legion who escaped with her?*

We hunt them down. This voice was Jenna's, yet not hers. A psychic projection of thoughts she wasn't even aware were hers. Because they weren't.

They belonged to him—the one whose alien skin she occupied now, in this nightmare landscape.

She didn't understand the words she was speaking, no more than she could comprehend the reason these creatures had done such a heinous thing to an entire community of people. But the four others standing with her on the cliff were looking to her now for direction, seeking counsel from the otherworldly kindred they saw before them.

Wherever they've gone, however long it takes, said the mind inside her skull, in the alien language that wasn't hers. *We hunt them down . . . until we claim the head of every last one.*

CHAPTER
Twenty-seven

A single, staccato rap sounded on the door of the room Lucan had taken over as his private office. He glanced up and heaved an aggravated sigh. "Enter."

Tegan came in, still dressed in his winter coat and weapons, fresh off his return from Boston. "Don't mean to interrupt."

Lucan shrugged and pushed aside the lab intel analyses Gideon had given him earlier that night. He hadn't even read the damn things yet, had just been sifting through the papers on autopilot for the past hour, glad for the excuse to shut himself away from the rest of the compound to wrestle with his thoughts. Grave, disturbing thoughts that probably weren't going to see any improvement, if Tegan's serious look was any indication. "How'd it go?"

"Could've been worse." Tegan arched a tawny brow. "Chase and the woman are both outside with the others."

"No resistance from him?" Lucan could hardly believe that.

"Oh, he resisted. Or would have, if Renata hadn't dropped him on his ass with a shot of instant obedience training."

"Shit," Lucan grumbled, raking a hand over his tense jaw. "And the female?"

Now Tegan's shrewd green eyes glinted with an ironic light. "Tavia Fairchild is everything Rowan told us she'd be—and then some. She's Breed, all right, and Gen One besides. No damn doubt about that. Got the *glyphs* and fangs to prove it."

"I'm not sure I want to know how you were able to confirm that."

Tegan grunted and shook his head. It took an awful lot to put the Gen One warrior in a state of awe, but there was no mistaking the amazement in his low voice. "You should've seen her, man. The instant Renata opened up on Chase with her mind zap, Tavia came out of nowhere, spitting venom and ready to take on all four of us at once." He exhaled a wry curse. "Maybe I should have let her try, just to see what she was capable of in raw, Gen One form. With training and a bit more time to get used to herself in her new skin, I think she could be one hell of an asset to us."

"She's not staying," Lucan said, already hating the idea that yet another civilian—and a female besides—was under the Order's roof. One more innocent life placed in his hands. A life unlike any other, if the facts about Tavia Fairchild's origins were even close to the truth. "I agreed to bring her in because we can't afford to let anyone connected to Dragos run loose and unchecked on the streets right now. She's here to provide whatever intel we can glean from her and to cool her heels until we ash that son of a bitch Dragos once and for all. Soon as we have what we need, she's going back to Rowan or a safe house somewhere. Either way, she's out of here ASAP."

"You gonna tell that to Chase?"

Lucan's dark look was met with a cool stare. "Ah, Christ . . . Harvard and her—"

Tegan inclined his head in confirmation. "Appears so. If the move she pulled, coming to his defense at Rowan's wasn't enough to convince me, the ride north only confirmed it."

"You talking sex, or sex and a blood bond between them?"

"That I don't know," Tegan admitted. "Harvard looks like shit, but he's keeping it together for the most part. I tested him on the way up, and I gotta say, I was surprised to see he passed. If not by much. No mistaking the feral vibe coming off him, but there was a new restraint about him that I haven't seen in a long time."

Lucan considered for a moment. "You think he needs solitary?"

"I think if we put him in a hole, that might just push him straight over the edge. Right now, Tavia seems like the only thing holding him together, and even that's precarious."

"Jesus." Lucan leaned back in his desk chair and blew out a long sigh. "Like things aren't bad enough around here. Harvard's outside, you say?"

Tegan nodded. "Hunter and Niko are keeping an eye on him while I headed down here to talk with you."

"And the female?"

"She's meeting the welcome wagon right now. Looks like we got back to base just in time. Everyone's about to head in with Dante and Tess for Xander's presentation ceremony."

Lucan's brow furrowed. "That's tonight?"

But, shit, of course it was. Gabrielle and the other Breedmates had been making preparations for the ritual for days now, trying to give Tess and Dante's son a proper introduction into the world despite the chaos that surrounded them. As leader of this household, Lucan would be the one officiating as tonight Xander Raphael would be officially presented to his kith and kin, and his godparents would publicly pledge themselves to his upbringing, should tragedy take Dante and Tess before he reached adulthood.

The ritual was steeped in tradition and honor among the civilian Darkhaven populations, more pomp than practical necessity. But it took on heavier meaning here, under the Order's roof, where combat and war could claim any one of their members on any given night.

Lucan stood up, unaware he was gritting his teeth until he heard the sharp grate of his jaws. His hands were fisted at his sides, knuckles white as bone.

Tegan's gaze narrowed on him. "What's going on with you?"

"Nothing."

When Lucan started to stalk toward the door, Tegan stepped in front of him. "Nothing, my ass. I don't need to touch you for an emotional well-check to know that something's got you freaked out. I don't think it's got anything to do with Chase or this new wrinkle Tavia Fairchild has caused. I don't even think it's got much to do with Dragos." The warrior stared harder at Lucan now, as though he could see right through him. "What's going on with you and Gabrielle?"

Lucan felt his chin go up in defense, a cold spark shooting through his veins. "Has she said anything to you? To Elise? What the fuck have you heard, Tegan?"

Tegan shook his tawny head. "Haven't heard a thing.

But I pay attention. She's walking around lately like there's a hole in her heart, and you look like you're about to lose your best friend."

Shit. He wanted to deny it, but there was little point trying to dodge Tegan now. Not when Lucan's face had to be telling Tegan how right he actually was. "I'm fucking things up with her. I knew when that female first came into my life that she deserved someone who could give her a life worthy of her. A safe life, a happy life. Not this endless upheaval and war."

Tegan narrowed a look on him. "Gabrielle's never struck me as the kind to go into anything with her eyes closed. When she chose you, she did it knowing exactly what she was getting into. Everyone under this roof knows there's nothing you wouldn't do for her."

"Except give her a son." Lucan felt the words slip out of his mouth before he could bite them back. Much as it killed him to admit it, he was glad his guilt was finally out there. Keeping it inside had been a festering sore that only bored deeper into his soul every second he held it back. "That's what she wants from me, Tegan—a child. And I can't give it to her. Not now. Not when I know this war with Dragos could eventually rip our son from her arms. And not when I can't see a clear future that isn't swamped with violence and corruption. This is no goddamn time to be bringing another innocent life into the world."

Tegan had gone very quiet now. Studying Lucan. Reflecting on something deep inside himself. Finally he gave a mild shrug. "Maybe it isn't, Lucan. Then again, maybe there's never been a better time. Maybe right now we all need a little hope."

Lucan stared, dumbstruck, realization dawning on him as subtly as a freight train. "You and Elise?"

"Yeah." Tegan's chuckle burst from him, full of a mystified wonder that Lucan had never heard in the warrior. Not in the five long centuries the two had known each other.

"Goddamn, T. Congratulations." He reached out and clapped his palm to his friend's thick shoulder, then pulled him into a brief, brotherly embrace. "How far along is she?"

Tegan's smile only deepened. "Not long. She conceived just a few nights ago."

Lucan thought back to the recent crescent moon phase, the brief cycle of fertility for blood-bonded Breedmates. While he was pushing Gabrielle away, Tegan and Elise were making a new life together.

Although Lucan was rife with shame for the fear that had kept him from sanctifying his own bond with Gabrielle, he couldn't deny his goodwill for Tegan and his beloved mate. "A Breed child couldn't hope for better, more loving parents. I mean that, my friend. I am truly happy for you and Elise."

The warrior nodded solemnly. "Knowing our son is on the way only gives me more cause to make this world a better place. For all our sons, Lucan."

He wanted to agree, to say he felt the same hope for the future none of them could predict, but Lucan's tongue stayed cleaved to the roof of his mouth. Tegan nodded. He understood. He, of all the warriors of the Order—down the many centuries since its original formation—knew the dread that was eating Lucan up inside.

Tegan knew it—he had to feel it himself—and yet he'd found the strength to put aside his fear and take an enormous leap of faith.

Lucan wanted to believe he had that in him too.

But the dread was an ache that refused to let him go.

Tavia had not been at all prepared for the familial atmosphere that greeted Chase and her on their arrival at the Order's headquarters. Based on the weapons and combat attire of their escorts out of Boston, she'd expected more of the same once she stepped inside the stone-and-timber fortress where they lived.

But it felt like a home more than the military-style bunker she'd anticipated. She could even see a roaring fire on the hearth of the great room just off the foyer and an enormous pine, trimmed with handmade ornaments, festive ribbon bows, and popcorn garlands. She didn't know what packed the bigger punch: the homespun Christmas vibe of the place, or the fact that she was standing in the midst of half a dozen heavily armed vampires and their mates yet had never felt more welcome or at ease.

Renata had made quick introductions for her while Nikolai and Hunter kept a close eye on Chase across the foyer. Tavia marveled at the beautiful women who were mated to some of the members of the Order: Dylan, with her mane of fiery red hair and peachy freckles; Alex, an athletic brown-eyed blonde with a quick, friendly smile; petite Corinne, whose long ebony hair and delicate features might have made her seem fragile if not for the steely resolve in her greenish-blue gaze; and Jenna, the human female Tavia had heard about on the drive north.

The pretty brunette had come into the foyer just a moment ago, leaning just a little on the arm of her mate,

Brock. The towering Breed male's dark face was drawn with unmistakable concern, all of it focused on her.

"How'd it go tonight?" Renata asked the pair after they'd had the chance to meet Tavia. "Any luck with Claire and the dreamwalking?"

Jenna gave an eager nod. "We got something new this time. I'm not sure what it means yet, but Claire and I documented everything. As awful as it was to be in the nightmare—to be living it like my own memories—I also can't wait to go in again and try to bring back something more."

Beside her, Brock emitted a quiet growl and muttered something about hardheaded females. Jenna wrapped her arms around him and gazed up into his dread-filled eyes.

"He worries," she told Tavia and the others, giving him a private smile.

"He loves you," the big warrior quipped right back, his voice as solemn as his gaze.

"Tavia, can I look at your *glyphs*?" The abrupt request came from Mira, a child of about eight or nine years who'd been among the first to greet Tavia on her arrival and had been watching her with rapt interest ever since.

"Mouse," Renata admonished her, shaking her head in exasperation. "Manners, young lady."

"Sorry." The flaxen-haired imp huffed out a remorseful sigh. "Tavia, may I *please* look at your *glyphs*?"

"That's not exactly what I meant, Mouse." Renata's expression was as mortified as any mother of a precocious child, even though her voice held a tinge of amusement. "It's not polite to ask something like that of someone. Or to stare."

"No," Tavia replied. "It's okay, really. I don't mind."

She inched up the sleeve of her sweater and let the child peer at the web of skin markings that tracked all around her arm. It didn't take long for the other children—teen boys, one a lanky ginger-haired youth and another, whose head was shorn to his *glyph*-covered scalp and whose face showed no emotion whatsoever— to drift over and have a look as well.

"These are real *dermaglyphs*," said the first boy, his hazel gaze suspicious under the fall of his drooping bronze hair. "So, you're really Breed, then?"

Tavia nodded. "Apparently, I am."

Mira rolled her violet-hued eyes. "I told you so, Kellan. He didn't believe me."

The boy shot her a sullen look. "I wanted to see it for myself, that's all."

"You said you needed proof, like you thought I was trying to trick you or something." There was a note of hurt in her tone. "How come you never believe anything I say?"

Kellan looked uncomfortable under the public accusation. When he finally spoke, his voice was quietly defensive. "It's stupid to take anyone on faith alone."

"Even your friends?"

He didn't answer, and while their argument faded into a silent standoff, the other boy, who was still studying Tavia's *glyphs*, moved closer. He had pushed up his own sleeve, revealing a similar pattern that swept around the lean muscles and tendons of his forearm.

His name was Nathan, and aside from his introduction as Corinne's son, the inscrutable young teen was a mystery. Tavia watched his long-lashed eyes take in her skin markings, cataloging them, one by one. He was serious and strangely detached, seeming vastly older than his years and nothing like any other boy she'd ever seen before.

When he glanced up at her, head cocked to the side, his blue-green eyes pierced her with the cool dispassion of a blade. "You are Gen One. Born in Dragos's laboratory."

She nodded.

"So was I."

The softly voiced confession sparked an instant kinship in her, and Tavia felt the absurd urge to hug the child who'd also been a victim of Dragos's evil. She wanted to talk with Nathan some more, ask him about his experience with the monster who created them, but the hauntedness of his gaze deepened, then was shuttered behind his dark lashes and gone altogether when he looked up at her again.

At that same moment, from a room down the corridor, Tegan and another warrior emerged and strode into the gathering in the foyer. Simply by breathing, the dark-haired male with Tegan commanded attention and respect, and there was no question that he was the leader of the Order, even before Tegan introduced him as such.

"Lucan, this is Tavia Fairchild."

She accepted the warrior's large hand and felt herself immersed in the stormy scrutiny of Lucan's shrewd gray eyes as he clasped her fingers in a firm, callused hold. "Mathias Rowan has filled us in on the basics, but I'm sure you understand we'll have questions for you now that you're here."

"Of course. Whatever I can do," she replied. "I need some answers myself."

He gave her a grim nod as he released her hand. "Until then, you'll be staying here, under the Order's protection. That means you remain on the grounds of this property at all times, and you make contact with no one beyond these walls without my express permission."

"Okay." It sounded a lot like imprisonment, but it was hard to balk at the offer when she had so few other options. Besides, she'd lived the first part of her life in one form of prison; now at least she had the truth. And she had Chase too. She felt him near her now, his presence behind her a warm comfort despite his radiating tension like a furnace.

Lucan sent a measuring look over her shoulder at him. "Unfortunately, we're in tight quarters and down to the last unclaimed room—"

"I don't need it." Chase's reply was dark and defensive, despite the negligent shrug that accompanied it. "I'm sure there's a locked cell with my name on it somewhere in here."

"That'll depend on you, Harvard."

"And we can figure all of this out later." The smooth female voice came from behind the group in the foyer, turning all heads her way. Tavia glanced at the auburn-haired beauty whose soulful brown eyes were fixed on Lucan alone. She was his mate; the palpable energy connecting the pair left no doubt. "You must be Tavia," she said, stepping forward to greet her with a welcoming smile. "I'm Gabrielle."

"Hello."

Gabrielle moved over to Lucan and twined her fingers through his. "Tess and Dante are waiting in the sanctuary with the others. Are you coming?"

Lucan inclined his head, brushing the back of his hand gently along the slope of her cheek. Such a simple gesture, and yet there was so much devotion in his eyes, it stole Tavia's breath. "Whatever you want, love. I mean that. As you just said, we can figure the rest out later."

She stared up into his gaze for a long moment, a question hanging between them unspoken. Then a tender smile broke across her face, warm and joyful and meant for him alone.

As they embraced quietly, Mira came over and took Tavia's hand in hers. "Come on. You have to meet the baby."

"The baby?" Tavia glanced to the rest of the women for explanation.

"Tess and Dante's newborn son, Xander Raphael," Renata replied. "He's not quite a week old now, and tonight he's being officially presented to his godparents. It's a tradition within the Breed."

"You're welcome to attend," Gabrielle said. "But I'm sure you must be exhausted too, so if you'd rather rest—"

"Not at all." Amazingly, she was anything but tired, even after all she'd been through lately. Her body felt stronger, more vital than ever, no doubt thanks to her otherworldly genes and the lack of medicines keeping that part of her suppressed. She had to admit, she was more than a little curious about this new side of her, including the rituals that were part of the strange new world in which she was suddenly submerged. "If you don't think anyone would mind me being there, I'd love to attend."

"Come on, then, let's go!" Mira gave her hand an eager tug, already charging ahead of the group as they started to move out of the foyer.

Yet despite Tavia's own interest in these people and the generous welcome they were extending her, she couldn't help noticing how Chase hung back. In fact, if anything, he seemed more uncomfortable now than he had on the drive north. His unease prickled through her veins like tiny needles under her own skin.

She paused and turned to look at him, waiting for him to join her. She couldn't leave him there alone when everyone else was moving into the other room—even if it appeared to be exactly what he wanted her to do. When he finally took the first step toward her, it was with the slow gait of a man making his way toward the gallows.

CHAPTER
Twenty-eight

It was the last place he wanted to be.

The fucking last thing he wanted to do was stand around like the interloper he was and watch as Dante and Tess presented their son to Gideon, his appointed godfather. Not that Chase begrudged the choice. It was the right thing to do for their child, the best thing. Should anything happen to Xander's parents before he reached adulthood, the Breed youth would want for nothing. Gideon and Savannah would provide him with all the love and care he could possibly need.

Dante had been insane to suppose that Chase could ever fill that role. Fortunately for him and Tess, Chase had shown them what a poor choice he was before their child took his first breath. And now he would stand by and try to feel unaffected—to feel nothing but relief—as the honor was bestowed instead on Gideon.

All the worse that Tavia would be there to witness it too.

She didn't know the tradition or politics of the ritual,

or the amount of fuck-ups and disappointments it took for Chase to have lost the privilege of being the infant's appointed guardian. But as they all entered the prepared sanctuary to take their seats in the wooden pews, he knew she could feel his shame, and that was enough.

Or so he thought, until Tavia's gaze lit on Elise across the candlelit room.

She held her surprise, but he felt her go a bit still beside him as she looked at the woman who had once been part of his family. Part of his life's deepest shame.

Elise stood at the front of the little sanctuary room with Gideon and Savannah and Dante, Tess and the baby. She'd been assisting with the silks to be used in the ceremony, but when her pale lavender gaze lit on Chase and Tavia, she whispered something to the waiting couples and started walking over. Tegan intercepted her halfway, wrapping a protective arm around her as he escorted her toward them. His expression was guarded and watchful, a male prepared to spill another's lifeblood right in the middle of the holy space if it meant keeping his mate safe from harm.

And little wonder he felt that way where Chase was concerned. Chase could still feel Elise's open hand cracking across his face from the last time he saw her. A strike he'd more than deserved for what he'd said to her in the days leading up to his separation from the Order.

But this was something different.

He watched the mated couple come toward him—Elise beatific and radiant, Tegan glowering and possessive—and he suddenly knew.

She was newly pregnant.

It should have hit him harder than it did. Maybe it would have, had Tavia not been standing beside him, her calm, nonjudging gaze watching him in quiet understanding as the couple approached. She was steady and serene, tranquil waters when he'd grown so accustomed to riding out his storms alone.

"Sterling," Elise whispered as she paused in front of him. She started to reach out to him, then seemed to think better of it, clasping her hands in front of her. "I'm so relieved that you're all right. The way you left us in Boston the other morning . . . we've all been fearing the worst."

"I'm sorry for the worry," he murmured. "That wasn't my intent."

"No," she said. "You intended to save us that day. And you did. What you did for all of us in that moment was—"

"Honorable," Tegan finished for her. "Fucking suicidal too, but that's beside the point."

Chase gave a vague lift of his shoulder, dismissing their gratitude. One noble gesture couldn't earn back everything he'd thrown away, no matter how badly he suddenly wanted to think it could. It would take time to prove himself fully to his brethren again. Time he wasn't sure he had when hunger was gnawing at him from far within the pit of his soul.

His hands were twitchy at his sides, his veins beginning to jangle, giving him the sudden, rising urge to hightail it out of the place and run deep and long into the night. As the dark impulse built inside him, he felt Tavia's fingers brush lightly against his. She knew what he was feeling, and her offered hand was just the mooring he needed. Their fingers twined, he cleared his throat and made the introductions.

"Tavia Fairchild, this is Tegan's mate, Elise."

"I'm also Sterling's former sister-in-law," she said, smiling with genuine kindness.

"Yes, I know," Tavia replied. "It's good to meet you."

"Likewise." Elise's gaze drifted down to their joined hands and a tender light came into her eyes. "Maybe after the ceremony, I can show you around the house and grounds?"

Tavia smiled. "Sure, I'd like that."

"I should go back and take a seat now. We were just about to begin."

As she and Tegan started to turn away, Chase reached out to take a light hold of Elise's arm. "Wait."

Tegan's answering growl was low and dark, well within his rights. His eyes flashed with amber sparks. Chase let go and blew out a hasty apology. "I just wanted to say congratulations. To both of you. About the baby. I'm happy for you both."

Elise beamed up at Tegan, then turned her joy on Chase. "Thank you. That means a lot to me, Sterling. It means a lot to both of us."

Tegan grunted and took Chase's offered hand in a firm shake. The blond warrior's hold hesitated, no doubt reading the emotional truth of Chase's words with the power of his touch. Chase didn't recoil under the extrasensory probe; he truly had nothing to hide. Tegan nodded, then drew his hand away and clapped Chase's shoulder. "Good to have you back, Harvard."

The pair walked off to take their seats near the front of the small sanctuary.

Chase turned back to Tavia. "She and Tegan have been mated for just over a year. I should've told you she was part of the Order now."

"It's all right. I was surprised to see her, but it's okay." She held his gaze, not with jealousy or anger, but with genuine care and concern. "What about you? Are you okay with Elise being here, and being mated to one of your friends?"

"Yeah, I am." He nodded, rubbing the pad of his thumb over the back of Tavia's hand, their fingers still entwined. "She's mated well. They both have."

For one insane moment, he pictured himself mated as happily as Tegan and Elise. It wasn't something he'd ever wished for himself, but now, with Tavia's hand enveloped in his, his mind was swamped with imaginings of what his future might hold if she were his blood-bonded mate. Impossible dreams.

His hope for any kind of future with Tavia would expire the first time he let his thirst rule him.

He told himself it didn't matter as the ceremony got under way and he and Tavia found their places by themselves in the last row of pews.

With Gabrielle holding the baby at the front of the room now, Elise and the other Breedmates lit eight white candles arranged in a large circle around Dante, Tess, Gideon, and Savannah—an infinite ring connecting them in this moment. There were no white-hooded tunics for the four of them; it was doubtful there'd been time to gather much of what they needed between the evacuation of the Boston compound and the ceremony tonight. But they had the eight thin lengths of virgin white silk, and as the candles were being lit all around them, Dante, Tess, Gideon, and Savannah braided the pieces together into a woven cradle they held suspended between them, a symbolic link between parent and guardian.

Lucan stood front and center, sober in his duty as officiant of the ceremony. "Who brings this child before us tonight?"

"We do," Dante and Tess answered in unison. "He is our son, Xander Raphael."

At Lucan's nod, Gabrielle carried the naked baby over to his parents and placed him in his mother's arms. With Dante holding one end of the woven cradle and Gideon and Savannah holding the other, Tess lifted Xander up to the gathered assembly.

Beside Chase on the pew, he could feel Tavia holding her breath, watching in awestruck silence as the ceremony unfolded.

"This babe is ours," Tess and Dante recited together. "With our love we have brought him into this world. With our blood and lives we sustain him, and keep him safe from all harm. He is our joy and promise, the perfect expression of our eternal bond, and we are honored to present him to you, our kin."

"You honor us well" came the singular reply from everyone gathered in the room.

Even Chase found himself murmuring the traditional reply, anticipating the ritual still to come. He'd witnessed countless such rites in the Darkhavens, for births and deaths and marriages, but ceremony among his warrior brethren was a rare thing. And this—a baby presented before the compound—was a first.

Which made it even more powerful as Tess returned her child to Lucan's arms and took her place once more beside Dante. Lucan's deep voice boomed heavy and unrushed as he pivoted toward Gideon and Savannah. "Who pledges to protect this child with blood and bone and final breath should duty call upon it?"

"We do," the pair replied together, words that tasted bitter on Chase's tongue as he pushed them back down his throat unspoken. He saw Dante's gaze search him out through the gathering, and he forced himself to offer a nod of acceptance, of sincere approval, for the decision his friend had made in the best interests of his son.

The soundness of that decision hit Chase even more pointedly in that next instant, when Lucan placed Xander in the center of the woven cradle and Gideon proceeded with the final step of the ritual. Bringing his wrist to his mouth, Gideon sank his fangs into his flesh, then turned and did the same to Savannah's wrist.

Chase knew it was coming, but as soon as the scent of fresh blood permeated the room, his body seized in a violent tremor. He struggled to get it under control, but the hunger was fierce. His fangs punched out of his gums to fill his mouth.

"Chase?" Tavia whispered softly beside him. "Are you okay?" She reached up to touch his cheek, her pretty face twisted in concern and bathed in the glow of his transformed irises.

At the front of the room, Gideon and Savannah were now holding their wrists above Xander, blood droplets raining down on his naked skin to signify their vow to surrender their lives for the protection of his.

Chase couldn't remain there. Not without losing his head and ruining the entire ceremony.

Miserable with himself, Chase pivoted off the pew and slipped out of the sanctuary as quietly as he could manage. He stumbled up the corridor to the great room and through the French doors leading to the deck outside. Leaping off it, he ran for the deep gloom of the surrounding trees.

By the time he took his first gasp of crisp night air, he was sick with hunger, lungs sawing, stomach feeling shredded to pieces inside him. He dropped to his hands and knees in the snow, dragging in one wheezing breath after another.

"Chase?"

Ah, Christ. Tavia. She'd followed him outside. It killed him to let her see him like this, weak and heaving like the junkie he was. He'd never forgive himself if he did anything to hurt her. "Get away from me, Tavia. Just—go back inside."

"What's happening to you? Talk to me, Chase."

"Leave, Tavia. Now." He flinched when she bent down to touch his hunched back. "For fuck's sake, stay away from me!"

She drew up short at his violent snarl, but there was no fear in her eyes, no pity or revulsion. Only concern. "You need help. I'm going inside to get someone—"

"Don't. Please. Not them." The words rasped out of him, raw and desperate. He shook his head, miserable as he looked up at her, knowing how he must appear to her now. So weak. So diminished. Pathetic. No shadows to conceal him, no bravado or fury to mask the truth of what he'd become. He groaned, whether from the anguish of his thirst or the depth of his humiliation, he wasn't sure. "I don't want anyone to see me like this."

Not even her.

Especially not her, but Tavia wasn't leaving. No, she knelt down next to him in the snow. Stroked her hand gently over his back, through his short, sweat-dampened hair. "I can feel your hunger . . . and your pain. You're shaking with it, Chase. My God, you're starving. If you need blood, take it."

"No." He choked the denial, even as his fangs tore farther out of his gums. His throat was ash, blood thirst raking him like nails over scorched earth. His fevered eyes lit on the pulse point ticking at the base of her neck.

Hunger spiked, hard and demanding. "Please, Tavia. Go back inside. Before I . . ."

"Before you drink from me?" Her gaze was steady on him, unafraid. "It's okay, Chase. I'm here for you. I would let you—"

"*No.*" He hissed a sharp curse and swung his head away from the temptation of her vulnerable throat. "No. Never with you."

"Because you don't want to bind yourself to me."

That quiet guess was so far removed from the truth, it brought his wild amber gaze right back to her. "Because once I have a taste of you, I don't trust myself to stop. You shouldn't trust me either." His voice was little more than a growl, animal and raw. "I'm sick, Tavia. This thing's had its talons in me for a long time. I'm not sure how much longer I can fight it."

She stared at him, studying the misery that had to be written all over his face and in the churning fury of his *dermaglyphs*. Some of the color drained out of her as comprehension dawned, cold and certain. "You're talking about Bloodlust. That's what this raw, shredding ache is that I feel in your veins all the time. It's your addiction."

No sense in denying it. She was the only person he couldn't hide from, the one person whose rejection would cut him the deepest.

He groaned, weathering another savage convulsion of his insides. Sweat popped all over his skin and across his brow, chill and damp in the cold winter air. When the worst of it gripped him, it was Tavia's tender hands that drew him back from his pain. She sat down on the frozen ground beside him and stroked his face with gentle care, courageous despite his feral condition.

"When did this start, Chase? How long have you been fighting it?"

Her touch gave him strength, brought the words up from his scorched throat like a balm drawing poison from a wound. "Six years," he admitted hoarsely. It all came up at once now, acrid and raw. "I've been hiding it from everyone since the night of my brother's death."

She ran her soothing fingers along the tense line of his clenched jaw. "What happened that night? I know you held something back when you first told me about Quentin's death. You said you didn't remember, but you do . . . you remember it all, don't you?"

He nodded, sick with the truth of his actions yet unable to deny them to her. He recalled every second of those blood-soaked hours surrounding Quent's death. Every one of the Rogues he'd slaughtered in his thirst to avenge his fallen kin.

And he remembered the shame of his actions afterward too, when his guilt had driven him to an even further low.

"I was the one who brought in the Rogue who killed my brother. Son of a bitch had drained two humans outside a Goth bar in Cambridge. I should've ashed him on the spot, but that was against Agency policy." He scoffed, still feeling the bite of fury like acid on his tongue. "So I hauled him in, and Quent put him on ice for questioning and processing. He was only in the room alone with the blood-crazed bastard for a few minutes. By the time Quent hit the alarm, he was already bleeding out from the gaping shank wound in his throat."

"Oh, Chase." Tavia's voice was a whisper on the chill night breeze, full of the same shock and anguish that he felt coursing through him now as he relived the awful moments.

"I'd done a weapons search on the Rogue when I brought him in, but somehow he got the makeshift blade past me. I failed my brother." He blew out a raw curse. "I might as well have stabbed him with my own hand."

"No," Tavia said, shaking her head as she caressed him. "God, no. You can't blame yourself."

"Really?" His voice was airless, as cold as the night around him. "Do you know how many times I wondered what it would've been like to live without the weight of Quent's shadow hanging over me? There were times I fucking *wished* for it, Tavia."

She stared at him, no doubt appalled now. Her fingers fell away from him, her exhaled breath clouding in the chill before being swept away into the dark. "You didn't kill him, Chase. Everyone makes mistakes."

"Not one of August Chase's sons," he replied, bitter with self-loathing.

He recalled the whispers that followed in the immediate aftermath of Quentin's death. Elise's horror had been the worst to bear. Her questions and confusion when she'd arrived at the Agency headquarters to see her dead mate still rang in his head: *How could this have happened, Sterling? Who brought the Rogue in? Who was responsible for searching him for weapons? Sterling, please tell me Quentin's not really gone!*

"I wanted to make it right somehow, but there was nothing I could do. Not even killing the Rogue who killed my brother made my guilt any lighter." He swore roughly and raked a hand over the aching bones of his face. His hunger still rode him, but as he sucked the wintry cold into his lungs, some of the burn had begun to ebb. "I went back to the Goth club where I'd picked up the Rogue earlier that night. There was another lurking outside, waiting for his prey. I took out some of my rage on him, then forced him to tell me where his nest was. A group of Rogues had squatted in a warehouse at the ass end of the Charles River. I killed them all, brutally, practically bathed in their blood. And I didn't stop there. I couldn't. The violence had me by then. By the time dawn started to break, I'd killed my first human and was teetering on the edge of a thirst I could barely contain. I've been fighting it ever since."

"Bloodlust," she murmured quietly.

He nodded. "Near enough to taste it. There's a tipping point in the disease that I haven't reached yet. If I cross that line and turn Rogue, I'm lost."

"Like Quentin and Elise's son?" she asked, her brow furrowing now. "You told me that's what happened to him, before you . . ."

"Before I shot him," he said, the admission bitter even now. "Yeah. But with Camden it was different. He'd gotten mixed up with a new club drug that had been making the rounds last year in Boston. It was called Crimson. The shit was potent, a speedball designed especially for the Breed. One whiff or taste of that red powder and it was all you could do not to fuck, fight, or fang everything in your reach."

"My God," Tavia gasped. "It sounds terrible."

Chase grunted. "Not if you're a young male bored out of his skull in the Darkhavens. They ate it like candy, and some of them learned that it was the fast lane to Bloodlust. Cam was one of them."

"I'm sorry."

He shrugged. "Me too. The Order and I took out the Crimson dealer's lab, destroyed all of the product.

Well . . . almost all of it. I kept a vial of it for myself. One last dose, enough to be lethal."

"The silver container I found in your desk in Boston," Tavia murmured. "Why would you want to keep something like that?"

He didn't have to answer. She would read his logic plainly enough. The dose of Crimson was his escape plan, his silver bullet, should Bloodlust finally pull him under all the way. Which more and more didn't seem so much a question of if but when.

He ground out a raw curse.

Walk away. That's what he should do—what he'd done every other time shit got too real for him, too heavy to deal with. And there was a part of him now that wanted nothing more than to vanish into the night and never look back. Just run . . . until he met daylight and all his problems—all his damnable failures, past, present, and future—were eaten by the sun.

That would have been the easy thing for him to do. Hard was making himself sit there and sweat through the shudders that were wrenching his body from the inside out. Hard was laying his weaknesses and his ugliest sins bare as he looked into Tavia's tender gaze and waited for the moment her concern mutated into justifiable contempt. Or worse, pity.

But Tavia's eyes wouldn't release him. Those clear, calm, spring-green eyes held him in the darkness like a caress. As he looked at her now, he realized the feral glow of his own gaze had banked. His irises no longer washed her in amber fire. Even the hungered throb of his fangs had eased in the time he'd been out there alone with her.

"You haven't lost the fight yet, Chase," she told him. "Isn't there anything you can do to help yourself get better? Maybe I can help you over time. I'd like to try, if you'd let me."

He stared at her, leveled by the genuine compassion— by the depth of feeling he could hardly fathom—that shone from her beautiful face. He couldn't resist reaching out to stroke her cheek. "How can you be so caring after everything you've just heard? When I've done nothing but make your life hell since the moment I first saw you?"

"You haven't made my life hell. Dragos did that." Her hands were warm and soothing against his face as she drew him close and pressed a brief kiss to his lips. "You gave me truth, Chase. You have from the very beginning. You've opened my eyes. I may not like everything I see, but it's real and it's honest and I feel like I'm finally alive. You've given me all of that."

He swore under his breath, wondering how it was possible that he'd allowed this female to get under his skin the way she had. Even worse, she had somehow gotten inside his heart, into his very blood.

Ironic that he should find her now, when the last thing he wanted—the very last thing he deserved—was a woman as extraordinary as Tavia Fairchild.

Whether or not he deserved her, Chase couldn't keep from wrapping his palm around her nape and pulling her close for his kiss. She tasted so sweet against his mouth. Felt so good and warm against him as she leaned into his embrace and parted her lips to accept the sweep of his tongue into her mouth.

He could have kissed her all night. Might have, if not for the sudden whoop and shouts of children racing out of the house to play in the snow. Chase pivoted his head to watch Mira, Kellan, and Nathan bound off the deck and into the pine-ringed yard with the compound's two canines—Alexandra's majestic Alaskan gray-and-white wolf dog and a scrappy brownish mutt terrier that belonged to Dante and Tess.

The kids tore right past, barely pausing to notice Chase and Tavia wrapped in each other's arms. Kellan stooped to grab a handful of snow and packed it into a ball. He lobbed it at Mira, missing her by mere inches as she dodged right and retaliated with a projectile of her own. The snowball nailed the teen dead center in the chest.

"Good arm," Chase called to her, which earned him a big grin from the pint-size blond imp.

More volleys were exchanged between Mira and the two boys, until suddenly Chase and Tavia found themselves under fire from the trio. They scrambled to their feet, Tavia laughing as Chase tried to pull her to safety behind the trunk of a thick pine. One of Nathan's snowballs smashed into the back of his head, raining icy powder down the nape of his neck and into the collar of his shirt.

"This means war," Chase shouted, grabbing a handful of snow and sending a ball shooting toward the kids and the dogs barking and jumping all around them.

Tavia's giggles were the most miraculous thing he'd ever heard. He wheeled around on her, full of empty bluster. "You think this is funny, female?" Her smile went wider, but her eyes glimmered with as much heat as humor. He stalked toward her, grinning now. Hotter than he should be, with the kids playing behind them in the woods. "You sure you want to take me on?"

Tavia's answering look was devastatingly inviting. "Think you can handle it?"

"Try me." He hauled her close and kissed her like there was no tomorrow.

CHAPTER
Twenty-nine

Deep in the woods now, Kellan, laughing, cheeks stinging with the cold, scooped up a handful of snow with his gloves and swung around to volley it at Nathan.

The kid was gone.

Mira's giggles trailed from several yards to his left, the barks of the two dogs following her farther into the cover of the dense forest. Kellan paused, silent, listening. Searching the dark for Nathan, anticipating the sudden cold explosion of incoming enemy snowball fire.

This was only mock warfare; Kellan knew that. But there was a spark of competitiveness inside him—a needling urge to prove himself a capable opponent, especially against this strange newcomer who'd been raised and trained by the villain responsible for the murders of Kellan's family.

His senses quirked with the faint stirring of the air. Nathan was moving through the trees now. Kellan's instincts prickled, sending him into a low, stealthy jog toward the subtle disruption of the boy's movement up ahead.

He found Nathan, stalking up on Mira in silence as she played with the dogs. Nathan held a snowball in his hand. In that next instant, he let it fly at Mira.

It shot toward her like a bullet, hitting her square in the back.

She went down as though it had been gunfire, letting out a surprised cry as the force of the impact knocked her flat on her face in a drift.

"Mira!" Kellan shouted, leaping out from his cover in the pines.

He saw the look of surprise on Nathan's face. He hadn't intended to hurt her. But that made no difference to Kellan's instincts. They lit up like a Roman candle, a confusing flood of concern and aggression coursing through his veins in an instant. With a roar, he lobbed his missile at Nathan, pelting the snowball at Mira's attacker with deliberate force.

Nathan dodged the assault and cocked his head in question. Then he reached down and returned fire. He launched one snowball after the other, a relentless hail that drove Kellan back with the force of a hundred fists.

Kellan's anger spiked. His sense of powerlessness kindled a raging fury inside him that exploded out of his mouth in a hoarse bellow. He got up and vaulted at Nathan, meaning to drive his fist into the stoic little killer's face.

Nathan coolly deflected. He moved so fast, Kellan didn't even see the defensive move coming until he found himself hitting the ground on his back, all the air leaving his lungs on a giant wheeze.

Nathan had him pinned, totally incapacitated.

A cold, wet hand was clamped around Kellan's throat,

a mere second away from crushing his larynx. Kellan couldn't breathe.

"Stop!" Mira cried. She raced over to them, eyes wild. She tugged at Nathan's arms, but his hold stayed firm and steady on Kellan's neck. "Nathan, please stop! You'll kill him!"

Her interference burned Kellan somehow. Embarrassment and humiliation, impotent outrage, rushed into his head as the pressure on his throat eased.

Nathan released him without apology. He stood up, watching without remorse as Kellan coughed and gasped, sucking in air. Mira's face was awash in worry as she hunkered down beside him and placed a tentative hand on his shoulder. Kellan brushed her off, hating that she should witness his degradation.

He dragged his gaze up to meet the silent, placid expression of the boy who had likely killed a dozen men, any one of them far more challenging an opponent than Kellan could ever hope to be.

Kellan admired that kind of lethal ability. He'd need it, if he meant to survive in this world Dragos's evil had created. If he meant to avenge the deaths of his kin, as a warrior of the Order one day or on his own, he would need that same cold talent—that same emotional detachment—that he saw reflecting down on him in Nathan's unblinking eyes.

Kellan rubbed his injured throat. Summoned his voice past the acid burn of his humiliation in front of Mira and looked up at the boy who dealt so efficiently in death. "Teach me everything you know."

Tavia lay in a pleasure-drowned daze, her limbs tangled with Chase's in the middle of the king-size bed in their room at the Order's compound. She'd lost track of how many times they'd made love. They'd started after the snowball fight of the night before, then picked up again after spending most of the day apart—Tavia with Elise and some of the other Breedmates, sharing meals and pleasant conversation; Chase sequestered in private meetings with Lucan, Gideon, Tegan, and the rest of the warriors.

Now another night was inching toward dawn on the other side of the shuttered windows and Tavia was blissfully, thoroughly spent.

Eyes closed, caught in a lazy, sated doze, she felt him shift slightly beside her on the bed. He kissed her eyelids, one then the other, his lips gentle even as his arousal nudged her hip in blatant demand.

"Mmm," she moaned, her mouth curving as she lifted her heavy lids. "Good morning. You're up early."

"If you're anywhere near me, guaranteed, I'm always going to be up."

She looked into his dark blue gaze and smiled. "Good thing I have Breed genetics too. Otherwise I'd never be able to keep up with you."

"Yeah, but I'd make sure you had fun trying." He kissed her, long and slow, rousing her senses into a heated rush of wakefulness. "Merry Christmas, beauty."

"Christmas?" She thought back on the days and realized it really was. "Never in a million years could I have guessed I'd wake up naked in a vampire's arms on Christmas morning."

He grinned. "Santa Claus has already been here and everything. Want to see what he brought for you?"

She laughed. "Is it a big present?"

His eyes gleamed devilishly, lit with amber sparks. "Very big."

"With a big red bow on it?"

He glanced down and shrugged, his mouth quirked in a sardonic smile that showed just the barest tips of his fangs. "How about a jaunty cap instead?"

She was still giggling as he kissed her again. When he slid into the wet cleft of her body, her giggles turned to sighs and then to moans of pleasure. He'd learned how to play every inch of her by now, and he was ruthless in his seduction. She surrendered to him wholly, crying out as he brought her to a swift, fevered orgasm.

"My God," she panted, her own fangs filling her mouth as he stoked her toward another shattering release. "Merry Christmas to me."

His answering growl was one of pure masculine pride. "You should see what I do for birthdays."

She laughed drowsily and gazed up at him. The sight of him this close and intimate felt so familiar now, so right. The feel of his naked body pressed against hers was as natural to her as her own breath, her own heartbeat.

And the warm knot that squeezed so tightly in her breast, and traveled lower still, into her very core, was an ache she hoped never to lose.

Deep down, she wondered if she should be afraid.

Because somehow, she realized she had fallen in love with Sterling Chase.

CHAPTER
Thirty

The dream roared up on Jenna from out of nowhere.

Asleep in Brock's arms, she'd been in and out of awareness, drifting from one fragile dreamscape to another.

Then came the blanket of dark gray fog. It swept her away without warning, taking her far from her conscious mind, into that of another being.

The Ancient.

The alien part of her that was merging with her humanity, strengthening the part of her that had once been mortal. Creating something . . . *other.*

It was this part of her that commanded her mind's eye now, as the thick fog carried her deeper into the realm of his memories. She rode it into the twilit shade of a dense primeval forest surrounded by jagged pinnacles of soaring sandstone rock. In the distance, great fires burned, choking the landscape with smoke and swirling ash.

She ran toward it, metal armor strapped to her *glyph-*

covered chest and thighs, jangling with every long stride of her bare, blood-spattered feet. Clutched in her hand was a long sword, a crude implement of mankind's world, with its hammered iron blade and leather-wrapped hilt. But it would suffice. It had bitten off more than one enemy's head tonight.

In a few moments, it would feed again.

Loose earth crunched beneath her feet as she ran toward the smoke of a burning encampment. Some of her brethren were there already, locked in combat with the legion they'd been hunting across continents and many long centuries.

Jenna's unearthly battle cry shook the spindly pines and basalt towers as she charged forward, through the curtain of thick black smoke and the bloodied carnage scattered on the ground.

In response, the massive silhouette of an enemy warrior came out of a crouch over one of the fallen. He pivoted to face her as she cleaved her sword in a powerful, killing arc. Long blond hair, gathered in thin braids that were stiff with drying blood and sweat, swung away from his face as he wheeled around to meet the threat she brought.

He wore no plates of armor over his bare chest, only hammered metal cuffs on his muscled forearms. Loose white sentry's pants were filthy with blood and gore and dirt, hanging in ragged tatters above his sandaled feet.

Jenna's inelegant blade descended on him, a blow he blocked with a swift, double-fisted twist of his polished spear. The weapons sparked off each other, the sword shrieking a metallic protest as the staff deflected its path and sent it sweeping downward.

Jenna felt her mouth move, the voice that wasn't hers speaking words in a long-dead language that didn't belong to the Ancient either. "Your queen cannot hide forever, Atlantean."

"No," the warrior replied, fierce eyes narrowed with fury. "But she doesn't need forever. She need only outlive you and your savage kind. And she will."

He brought up the long staff and, in the glow of flames licking skyward all around them, firelight glinted off the symbol that adorned the spear's hilt and the shining metal cuffs on his arms: It was a crescent moon, poised to catch the falling teardrop that hovered above its cradle.

The same symbol that every Breedmate bore as a birthmark somewhere on her body.

Jenna had no time to process the uncanny revelation or the stunning implications of what it could mean.

Her arm came up, sword raised high.

She swung, using all of the preternatural power at her command. Her enemy dodged. A mere fraction too late.

The iron blade cleaved into flesh and bone and sinew, a punishing hit to his shoulder. Blood surged like a fountain from where the sentry's arm dangled uselessly at his side, all but severed. In the cradle of his palm, a bright light began to glow in the shape of the same symbol he wore on his weaponry and armor. He was injured and weakened now, but it would take more than a lost limb to end the warrior's immortal existence.

Jenna breathed in the scent of spilling enemy lifeblood and felt the rush of a savage exhilaration race through her.

She roared with it, victorious. Conquering.

Unstoppable.

She hauled back on the blade again and let it swing, burying it deep in her enemy's neck. Light erupted as his head broke away from his body. The glare of it was blinding, as pure and milky white as the full moon hanging in the night sky.

The beam flared brighter, impossibly so . . . and then it was gone.

An immortal flame snuffed forever by the sword she held in her alien hand.

"Jenna!" The deep voice called to her through the billowing soot and the clash of weapons not far from where she stood. Strong hands took hold of her, shook her hard. "Jenna, can you hear me? Jenna, damn it, wake up!"

She came out of the dream gasping, clutching onto Brock, who was now sitting up on the bed beside her. His eyes were wide and worried. His big hands roamed over her face, brushing aside the strands of hair that clung to her damp brow.

She stared at him, trying to make sense of what she'd just witnessed. In the end all she could manage was a trembling couple of words. "Holy shit."

Lucan paced the confines of his bedroom, edgy and restless, despite the physical satisfaction of his body. It was early morning outside the temporary compound's sheltering walls and shuttered windows. Christmas, for fuck's sake.

He didn't feel like celebrating. He felt like strapping on weapons and combat gear and taking this damned war straight into Dragos's face. He wanted it ended, preferably with Dragos under his boot heel, bleeding and broken, begging for mercy he would never receive.

He wanted that with a ferocity he could barely contain.

All the more so when he considered the promise he'd

given Gabrielle in the hours they'd lain together, making love in the bed where she slept now, as sweet and lovely as a dream.

At the next crescent moon cycle, Lucan would give her a son.

As much as he'd been fighting the idea, there was a part of him that had wanted it as much as she did. Maybe more. For nine long centuries, he'd walked alone by his own choosing. He'd had his warrior brethren, but family—a Breedmate and children—was nothing he'd ever craved. Until an auburn-haired beauty with melting brown eyes and the fearless heart of a lioness had strode into his world and laid all his intentions to waste in an instant.

He'd never imagined he could love so fully, so completely. His dread of an unknown future was hardly a match for his devotion to the incredible female who'd taken him as her mate.

And as Tegan said, knowing the world they were fighting for belonged to their sons only made his determination burn all the brighter to see it thrive in peace.

Lucan walked back to the bed and leaned over to press a gentle kiss to her cheek. The brief brush of his lips made her stir, then smile, still caught in a light slumber. "Good morning," he murmured softly. "Sleep, love. I didn't mean to wake you. I'm heading down to the tech lab for a while to review some of the intel that came in from New Orleans."

"It's a holiday," she reminded him, her voice thick and drowsy. Far too inviting, as she stretched with feline grace and rolled onto her back to face him. "Come back to bed?"

God, he was tempted. "I'll only be a couple of hours.

I want to put in some time while the rest of the house is asleep. You rest, and I'll come back before too long."

Her answering moan was languid and breathless. It made him want to crawl under the covers and make her do it again. Preferably as she climaxed against his mouth.

He stepped away from the bed and pulled on a fresh black T-shirt and fatigues. Gabrielle was already fast asleep once more, her breath puffing softly between her parted lips. He smiled, content simply to look at her.

Christ, he had it bad for her.

And he wouldn't want it any other way.

He was still smiling like a love-struck fool as he walked out to the corridor and silently closed the bedroom door behind him. Another door opened down the way and Mira came sneaking out on her toes, her pink nightgown swishing around her ankles as she hurried up the hall.

Her flaxen hair was a wild tangle on her bed-rumpled head, her eyes half-closed and bleary with sleep. She ran headlong, practically blind with purpose as she crashed right into him. "Oh!" she gasped as he caught her in both hands and kept her from bouncing off her feet. "I thought I heard Santa out here."

"Not Santa." Lucan chuckled and stooped down to her level. "Just . . . me . . ."

As he brushed the tousled mop of hair from her face, Mira's eyes met his. He'd been expecting to see the opaque violet of her custom-made contact lenses. Lenses that had been specially crafted to mute the young Breedmate's talent for prognostication. Instead, Lucan found himself staring into the clear, mirrorlike pools of the child seer's powerful gaze.

A vision slammed into his brain like a bullet.

Blood-soaked.

Horrific.

"Oh, no!" Mira cried. She realized her mistake at once, bringing her hands up to shield him from the power of her eyes. "My lenses. I forgot to put them in. Lucan, I'm sorry!"

"Shh," Lucan soothed as she burst into tears. He pulled her close, offering a comforting embrace as the little girl sobbed with remorse. "It's all right, Mira. You did nothing wrong."

She drew back, careful now to hold her arm up over her eyes. "What did you see, Lucan? Was it something bad?"

"No," he lied. "It was nothing. Don't you worry, everything's all right."

But even as he spoke, a pit of black, yawning dread cracked wide open inside him.

Mira's gift had just shown him a glimpse of a future more bleak than anything he'd imagined in the worst of his countless nightmare scenarios.

CHAPTER
Thirty-one

"One more vial and that should do it, Tavia," Gideon said from the other side of his makeshift tech lab. "How you hanging in over there, Harvard?"

Chase grunted his response, all he was capable of as he watched the other warrior withdraw the last of half a dozen blood samples he'd collected from Tavia's arm. Chase felt like a pussy having to sit clear across the room during the clinical procedure, trying his damnedest not to let the sight of those filling vials awaken his feral side. His fangs had erupted from his gums at the first pinprick that scored her skin, his hunger worsening to a fevered throb at the trace exotic scent of her blood.

Hard as it was for him to be there when his body was taut and on edge with thirst, sitting it out in the hallway while Tavia was run through a variety of exams and tissue samplings was out of the question.

Fortunately, Gideon kept everything quick and efficient.

"All set," he announced a moment later.

Chase stalked over as the blond warrior took away the containers of blood and DNA swabs to prepare them for testing. "You okay?" he asked Tavia, thoughts for his own well-being eclipsed by concern for her.

"Piece of cake," she said, rolling her long sleeve down over her *glyph*-covered forearm. "I spent the first twenty-seven years of my life in and out of private clinics and medical trials. I'm used to being poked."

Chase's grin was filled with another sort of hunger now. "I don't want you getting used to anyone poking you, unless that someone is me."

It was a possessive thing to say, and even though he had no right to think it let alone let the words roll off his tongue, he couldn't apologize for it. The past hours he'd spent with Tavia—baring his soul to her, laughing with her, making love to her, then making love some more—had set a hook in him so deep, he wondered if he'd ever be able to shake it loose.

Not that he wanted to.

And that was the hell of it, right there.

He craved this woman, cared for her more than he had anyone or anything in all his life before her. Some desperate, hopeful part of him wondered if the hole she filled in his heart might someday grow to fill the other, more ravenous one that threatened to consume him.

"Okay, kids," Gideon announced as he came back into the room. "I'll run the blood work and tissue analysis later today. We should have full results in a few days, but based on what I've already seen here, coupled with the data you found in good old Dr. Minion's clinic records, I think it's pretty obvious what they're going to return." He raked his fingers through the blond spikes of his cropped hair and exhaled a marveled chuckle. "Never dreamed there'd come a day when I'd be up close and personal with a female Breed—never mind a female Gen One with Breedmate DNA. You can blend in with humans if you have to, you can subsist on blood or food, and you can walk in the daylight without getting cooked after a few minutes. My God, Tavia. You're absolutely remarkable."

She smiled. "Hey, I've seen you working magic on these computers, Gideon. You're not so bad yourself."

Chase grunted, slanting an arch look at the warrior. "Yeah, and come to think of it, you've been up close and personal enough for one day."

Gideon smirked in Tavia's direction. "What can I say? He gets wicked jealous when I flirt. It's a problem for us."

She laughed along with him, as aware as anyone by now that the Order's resident genius only had eyes for his Breedmate, Savannah.

Gideon studied Tavia in open wonder, his head cocked to the side now, arms crossed over his gray Boondock Saints T-shirt. "Have you considered offspring?"

"Offspring?" Tavia shot an uncomfortable look at Chase. "Uh . . ."

"Oh, not that I'm suggesting," he quickly interjected. "I just mean, from a purely genetic standpoint, the possibilities are . . . well, exciting. Intriguing, to say the least. Don't you think so, Harvard?"

Chase couldn't have replied if he wanted to. The thought of Tavia pregnant had struck him both mute and stupid. He could imagine nothing more powerful than the idea of her giving birth. The fact that her children would mark the beginning of an entirely new generation of the Breed paled in comparison to the feeling that swamped Chase when he pictured himself as the father of her sons.

Or, Christ . . . her daughters.

Tavia's eyes were steady on his, and he wondered if her bond to him would betray the depth of his reaction. He couldn't hide what he felt, not with her. And even without the blood bond to tell her how powerfully she affected him, his unflinching, heat-filled gaze would have given him away.

Gideon cleared his throat in the weighted silence of the room. "You say there were clinic records documenting other cases like yours, Tavia?"

She nodded. "Dr. Lewis was treating others like me, but according to the files we found, the patients had all died over the years. If there were files on others who are living, I didn't see them when we searched the clinic."

"But there could be others like you out there," Gideon said. "Knowing Dragos, I'd lay odds there definitely are others. Women who are embedded in normal human lives as you were. Women who will soon run out of their meds and begin transforming into their true Breed natures, the same way you did."

"Oh, my God," she replied. "If that's true . . . if something like that were to happen . . ."

Gideon nodded. "Disaster time."

"And assuming there are others," Chase put in, "there's no telling what Dragos might be using them for. In Tavia's case, it was her photographic memory. Dragos was using her to collect various human government intel through her work for the senator."

Tavia inclined her head in agreement. "When I'd go in for treatments at the clinic, they also used that time to harvest details about places I'd been with the senator, security-sensitive things I'd been privy to as his assistant. It wasn't enough to exploit me as some kind of secret science experiment, they had to mind-rape me too."

Chase heard the anger in her otherwise calm voice. He reached over and slipped his fingers through hers. "Wish like hell I'll get the chance to deliver a little payback on that sick bastard. The more painful, the better."

"You, me, and the rest of the Order," Gideon said. He glanced to Tavia once more. "I don't suppose you have any knowledge—even the slightest bit of intel—about Dragos's operation?"

"No. I didn't even know he existed until Chase tried to warn me about him." She shook her head, brow furrowed. "If I could get anywhere near Dragos, I'd love to use my new skills against him. Especially the lethal ones."

Although Chase understood her need, he bristled at the notion of her even considering getting close to evil like Dragos. "Not gonna happen so long as I have anything to say about that. Dragos is deadly, Tavia. You can never underestimate what he's willing to do."

"Harvard's right," Gideon said. "As much as I agree with him, though, I have to admit having a mole in his operation would be damned useful right about now." He gestured to a computer monitor with a program running some kind of split-screen script. "The data Hunter and Corinne brought back from New Orleans is password-protected and encrypted. I created a routine to break it down, but the damn thing has been cranking on that character sequence for a couple of days and we're barely halfway there."

Chase looked at the display. Of the thirteen-digit

placeholders on the screen, only six of them were locked into place: 5, 0, 5, 1, 1, N.

Tavia's mouth curved into a sly smile as she turned to look at Gideon. "May I try?"

He held out his hand in invitation and let her take the seat in front of one of his computers. He typed something on the keyboard, and the machine beeped, popping up an "Access Denied" screen that prompted for a password. "Knock yourself out."

Tavia entered the six digits from the deencryption program, Chase and Gideon taking positions behind her to watch her work.

She typed another seven characters to complete the sequence: 1, 5, 2, 5, 1, 2, E.

And just like that, she was in.

"It's the same password that opened Dr. Lewis's clinic records," she said, looking fairly pleased with herself.

Gideon slapped Chase on the back of his shoulder and let out a whoop. "Well, fuck us both, Harvard. She's bloody brilliant." He pivoted away suddenly and grabbed a notepad and pen from his workspace. He handed both to Tavia. "Jot that whole thing down for me again."

She did, and when she passed it back to him, he hissed out a slow curse. "Bugger. I might have guessed it would be something like this." He brought up a browser and typed the sequence into a search engine map. "It's GPS coordinates."

Chase watched as the screen displayed a close-up of an area he immediately recognized. "It's a mountain region in the Czech Republic. Isn't that the area where we found the cave the Ancient had been hibernating in before Dragos woke him and imprisoned him in his lab?"

"The very one," Gideon confirmed. "And Dragos has

been using its coordinates as the password to his entire operation." He barked out an incredulous chuckle. "That's the megalomaniac villain version of using your favorite pet's name, for crissake. Maybe there's hope of beating this asshole yet."

Gideon began clacking away at three keyboards, sliding from monitor to monitor, cracking open data files and laboratory intel on multiple computers like a maestro conducting an opus. Chase and Tavia were all but forgotten in the midst of his geeked excitement.

"I'm impressed," Chase told her, proud and more than a little turned on.

She gave him a smile that went straight to his cock. "We all have our talents."

He was about to ask her if she wanted to see one of his favorites when the thud of approaching boots sounded in the corridor outside. Lucan came in dressed for combat in fatigues and heavy arms, the rest of the warriors garbed likewise, trailing close behind him. They all wore grim expressions, steely-eyed looks that Chase recognized well.

The Order was preparing to head into battle.

"I'm in," Gideon said, wheeling around in his chair to meet them. "Tavia just got us past the security on the lab intel. I'm in it with both hands now."

Lucan's gray eyes swung to her in approval. "Good work."

She gave him a faint nod. "Whatever I can do to help."

"Appreciated," he said, then glanced to Chase and offered a neutral nod of greeting. "I've just spoken with Mathias Rowan to let him know our plans," he told Gideon. "We roll out at sundown tonight to sweep every Enforcement Agency hangout in Boston."

"You mean raid them?" Chase asked.

"Raid them. Raze them. Mow the motherfuckers to the ground, if that's what it takes," Lucan replied, his deep voice vibrating with violent intent.

Chase swore under his breath. "You can't be serious. The truce between the Agency and us is tentative at best. It always has been. If the Order goes into their turf with guns blazing, you'll be doing battle not only with Dragos but with the entire vampire nation."

"We didn't start this war," Lucan snarled. "But we're damned well going to finish it. Even if I have to hack through the ranks of the entire Enforcement Agency to finally get my hands around Dragos's throat. As far as I'm concerned, he and the Agency are two heads on the same snake. I'll gladly sever either one. Let Mathias Rowan sort the bodies after the dust settles."

Chase had never seen Lucan so virulent. Menace rolled off the Order's leader like a dark current, the cold of his rage a palpable force in the room.

"We have patrol tactics to discuss."

We, he said, but Chase could read Lucan's meaning in the level command of his gaze alone. *We* meant the Order, which didn't include him.

"Sure," he said, no animosity in his voice or his veins. He was a liability to the Order now, at a time when they could least afford them. He got that. And he couldn't blame Lucan for shutting him out from this mission.

As much as he might have wanted to think he hadn't lost his brethren completely, Chase understood that he still had a long road ahead of him if he wanted to prove himself worthy of their trust. He only hoped they'd one day give him that chance.

Tavia walked with him out to the corridor, saying nothing as she slipped her hand into his. She didn't need to say anything. She understood. She cared, and he wondered for the hundredth time how he could ever think he deserved her.

"Hey, Harvard."

The low male voice drew him up short in the hallway. Dante stood there, the dark-haired warrior's arms crossed over his chest. His curved titanium daggers—weapons that had taken out countless Rogues and had even found their way under Chase's chin not so long ago—were sheathed like huge claws on his weapons belt. His whiskey-colored eyes narrowed beneath the harsh slash of his dark brows. He gestured over his shoulder with a tilt of his chin. "About what just happened in there . . ."

"Forget it," Chase said. "I want what's good for the Order too. Right now, that's not me."

He started to walk away, but Dante met up with him. Stilled him with a brotherly hand coming to rest on his shoulder. "I just wanted to tell you that it's good to have you back in the compound again. I'm glad you're here."

Chase felt Tavia's eyes on him as he absorbed the offer of truce from the warrior who had once been his tightest ally in the Order. His closest friend. A brother, in every sense of the word. "Thanks." Feeble reply, but all he could muster on his suddenly dry throat.

"Listen, Tess would love it if you and Tavia came around to our quarters sometime. I'd like it too. I'd like to give you a proper introduction to my son."

"Sure." Chase nodded. "Yeah, sure. Of course."

"We'd be honored to meet him," Tavia said, speaking the words that seemed to fail him so spectacularly in that moment.

"Great," Dante said. "That'll be great." He backed away, then abruptly pivoted around again, a wide smirk breaking over his face as his eyes met Chase's across the length of the corridor. "By the way, Merry Christmas, dickhead."

"Same to you." Chase chuckled, falling back into the easy camaraderie they once had. God, he didn't realize how much he'd missed that until just now. "Try not to get your ass handed to you tonight on patrol, yeah?"

Still grinning, Dante gave him a one-fingered salute. His deep laugh rumbled as he headed back to rejoin the other warriors.

CHAPTER
Thirty-two

It was long past midnight and the Order had been on patrol from the moment they arrived in Boston. In that time, they'd smashed down the doors of a dozen Enforcement Agency sip-and-strips and known hangouts in and around the city.

Lucan had no intention of calling it a night until they'd raided every last one.

Few of the Agents they'd interrogated had confessed to knowing anything about traitors within their ranks. But there was one name that came up on battered and bloodied lips more than once: Arno Pike.

"His Darkhaven is in the North End," Mathias Rowan reported. Lucan had called the Agency director for a quick rundown on the bastard as Kade, Brock, and Hunter cleaned up the carnage they'd left in the most recent raid.

"Any kin at his place?"

"None," Rowan said. "Pike lives alone, no immediate family. He had a mate until about a year ago, but she died. Says here she was mugged in Dorchester, strangled."

Lucan grunted. "Convenient. Address?"

Rowan rattled off a swanky street in an area of multimillion-dollar brownstones. Lucan typed it into a text on a second phone he carried and sent it out to the rest of the Order's boots on the ground.

"Lucan, look. You know I'm on board with whatever you deem necessary to stop Dragos. And I mean stop him dead. But my dispatch lines are out of control. You've got civilians calling in, terrified of what they're hearing. The word among the Breed population here in Boston is that you've lost your goddamn mind. They're saying you've finally snapped, that on your command the Order is kicking down Darkhaven doors and hauling unarmed civilians into the streets at gunpoint."

Lucan exhaled a ripe curse. "The same shit they've been saying about the Order for years, decades."

"Except now it's true." Rowan's voice sounded weary. "And it's Christmas, for fuck's sake. How long do you mean for this mission to go on?"

"Until I rout Dragos and all his followers out of hiding, once and for all."

Rowan's answering silence stretched long. In the pall of his heavy contemplation, Lucan's cell phone rang with another incoming call. He told the Agent to hang on and switched over to accept the other line.

Niko's voice answered his clipped greeting. "Lucan, we've got Pike."

"Where are you?"

"Southie, down by the Mystic. Rio and I chased the son of a bitch into a vacant warehouse. Want us to hold him for you, or can we start hurting him for intel now?"

"Hold him," Lucan growled. He was already moving,

motioning into the sacked Agency club for Hunter to follow him. "I'm on the way now. Bringing along backup for the interrogation. If hurting Pike doesn't get us anywhere, I'll have Hunter bleed the truth out of him."

He disconnected, then informed Rowan of the situation as he and Hunter jumped into the waiting Rover and sped for Southie like a bat out of hell.

Although Arno Pike hadn't suffered more than a few scrapes and bruises in his detainment, the male looked like shit. Smelled like it too. Piss anyway, and a bitter acridness that went beyond fear. Lucan could hardly stand the rank stench that rolled off the vampire as he and Hunter walked into the warehouse where Nikolai and Rio waited with the Agent.

"You're a popular guy, Pike," Lucan said as he approached the male who slumped on a rusted metal chair. "You'd be shocked to hear how many Agents mentioned your name tonight when we asked them who they'd point to as someone most likely to turn traitor to his own race. You're the undisputed winner. Congratulations."

"I can't wait to see what he's won," Niko said, his teeth and fangs gleaming in the gloom of the abandoned building.

"You've overstepped your bounds this time," Pike charged, his voice thin but nonetheless malicious. Sweat beaded on his pale face and throat. His cheeks were sallow and drawn, his lips white, bloodless, as he spoke. "The Order has made many enemies tonight. The Enforcement Agency will not let these unwarranted raids and harassment go uncontested."

"The Agency can contest all they want," Lucan replied. "Meanwhile the Order intends to turn the fucking organization inside out to shake loose the traitors."

Pike started to laugh, wheezing a bit. "You're too late, warrior. You'll never stop him now."

Lucan's mind went dark with the vision Mira had shown him. So much blood in the streets. Countless lives lost, Breed and human alike. The screams of terror and mourning, the wails of the dying, filling the night.

Before he knew he'd taken the first step, Lucan was bearing down on Pike where he sat. "What do you mean, I'm too late?" he snarled, fury seething through his veins. "Tell me what you know about Dragos's plans!"

Pike's jaw clamped tight. His bleary eyes were mutinous, stubbornly resistant. "I'll never tell you. You'll have to kill me."

"Not a problem," Lucan growled. "But first, you will talk. Or I promise you, you'll be begging for death."

Pike tittered, maniacal now. "You'll never get anything out of me. Not from any of us who are loyal to him."

God help him, Lucan wanted nothing more than to rip out the male's throat. But he held his rage in check, if only by a fraction. "There are other ways to get what we need from you, asshole."

He nodded to Hunter. The Gen One assassin could read a Breed male's memories through blood. One bite and all of Pike's secrets would be known. Hunter strode forward, baring his fangs as he neared. "Hit him," Lucan commanded blandly.

Hunter took hold of Pike's wrist and struck it hard. He recoiled an instant later, spitting out the blood on a curse. He looked at Lucan, his golden eyes furious as he wiped away the red stains on his mouth. "He's taken poison."

"Son of a bitch," Lucan hissed.

They all stared at Pike, who was laughing now, even as he dropped to the floor and began to convulse. Foam curdled around his mouth as the poison tightened its hold on him. "You're too late, Lucan. Just like I told you." His giggle cut short on a pained groan. He started gasping for air, already in the throes of death.

"Come on," Lucan said, motioning for the others to follow him. "Let's get the fuck out of here."

As they left Arno Pike writhing and dying in the middle of the vacant warehouse, the vampire's taunts echoed behind them.

"You're too late . . . Dragos has already won."

CHAPTER
Thirty-three

Tavia cried out in pleasure as she arched beneath Chase, swept into the thrall of her third orgasm in as many hours. Her bliss was sharp-edged and raw, untempered. She rode it with abandon, curling her fingers into the hard muscles of his shoulders as he rocked into her body at a fevered, animal pace.

She loved the way he fucked her. Loved how strong and powerful he was, something unearthly and dark. She loved that he coaxed the same from her. Loved how he welcomed the savage, needful part of her that was anything but human. Demanded it from her. And she loved how every touch and kiss and fevered thrust claimed her as his.

She *was* his; her heart knew it as surely as did her molten blood and body.

A hiss escaped her as he plunged deep into her core, filling her, touching a place that belonged only to him. She threw her head back on the pillows, lips peeled back from her teeth and fangs as she gave a ragged shout of release. "Yes. Oh, fuck, Chase . . . harder. Don't stop."

With a roar boiling from between his gritted teeth, he grabbed her ass in his hands and hauled her to him, lifting her hips up to meet the crashing intensity of his thrusts. He pounded her with unbridled fury. His cock stretched her tight around him, as hard as steel inside her, relentless, dominating.

A snarl tore loose from him as he pumped harder, deeper, their amber gazes locked. His *glyphs* were wild and alive with dark colors, all the shades of desire and need. Hues that rode her own bare skin as he pushed her toward the crest of another orgasm. He bore down on her with tight, fevered strokes, his fangs huge and gleaming under the harsh twist of his beautiful mouth.

"Tavia," he rasped, shuddering against her with the force of his release. The hot rush of his seed flooded her, and she came with him, panting and mewling as her body detonated around him, her senses shattering into a million glittering pieces.

In its wake, there was hunger.

She hadn't fed since the first time with him. Now, with her every nerve ending alive and electrified, she craved his blood with a ferocity that bordered on madness. She couldn't keep her eyes from the throbbing pulse at the side of his strong neck.

Her mouth was tinder dry. Her gums pounded at the base of her extended fangs. She wet her parched lips, gazing up at him from under the thirst-heavy droop of her eyelids.

He understood her need. His amber irises flared brighter, pupils thinning to slivers as he watched her home in on his drumming heartbeat.

"Christ," he whispered, reverence and profanity all in the same breath.

She lifted up from the bed, bracing her palm against his chest and shoving him onto his back. His lungs sawed as she crawled up onto him, his body hot and powerful beneath her. She bent forward, licked a slow path along the taut column of his throat, playing the tip of her tongue over the fat vein that ticked so deliciously below the surface of his smooth skin.

She teased it with the sharp tips of her fangs, wringing a strangled groan from him in the instant before she sank her teeth deep into his flesh.

She moaned as his blood gushed over her tongue, hot and tingly and dark. She swallowed it greedily, relishing the spicy, exotic taste of him. As she fed, he lay rigid beneath her and stroked her back and unbound hair. She didn't know if her feeding brought him the same contentment it did her. All she knew was the thrumming beat of his pulse against her lips and in her ears, the drowning roar of his blood as it flowed into her muscles, bones, and cells. It quelled the savage pound of her senses. Nourished her as though she'd been starving for it all her life.

When she'd had her fill, reluctantly she swept her tongue over the punctures to seal them.

She didn't realize his anguish until she dragged her sated gaze up to his face. His lips were bloodless, drawn back from his teeth and fangs in a tortured grimace. He rolled away from her on a rough curse, his big body shuddering as he swung his legs over the edge of the bed and raked his trembling fingers into his damp hair.

His hunger owned him. It raked through her now, the savagery of his blood thirst eclipsing all the pleasure and comfort she'd taken so selfishly from his vein. It tore her open inside, bringing with it a cold, empty ache in the pit of her soul.

God, how he suffered now.

She didn't know how he could withstand such agony. Just the echo of it in her own blood was enough to suck the air from her lungs.

She gasped, clutching at her abdomen as his pain knocked her down onto the bed. She writhed with it, her body jackknifing as the anguish of his hunger swam through her like black, burning acid.

He was hurting her.

The thought slammed into his hungered mind even before he pivoted to find Tavia's naked body constricted in an anguished ball in the middle of the bed.

Ah, Christ.

"Tavia?"

It killed him to see her in such pain, to know that it was his agony clawing at her. His affliction transferred to her through the blood connection of Tavia's bond to him. Because of that bond, his suffering was hers.

And his regret for that was fathomless.

"Tavia, look at me," he murmured, moving back toward her on the bed. He smoothed his hand over her head, hissing as he felt the fevered heat of her skin when he brushed his fingertips across her sweat-sheened brow. "Tell me you're all right."

She moaned as another wave of hunger burned through him like wildfire. When she opened her eyes, he saw pure misery in the bright amber pools of her irises. Her *dermaglyphs* were churning furiously, steeped in the same angry hues as his own skin.

His choked curse was ash on his tongue. He'd never

felt so helpless, so full of hatred for himself and the disease he knew would one day destroy him. But not even Bloodlust compared to the agony of seeing Tavia in distress. Knowing he was causing it.

He had to feed.

The reality arrowed through him, cold and undeniable.

He needed blood to ease the pain—for her. His own pain meant nothing except for the hurt it was delivering to the woman he cared about more than life itself.

The woman he loved.

Tears streaked Tavia's cheeks as she looked up at him from her tight fetal position on the bed. Her breath rushed between her parted lips in rapid pants, her body shuddering and writhing.

Goddamn it. And damn him as well.

He couldn't leave her like this to go and hunt. There was no telling how long he'd have to run before he found prey, and meanwhile Tavia would be suffering alone.

"Help me, Chase." Her voice was a threadbare whisper, frayed and fragile. So naked and trusting. She reached out to him, letting her hand fall open before him on the bed. "Please . . . do it. Make this pain go away."

He stared at her, feeling the last scrap of his questionable honor slip away as his hungered gaze settled on the pulse that throbbed between the delicate bones and tendons of her outstretched wrist.

He should have refused the temptation. He should have found another way—anything but the solution that was offered before him now. The one that would bind him to Tavia irrevocably. Eternally.

But even as he struggled to deny the thing his heart craved most, Chase found himself positioned above her on the bed. With utmost care and trembling hands, he lifted her arm up toward his mouth. Set the sharp tips of his fangs against her tender skin.

Swore under his breath as he sank them into her vein and drew the first taste of her blood.

Holy hell, she was sweet.

Her blood hit his tongue like nectar from a forbidden vine. He drank her down, feeling a rush of electricity and power blast into every starving cell of his body. The strength of it hit him like a blow to the chest. An explosion that awakened his senses, lit them up with the force of a supernova.

He'd heard the blood bond was a powerful thing, but he hadn't been prepared. Not even close. Some distant bit of logic reminded him that Tavia was not only Breedmate but Breed, the intensity of that combination making itself known to him now, as he felt her blood rocketing through him.

The humans he'd fed upon to excess so often before could've been made of dust for all he knew now. Tavia's blood was a drug unlike anything he'd ever tasted before.

He couldn't get enough of her.

His mouth fastened tightly over her wrist, he drank hard and deep.

He couldn't make himself stop.

Not even when her hand curled into a fist and the tendons in her arm went taut beneath his lips. Not even when she gave a little moan, calling his name on an uncertain gasp.

It wasn't until he felt her fear, bone-deep and chilling, seeping through their bond that he found the strength to release her. Barely.

Her eyes were wide, dread-filled as she stared at him now. No longer glowing amber with pleasure and desire, but bright green and full of a terror that tore him apart inside.

Her cheeks were pale, her *dermaglyphs* drained of most of their color. She held her bleeding wrist to her chest, her finger wrapped around the wounds. "Chase," she whispered brokenly. "I'm sorry I panicked. I was afraid. You were taking so much and I . . ."

Jesus Christ.

He could hardly bear to think what he might have done if the blood bond hadn't alerted him to her terror. It was his greatest fear, causing her any kind of harm.

To realize how close he'd been just now was more than he could take.

All the worse when what he craved more than anything was to take her beneath him once more and lose himself in the pleasure of her body while he drowned in the sweet intoxication of her blood.

"I can't be near you like this," he heard himself tell her, although his voice was hardly recognizable, even to his own ears. The words sawed out of him in a feral tangle, harsh and sharp-edged. "I can't do this ever again. I *won't*."

"Chase," she said, reaching out to him with her wounded arm.

The scent of her blood slammed into him like a bullet. He flinched away, averting his gaze as he backed toward the far wall. As far from her as he could get. He glanced to the window and the predawn morning outside. A mental command flung the glass open, bringing with it a rush of bracing winter air.

Tavia got up from the bed and started toward him. "Chase, please. Don't shut me out . . . let me help you."

He allowed himself one last look at her. Then he pivoted out the window and vanished into the darkness.

CHAPTER
Thirty-four

Tavia took her time showering and getting dressed, listening for Chase's return.

But it had been more than two hours. Daybreak would be coming soon, and he was still gone. Possibly gone from her life for good.

She staggered under the weight of that thought.

It was impossible to think of her life as it was now—her new life, the one based finally in truth—and not imagine Chase as part of it. She was bonded to him, not only by blood. She cared about him deeply. She loved him, and would have done so even without the unbreakable connection that linked her to him on a visceral, preternatural level.

And because she loved him, she couldn't stay there now.

He was right; what happened between them earlier could never happen again. She'd felt the power of his hunger, the depth of his mounting addiction. She'd felt how intensely he had reacted to her blood. How easy it would have been for him to lose control completely and slide over the edge of an abyss from which he might never return.

She couldn't bear to contribute to his struggle.

As she stepped out into the corridor from the bedroom, she heard some of the Order's women talking where they'd apparently gathered in the kitchen. The aromas of freshly brewed coffee and breakfast drifted toward her, along with the Breedmates' quiet conversation.

"Think about it for a minute now. Haven't you ever wondered what it is that makes us different from other women?" The velvety voice belonged to Savannah. "What if Jenna's dream can explain some of that?"

"Atlanteans? You can't be serious." This from Rio's mate, Dylan.

Gabrielle answered her. "It wasn't that long ago that most of us were saying the same thing about the Breed. Not that I'm finding it any easier to wrap my head around the idea that the birthmarks we all share have some kind of link to an immortal race of warriors."

Tavia took a few steps up the corridor and saw Hunter's ebony-haired Breedmate come out of the kitchen with plates for the dining room table. Corinne spoke as she set the places. "I was orphaned as an infant and taken in by a Darkhaven family. Never knew either of my birth parents. Neither did my adopted sister, Charlotte."

"That's true of you and Elise and Renata and Mira," Dylan replied. "But how do you explain the rest of us?"

"You can add Eva and Danika to that list too," Savannah said. "Both of them were foundlings, raised in the Darkhavens."

Tavia really didn't want to be noticed, particularly

creeping out from the bedroom like a wraith, but there was no clear shot to the front door without someone seeing her. She paused as Elise came out of the kitchen with a tray full of stacked cups and saucers.

"Actually, most of the Breedmates I've known were either orphaned or abandoned as babies or young children. That's how so many of us end up in foster care or runaway shelters."

Dylan came out carrying a steaming mug of coffee. "Well, I knew my dad, and he was nothing special. Just a garden-variety huckster, con man, and drunk who caused my family a lot of heartbreak before he split for good. Tess's father died in a car crash when she was a teenager. And didn't Alex's dad pass from Alzheimer's?"

"He did," Kade's Breedmate from Alaska replied as she handed off silverware to Corinne. "Hank Maguire was the only dad I ever had, but he wasn't my birth father. My mom never told me who my real father was. She took that secret with her when she died."

"I never knew my parents either," Gabrielle put in. "My mother was institutionalized as a teenage Jane Doe soon after I was born. All my records are sitting in DCF files somewhere in Boston."

"We can't forget Claire's father," Dylan added, obviously unswayed. "He and her mother were both killed in Africa by rebel warfare. So that rules him out as an immortal."

"Look," Jenna said, coming out of the kitchen now too. "I'm not trying to say I know all of this for sure, but I know what I saw. The Ancients were at war with a race of beings that were something other than human. They hunted these warriors over centuries, across continents. And the only way to kill them was by taking their heads."

"Hi, Tavia." Mira had come out of a room off the hallway and strode right past her with a little wave of greeting. "Are you going to have breakfast with us?"

"Oh. I . . ." She glanced up to find several pairs of eyes on her now. Elise, Dylan, and Gabrielle had come into the corridor to look at her questioningly. "I was just . . . taking a little walk, that's all."

Mira shrugged. "Okay. But you won't want to miss out on blueberry pancakes with whipped cream."

As the girl wandered into the kitchen with the other Breedmates, only Elise remained. Her soft eyes were sympathetic. Far too knowing for Tavia's comfort. "Something happened with Sterling." Not a question, a gentle statement of fact. "Is he gone again?"

Tavia nodded, seeing no sense in denying it. "A couple of hours ago. I don't know if he'll be coming back."

Elise let out a small sigh. "I'm sorry. I saw how he was with you. If he left, don't think it's a question of whether or not he cares for you. It was plain to me—to everyone—that he does."

Tavia shrugged, managed a faint smile. "I can't stay now either."

The female's expression went a bit cautious. "Perhaps you should talk with Lucan first."

"Is that a polite way of telling me I'm not allowed to leave?" She exhaled a soft apology. "When Chase comes back—*if* he comes back—I don't want to make things harder for him. He needs the Order."

"Yes," Elise agreed. "I think he needs you too."

Tavia shook her head, wishing that was true. "I have to go."

"Stay for breakfast, at least," Elise offered. "The warriors and Renata will be here before sunrise. Perhaps Sterling will be back by then too."

"I can't," Tavia replied. She glanced past Elise as Dylan popped her fiery red head out from the dining room.

"Are we setting another place at the table?"

"That's what we're discuss—" Elise's words were left unfinished.

Because in the time it took for her to swivel her blond head around to answer Dylan, Tavia had summoned the speed given to her by her Breed genetics and had disappeared out the front door.

He was an idiot.

It had taken him several hours to arrive at that realization. Several dozen miles of running like a wild animal through the cold, dark wilderness to understand he would never be able to get far enough away from his biggest problem: himself.

He had to face his demons, not hope he could outpace them or deny them.

Tavia had been teaching him that by example from the moment he first laid eyes on her. He'd just been too thick-headed to grasp the concept.

He'd hurt her earlier, scared her, and he needed to repair that damage—if she'd let him.

He didn't know how to live with someone, how to love someone the way a special female like Tavia deserved, but he wanted to try. As unsure as he was about proving himself worthy of her, he could not imagine his life without her.

He loved her, and if it took locking himself up below the Order's new compound to starve the Bloodlust out of him, then he was damn well good and ready to get started.

His bare feet flew over the snow and ice of the forest floor. He felt none of the cold, only the warm promise of a future he hoped to convince Tavia to share with him as his mate.

But as the sprawling bulk of the stone-and-timber compound appeared in the distance ahead of him, Chase realized she was gone.

He felt her absence even before he climbed back in through the window she'd left open in the bedroom where they'd made love. Where he'd fallen on her like the animal he was and fed until she was weeping and terrified. His blood told him she was nowhere near now.

By the vacant chill of his veins, he guessed that she was easily miles away. He'd lost her, probably forever.

He should be relieved, for her, if not himself. She'd made the decision for him. The safest one. The only one that wouldn't put her life at risk every time she got near him.

He sat down on the edge of the empty bed, naked, bereft.

Dawn was rising, sending slivers of pale pink light down through the thick canopy of pines outside. He watched it for a moment, unable to summon the desire to close the shutters. The house's electronic security took care of it for him, automated steel louvers locking tight, blotting out the morning.

He didn't know how long he sat there. When the hard rap sounded on the door behind him, his voice was a rusty sound in the back of his parched throat. "Yeah."

"Harvard." Dante spoke through the closed slab of hand-hewn wood. "You two decent in there, man?"

Chase gave a faint scoff. "She's gone," he murmured.

The door opened and Dante stepped inside. "Jesus, it's freezing in here. What do you mean, she's gone?"

Chase pivoted his head to meet his old friend's confused frown, turning amber high beams on him. The warrior lifted his chin, dark brows rising as he took in Chase's feral appearance. "Ah, shit. You didn't—"

"I drank from her," Chase admitted. "Things got . . . out of hand. I scared her pretty bad. I hurt her, and now she's gone."

Dante stared at him for a long moment, studying him. "You care about this female."

"I love her. That should be reason enough for me to let her go, right?" He slowly shook his head, considering how much better off she'd be without him. "I'm the last thing she needs in her life."

"More than likely," Dante replied, grave. No mercy in his voice or in the sober eyes that held Chase's amber-swamped gaze. "She doesn't need you in her life like this, my friend. Nobody who cares about you wants to be there to watch when you crash and burn. I'd say least of all her. I don't mean to be harsh. You're trying to get your shit together, I can see that."

"Yeah," Chase agreed. "I have to. I want to prove to her that I can beat this."

Dante shook his head. "No, man. First, you have to want to prove it to yourself."

CHAPTER
Thirty-five

Dawn was cold and brittle, clouding Tavia's breath as she stood on the stoop of the little house she'd called home until roughly a week ago. Yellow crime scene tape sealed the front door, which was still festooned with a ribboned Christmas wreath and sleigh bells that jangled as she broke the tape and stepped inside.

The house was silent, tomblike. A shell that now felt as empty and foreign to her as the life she'd been living inside its walls.

The lies she'd been living.

Tavia moved through the place with a sense of detachment. None of what was here belonged to her. Not the homespun furniture or cheery fixtures. Not even the photographs on the walls—snapshot collages of another time, a scattered chronology of her childhood and teenage years. Time that had been carefully monitored and manufactured, constructed of countless falsehoods and betrayals.

These mementos of her past had seemed so real once.

Her life had seemed so normal until a week ago. She'd been happy for the most part, enjoying her home life and her career, accepting that the world she lived in was the one in which she belonged. How could it have seemed so real for so long, yet been nothing more than a monstrous lie?

It didn't matter anymore.

She let all of it go, here and now.

There was no bitterness as she looked around her, nothing but calm acceptance as her gaze panned the kitchen, its cream-colored floor marred by a ghastly brown bloodstain where the Minion pretending to be her aunt had fallen after taking her own life at Dragos's command.

It was only when she thought of him—Dragos, the chief orchestrator of her betrayal, who'd ruined or taken so many other lives through his unconscionable actions— that Tavia felt a flare of rage ignite in her gut. For what he did to her and the others like her, for what he'd done to the Order during their quest to defeat him, for the evil he was certain to be perpetrating even now, she hoped his end was coming soon.

A dark part of her—a powerful, predatory part of her that was becoming more familiar to her than one she'd known for the past twenty-seven years—wanted to be there the day that Dragos took his last breath. She growled with the need for bloody, final vengeance, her *glyphs* churning with palpable fury beneath her clothes.

But as much as she wanted a hand in Dragos's demise, she couldn't let a personal need for retaliation get in the way of the Order. This was their battle, not hers. The same way Chase's battle with Bloodlust was his to fight. He hadn't invited her help, nor did he want it. A point he'd made abundantly, heartbreakingly clear to her.

She wasn't a part of Chase's world or the Order's, no more than she was a part of the one surrounding her in the cramped confines of this dead Minion's house.

She needed to find her own place of belonging now, wherever that might be. The problem was, no matter how she tried to picture her life going forward, it was Chase's handsome, haunted face she saw in front of her.

She loved him. She belonged to him in every way, and she would for always.

Even if his disease never let him go.

A deep foreboding had settled over the compound as the morning crept by. The news of Chase and Tavia's conflict and her subsequent departure earlier that day was only another complication in a situation that had everyone sober and on edge.

Dragos was hatching something big.

No one could be sure just what he had in store, but the Order's interrogation of one of his lieutenants in Boston last night had left all of the warriors in a state of grim expectation. It didn't help matters that, at barely ten A.M., daylight would keep the Order hostage indoors for the next five or six hours.

While most of them were gathered elsewhere to run through intel and patrol tactics with Lucan, Gideon and Lazaro Archer sat in the makeshift tech lab along with Dylan and Jenna. At roughly a thousand years old, Archer was one of the eldest of his race, older even than Lucan. Not that anyone would guess the handsome, jet-haired Breed male with the midnight blue eyes was more than a day over thirty.

It was only when he spoke of witnessing the Norman Conquest of England and the Christian Crusades as though they happened last year that the disparity between his staggering life experience and youthful appearance made Jenna's mind boggle.

"So, you think it's possible that the Ancients might've been actively hunting a race that wasn't quite human?" she asked him.

Archer considered for a moment. "Anything is possible. It might help explain the many times my own father—one of the original eight otherworlders—would disappear for months on end when I was a boy. He spoke from time to time of gatherings with his brethren. They could have easily been hunting operations as you saw in the dream."

"Why kill them?" Jenna wondered aloud. "I mean, what was the problem between them?"

Archer lifted one bulky shoulder. "The Ancients were a conquering race. We've seen that in your journals, in the history we've collected from your other dreams. My father and his kind had no humanity in them, even less mercy."

"He's right," Gideon put in from across the room, where he was typing on his computer keyboards, hacking through what had to be thousands of records recovered from Dragos's dead lieutenant in New Orleans. "Before the Order took them down, the Ancients blew through human settlements like locusts. They fed, they raped, they slaughtered. Resist their will, and they would annihilate you."

Jenna nodded, recalling the nightmare of the wave that consumed an entire population. The mention of the escaped queen who'd refused to surrender to the Ancients. Her city had been toppled in response. Her legion pursued with a dogged purpose.

"Let's say all of this is true," Dylan added now, swiveling around in her chair. "Even if there was another nonhuman race of beings on this planet and some kind of supernatural grudge match between them and the fathers of the Breed, that still doesn't mean every Breedmate has an Atlantean father hiding in her closet."

Gideon smirked. "Speaking of which, how'd that hack I wrote for Gabrielle with Department of Children and Families work out?"

"She accessed her records, but there wasn't much to discover," Jenna replied. "Both parents are listed as J. Does. Her teenage mom was too far gone mentally to provide any specific detail when she was committed. As for Gabrielle's father, it's anyone's guess. Her mom mentioned a boyfriend, a seasonal worker who disappeared soon after she became pregnant."

Gideon's brows lifted, his blue eyes intrigued. "Male of unknown origins who disappeared after getting a young woman pregnant?"

"Oh, come on," Dylan interjected. "Don't tell me you actually think this is possible too? Of everyone, I expected you to be the voice of reason."

"There is logic in the notion." He lifted his hands in surrender. "I'm just saying."

"Claire is looking into details about her parents' deaths in Africa," Jenna added. "It's been some fifty years now, but the relief group her mother worked for kept pretty good accounts. She thinks she might have answers in a couple of days."

Dylan stared, still skeptical. "And there's the matter of Tess's father. Dying in a car accident is a pretty mortal way to go."

Jenna shrugged. "I know. I need to get some more information from her about that before I can rule anything out."

Dylan gave a shake of her thick red hair. "Meanwhile, it makes perfect sense to you all that these immortal warriors—this Atlantean legion that serves an exiled queen—have been walking around the planet undetected for thousands of years."

Everyone glanced her way now, three pairs of eyebrows lifted in question. She blew out an exasperated gust of air and threw up her hands. "Yeah, yeah, I know. But the Breed is different. The Breed banded together, colonized. They protect their own. If there's some kind of immortal race out there who's fathering offspring and walking away without ever looking back, then I want no part of it."

"Maybe it's safer for them if they leave," Jenna guessed.

Dylan frowned. "Safer for an immortal?"

"No," Lazaro Archer replied. "Safer for their daughters if they never know who their true fathers are. At least until the last of the immortals' sworn enemies is dead."

Jenna looked at him. "The last of the Ancients may be dead, but his memories and history are still alive and well inside me. Possibly somewhere close to forever, if Gideon's right about my longevity odds."

"Maybe that was the point." Archer's ageless eyes glimmered with shrewd intellect. "He was the last of his kind on this planet. For all he knew, he could have been the last of his entire race. If the Ancient understood his death was coming, ego may have made him seek out some way to keep a part of him alive."

"So, why would he make me choose if I wanted to be his walking, talking memory box?" Jenna asked. "He gave me a choice between life or death that night. What did he mean by that?"

Archer grew more serious, grimly so. "Maybe we have much to learn about these immortals. And through you, the Ancient has given us that chance."

As that statement hung over the room, one of Gideon's computers beeped. He swung around and typed a flurry of keystrokes. "You gotta be kidding me. Can it actually be that easy?"

While Jenna and the others watched, he jogged over to a table containing half a dozen thick black collars. Ultraviolet obedience collars engineered by Dragos's operation and outfitted on all of his laboratory-raised Gen One assassins. Hunter and Nathan had both worn them while they served Dragos, and they'd both been damn lucky to be free of them without having lost their heads in the process.

As for the assassins who'd once worn the assortment of collars on Gideon's table? Not so fortunate. Hunter had been collecting the devices from every one of Dragos's personal army that he killed. Most of the polymer rings had been detonated beyond repair—a hazard of retrieval. But there were a couple that Gideon had reengineered. It was one of those he fetched now.

"Thanks to Tavia, I was able to get past some password-protected, encrypted files," he explained as he carried the collar over to a lidded, large metal box beside his workstation and placed it inside. Then he picked up a cell phone he'd jury-rigged as a remote control. He started typing a sequence on the keypad. "If my calculations are correct, this code should reset the detonator to neutral."

The device in the box emitted a low hum in response.

"Ah, shit." Gideon's expression went a bit slack. "Archer, hit the deck!"

Before Jenna knew what was happening, she and

Dylan were whisked to the floor beneath the sheltering bulk of two Breed males—just as a beam of intense UV light burst from under the lid of the metal box. It was gone just as quickly, evaporating like a brilliant ray of sunlight doused by shadow.

"Holy hell," Gideon said, rising to let Jenna loose from beneath him. The protection was unnecessary for Dylan and her, but Gideon and Archer were a different story. Gideon raked a hand through his mussed spiky blond hair, giving his geeky genius look an added dose of dishevelment. "Well, I'll be damned. That's a first."

"You've never seen one of those things detonate before?" Archer asked, giving Dylan a hand up from the floor beside him.

Gideon grunted, shook his head. "No. I've never been wrong before." He cracked a cockeyed smile a second later. "But now I know how to blow these suckers up on demand."

Just then, Tess appeared in the open doorway of the tech lab. She glanced at all of them, then looked around the room as if she sensed something recently amiss. "Savannah said you wanted to see me, Jenna?"

"Yeah," she said, meeting the Breedmate's gentle aquamarine gaze. "I wanted to ask you a couple of questions about your father."

"Sure, but there's not much to tell. He died back in Chicago when I was fourteen."

"Car accident," Dylan said from beside Jenna.

Tess nodded. "That's right. Why do you want to know?"

"Are you sure it was a car accident?" Jenna pressed.

"Positive. He was in a convertible, speeding. My father always loved driving too fast." She smiled sadly. "He was larger than life. Utterly fearless."

Jenna felt sorry for the young girl who lost a parent she obviously adored. "How did the accident happen?"

"Witnesses said he dodged to avoid hitting a dog that ran in front of him. He swerved into oncoming traffic. There was a semi coming the opposite way."

Jenna had seen enough head-on collisions in her work as a Statie in Alaska. She could imagine what had happened. But she still needed to hear the answer from the Breedmate herself. "How did he die, Tess?"

"He was decapitated. He died instantly."

CHAPTER
Thirty-six

"I sure hate to see a pretty woman drinking alone."

Tavia didn't bother to glance up when the middle-age suit down the bar from her at the hotel lounge finally worked up the nerve to saunter over and attempt to strike up a conversation. Her drink was long gone and her burger-and-fries lunch sat barely touched in front of her. "I'm not looking for company."

"I hear ya. Had my fill of people the past couple of days too. Holidays are a bitch like that." His domestic light beer sloshed in the longneck bottle as he gestured to the empty seat beside her. "Care if I sit down?"

She practically snarled. "Would it matter if I said yes?"

He chuckled as if that was invitation enough and plopped down next to her. Without looking at him, she sized him up by scent alone. Cheap hotel soap and designer cologne on his skin, neither of which masked the trace musk of recent sex that clung to him. Fabric softener and spray starch on the white button-down he wore under his discount outlet suit that still carried the tang of jet fuel exhaust from being packed in his luggage on the flight. He wasn't wearing a ring when he came over, but she didn't have to check to know that she'd find a faint outline of one against the tan he probably picked up at Disney World with the family not too long ago.

"You in Boston on business?" she asked.

He set his empty on the bar and pivoted in his seat to face her. "Sales convention here in the hotel the next couple of days. Just got in this afternoon."

Tavia gave him a tight smile, barely resisting the urge to flash a little fang. "You sure don't waste any time. Your wife know you fuck around on her when you're out of town?"

He got quiet all of a sudden. "My . . . what the hell do you know about my wife?"

She smirked into her plate as he slid off the stool in a huff and shuffled away to rejoin some of the other men in his pack.

Alone once more, Tavia couldn't suppress her soft bark of laughter. Heightened senses could prove quite amusing in this new life she was going to be living as one of the Breed.

She motioned for the bill and began digging in the pocket of her jeans for her money. Before she'd left the house that day, she'd taken the two hundred dollars emergency cash from the kitchen drawer. Not like anyone was going to miss it, after all. Unfortunately, it wouldn't last long, and then she'd have to figure something else out.

She already felt guilty enough, having appropriated a room on her own when the hotel refused to give her one without a credit card and proper ID. It had taken her only a few tries to mentally unlock a vacant room near a stairwell exit. Easy escape, in case someone opened it legitimately with a key and she had to get out of there fast.

"Need anything else here?" the bartender asked as he came over with the check.

Tavia shook her head. "I'm all set." She eyed the total and left him a healthy tip, more than ready to be gone from the place now that the bar was filling up with a dozen more businessmen who reeked of cheap beer, cigarettes, and bad cologne.

She swung off the stool and could hardly get through the crowd that was thickening inside the cramped lounge. They moved en masse toward a flat-screen monitor mounted in the corner of the place at the other end of the bar. She thought maybe there was a big game under way, until several of the gathered men crossed themselves, eyes wide, transfixed by the television.

"Holy shit," someone muttered darkly. "Turn that up, will ya?"

The volume bar inched up to full blast and Tavia stared, horrified, as a live newscast played from a satellite link overseas. The reporter was speaking in German, but there was no need to understand the language in order to comprehend what was being said.

The scene taking place on several simultaneous video feeds behind him was utter chaos.

People racing through the darkened city streets, screaming, wailing. Running for their lives. Wild gunfire popping in the distance. Smoke rising from storefronts and high-rises. Cars abandoned in the middle of intersections, doors flung open, metal twisted and crushed by a brute force unlike anything mankind had ever witnessed before.

And the bodies. Dozens of them, strewn about like broken, bloodied dolls.

The reporter went on, his voice cracking with emotion as he attempted to choke back tears while his city was being sacked in front of the world at large. In the end, he lost it. A sob ripped out of him, and in the moment before he dissolved into an unintelligible howl of anguish and terror, one word echoed like a scream in Tavia's heart.

"*Vampires.*"

Lucan couldn't feel his legs.

For the first time in his life, he felt utterly powerless. He stood in the great room of the makeshift, inadequately equipped compound and listened on speaker phone with the rest of the Order's household as Andreas Reichen reported in from Berlin.

At sundown, Enforcement Agency rehabilitation facilities all over Europe were thrown open, setting loose hundreds of blood-addicted Rogues on an unsuspecting, unprepared human public.

"It's primarily the larger cities that are seeing the worst of the carnage right now," Reichen said, his accented voice grim and wooden. "In Germany: Berlin, Frankfurt, Munich. France is reporting scores of casualties as well. Poland and the Czech Republic too. More reports are being broadcast live every hour."

Lucan wanted to roar his fury. He wanted to destroy something, bellow his rage until the house came down around his ears in a pile of burning rubble. But he couldn't even unfist his clenched hands. He could hardly form words in his throat, which had gone dust dry and thick the moment the first newscasts delivered word of the vampire attacks overseas only a few minutes ago.

And now Reichen had confirmed the worst.

Dragos was behind it all. This was his checkmate move. The one Lucan hadn't seen coming. The one he never would have believed Dragos capable of, it was so incomprehensible. So final.

Arno Pike's taunting words from last night came back to him like a punch to the gut.

You're too late . . . Dragos has already won.

How could the Order fix this?

How could they contain the situation when the number of freed Rogues surpassed them by scores and were spread throughout multiple regions across the globe?

How could anyone hope to undo the damage Dragos had wrought in this single act of retaliation?

The veil of secrecy—of tentative peace—the Breed had lived behind for so long, for millennia—had been ripped away. And it could never be put back. Their kind were exposed to the human world in the worst possible way.

As monsters.

As killers without conscience, without souls.

And the hell of it was, the attacks in Europe were only the beginning. Lucan knew Dragos well enough now to expect that the same carnage and terror would soon be visiting the United States. Canada and Mexico too.

Less than three hours of daylight left.

Nightfall was coming fast.

"Get Mathias Rowan on the phone," he told Gideon. "I want a lockdown placed on every Agency rehab facility across North America. Tell him to get it done now!"

While Gideon ran to make the call, Lucan looked at

the warriors and their mates gathered around him now. Dante and Tess, cradling their newborn son. Tegan and Elise, grim with the awareness of the dark world their own son would be inheriting. Rio and Dylan, hands clasped tightly, Rio's scarred face taut and sober. Niko and Renata, both putting on a courageous front as they clutched Mira in a protective embrace. Kade and Alex, huddled close where they stood with Brock and Jenna, his arms wrapped around her as she wept silent tears. Hunter and Corinne, stoic, even though they held each other's hands with white-knuckled intensity, the pair grouped closely with Corinne's son, Nathan, and the Archers. Savannah and Gabrielle stood together on the other side of Lucan, the two women straight-spined and resolute, as brave as any warrior.

And there was Chase as well. He lingered at the edge of the room, uninvited. Nevertheless, he was dressed for battle in night fatigues and combat boots. Weapons bristled from the belt at his lean hips and from the straps that crisscrossed his chest.

Lucan inclined his head in acknowledgment. In trust and thanks. They were going to need all hands on this mission. Chase would never have a better chance to prove himself. Lucan could see from the warrior's gaze that he intended to do just that. Or die trying.

Every pair of eyes was on Lucan, waiting for his decision. Trusting him to make this better. To lead as he'd never been called upon to do before.

He could not fail them.

He would not.

Gideon came back into the room and held a cell phone out to Lucan. "It's Rowan. He says all the North American facilities are offline. Communications are shut down all over the grid. There's no way to call for a lock-down."

Which meant Dragos had anticipated as much and had already covered that base. Lucan cast a grave look at his assembled brethren. "Everybody suit up. We're rolling out before dusk."

CHAPTER
Thirty-seven

Tavia was still shaking as she made her way across town late that afternoon. Everywhere people were talking about the atrocities taking place in Europe. Countries overseas were calling for emergency assistance and disaster relief, desperately pleading for the governments of the United States and other nations to provide immediate military support.

It was horrific and surreal, the shape of the world after just a few hours of unprovoked carnage and bloodshed.

And Tavia was certain that Dragos was at the center of it all.

She'd seen more than one photograph and news video that had captured the feral, bloodstained faces of some of the attackers. The vampires, as the whole of mankind now knew them to be.

They were Rogues, all of them.

For what hadn't been the first time since the word of the attacks, she thought back to what Chase had said about the rehabilitation facilities controlled by the Enforcement Agency. He'd mentioned how widespread the violence would be, how total the carnage, should blood-addicted Rogues suddenly break loose on the human world.

And now Dragos had instigated that very nightmare overseas, Tavia was sure of it.

He had to be stopped. Before he had the chance to wreak any more terror or to put the planet's inhabitants in any more danger.

If only she could find a way to get close to him, she would find a way to kill him.

The seeds of a plan to do just that had been forming in her mind for the past few hours.

She hurried into the Back Bay residential area on foot, sundown having just kissed the city in cool shadows. A light snow fell, muting some of the din from the traffic-clogged streets and anxious, chattering pedestrians on the sidewalks and alleyways.

Tavia saw the familiar brownstone mansion up ahead on the other side of the street. She waited for a mass transit bus to pass, then stepped into the one-way street to cross.

As the great belch of noxious exhaust and steam cleared away, she found herself staring into the face of a monster.

The Rogue stood on the twilit curb, dressed in a tattered, bloodstained institutional jumpsuit. He cocked his head as he stared at her, his face and neck slick with gore from a fresh kill. Tavia's fangs throbbed at the scent of wet red cells, but the spike of adrenaline running through her had nothing to do with hunger. Fear needled her veins, racing up her spine.

Oh, God.

The carnage was about to happen here too.

With an animal sniffle and a low grunt, the Rogue stepped off the curb toward her. Tavia ducked out of his path and ran for the nearest alley. She looked back, making certain he followed.

The knot of dread that formed in her stomach when she saw him loping after her with fangs bared was as cold as ice and put a chill in her blood. She ran deeper into the alley, reaching for the weapon concealed in the back waistband of her jeans.

The Rogue's footsteps were heavy, crunching on the ice that crusted the old pavement.

Tavia slipped behind the corner wall of a brownstone and waited the few seconds before the lumbering bulk of the vampire appeared. Then she struck—silently and swiftly.

The blade stabbed into the Rogue's chest, stopping him dead in his tracks. He grunted something unintelligible, his hands coming up to the wound that was blossoming over his heart.

Already the titanium was doing its business on the Rogue's bloodstream. Racing through the diseased veins and arteries like poison, just as Chase said it would.

It was thanks to that advice that Tavia had paid a visit to an area pawnshop earlier that day, spending half her remaining cash on the blade. So worth it, she thought, watching the Rogue drop to his knees as the metal made quick work of him.

Used titanium hunting knife: sixty-three dollars.

Value: priceless.

She didn't wait to watch the Rogue's body disintegrate into a heap of sizzling goo, then ash. Instead she cleaned the blade and stowed it, then ran for Chase's Darkhaven.

As she reached the front door of the empty brownstone estate, a soul-rending scream went up in another part of the neighborhood.

More Rogues on the prowl.

More human deaths taking place even now.

Night was coming, and the terror it was bringing had already arrived.

The world was ablaze and bleeding in the dark.

Chase eyed the terror-torn landscape from the backseat of the Order's speeding black Rover. Dante and Renata sat beside him in silence. Rio was grim-faced in the jump seat in back, Lucan stoic, jaw clenched, where he rode shotgun next to Nikolai up front.

They had miles of travel behind them, five-plus hours of drive time packed into barely three at Niko's breakneck speed. Brock followed fast in the second vehicle, carrying the rest of the Order's mission crew toward Boston. Even Lazaro Archer had strapped on arms and combat gear to accompany the warriors into the night's battle.

God knew they were going to need all the help they could get.

By Mathias Rowan's account, the Rogue population let loose from rehab facilities along the eastern seaboard alone numbered close to a hundred. It would take weeks to contain them all, possibly longer. And that didn't factor in the scores of others likely released in other parts of North America tonight.

The odds against the Order's success were staggering. Eventually, they would have to split up, tackle the problem from multiple directions.

But Boston was the immediate concern. It was there

that Dragos had seemed to deliver the hardest hit, no doubt to flaunt his power in the warriors' faces, unleashing unholy hell in the Order's home turf.

The closer they got to the city, the worse the chaos became.

Scattered house fires shot bright orange flames skyward on both sides of the highway. Traffic was crazed in both directions as panicked drivers fought their way in and out of the various city arteries. Sirens blared from everywhere. And in the neighborhoods and surface streets, packs of humans rushed on foot in a blind confusion, eyes wild, faces contorted in terror, fleeing a danger they would never outrun.

Everywhere Chase looked, the scene was utter, bloody madness.

"Cristo," Rio hissed in the tomblike quiet of the Rover. In his peripheral vision, Chase saw the formidable Spanish warrior cross himself and lift a religious pendant on a thin chain around his neck, pressing the small medallion to his lips in silent prayer.

The Boston skyline loomed just ahead now, black smoke rising from smoldering buildings and the crumpled wreckage of cars left abandoned in the streets by their fleeing drivers. Screams rent the air, adding to the cacophony of violence that hung over the entire city.

Chase's thoughts went to Tavia. She hadn't left his mind for a moment in the time since he'd set out with the Order for Boston. He knew she was near, somewhere in the city. He could feel her in his blood. His veins still tingled with the pang of fear he'd picked up from her not long after the Order had set out for Boston. The jolt had been visceral but brief, and long diminished. The knowledge that she was safe now—that she was alive and unharmed—was a reassurance he clung to as the rest of the world was dissolving into bloodshed and ruin before him.

Still, the urge to wrench open the vehicle door and run to her was strong. Overwhelming. But his duty was with the Order right now, more than ever. So long as he knew she was breathing, he could do what he had to tonight.

Tavia was a strong, capable woman. She had been even before the astonishing revelation of her Breed lineage. She was smart and levelheaded. He knew that. He took comfort in the fact that his beloved—his mate, if he should ever prove worthy of the honor—was the most extraordinary female he would ever know.

But she was also courageous and determined. Two things that put a knot of worry in his chest when he considered what she might do if the violence Dragos had unleashed here tonight were to find its way to her. He prayed she'd lie low until he and the Order could clamp a lid on this hellish situation and he could break away to find her.

From the passenger seat up front, Lucan radioed the others in the second vehicle. "Tegan, take your team into the North End. Start your sweep there. The rest of us will begin in Southie, drive the Rogues together from both ends and take out as many as possible."

"On it" came the warrior's grim reply.

Behind them, the Rover's headlights veered away as Brock gunned the SUV through an obstacle course of clogged and chaotic traffic.

"Lock and load, everyone," Lucan said, casting a grave look at the rest of them. "It's gonna be a long, bloody night."

CHAPTER
Thirty-eight

The terror continued until dawn.

Tavia hadn't slept at all. Probably no one in the city had. Probably no one across the entire bleeding nation had found a minute's rest so long as the screams and violence played out in what seemed an endless, hopeless night.

It wasn't until daybreak pushed the attacking Rogues to ground that the terror had paused. With morning came the cries of the grief-stricken and the lost—the war zone aftermath of an assault few human minds could fathom.

And it wasn't over yet.

When the sun set again, a fresh wave of carnage would come.

Tavia knew it with a dread in her marrow as she opened the front door of Chase's Darkhaven and stepped outside into the daylight. Her plan to seek out Dragos had solidified overnight. She'd taken the necessary steps, devised the method she would use to put herself in his presence and, with opportunity and any luck at all, kill the son of a bitch.

The scene outside the brownstone mansion as Tavia walked briskly was nothing short of Armageddon. Vacated cars lay scattered everywhere, headlights flashing, alarms bleating in a discordant symphony with the musical rings of what seemed to be a thousand unanswered cell phones. Smoke and ash billowed from the smoldering shells of looted storefronts and residences that had been smashed open during the worst of the attacks. Huge pools of blood soaked the snow-filled neighborhood yards and empty sidewalks.

The city was a ghost town. No one risked being out, except for Tavia and the grim-faced emergency workers patrolling the shambled streets, or the medical examiner's office personnel who soberly covered and collected the many dead.

Tavia hurried to her destination, head down, eyes stinging from the barrage of so much ugliness and destruction. She went across town, back to the Suffolk County Sheriff's Department, the same police station where she'd been just a week earlier. It seemed as though a decade had passed since she'd been summoned to identify the unnamed shooter from Senator Clarence's holiday party. Her world couldn't have rotated any farther on its axis than it had in the handful of days that followed.

Reality had shifted, and now that same alleged madman was the person she loved more than any other. The one she didn't want to live without. And she was determined to reunite with him, once she did her part to destroy their shared enemy.

"Miss Fairchild—Tavia?" Detective Avery's voice carried across the bustling station a moment after she'd entered. She glanced up and saw him hurrying toward her, his middle-age face drawn and haggard. He looked her over with obvious concern. "My God, are you all right?"

She was, but the bruises and lacerations on her face and body would have indicated otherwise. Which had been the entire point, after all. In addition to her assortment of self-inflicted injuries, her jeans and long-sleeved black sweater were torn and ragged. Her grimy leather flats were soaked with blood, the latter effect coming courtesy of her trek into the station.

"Come with me. I'll find someone to look after your wounds," the kind detective said, obviously taking her silence for shock. He led her deeper into the station, through the throngs of anxious officers coming in and out of the place in a collective daze.

"At least you're alive. Thank God for that," he went on, taking her over to an empty chair in a vacant office. His hands were shaking as he lifted the receiver of the black desk phone and dialed a number. He swore and slammed the thing back into its cradle. "Busy signal. Lines could be down. The whole damn city is falling apart out there. I can't even comprehend what's going on these past several hours. I mean, none of this can really be happening . . ."

Tavia felt sorry for the horror of what this man and the rest of his kind were suffering. But she had no words of sympathy to offer. Nothing was adequate anyway. Her mind focused wholly on her purpose in being at the station, she scanned the dozens of faces passing through.

She found one she was looking for: Cold, dead eyes met her narrowed gaze across the sea of churning bodies.

The Minion knew her on sight, recognized what she was.

"I'll be right back," Tavia murmured to the detective. "I need a drink of water."

Avery didn't protest or get up to follow her, already pulled in another direction as a uniformed officer swept in to relay more grim news from the trenches. Tavia beelined it for the Minion, breezing her way past the humans until she was standing right in front of Dragos's mind slave. "I need to see your Master."

His mouth twisted. "I don't take orders from anyone but him."

"I've just come from the Order's compound," she pressed. "I think Dragos will be very interested to hear what I have to tell him."

The Minion in uniform stared for a long moment, considering. "Follow me."

She went with him, out a back door and into the parking lot. The Minion dialed a number, let it ring once, then disconnected. A second later, the cell phone chirped with an incoming call. Tavia could barely contain her contempt as Dragos's voice came over the line, demanding to know why he was being disturbed. The Minion informed him that Tavia was there, then received clipped instructions to search her for weapons.

He pocketed the phone with Dragos still on the line and started patting her down. He found the titanium blade right away, pulled it from behind her with a smug sneer and shoved it beneath the leather belt of his cop's uniform. His hands were rough on her, skimming both legs and thighs before climbing up her torso. He lingered a bit too long around her breasts, and Tavia growled her disapproval, showing him a bit of fang in the process.

The Minion backed off and put his cell phone up to his mouth. "She's clean. What would you like me to do with her, Master?"

Dragos's voice was menacing, edged with an intrigue that made her skin crawl. "Hold the female there. Await my further instructions."

"The number of confirmed dead worldwide is in the thousands."

Lucan nodded as Mathias Rowan delivered the sober news that morning at his Darkhaven. The Order had finally sought shelter there after the long night of combat. Not even Dragos's evil could trump the rising sun. With daybreak, all of the Breed—warrior, civilian, and Rogue alike—were forced to look for cover.

In the background, Tegan, Chase, and the rest of the warriors were flipping through television coverage of the attacks and their aftermath. It seemed impossible, not only the accounts of widespread slaughter and destruction over the past eighteen hours but the open talk by human law enforcement and government officials about the indisputable existence of vampires.

And mankind had, understandably, deemed them their enemies.

Savage.

Monstrous.

A deadly scourge that required a focused and swift extermination.

Lucan saw Mira's vision in the graphic video coverage and photographs being broadcast all over the world. He'd lived it last night, when his boots had been soggy with spilled blood, the bodies of dead humans and slain Rogues spread out as far as his eyes could see. He tasted it now, in the bitter tang of regret on his tongue, regret that he hadn't put a stop to Dragos before he'd unleashed such hell. Regret for the fact that the nightmare had only just begun.

Europe was bracing for nightfall again, calling in military forces to help secure the largest cities in case of another attack. Everyone was praying it wouldn't come, but Lucan and the rest of the Order knew it would. Although none of the warriors or Mathias Rowan had said as much, they had to be wondering, as he was, how they would be able to combat another attack of the magnitude seen yesterday.

They were roughly a dozen gathered here against hundreds loose on two continents. Twenty against hundreds, if they counted Rowan and the handful of Agents he'd vouched for, good men who'd immediately pledged themselves to the cause. A scant few more overseas, headed up by Reichen. But the Order and their new allies couldn't be everywhere at once. They would need ten times their current number to eradicate the freed Rogues before they took more innocent lives.

Before the humans decided to go on the offense.

"Are the curfews in place?" Lucan asked. With the humans in a state of terror and suspicion, no Breed male would be permitted to feed while the Rogues still posed a threat. To mankind right now, there was no distinction between a law-abiding Breed civilian and a Rogue. For the safety of all the Breed, Lucan had demanded that Darkhavens comply with a nighttime lockdown until further notice.

Rowan gave him a dubious look. "We're doing our best to get the word out, but it's a slow process with most of the Agency infrastructure shut down since the first attacks."

"Keep on it," Lucan told him. "We've got our hands full enough without having to worry about civilians getting caught in the crossfire."

As for the Enforcement Agency, it had virtually disintegrated overnight. Communications had gone dark. Dragos's hidden network of followers—including two known Agency directors, one in Seattle, another in Europe—had come out from the shadows to openly proclaim their allegiance to him and his goals. Countless other Agency personnel had defected too, either to place their bets on Dragos or to withdraw from service altogether and focus on seeing their families through this dark time.

Lucan's heart was several hours north, with Gabrielle. He worried for her and the rest of the Breedmates and the children, alone with Gideon through all of this unrest and chaos. He had no doubt that Gideon would keep them safe, but it killed Lucan to be away from his mate when her deep anxiety rode him like spurs. All of the warriors were sober today, contemplative.

Especially Chase.

Lucan felt for him probably the most right now. The warrior stood alone at the back of the room, stoic and controlled, a marked change from the male who'd been so volatile in recent months. Reckless and insubordinate. A liability to his patrol partners and himself.

There was little left of that Chase in the cool, capable warrior who'd fought side by side with him last night, despite all the blood that was spilled. It had been a testing, taxing night for all of them, but Chase in particular. Yet he'd stood strong. He hadn't broken. Nor would he, Lucan guessed, meeting the warrior's clear, focused gaze across the room now.

Chase's eyes were steady, filled with a steely determination.

A single-minded, unflinching purpose that gave Lucan a glimpse of the leader Sterling Chase had been born to be. The leader he could be again one day in the future, if any of them survived to see that future arrive.

Lucan inclined his head, an approving nod that said more than he could have managed with any amount of words.

Chase nodded back, sober, understanding.

Lucan was proud to have Harvard on the Order's side again. Proud to be able to call Sterling Chase his brother and his friend.

CHAPTER
Thirty-nine

Jenna hung up the phone and leaned back in her chair. Even though her heart was banging with adrenaline over the news she'd just heard, a heavy weariness settled over her like lead anvils perched on her shoulders.

"How's Claire hanging in down there in Newport?" Gideon asked, looking over from his continued experiments on the UV collars across the room from her in the tech lab.

"She's all right. She's safe, and things are quiet for now."

While the rest of the compound was glued to television reports of the Rogue attacks, Jenna and Gideon had thrown themselves into their work. After the inadvertent detonation of the other collar, he had chased down the programmical key to all of the collar activation sequences. Gideon had even managed to get one of the collars in his collection to show up on a GPS map, which had him very excited. It helped, having something to do besides wait for word, and then wait for some more.

Jenna rubbed at the ache in her *glyph*-marked neck, a product of too many hours without sleep and too much worry about Brock and rest of the Order. Worry for the entire world, in fact. Nothing else seemed important at all in light of the events of the past twenty-four hours. At least everyone she cared for was safe and accounted for. "Lucan and Mathias Rowan sent a pair of Agents down to Newport to guard the Darkhaven while Reichen is overseas. Claire says she's in good hands."

Gideon nodded. "Glad to hear it. I gather she was able to do some digging into the question of her parents' deaths before all hell broke loose last night?"

"Yeah," Jenna replied. "That's why she called, actually, aside from letting us know she's okay. Claire contacted the relief organization her mom worked for back in the fifties and they looked up information about the rebel raid on the village. It turns out several people were killed that day, three from the relief organization and four more from the village."

"Claire's father being one of them?" When she shrugged, Gideon set down the broken ring of black polymer he'd been working on. With lowered brows, he regarded her over the rims of small, pale blue sunglasses perched on the end of his nose. "Claire's father wasn't killed?"

"No one seems able to say for sure. According to accounts at the time from the villagers who witnessed the raid, he was shot multiple times. Mortally wounded, the same as Claire's mother and the others."

"But?" Gideon prompted, scowling now.

"But there's no record of his body being recovered."

"Holy shit."

"Yeah." Jenna shook her head, still a bit numbed by the idea. "He was declared dead like the rest of the victims and simply ceased to exist from that day forward. For all anyone knows, he could have gotten up and walked away."

"Not if he was mortal," Gideon replied, his eyes serious, devoid of doubt.

"Right." This news from Claire had only added to Jenna's certainty that she was on the right track. If it weren't for Dylan's steadfast insistence that her father was just an average, human, run-of-the-mill asshole, all the question marks on Jenna's theory would be eliminated.

"Jen?" As if conjured by thought alone, Dylan now stood in the open doorway of the tech lab. She looked shell-shocked and pale. In her hand was a yellowed square of paper.

"Hey," Jenna said, getting up to meet her. Dylan looked so stricken and upset, Jenna pulled her into a tight hug. "What's wrong? Did something happen?"

The Breedmate's eyes were searching, a little lost. "With everything that's going on, I guess I was feeling kind of homesick today. I started missing my mom. After she died last year, I took a small box of mementos from her apartment. I hadn't looked through all of it, just enough to see that it contained some letters and postcards, souvenirs from her travels. Silly things, really. She was sentimental, had the most open, loving heart I've ever known."

Jenna brought Dylan inside and guided her to the empty desk chair. "Tell me what this is about."

"I just went through everything in that box. At the bottom, I found a sealed envelope. This was inside it." She placed the piece of paper on the desk. Something was written in the upper right corner in loopy, buoyant handwriting: *Zael. Mykonos, '75.* Dylan stared up at Jenna meaningfully. "I was born the following year."

No question what she was getting at. "But your mom and dad were already married, I thought. You have two older brothers."

Dylan nodded. "And in 1975, my mom left for a few months. She went to Greece all by herself, just picked up and left. She told me a few years ago that she'd wanted to divorce my dad, but he begged her to take him back. But she never told me about this. She never told me about *him*."

Dylan flipped the piece of paper over. It was a close-up photograph of an impossibly beautiful man, bare-chested and tanned golden brown, sitting on a white sand beach. His sensual mouth curved in a knee-melting smile for the person who took the snapshot, presumably Dylan's mother.

"You think she had an affair with this guy?"

"Yeah," she said. "I'd say the odds are pretty damn good."

Jenna picked the photo up so she could look closer. Purely for clarification purposes, of course. She stared transfixed at the flawless, muscular body and the mane of copper-shot blond hair. His face was unlined, ageless. His dark-lashed eyes were piercing blue, the color of tropical, turquoise waters. Wise and unearthly.

And slung around his strong wrist was a tooled leather band with a hammered silver emblem affixed to it . . . a teardrop suspended over the cradle of a crescent moon.

Tavia's stomach lurched as the black helicopter swooped down over the sunlit water toward an isolated, tree-choked island several miles off the coast of Maine. Twenty minutes after the Minion at the police station had contacted Dragos, the dark-suited pilot, also Minion, arrived to take her to a private helipad at the top of a Boston high-rise.

She absorbed every detail of the journey, cataloging landmarks and locations in case she needed to pass the intel along to the Order. Although none of it would matter if her plan to kill Dragos failed and she ended up dead in the next few hours.

The pilot put the helicopter down on a slab of cleared concrete behind a fortresslike residence. It was the only building on the forbidding crag of granite and tall pines. No way off the island on her own, unless she wanted to swim a freezing Atlantic current or sprout wings.

"This way." The Minion climbed out of the cockpit and waited for her to follow. They crossed the yard against a howling, brittle wind, and up toward the back of the sprawling house.

The door opened from within, and another Minion, this one bristling with a semiautomatic rifle in his hands, motioned for her to enter.

She thought she'd been prepared to face Dragos, but the sight of him waiting for her inside the house put ice in her marrow. "Miss Fairchild. This certainly is an unexpected pleasure."

He was flanked by four Gen One assassins, dressed in head-to-toe black. They had weapons too, guns and knives at the ready, strapped across their hard chests and fastened to their muscled thighs. But it wasn't the arms that gave them their lethal air, nor their severe, shaved heads and black UV collars clamped around their powerful necks. It was the lack of mercy in their eyes. The lack of any emotion whatsoever.

They were killing machines, and any hope she had of ending Dragos's life swiftly on her arrival was stalled by the understanding that these four Hunters would see her dead in less than an instant after she made the first move.

As threatening as the group of them was, it was Dragos's presence in front of her that put a shudder in her bones. Something about him had chilled her instinctively when she first met him at the senator's office. Now, understanding the depth of his depravity and evil, she was physically repulsed. She used the faint convulsion to effect fear and relief. "I had nowhere else to go. Thank you for allowing me to see you."

Dragos eyed her suspiciously. "You've been with the Order all this time."

Not a question, an accusation. "I didn't think I'd ever escape them."

"And here I'd guessed you'd gone willingly," he replied, guarded, scrutinizing. "I thought perhaps Sterling Chase had found a way to charm you."

"Charm me?" She forced an affronted scoff. "He abducted me. Interrogated me. He . . . beat me."

He studied her bruises and the lacerations that were already healing. Nostrils flaring, he sniffed slightly, testing the scent of her against what she was telling him. "Did he seduce you?"

She couldn't hope to deceive him completely. He could smell the truth on her skin, she knew that much without a doubt. She hung her head as if in shame. "He used my body against me. He made me drink his blood."

"Hmm." He sounded satisfied with her answer but displeased with the facts. "That is unfortunate, Tavia. The bond is unbreakable."

"Only by death," she replied, the words catching in

her throat, though not out of regret as she hoped he would be tempted to believe. He lifted her chin and she forced a cold hatred into her eyes—not so hard when the hatred was reserved for the vampire standing before her. "Why didn't you tell me who I was? Why did you keep the truth of my origins a secret from me?"

He backed away, out of her reach. His icy eyes narrowed in calculation, that spark of suspicion visiting them again. His Gen One guards inched forward, ready to protect their creator.

Tavia's heart rate sped as she fought to keep Dragos engaged, to keep him intrigued enough to trust her. This was her only chance; she couldn't give him any room for doubt.

"Why did you keep me weak when I could have served you so much better if I was strong?" The vehemence of her determination to win him over made her eyes flash with hot amber. "I could have been something more to you if you'd only allowed me the truth."

His dark brows rose slightly. A slow smile put a faint twist to his mouth. "You served me very well, Tavia. You were more than useful. And I would have told you everything—I would've freed this glorious part of you—when the time was right."

"Instead you left me defenseless. You didn't give me any chance." She played to his ego, and to the obvious attraction she felt radiating from him as her disgust for him made her Breed nature spike to life inside her. "You had to know the Order held me. You had to know they would question me about you, abuse me. They refused to believe me when I told them I didn't know who you were or where they could find you."

"And if they'd known the truth about you, they would

have killed you for it," he replied evenly. "I would have, if I'd been them."

Cold words from a cold, black heart. She believed him, and it took all her strength of will to force the next words from her lips. "You were the first person I thought of after I escaped. I sought you out because you're my creator. The only one I can turn to. You are the only one strong enough to defeat the Order."

"And so I have," he answered, smiling with self-satisfaction. He considered her long and hard now, his obvious interest making her skin crawl. "I've been fascinated with you from the time you were a child, Tavia. You're so lovely. My homegrown, personally designed Eve." He shrugged. "Oh, the others have their charms as well, but I find I am particularly attracted to you."

The others, he said. Not past tense, but present. She thought back to Dr. Lewis's files—the ones detailing deceased patients and the ones she hadn't had the chance to read before the clinic was destroyed. So, there were other lab-created Breed females who'd survived the prolonged medical trials and treatments? She had to be sure. If she had sisters, she had to find a way to help them.

Dragos was still studying her, his chilling eyes like dead fingers on her skin. "When I am king and all the humans and Breed alike bow to me—very soon now," he added, grinning with arrogant certainty, "I will require a suitable queen."

Tavia swallowed the bile that crept into her throat at the very idea.

"I think I would enjoy having you at my side, in my bed." He grunted, amused by something. "My gift to you will be the Order in chains. You can kill Sterling Chase personally if you like."

The words—the very thought of Chase or the others in the Order falling into Dragos's hands—hit her like a slap. He reached out, lightly stroked her cheek. She struggled not to gag, aware of the Gen One assassins watching her like hawks.

She could chew Dragos's hand off in an instant, but she needed to kill him. And for that, she needed to get close. God help her, intimate, if necessary.

"Come," he told her. "It's past sundown overseas. I was just about to sit down and watch the news coverage. You will join me, Tavia, and witness the kingdom that is soon to be ours."

CHAPTER
Forty

The Rogue had a woman cornered in the stairwell of her posh apartment building when Chase smashed into the vestibule and ashed the suckhead. The titanium blade raked across the feral vampire's throat sent him sputtering to the floor, dropping in an oozing, sizzling heap of melting flesh and bone.

Chase stood over the dead Rogue, his fingers sticky on the blade's handle, his black fatigues and combat boots awful with blood and gore from the other kills he'd already made in the couple of hours since the sun set that night. He stared down at the fright-stricken woman who huddled in the far corner of the stairwell. The amber glow of his eyes cast her face in fiery color. Her brown hair was in disarray, fallen out of its conservative twist at her nape. Her dark, skirted business suit and frothy white blouse were disheveled, torn in places and smudged with the filthy handprints of the suckhead who'd attacked her.

"You're okay," he assured her as he cleaned the edge

of his blade on his pants. "The Rogue can't hurt you now."

She gaped up at him in horror. Shook her head frantically as she shrank farther back, eyes wide and mistrusting. "You—oh, God, you're one of them too!"

"No," he said, then blew out a curse when he considered how close he truly was to being the same ravenous beast as the ones cutting a bloody swath through the night. "I mean you no harm. Get up."

She pulled in a hitching breath. "I don't understand."

"No time to explain," he growled. "Now get the fuck inside your apartment and bolt the door. Don't come out until daybreak, you understand? Go. Now!"

She scrambled away from him in a clumsy rush, one high-heeled pump lost during her attack. As she hurried toward her apartment, she found the wherewithal to fumble her cell phone out of her purse and snap a quick picture of him in all his vampy glory. Wonderful. Not like he didn't already have enough photos on file with human law enforcement.

He stalked outside and took a cleansing breath. Or rather, it should have been cleansing. But the wintry air was ripe with the undercurrent of spilled red cells, some of it fresh, some of it coagulating in ice-crusted puddles on the streets and sidewalks.

The presence of so much blood, for so many hours at a time, was making him crazy.

But he pushed through it anyway, his mind centered on his responsibility to the Order. His heart was grounded in his love for Tavia.

It troubled him that he couldn't feel her near anymore.

He wanted to see her, touch her. Have irrefutable proof that she was safe. And he wanted her to know that he loved her. More than anything, he wanted her to know that.

Damn Dragos. And damn this war that had finally exploded in the Order's face. They were doing their best to get the situation cleaned up, but the battle had only just begun. With Boston's streets having come under some degree of control earlier that night the Order had since moved on to New York City, where there'd been reports of vicious attacks in Manhattan and every surrounding borough. Between the Order and Rowan's guys, they'd smoked upward of thirty Rogues the past two nights. A lot more to go. And a lot more cities still under heavy siege, in the States and abroad.

"Harvard." Dante's deep voice cut through the darkness. He jogged up, curved daggers in his hands, his face smeared with the grit of recent combat. "You get the suckhead that came this way?"

"He's dead," Chase replied. His vision was still flooded with amber, fangs thick in response to the stench of blood that permeated the night. "Ashed the bastard just as he was moving in for the kill. Victim walked away with her carotid intact—and a picture of me standing over the smoked body."

It wasn't the first time the humans the Order were trying to spare had stopped to take snapshots or cell phone videos of the warriors attempting to sweep up this mess. Nor would it be the last.

Dante raked a hand over his begrimed face. "Fucking modern technology. Inconvenient as hell sometimes, eh? Well, it's not like the Breed has to be concerned with keeping a low profile anymore. We're about as out as we can be."

Chase nodded and absently rubbed at the center of his chest.

"You okay?" Dante asked, studying him.

"Yeah. It's just . . ."

"Tavia," the warrior said when Chase's voice trailed off.

"I hate that I'm not with her right now." Their blood bond thrummed through him, but her physical distance from him left a hollowness in his chest. "I hate that I can't feel her close."

Dante nodded, sympathetic. "If she's in trouble, you'll know. And if that time comes, I'll have your back. All of the Order will have your back."

The promise—the renewed bond of friendship, and kinship with the Order—made Chase's throat go dry. It humbled him, knowing that Dante and the others were ready to accept him again. Willing to bleed for him, the same as he would do for any of them.

He'd found his family in these good, brave men.

He wouldn't risk losing that for anything.

And he couldn't know his true home until he had Tavia standing at his side.

Just then, Dante's cell phone began to vibrate with an incoming call. He picked up, greeted Niko, then swore low under his breath. "You gotta be shitting me. Yeah, we can bounce. Harvard and I are five minutes away from you. Be right there." He ended the call and shot Chase a grave look. "Rock and roll time. Order's moving out, ASAP."

"Problem?" Chase asked, rhetorically, when they were surrounded by little else.

"Fresh wave of Rogues just swept into D.C. They're torching the place, smashing up the foreign embassies and dragging people out of their homes. Human fallout is off the charts."

Chase snarled a raw curse, then fell in alongside

Dante to meet their brethren for the next round of battle.

She was never going to get near enough to kill him.

Dragos kept his Hunters close at all times. Yet as cautious as he was, he didn't seem to view her as much of a threat. How could she be, when getting to him would first require that she simultaneously disable four highly trained soldiers?

Right now, he was behind closed doors in his private study, conferring with his lieutenants. No doubt they were gloating over the most recent terror they'd unleashed—setting loose even more Rogues into thickly populated areas, including a massive attack on Washington, D.C. Dragos had been giddy with the prospect of more death and destruction to come.

And Tavia had been forced to bite back her horror as the body counts began to soar for the second night in a row.

In the hours since she'd arrived at his lair, she'd resolved in her mind that there was likely only one place that she would have the opportunity to be alone with Dragos. It turned her stomach to think of letting him touch her, of putting herself anywhere near him, let alone in his bed, but she would do it if that proved the only way.

She sat on a sofa in his beautifully appointed living room, listening to his sadistic laughter and animated conversation on the other side of the closed door. The Minion posted in the room kept an eagle eye on her, the dull glint of his soulless gaze sending a ripple of contempt crawling up her spine. The inaction and sense of powerlessness over everything Dragos had accomplished was driving her crazy. She had to do something to thwart him, if her plan to kill him would have to wait any longer.

She stood up abruptly, sending the Minion across the room into stiff alertness. "I've been sitting here for more than an hour. I need to use the bathroom."

The Minion hesitated, then gestured toward a powder room just outside in the hallway. Tavia walked over at a nonchalant pace, sagging against the door as she closed it behind her. She felt inside her bra for the item she'd been carrying with her since she'd left Chase's Darkhaven earlier that morning.

The silver vial of Crimson was warm from her skin, the wax-sealed cork stopper still snugly in place on top of the deadly dose. All she needed was the chance to put the powder down Dragos's throat. The fact that the drug would deliver a writhing, agony-filled death probably shouldn't have given her so much satisfaction. But she wanted him to suffer. For all the evil he'd enacted during his too-long lifetime, she wanted Dragos to die slowly and horrifically.

She tucked the vial back into her bra and carefully opened the door, peering around it to the living room. The Minion hadn't moved. Genetically speaking, he was only human, so he didn't so much as blink with notice when she flashed out of the bathroom and down the hall with swift Breed agility.

Tavia followed the electronic vibration of computer equipment emanating from the stairwell at the far end of the hallway. Dragos's operation command center, she guessed.

Someone typed on a keyboard, machinery humming nearly imperceptibly from below. Tavia took the steps silently, faster than the Minion technician could track her. Her strength was gaining every day now, along with her inhuman speed and dexterity. She grabbed both sides of his head and gave his neck a hard, lethal twist. She eased his dead bulk down without a sound, then stowed his body in a nearby supply closet.

A wall of monitors glowed with various security feeds and running programs. Tavia scanned them all, absorbing as much of Dragos's command center data as she could. One of the computers—the one the Minion had been typing on—showed an open database, accessed by his log-in credentials. Tavia searched the system menu for applications that might shed more light on Dragos's operation.

After a couple of tries, she'd pulled up a wealth of intel, including the records on three other Gen One females still active in Dragos's program. She read their names and locations with an ache in her chest—three half sisters, none of whom knew of the others' existence. "I will find you," she promised them all now in a fierce whisper. "This will be over one day."

Still more data opened to her as she searched deeper into the hard drive. Reams of Dr. Lewis's study findings, treatment procedures, and prescription formulas. Records on the Hunter program, including dossiers on the entire assassin population.

Good lord, everything the Order needed to crush Dragos's operation from the inside was located right here in front of her.

She had to find a way to get it to them. Calling it in would be impossible. There was simply too much intel and too little time. There had to be a better way.

And so there was, she realized.

She brought up a DOS prompt on the computer and typed in a command. The dark screen filled with line after line of code and parameters. When she saw the one she needed, she committed it to memory in an instant.

But how to get this to the Order?

She raced over to the dead Minion in the supply closet and searched him for a cell phone. Found it in the front pocket of his Dockers. Her fingers flew over the touch pad.

No sooner had she finished and sent the message than she sensed a shift of movement in the hallway above. She shoved the phone back in the Minion's pocket and dashed upstairs . . . right into Dragos and his four assassin guards.

CHAPTER
Forty-one

"Lost your way, Tavia?"

The female's expression didn't falter even for a second as Dragos stared at her. If it had, he would have commanded his Hunters to kill her on the spot. But she held his gaze without a speck of guilt or fright.

No, the look she gave him was level and unfazed. Lit with an elusive intrigue that made him want to study her some more. He could think of many amusing ways he'd like to study the beautiful Tavia Fairchild.

"My Minion said you'd gone to look for the bathroom."

"Your Minion is a bore. I got tired of waiting for you to be finished with your meeting, so I went exploring." Her mouth curved in a cool, confident smile that went straight to his cock. "Your operation here is impressive. I hope you don't mind my curiosity."

He wasn't sure if he did or not, but the way she looked at him now—part willing seductress, part leashed predator—made it easy to forgive her. Besides, he was too exultant to care if she was attempting to play him or not. Everything he'd been working toward was now falling into place.

Violently, bloodily, perfectly into place, just as he'd intended.

"How did you enjoy today's continued spectacle?" he asked, gauging her reaction with a shrewd eye.

"Incredible," she answered without inflection. But she moved closer now, her clear, crisp green gaze fixed on him with single-minded purpose. "To see that much bloodshed—" She shivered a little, and when her eyes lit on him again, they sparked with amber fire. "It does something to me, seeing that kind of power. Being near it makes me feel things I can't really explain."

His approving growl curled up the back of his throat. "It turns you on."

He understood that reaction. And it didn't surprise him to hear this female admit as much to him. She was Gen One, her predator's genes nearly pure. She was also bred of the same otherworldly line that he was, the Ancient used to create her having been the very one who sired his own Gen One father several centuries past. Tavia Fairchild shared his genetics; the idea that she might share some of his same dark instincts and hungers was a seduction he could hardly wait to explore.

"I hoped you might show me more," she said, then glanced to the four assassins who flanked him as though they were annoyances she couldn't wait to be rid of. "In private, I mean."

Dragos hadn't lived to be in the neighborhood of seven hundred years old because he was a fool. Nor did he tend to let his dick make decisions for him. There was a calculating part of him that knew if he went downstairs to his control room, he'd find his Minion technician no longer breathing and a security breach detected in his computer systems.

He also knew that Tavia's captivity with Sterling Chase and the Order likely hadn't been as noncomplicit as she would like him to believe. But the Order no longer mattered to him. His plans were too far gone to be halted, and Lucan's warriors had their hands more than full with the havoc being wreaked in various parts of the world.

Tavia wanted him to think she couldn't wait for him to take her to his bed. He saw no need to disappoint. He would fuck her senseless and repeatedly—until she bled and begged for mercy—but not until after his ascent to power was assured.

He reached out to stroke her velvety cheek. "I intend to show you a great many things, Tavia. Beginning with the moment I become lord and master of every living being on this planet." He took pleasure in the flicker of uncertainty in her unblinking eyes. "We're leaving now for Washington, D.C. If you're to be my queen, I want you with me when I seize the crown."

The scene in D.C. made the attacks in Boston and New York City look like a walk in the park.

Rogues flooded the downtown streets and outlying neighborhoods from all directions. Casualties were heavy, collateral damage off the charts. To combat the onslaught of scores of ravenous vampires set loose on the densely populated urban areas, the Order had split up into three teams: two on the ground with guns and knives; another on sniper duty atop a high-rise corporate building, taking out Rogues with high-powered assault rifles while keeping an eye on the situation for the teams on foot.

Tegan, Hunter, Brock, and Kade were taking care of business in Columbia Heights when Niko radioed to Chase's team that a swarm of Rogues had just knocked over a Metrobus full of commuters.

"Down on Pennsylvania Northwest," Niko advised from his rooftop lookout perch with Renata and Rio. "Shit, there must be thirty humans on board. It's gonna get ugly fast."

"Heading there now," Lucan told him, motioning to Chase, Dante, and Archer, the team already moving out.

They were at the location in a matter of minutes, but the carnage had already begun.

The boxy silver, red, white, and blue bus was on its side in the street, a dozen Rogues climbing all over it, smashing out windows and grabbing for the screaming, terrified people trapped inside. More Rogues crept in from surrounding streets and alleyways, drawn to the scent of spilling blood.

Chase's own physical reaction was swift as well, nearly overwhelming. His head drummed with hunger, veins lighting up with the urge to feed, to gorge like the mad beasts clawing and tearing at the toppled bus. He pushed past his body's fevered response, leaping into the fray with the rest of his team as they charged the downed vehicle and starting kicking Rogue ass.

Lucan seized the largest of the assailants and threw the suckhead down to the pavement with a roar. Two rapid gunshots and the Rogue's skull exploded, killing him even before the titanium rounds could do their damage. Lazaro Archer stormed the fallen cab of the bus at that same moment, blasting deadly fire on the pair of Rogues who were climbing in through the shattered windshield, slavering to join four others who had already managed to break inside to feed.

Chase and Dante vaulted onto the back of the bus in tandem, a tag team of slashing titanium blades and fury. They mowed down three suckheads in mere seconds, then swung down into the bus to deal with the other assailants while Lucan hacked his way through the ones on top. Up front, Archer cleared away the ruins of the broken windshield and started pulling the terrified humans out to safety.

Screams and roars mixed with the staccato crack of gunfire as the battle raged. People streamed out of the bus in hysterics. It was pandemonium, blood-drenched and savage. When the dust finally settled, only four human victims lay dead inside the bus, another two dropped broken and lifeless in the street nearby. The Rogues' losses had been greater: The oozing remains of nearly a score of smoked blood addicts pooled like black oil on the pavement.

No sooner had they contained the situation than Lucan's cell phone hummed with an incoming call. The Order's leader paced away from the bloody fallout to answer. His deep voice was serious, hushed. When he slid the phone back in his coat pocket and turned to look at Chase, his stern, gore-spattered face was grave.

"What's up?" Dante asked from where he stood beside Chase. Archer drew to a pause beside the other warriors then too.

"That was Rowan." Lucan gave a sober shake of his head. "He received a text with intel for Gideon. Apparently we've got the IP address for Dragos's command center."

"Holy shit," Dante breathed. "From whom?"

Lucan's sober gaze swung to Chase and stayed there, making his heart take a swift, cold drop into his gut. "It was from Tavia. She sent it from Dragos's headquarters. He's got Tavia."

CHAPTER
Forty-two

The white-brick, Queen Anne–style mansion and parklike grounds occupied a large, dedicated section of the circular United States Naval Observatory property in the heart of Washington, D.C.

Tavia knew it on sight, had been inside its thirty-three-room splendor more than once during her employment as Senator Clarence's aide. As the blades of Dragos's Minion-piloted helicopter chopped the night sky above the vice president's residence, she peered out the window to the snowy, tree-filled ground below and felt some of the air leave her lungs on a gasp of heartsick astonishment.

Military and Secret Service vehicles sat vacant at their posts around the property. Dark shapes lay unmoving on the ground, the obvious signs of struggle—of armed conflict and unanimous human losses—grimly evident as the aircraft slowly descended into a clearing several hundred feet from the house.

Dragos's assassins had already been here.

She understood that even before a pair of them came out from the cover of the trees to meet their arriving commander. "Everything is secured," one of the massive Gen Ones in head-to-toe black informed him. "The human awaits you inside."

"Excellent," Dragos replied. With the two Hunters leading the way, Dragos took Tavia by the arm in a none-too-gentle grip as they exited the helicopter. Following close behind was the assassin who'd made the trip with them, watching her every move.

If the scene outside the mansion made her heart catch with sick dread, the reality of what had taken place inside hit her even harder. The vice president sat at gunpoint on the ivory-colored sofa in the tastefully appointed living room. Behind him on the wall, the celadon and cream palette of an oversize abstract painting was sprayed with blood, no doubt belonging to the dead Marine who sprawled on the floor just a few paces away.

"Tell me what you want from me, damn it!" the graying government official shouted to his emotionless captors. "Please, let me at least see my wife and family. Let them go."

"Relax," Dragos replied smoothly, catching the vice president's full attention as he strolled into the room. "Your family is upstairs, unharmed, with some of my men. I have no need of them."

The man's face sagged into a visibly incredulous stare. "Drake Masters? For God's sake . . . and Tavia?" He moved as though he meant to stand up, but the assassin standing beside him persuaded him otherwise with a nudge of his semiautomatic pistol. "What is this about, Drake? I demand to know what the hell is going on!"

Dragos chuckled. "You no longer demand anything.

And you can call me Dragos. In a few minutes you'll be calling me Master."

"I don't understand," the vice president murmured. "I don't understand anything that's been happening these past couple of days—"

"Don't you?" Dragos mused darkly from beside Tavia. He strode forward, radiating a cold menace. "Don't you finally understand how powerful I am? Now that you've seen what I can do—now that the entire world has seen the magnitude of my wrath—perhaps mankind will finally realize that they control nothing. This world belongs to us now. To me."

Stricken eyes went a bit wider. "What are you saying, that all of this madness is somehow your doing?"

Dragos's reply was a low growl of sound that made Tavia's veins turn to ice. "The Breed has lived in the shadows long enough. I am resetting the order of things. I am putting the Breed on the top of the food chain where we belong. And you are going to help me do that."

Tavia's fists clenched at her sides. Anxiety spiked through her like acid as she felt Dragos's mood go from mildly amused to dangerously determined.

"Tonight, I am seizing my rightful place as master of all mankind and Breed alike," Dragos went on. "For your part, you will make the call to help me begin my ascent to power. You will deliver the president to me right here and now."

A look from Dragos prompted one of the guarding assassins to wrest the human's cell phone from his suit coat pocket. The Gen One held it out to the vice president, who merely stared at it in abject refusal. "You're insane," he said sharply. "You may have found a way past my security outside and killed my staff, but more will come. They're on the way now, I can guarantee that. You've just brought down the entire United States military on your head."

Dragos laughed. The air around him vibrated with ominous cold before his eyes flashed bright amber and his fangs erupted from his gums. "Make. The. Call."

"I can't," the human protested. "I won't do this—"

In the fraction of an instant between those damning words and Dragos's leap forward like a viper ready to strike, Tavia sprang into action. With superspeed motion, she placed herself between Dragos and his intended victim, the vial of Crimson retrieved from its concealment on her person and uncorked in her hands.

She held a bunch of the red powder in her palm—all the weapon she had in that moment. She exhaled the breath that would blow the massive dose into his face, praying it would be enough to disable him, if not kill him in a blast of writhing agony.

But she never got the chance.

Moving faster than she could track them or react—faster than she could fathom, even though she herself was gifted with similar genes—two of the Hunters protecting Dragos grabbed her.

One wrenched her arms back behind her. The other held the vial of Crimson. With a single command from Dragos, she understood with cold certainty that she would be dead.

His expression was too mild to be trusted, his movements very calm as he took the Crimson away from his guard and held it up to his nose. He gave it a faint sniff, then sneered with cold malice. "Now, this was an incredibly stupid gamble on your part, Tavia. A pity."

Before she could react, he lunged forward and shoved the open vial into her mouth. She choked on the dry dust of the powder as it hit the back of her throat. Coughing, sputtering, she went down on her knees as a rush filled her head like the buzz of a million stinging bees.

Oh, God, she thought, desperate with fear as the Crimson hit her bloodstream and agony arrowed through every cell of her body.

She'd failed.

She'd failed Chase and the Order miserably, and now she was certain that Dragos had just killed her.

Chase's knees buckled beneath him in the street. A pain racked him, so violent it felt as though his chest were breaking wide open.

"Tavia."

Ah, Christ.

Her agony was everywhere inside him. Fire and daggers and poison—a suffering so intense it was a wonder his heart didn't cease beating in his chest.

No, the wounded organ wanted to explode behind his sternum.

The ferocity of what she was feeling in that moment was the most terrible thing he'd ever known. Not only because of the raw anguish of her pain, but because of the fact it was she who felt it.

His female, his mate, hurting—God forbid, dying— and he unable to be at her side.

"Tavia!" Her name ripped out of his mouth on a roar.

"Chase," Dante shouted, right beside him as he stumbled under the weight of her agony. "Jesus Christ. Talk to me, Harvard. What's going on?"

"She's hurt. Ah, fuck . . . I've got to get to her!"

His desperation to reach her after hearing a moment

ago that she was with Dragos now went nuclear. As Niko and Brock rolled up in the Order's two SUVs with the rest of the warriors, Chase broke for the vehicles. Dante, Lucan, and Archer were right behind him.

Tegan was on the phone with Gideon as Chase and his team piled into the Rover. "We're moving out right now," he said, then glanced to Lucan and the others. "Gideon got a bead on the IP address Tavia provided. It's originating in Maine, a private island off the middle of the coast."

Chase's agony worsened, wrenching him from within. He growled with the fury of his helplessness. "Get me to her. Please . . ."

The vehicles started rolling, tearing through the smoke-wreathed streets of D.C.

"Gideon says he's got more intel on those detonation sequences for the UV collar codes. He's trying to grid them to GPS signals, work up some kind of road map to all the active Hunters," Tegan reported.

Lucan grunted. "Tell him he'd better step on it. We may need those codes when we get to Dragos's lair."

As they sped through the chaos and carnage of the dark capital city, the heavy ache in Chase's chest burrowed deeper. His blood bond to Tavia was throbbing, pumping through his senses like the beat of a drum. It felt near enough for him to touch. "We're not going to Maine."

Niko's questioning gaze met his pained stare in the rearview mirror.

"Stop the car!" Chase rasped, hardly able to speak for the shredding intensity of his realization now. "We gotta turn around. I feel her. She's here. She's somewhere in this city."

CHAPTER
Forty-three

She could hardly stand the pain.

It swam through her veins, through her mind, draining her of all strength. Chewed away at her sanity with tiny, shredding teeth.

This was death.

This was true agony, a swift and thorough addiction that left her writhing on the floor. Gasping as though she was dying for air.

This was hell unlike any she could have imagined, to feel her body lost to a hunger—a savage, consuming thirst—that no amount of drink could quench.

Through bleary eyes, her face resting heavily on the floor where she writhed in helpless despair, she watched as Dragos's newest Minion made the call to the man he once served as his loyal second. The vice president's neck still bled from the twin punctures Dragos had made there, but he no longer felt pain. He knew only to please his Master.

"The president is on the way," the Minion said, hand-ing the cell phone back to Dragos with a dead man's smile. "He was suspicious of the request. He will come with heavy military guard, Master. They will be on shoot-to-kill orders if he senses anything amiss."

Dragos nodded. "We are prepared for that. All I needed was to get him close. Soon I'll own him too. And with his allegiance will come the rest of the world's leaders, one by one. You've just helped put the last nail in the coffin of the humans' control over the Breed."

The Minion inclined his head in a servile bow.

Tavia tried to get up, desperate with the hope that something—anything—would thwart the evil Dragos still intended. She no sooner lifted her head than a heavy boot came down on the back of her neck, pinning her there.

The Hunter's boot heel promised to crush her throat if she even thought of rising up against his commander.

She sagged back down and felt a new agony bloom to life inside her. It was Chase. Her blood surged with the power of his fury—his fear for her. It shook her to her core, how deeply he longed to be near her now.

And he was coming. She could feel that too. She felt every mile that shrank between them—could almost feel him urging her to hold on, to stay alive, until he could reach her.

It was only then that her tears started to fall.

Chase was coming for her, and Dragos and his army of killers would be waiting for him.

"You're sure this is it?" Nikolai asked from behind the wheel as they sped toward the sprawling United States Naval Observatory compound.

Chase's blood thrummed hard with the answer. "I'm sure. She's in there somewhere."

"The vice president's house is on these grounds," Dante said from next to him in the Rover's backseat. "This place should be swarming with military."

"Not if Dragos is here too." Lucan's reply was an ominous mix of foreboding and thinly leashed menace. "Good God. Tavia's brought us right to the son of a bitch."

Lucan's cell phone hummed with an incoming call and he pressed the button to put it on speaker. It was Gideon again. He'd been keeping a pulse on the situation since they'd set out a few minutes ago. Now his voice was tight with an eager intensity.

"We got pay dirt on those collar signals at last," he reported. "I've got a map online and I'm seeing a whole lot of signals coming out of the D.C. area right now."

"Where at?" Lucan asked as Niko took a fast corner and gunned it onto the circle, Brock keeping close behind.

"I've got literally dozens of blips a couple miles northwest of the White House. The area's lit up like a goddamn Christmas tree."

Lucan glanced to Chase and the other warriors, dark brows low over his steely gray eyes. "We know exactly where that is. We're rolling up to it now."

"Holy shit, this can't be good," Gideon murmured, running his hand over his disheveled blond hair as he slumped back in his seat in the tech lab. "It could be a trap, guys. You could be walking right into Dragos's hands."

A muscle ticked in Lucan's jaw as he met Chase's determined gaze. "Guess we're gonna find that out soon enough. Chase's female is inside. We're not leaving without her."

A look to Niko dropped the warrior's foot hard on the gas.

With a screeching wail of rubber on asphalt, both of the Order's Rovers surged up onto the parklike lawn of the vice president's compound.

Chase leapt out halfway up the yard and raced toward the mansion with all the preternatural speed he possessed.

Dragos heard the sudden shriek of tires on the grounds outside the house. He wheeled toward the noise, knowing that the president and his security detail would not come barreling into the place hell-bent for leather.

It was the Order.

He threw a glance at Tavia, recalling her admission that she'd taken blood from Sterling Chase. He might have guessed the half-Rogue former Agent might've also sampled her blood. They were bonded, and when Dragos saw the tears streaking the female's contorted face, he understood that Chase and she were bonded by more than blood. She loved him.

And Dragos was betting by the cacophony of gunfire and combat rising up in the yard outside that Sterling Chase loved her too.

"You led them here." He let his laughter boom out of him as he clapped his hands in mock applause. "Congratulations, Tavia. You've done what I've been unable to accomplish all this time. You brought the Order to me, right to their certain deaths."

He swung a hard look on one of the Hunters who stood nearby in the living room. "No survivors. Under-

stand me? Tell the others to do whatever they must to
see it done. I want Lucan and his warriors dead right
now, goddamn it!"

As the assassin pivoted to carry out the command, a
window at the front of the residence shattered. Rapid
gunfire and a massive bulk of roaring fury crashed inside, taking the Gen One down to the floor in a blurred
confusion of motion and savagery.

Dragos gaped at the unexpected invasion. He dived
for a weapon as his Hunter took the brunt of a punishing assault by Sterling Chase. The warrior was crazed
with violence, purely animal. Almost magnificent in his
lethality.

Another warrior vaulted in behind Chase, then another, the mad exchange of incoming gunfire and deadly
force taking on two more assassins by what seemed to
be sheer bloody-mindedness alone. The battle was brutal, and Dragos knew a pang of uncertainty when he
saw his highly trained killing machines taking a beating
from Chase, Dante, and Rio of the Order.

Behind him, Dragos saw Tavia using the moment of
inattention to push herself up from the floor. The bitch
was in bad shape, but she wasn't about to go down
without a fight. Her amber eyes skewered him from
across the room. Her fangs were sharp white daggers,
dripping with the red foam of Crimson that would
eventually consume her sanity and her life.

But not soon enough.

She came out of her crouch and sprang off her toes
toward him. Dragos went down beneath her, his pistol
skittering out of his grasp as the seething female vampire perched on his chest like a she-dragon about to
eviscerate him.

She didn't get the chance.

Before she could do her worst, his last remaining Hunter in the house plucked her off him and threw her against the wall. She crashed to the floor in a broken, moaning heap. Dragos was right there as she tried to lift herself for another round.

"Not so fast," he warned her, the butt of a semiauto 9 mm pushed up hard against her temple. A nod to his Hunter saw her yanked to her feet. Dragos kept his pistol leveled on her, ready to blast her brains all over the wall if she so much as blinked in a way that displeased him.

Across the room, Chase and the others had finished his two assassins. In the yard beyond, the combat raged on, gunfire blasting, sirens wailing in the distance as the rest of the city remained under siege at Dragos's command.

Dragos grinned as Chase realized he'd taken his battle as far as he could.

The warrior's eyes flashed hot amber as he glared at the pistol that could end his female's life at any second. "You have lost," Dragos told him. "You and the Order were never going to win this."

"Let her go." Chase lifted his own weapon now, training it on Dragos's head.

"Let her go?" Dragos scoffed at the tight command and the threat of the bullet he knew the male would never risk. Not when his woman's temple could so easily eat a bullet at the same time. Not that it would take a bullet to kill Tavia Fairchild now. "She's already gone, warrior. Look at her. Foaming and panting like a rabid dog. Put down your weapon."

"Tavia," Chase said now, his gaze pitiful with love and concern. "Tell me you're okay. Ah, Christ . . . tell me I haven't lost you."

Dragos chuckled, enjoying the wasted sentiment like the villain he truly was. "I said put down your—"

The words clogged in his throat, then leaked out of him on a wheezing cry as a jolt of pain stabbed his skull. It was debilitating. A fiery-hot stake that skewered his brain made every muscle in his body convulse in agony. The pistol fell out of his hand. His legs disappeared from beneath him. His head felt squeezed in a vise, about to pop under the extreme pressure and pain.

As Dragos crumpled to the ground, he saw the slender outline of a female in black leather. A Breedmate with chin-length black hair and piercing jade green eyes that held him in a mind-blasting web of extrasensory power.

As soon as Renata's talent dropped Dragos, Chase flew at him in a furious leap.

He couldn't curb his savagery.

His roar was purely animal as he clamped his jaws down on the vampire's throat and tore out his larynx with his teeth and bared fangs. Dragos's scream died along with him. The orchestrator of so much violence and misery, dead in a bleeding mash of frayed tendons, spurting arteries, and wide-eyed, slack-jawed fear.

Chase had wanted to make the suffering last. He'd craved a brutal, punishing demise for Dragos, but not with Tavia's life on the line. Chase let Dragos's body fall, rubbish discarded without a single backward glance.

As the life left his body, all his Minions would perish too. Behind Chase, the human who'd been the vice president slumped lifeless to the floor. Elsewhere in the world, wherever Dragos had sown his seeds of revolt, the humans he owned would all die in a similar manner: abruptly, quietly, inexplicably.

Not so his homegrown army of assassins. Between Dante, Rio, and Renata, the last Hunter remaining in the house was no longer a threat, but those still battling the Order on the grounds outside would not relent until they carried out their commander's wishes.

Chase knew his brethren needed him out there.

He knew it, yet all he could do was race to Tavia's side and pull her Crimson-ravaged body into his arms.

"Stay with her," Dante said, no judgment in his whiskey-colored eyes. Only friendship, and the understanding of a mated male who would do the same thing if it were Tess lying there now. "Keep her safe. We'll handle the rest."

Chase hugged Tavia close as Dante and the others pivoted to head out into the fray.

In the next instant, the night outside was illuminated with the sudden flash of intense, retina-searing light.

CHAPTER
Forty-four

Lucan hit the ground and shielded his eyes along with the rest of the Order as soon as they heard the sudden, tandem hum of the UV collars on the army of attacking Gen One assassins.

Still, the impact of their detonation came as a shock.

The emitted light was so bright—like a bolt of lightning taking out the entire offensive assault in one fell swoop.

When it was gone a moment later, the remains of dozens of Hunters lay where they'd fallen, their heads cleanly separated from their bodies by the shearing power of the collars that ensured their loyalty—and their indenture—to Dragos.

"He's dead." Dante jogged out alongside Rio and Renata, the latter being swept into a fierce embrace by Nikolai as soon as he saw her. "Dragos is dead."

"Chase and Tavia?" Lucan asked, glancing back toward the house when neither of them came out.

"She's in bad shape, Lucan." Dante's tone didn't hold

a lot of promise. "By the look of her—the way she's acting, the pink spittle around her mouth . . . I've only seen that kind of reaction one time before."

"When the Order was asked to stop the Crimson dealer who was ruining all those civilian kids' lives," Lucan finished, recalling that night—and the uptight Enforcement Agent who came to them reluctantly a year ago and had somehow become an integral member of the Order. A member of the extended family that Lucan would protect with his life. Seeing how deeply Chase cared for Tavia Fairchild, recognizing their bond, that made her a member of that family now too. "We need to take her back to the compound, find a way to help her."

Dante nodded, but there was worry in his gaze, not only for Tavia but for Chase as well. "If she doesn't make it . . ."

"Then we'll have to make sure she does."

Lucan's cell started ringing. Gideon, phoning in from headquarters. "Since you're taking my call, I'm gonna go out on a limb and guess that my hack of the detonation codes worked."

"It worked," Lucan confirmed, nodding to Tegan and the others who'd just witnessed the same miracle of Gideon's genius and were coming to join the rest of the group. "The worst of this war with Dragos is finally over. Now we have to deal with the fallout."

As he spoke, a large black SUV with flashing headlights and a military vanguard escorting it came roaring up the drive toward the house. Lucan felt his brethren tense around him, readying themselves for a continuation of the battle.

"Stand down," Lucan advised them coolly. "We must

show the humans we are their allies, not the enemy. Hopefully they'll afford us that chance despite everything Dragos has done to undermine it."

Dozens of soldiers ready for combat surrounded the Order as the SUV came to a halt a few yards away from the gathered Breed warriors. A gruff-looking man in military uniform came out of the back and walked crisply toward them. Four embroidered stars rode down the front insignia pad of his camouflage army fatigues, another set of stars ran across the visored camo cap that covered his high-and-tight, graying hair. As the officer made his approach, shrewd eyes scanned the unexplainable destruction and body count that littered the grounds.

"General," Lucan said, giving him a slight nod of greeting.

The human remained silent, gauging the situation. "Where is the vice president?"

"He's dead. You'll find his body inside, along with that of the one responsible for everything that's happened here tonight." Lucan held the high-ranking officer's appraising stare. "The one who orchestrated all the carnage in this city and others around the world will do no more harm. My brethren and I destroyed him. But evil is still running loose in your streets and there is more work to be done to stop it. Work that needs to be done by all of us together, mankind and ours."

The general's eyes narrowed. "Your kind. Just what is your kind? Savages. Vampires, slaughtering our citizens. Spilling blood all over the world, feeding on us like parasites, for God's sake."

"My kind is called the Breed," Lucan replied evenly. "We have lived among you for many hundreds of years.

We are not monsters. In fact, part of us is human, not so different from you."

"I've seen no humanity in the killings taking place over the past couple nights."

Lucan nodded, unable to deny it. "There were some among us who felt mankind should serve us, instead of sharing this world together in peace. Their leader is now dead."

The general stared, hardly convinced. "After what we've seen, how can we ever trust any of you?"

Lucan let the contempt and suspicion wash over him without reaction. He wasn't blameless, after all. The fear that had been stricken into the humans' hearts the past couple of days could take years to assuage. It could take centuries to rebuild some sense of order now. It could take longer still to achieve any kind of peaceful coexistence between their races.

But they had to try.

For the future of everyone.

For the future of all the unborn children of the Breed and humankind alike.

"I know that trust will not be an easy thing," Lucan said. "But for the good of all, we need to try."

The general started to say something—a protest, judging by the hard look that entered the old soldier's eyes. But at that same moment, he paused to listen to the communication device tucked into his right ear. "Yes, sir," he murmured quietly. "Of course, Mr. President."

He stepped to the side as the back door of the SUV opened and another man climbed out. Lucan drew in a breath, watching cautiously as the military detail parted to clear a path for the most powerful man in the United States.

The president stood before Lucan, dressed casually in street clothes and a fleece-collared, dark olive bomber jacket. He looked haggard, as if the weight of the world rested on his shoulders. Lucan offered a faint, knowing smile as he inclined his head in greeting.

"You say the one who caused all of this is dead?"

"Yes, sir," Lucan said with a nod, realizing the president must have been monitoring the conversation with the general from inside his SUV.

"And you and these men—this woman too," the human leader added, glancing at Renata, who looked every bit as fierce as the rest of the warriors. "You say you had a hand in taking him down?"

"We did," Lucan replied.

The United States' commander in chief fell silent, considering. "I've seen scattered reports of a group of soldiers—a group of vampires—who've been saving human lives since the carnage began here two nights ago. I've seen photographs, video clips. Do you know anything about this group?"

"They are my brethren," Lucan replied, pride swelling in his chest. "We are the Order. And I am their leader, Lucan Thorne."

The president studied him now, for so long Lucan wondered if a new war would begin right here, in that moment. Then the human slowly lifted his hand and held it out to Lucan in greeting. In thanks. "We owe you a debt, Lucan Thorne. You and your Order."

Lucan accepted the offered show of trust. He pressed his bloodstained, combat-hardened hand to the human's palm and gave it a firm shake.

*　*　*

Tavia felt too warm in his arms, fevered, even as she shivered.

The Crimson had a strong hold on her, too strong. She was sinking into it, drifting further and further out of his reach. "Stay with me, beautiful. Don't let go."

"So tired," she murmured, her lips cracked and parched, the corners of her mouth coated with pinkish foam. "So thirsty . . ."

"I know," he whispered. "I know you are, but blood can't help you now. It will only make it worse."

She moaned, and in that broken, needful sound he heard echoes of his own struggle. How ironic that it should be Tavia facing Bloodlust, just when he felt he might actually stand a chance of beating his.

How cruel to think that she was suffering as he had, all for her desire to help him and the Order defeat Dragos.

And she had helped.

Without her risking so much, her life itself, there was no telling how far Dragos would have been able to take his twisted plans.

Outside the din of combat had settled. The bright explosion of light that Chase had seen several minutes ago had left a strange calm in its wake. No more close gunfire or fighting. Dragos's assassins were no more either; Chase knew that had to be fact. As for the Rogues who remained uncaged and loose in the cities around the world, the Order would continue taking them out until the last one was ash in the street.

The world would be better tomorrow, thanks to Tavia's courage and that of his brethren.

There was so much to look forward to—so much hope for a better world for all. He didn't want to imagine that world without Tavia in it. He refused to think it could be possible.

He would nurse her back to health, even if it took locking himself up with her until the fever of her hunger finally passed. If it passed.

He would gladly trade his life for hers right now, if he could turn back the clock and take the deadly Crimson in her place.

"No," she murmured, her voice thick around her fangs. Even through the ravages of the drug, she must have felt the depth of his emotion as he held her in a careful, despairing embrace. She gazed up at him, her feral amber eyes sad and moist with welling tears. "Leave me here, Chase. Go with your brethren."

"No." He shook his head once, then again, more fiercely. "No. I'm never leaving you. Not ever again." His voice cracked, too full with the emotion he felt for this woman. His woman. His mate. "I love you. You are mine. In my heart, I knew that from the beginning. You are my beloved, Tavia, my only one."

"Chase," she whispered. Her tears spilled over now, streaking down her cheeks and chin. "I love—"

A convulsion racked her as the Crimson burrowed deeper into her blood. Chase felt it, hot and seething in his own veins. And he felt her love. Running under the current of the thirst that was savaging her body, Chase felt the strong and steady beat of her heart . . . and it was filled with love for him.

It was all he needed to know.

It was all the hope he required.

She would get better.

She would heal.

And she was his, forever.

He gathered her up into his arms. He kissed her parched mouth, then rose with her and carried her out of the house, away from the carnage, and back to the warriors who were his kin. "I'm taking you home now, Tavia."

EPILOGUE

One Year Later. New Year's Day.

Chase made good on his promise to be at her side until she was well again.

Tavia had felt his strength holding her, protecting her, anchoring her during the time her body struggled to come back from the edge of a dark abyss.

Tess had helped heal the organs that were ravaged by the Crimson's poison, but there was little her unique Breedmate talent could do for the hunger that had gnawed at Tavia, chewing away at her will and sanity hour by hour, day by day . . . week by week.

For that they'd had to turn to an unlikely source: Dragos. Or, rather, his Minion doctor's treatment formulas and procedural logs, documenting the twenty-seven-year-long suppression of Tavia's Breed nature. They'd used Dr. Lewis's medical treatments to curb her blood hunger and quiet her body's fever so she could purge the Bloodlust from her system and rest the months required for her to mend.

Ironic, and yet somehow fitting, that the same insidious practice that had been a betrayal of her trust from the moment of her birth had, in the end, been the very thing that saved her.

That, along with Chase's love.

It flowed through her now, where he stood behind her, sheltering her in the circle of his arms. His heartbeat echoed in her own blood, steady and strong, whole and hale. She nestled deeper into his embrace, sighing softly as his warm breath skated along the side of her neck.

"Have I told you today how much I love you?" he murmured, low, private words meant only for her.

"You have," she whispered, smiling at the kiss that settled briefly below her ear and sent a tingle of heat racing through her. "But I don't think I'll ever tire of hearing it."

His answering growl vibrated against her spine like a sensual purr. "Good thing we've got forever. We've already missed too many days."

Six full months—that's how long it had taken for Tavia to make the journey back to the living. It hadn't been easy, but it was time and agony she scarcely recalled now; a rare, merciful reprieve from the power of her faultless memory. But through their blood bond, Chase had weathered it all. It had to have been hell for him, finding the strength to combat his own affliction while experiencing hers as well, but somehow he'd done it.

With the help of his brethren of the Order, his family.

And now her family too.

Tavia glanced at the people gathered with them tonight in the dimly lit observation room in the General Assembly Hall of the United Nations headquarters in

Manhattan as Lucan prepared to address the delegation.

All of the Order and their families were there. Seated in the front row of the private balcony suite were Gabrielle, Savannah and Gideon, Dante and Tess with little year-old Xander Raphael. Tegan held his infant son in the cradle of his muscled arm, his other wrapped lovingly around Elise. Rio and Dylan, Kade, Alex, Brock, and Jenna stood by the large glass window beside Niko, Renata, and Mira, peering down with Andreas and Claire Reichen, Hunter, Corinne and Nathan, Lazaro and Kellan Archer, at the crowd of eighteen hundred delegates from all over the world who occupied the seats below.

The assembly was filled to capacity, buzzing with excitement and anticipation. Because, today, as night fell over North America on a crisp, clear January 1st, the 193-nation coalition had amended its charter to admit its newest member:

The nation of the Breed.

Chase's heart beat with an anticipation Tavia shared as Lucan moved toward the microphone to accept the evening's honor. Alongside him were the president of the United States and several other world leaders.

"My name is Lucan Thorne." His piercing gaze panned the faces of the delegation, all of whom stared at this formidable male in his conservative black suit, which did little to soften the air of dark power that radiated from him. "I stand here before you tonight, addressing the world on behalf of my kith and kin . . . my long-lived race, called the Breed."

As his deep voice filled the chamber, the room fell into an immediate, complete silence.

"We have existed alongside you for a very long time.

And we have never meant you harm, though it will take time to build that trust, when we are starting on blood-stained ground." He paused as though to let his words be absorbed, everyone in the room aware that his message was going out to many millions of ears around the world. "There have been casualties on both sides over the past year—those humans who have been attacked at night by Rogue members of our kind, and those of us being hunted by day and torn from our Darkhavens in the weeks and months that have followed the first waves of violence. We need to agree to move past these dark beginnings and set the course for a new path forward. This will not be easy. It may not be fully accomplished for years to come, nor without any more lives lost."

As the capacity crowd rumbled with unease at the hard honesty of words that could be conceived as more threat than warning, Lucan looked to the president and the other leaders. "From the shadows we have watched as man over the centuries has made war on themselves over borders and mistrust of one another. I come here tonight asking for unification across all divides, for the good of humankind and my own. I come here tonight with the hope that all residents of our world will find a way to coexist, to get along with one another. And I come here tonight because I believe that we *will* find common ground and that we can, eventually, forge a lasting peace between us all."

Gabrielle turned a smiling, tear-filled look on Chase and Tavia and the others in the room. "When I first met Lucan, he told me he was just a warrior, not an emissary for his race. Later on, when Dragos was doing his worst, Lucan worried that he didn't think there was any hope for what the future might hold." She glanced down lovingly at her three-month-old son, who nestled snugly against her in a peaceful sleep, tiny pink fist tucked under his chin. "I've never been more proud to be his mate than I am right now."

"This was Lucan's true destiny," Tegan said, the forbidding Gen One looking out at his leader, his friend, with respectful, admiring eyes. "It's always been in him to lead, to be the one clearing the way toward a better future. It's what he's done from the very beginning. He honors his race well."

"You all do," Elise added, beaming up at her mate while their baby boy took in the room with wide, inquisitive eyes the same lavender shade as his mother's.

Everyone nodded or smiled in response, no doubt every heart full with pride—and hope—for the future they were seeing forged in this hall tonight.

But Lucan's words of warning were true.

Although Tavia had awakened six months ago healed and stronger than ever through the love she shared with Chase, the rest of the world still bore deep wounds from the violence and terror that Dragos had unleashed on it.

There would be much to do in the months and years to come. There was still mistrust between mankind and the Breed. Pockets of unrest and violence still existed on both sides.

With the help of Andreas Reichen, Mathias Rowan, and the dozens of Enforcement Agents who'd come together in the fight to end the bloodshed, the Order had swept the cities clean of all Rogue violence. Together they'd also eradicated Dragos's remaining lieutenants and their known accomplices. But there was no telling if his seeds of dissent had taken root in secret elsewhere.

With the top ranks of the Enforcement Agency neutered and its membership in shambles, it was the Order that had taken charge of enforcing all Breed law now.

There was much left to be done, many questions yet to be resolved, but things were off to a good start.

There was hope.

Tavia felt it as she met the earnest, caring faces of her Breedmate friends gathered around her. She felt it when she looked at the warriors, standing so firm and courageously behind Lucan's resolute lead, all of them prepared to embark on this new, uncharted way of life. A new world to be formed and shared by all, human and Breed alike.

Most of all, she felt hope bloom inside her, warm and abiding, when she looked up into Chase's steady blue eyes and felt his love moving through her . . . growing inside her.

Love that would take physical form when their twins were born in the spring.

Tavia felt joy, and as her gaze held her mate's now, she felt a perfect peace swell to fill her. They'd found love in each other and an eternal bond that transcended the one that linked them through their blood.

She and Chase had both, finally, found home.

CHAPTER
One

Humans.

The night was thick with them.

They choked the dark sidewalks and intersections of Boston's old North End, overflowed from the open doorways of dance clubs, sim-lounges, and cocktail bars. Strolling, loitering, conversing, they filled the near-midnight streets with too many voices, too many bodies shuffling and sweating in the unseasonable heat of the early June evening.

And damned too little space to avoid the anxious sidelong looks—those countless quick, darting glances from people pretending they hadn't noticed, and weren't the least bit terrified, of the four members of the Order who now strode through the middle of the city's former restricted sector.

Mira Nikolas, the lone female of the squad of off-duty warriors, scanned the crowd of *Homo sapiens* civilians with a hard eye. Too bad she and her companions were wearing street clothes and discreetly concealed weapons. She'd have preferred combat gear and an arsenal of heavy firearms. Give the good citizens of Boston a real excuse to stare in mortal terror.

"Twenty years we've been outed to mankind, and most of them still gape at us like we've come to collect their carotids," said one of the three Breed males walking alongside her.

Mira shot him a wry look. "Feeding curfew goes into effect at midnight, so don't expect to see the welcome wagon down here. Besides, fear is a good thing, Bal. Especially when it comes to dealing with their kind."

Balthazar, a giant wall of olive-skinned thick muscle and ruthless strength, met her gaze with a grim understanding in his hawkish golden eyes. The dark-haired vampire had been with the Order for a long time, coming on board nearly two decades ago, during the dark, early years following First Dawn, the day the humans learned they were not, in fact, the ultimate predator on the planet.

They hadn't accepted that truth easily. Nor peacefully.

Many lives were lost on both sides in the time that followed. Many long years of death and bloodshed, grief and mistrust. Even now, the truce between the humans and the Breed was tentative. While the governing heads of both global nations—man and vampire— attempted to broker lasting peace for the good of all, private hatreds and suspicions still festered in either camp. The war between mankind and Breed still waged on, but it had gone underground, undeclared and unsanctioned, but nonetheless lethal.

A cold ache filled Mira's chest at the thought of all the pain and suffering she'd witnessed in the years between her childhood under the protection of the Order, through the rigorous training and combat experience that had shaped her into the warrior she was now. She tried to sweep the ache aside, put it behind her, but it was hard to do. Tonight of all nights, it was next to impossible to shut out the hurt.

And the part of this war that was personal, as intimate as anything in her life could be, now gave her voice a raw, biting edge. "Let the humans be afraid. Maybe if they worry more about losing their throats, they'll be less inclined to tolerate the radicals among them who would like to see all of the Breed reduced to ashes."

From behind her, another of her teammates gave a low purr of a chuckle. "You ever consider a career in public relations, Captain?" She threw a one-fingered salute over her shoulder and kept walking, her long blond braid thumping like a tail against her leather-clad backside. Webb's laugh deepened. "Right. Didn't think so."

If anyone was suited for diplomatic assignment, it was Julian Webb. Adonis-handsome, affable, polished, and utterly devastating when he turned on the charm. That Webb was a product of a cultured upbringing among the Breed's privileged Darkhaven elite went without saying. Not that he ever had. His background— along with his reasons for joining the Order—was a secret he'd shared only with Lucan Thorne, and the Order's founding elder wasn't telling.

There were times Mira wondered if that's why Lucan had personally assigned Webb to her team last year—to keep a close eye on her for him and the Council and to ensure the Order's mission objectives were being met without any . . . issues. Since her humiliating censure for insubordination by the Council eighteen months ago, it wouldn't surprise Mira to learn that Lucan had entrusted Webb to smooth out any potential rough patches in her leadership of the unit. But she hadn't worked her ass off, trained to the brink of killing herself to earn her place with the Order, only to throw it away.

It was highly unusual—all but unheard of, in fact—that a female like her had come through the ranks with the Order to be awarded a place as captain of a warrior team. Her pride swelled to think on that, even now. She'd lived to prove herself capable, worthy. She'd pushed herself ruthlessly to earn the respect of the Order's elders and the other warriors she'd trained with—respect she'd eventually won through blood, sweat, and stubborn determination.

Mira wasn't Breed. She didn't have their preternatural speed or strength. She didn't have their immortality either, something she, as a Breedmate—the female offspring of a *Homo sapien* mother and a father of as-yet-undetermined genetic origins—could only obtain through the mated exchange of a blood bond with one of the Breed. Without that bond being activated, Mira and those other rare females born like her would age, and, ultimately die, as mortals.

At twenty-nine and unmated, she was already beginning to feel the physical and mental fallout of her taxing career choice. The wound she'd been carrying in her heart for these past eight years probably didn't help either. And her "conduct unbecoming" reprimand a year and a half ago was likely more than enough excuse for Lucan to want to reassign her to desk duty. But he hadn't yet, and she'd be damned if she gave him further cause to consider it.

"Storm's coming," murmured the third member of her team from beside her. Torin wasn't talking about the weather, Mira knew. Like a lion taking stock of new surroundings, the big vampire tipped his burnished blond head up toward the cloudless night sky and drew in a deep breath. A pair of braids woven with tiny glass seed beads framed razor-sharp cheekbones and finely chiseled features, an unconventional, exotic look for someone as expertly lethal as Torin, one that hinted at his sojourner past. The glittering plaits swayed against the rest of his thick, shoulder-length mane as he exhaled and swiveled his intense gaze toward Mira. "Bad night to be down here. Something dark in the air."

She felt it too, even without Torin's unique ability to detect and interpret shifts in energy forces around him.

The storm he sensed was living inside her.

It had a name: Kellan.

The syllables of his name rolled through her mind like thunder. Still raw, even after all this time. Since his death, the storm of emotion left in his wake grew more turbulent inside Mira, particularly around this time of the year. Whether in grief or denial, she clung to Kellan's memory with a furious hold. Unhealthy to be sure, but hope could be a cruel, tenacious thing.

There was still a part of her that prayed it was all a bad dream. Eventually she'd wake from it. One day, she'd look up and see the young Breed male swaggering in from a mission, whole and healthy. One day, she'd hear his deep voice at her ear, a wicked challenge while they sparred in the training room, a rough growl of barely restrained need when their bouts of mock combat sent them down together in a tangle of limbs on the mats.

She'd feel the formidable strength of his warrior's body again, big and solid and unbreakable. She'd gaze into his broody hazel eyes, touch the crown of tousled waves that gleamed as copper-brown as an old penny and felt as soft as silk in her fingers. She'd smell the leather-and-spice scent of him, feel the kick of his pulse, see the sparks of amber heat fill his irises and the sharp white glint of his emerging fangs, when the desire he held in check so rigidly betrayed itself to her despite his best efforts to contain it.

One day, she would open her eyes and find Kellan Archer sleeping naked beside her again in her bed, like he had been the night he was killed in combat by human rebels.

Hope, she thought caustically. *Such a heartless bitch.*

Angry at herself for the weakness of her thoughts, she picked up the pace and glanced at the intersection ahead, where half a dozen human couples had stumbled out of a trendy hotel bar and now stood paused for a traffic signal. Across the street from them, one of the city's ubiquitous Faceboards took the liberty of scanning the group's retinas before launching into an obnoxious ad, custom-tailored for the interests of its captive audience trapped at the crosswalk, waiting for the light to change.

Mira groaned when the digitally rendered 3D image of business tycoon Reginald Horne, one of the wealthiest men on the planet, addressed the couples by name and proceeded to hawk discounted stays at his collection of luxury resorts. Horne's face was everywhere this year, in press releases and interview programs, on entertainment blogs and news sites . . . anywhere there was a webcam or a broadcast crew willing to hear him talk about his newly unveiled technology grant—the biggest science award of its kind. It probably irritated him to no end that neither that story, nor the announcement that Horne was helping to champion the upcoming Global Nations Council summit, enjoyed the same depth of coverage as the ones concerning the billionaire's recent divorce from Mrs. Horne the sixth.

"Come on," she said, stepping off the curb to avoid the pandering wait at the light.

She led her team across the street, heading up the block toward Asylum, a local watering hole that in recent years had become an unofficial neutral ground for its mix of vampire and human clientele. Another squad from the Order was meeting them tonight. Mira hadn't been much in the mood to socialize—least of all in this city, on this night—but the teams deserved to celebrate. They'd worked hard together for the past five months on a joint mission: Black Ops stuff, the kind of covert, specialized assignments that had become the Order's stock-in-trade over the past two decades.

Thanks to the combined effort of Mira's squad and the one she spotted at a back table as she entered Asylum, the GNC had one less international militant group to contend with. It was a victory that couldn't have come at a better time: Just ten days from now, government leaders, dignitaries and VIPs from all over the world, representing Breed and humankind alike, were scheduled to gather in Washington, D.C., in a much-publicized show of peace and solidarity. All of the Order elders would be in attendance, including Mira's adoptive parents, Nikolai and Renata.

Back home in Montreal, the mated pair were still waiting for her to confirm if she'd be going with them too. Although neither had said anything, she knew their invitation was given in the hope that she might expand her social circle, maybe meet someone she might consider bonding with someday. It was also their well-meaning, but none-too-subtle attempt to take her off the battlefield, even for a little while.

She must have been scowling when she arrived at the table with her team, because as she sat down, the captain of the other squad narrowed a concerned look on her from his seat across from her.

"You all right?" Nathan Hunter's voice was level and unreadable beneath the thump of music and the din of noise rising up from Asylum's bar and dance floor. His greenish-blue eyes were steady and unblinking beneath the military-short cut of his jet-black hair. "I wasn't sure you'd be up for this."

Not sure she'd be able to handle being back in Boston. Especially on the anniversary of Kellan's death.

She caught his meaning, even though he didn't specifically say the words. He knew her too well, had been one of her dearest friends for almost as long as Kellan had. Longer, now that Kellan had been gone eight years. Nathan had been there that night too. He'd been right next to Mira, holding her back from the flames and falling debris when the warehouse exploded into the dark sky. And he'd been standing at her infirmary bedside days later, when she woke up and learned there'd been no trace left of Kellan or the human rebel scum he'd pursued inside the booby-trapped building.

Mira cleared her throat, still tasting ash and smoke all these years later. "No, it's fine. I'm good." He didn't believe her, not at all. She looked away from his probing stare and took in the rest of the warriors gathered around the table. "In case I didn't say it already, nice work, all of you. We kicked some serious ass out there together."

Torin and Webb nodded in agreement, while Bal shot a crooked grin at the three members of Nathan's crew. "Captain's right. Damn good working with you ladies. After all, every skilled surgeon needs someone to mop up the spilled blood and guts, or hand him the right tool when he calls for it."

"I got a tool for you right here," quipped Elijah, Nathan's second-in-command, a brown-haired Breed warrior with cowboy rugged looks, quicksilver smile and a slow, Texas drawl. "And if you want to talk surgical precision, we've got you beat in spades. My man Jax over here? Poetry in motion. Two of those rebel bastards had the bad judgment to open fire on us, but Jax took them both out with a single toss of his hirashuriken." Eli made a low whistling sound as he drew his finger across his neck and that of Rafe, his teammate seated next to him. "Thing of fucking beauty, Jax."

Jax gave a mild bow of his dark head at the praise. Half-Asian and one-hundred percent lethal, the big, ebony-haired vampire was renowned for his deadly grace, and for his skill with the razor-edged throwing stars he handcrafted and carried with him wherever he went. Mira knew without checking that Jax likely had half a dozen of his hira-shuriken on his person now.

She carried her own pair of custom blades too, daggers she'd had since she first learned how to properly use one. They were always within her reach, even though it was illegal to discharge weapons of any kind in civilian sectors of the city. Only uniformed officials with the Joint Urban Security Taskforce Initiative Squad, a government directed police detail comprised of handpicked Breed and human officers, were licensed to carry unconcealed arms or use deadly force in non-military situations.

Reflecting back on the success of their completed mission, Mira nodded to Nathan's other squad member, blond, blue-eyed Xander Rafael. "Good job providing the cover we needed to breach the rebel's compound," she told him. "You've got serious skills, kid."

"Thanks." Though hardly a child, Mira had known Rafe since he was an infant. Of the group seated around the table now, he was the newest recruit, fresh out of training ten months ago. Mira was almost a decade older than him, but the young Breed warrior was capable and wise well beyond his years. He was also the son of an Order elder, Dante, and his mate, Tess. Like all Breed offspring, Rafe had been gifted with his mother's unique extrasensory talent. Tess's ability to heal with her touch was a conflict for her son, who had also been born with his father's innate courage and virtually unmatched fighting skills.

Rafe's other gift from his mother was his fair hair and eye color. On Tess, the honeyed waves and aquamarine gaze was stunning, infinitely feminine. On Rafe, six-foot-six and wrapped in lean, hard muscle, the combination turned every female head in the vicinity of him.

One such female, a twenty-something brunette who'd been watching their table from the bar with a gaggle of her friends, was doing everything she could to catch Rafe's eye. He'd noticed. And there was no doubt he knew what the pretty girl would be offering him, too; Mira saw that spark of male arrogance lift the corner of the warrior's mouth in the moment before he and a few other males at the table swiveled their heads to greet her.

"Hey," the young woman said, eyes on Rafe for the longest. She'd made her choice, no question.

"Hey, yourself," Eli answered for the rest of the table. "What's your name, beautiful?"

"I'm Britney." A smiling glance at him and the other males, then back to stay on Rafe. "My friends have been daring me to come over here and talk to you."

Rafe smiled. "That right?" His voice was smooth and unrushed, that of a male totally at home with his effect on the opposite sex. Or another species, in this case.

"I told them I wasn't afraid," Rafe's admirer went on. "I told them I was curious what it was like—" She gave a quick toss of her head, flustered, but flirtatious. "I mean, I was curious what you were like . . ."

Fang-girls, Mira thought with an amused roll of her eyes. Despite the ongoing civil unrest between human and Breed, there was never a shortage of women—and a large number of men—looking to donate their fresh red cells in exchange for the sensual high of a vampire's bite.

Balthazar chuckled. "Very brave of you to come over all by yourself, Whitney."

"It's Britney." She giggled, nervous but determined. "Anyway, they said I should do this, so . . . here I am." Licking her lips as she inched closer to Rafe, she pushed her long brown hair back over her shoulder. The adjustment bared the delicate white column of her neck and Mira felt the air go sharp with the instinctual reactions of more than one Breed male at the table.

"No reason for your friends to be shy." Torin's voice was a smoky, dark invitation that made even Mira's dormant senses prickle with awareness. He drew in a breath through parted lips that didn't quite hide the pearly white points of his fangs. "Call them over and let's see if they're as daring as you are, Britney."

When the girl excitedly motioned for the others to join her, Mira got up from the table. Fresh off a mission and deserving of some kind of reward, the warriors had a right to accept the indecent proposal being extended to them here. But that didn't mean she wanted to watch. "Feeding time ends at midnight, boys. That's ten minutes from now, in case any of you were worried about breaking curfew laws."

Nathan stood now too, the only one of the vampires

seemingly unfazed by the approach of several warm, pretty females willing to play blood Hosts to them to-night. "What are you doing?"

"Getting out of the way. I'll be back in a few."

He frowned. "I should go with you—"

"No, stay." She held up a hand, gestured with a nod toward the arriving women. "God knows, these fools can't be trusted without adult supervision." The taunt got the anticipated rise out of Eli, Bal, and the others, but Nathan's gaze remained solemn on her. When his broad mouth went flat in disapproval, she reached out and cupped his jaw in her palm. She felt him tense at the contact, and suddenly wished she could take back the tender gesture. "Have some fun, Nathan. You earned it too, you know." She started walking away from the table. "Ten minutes," she called over her shoulder. "Somebody be nice and have a drink waiting for me when I get back."

She was fine until she reached the exit. Then the weight she'd been holding off all night settled on her chest and brought hot tears like needles in the backs of her eyes.

"Shit. Kellan . . ." She let his name escape her lips on a rasped breath as she leaned against the brick exterior wall several yards away from Asylum's crowded en-trance. God, she hated how much it hurt to think of him. Hated that she hadn't been able to find her way free of the hold his memory still had on her. No, his death had killed something in her, too. It had broken her somewhere deep inside, in a place no one but him had reached, before or since.

Mira hung her head, not bothering to sweep aside the loose blond tendrils that had escaped her braid and now swung into her face like a veil. She cursed under her breath, struggled to pull herself together. Her fingers were trembling as she wiped the moisture from her cheeks. She blew out a frustrated sigh. "Damn it. Get a grip, warrior."

The angry self-rebuke worked well enough to lift her head and square her shoulders. But it was the high-pitched, human chortle from within the nearby throng that really snapped her out of her pointless sulk. Mira would know that barnyard hoot anywhere. Just the sound of it made her veins go hot with contempt.

She spied the young man's head—his ridiculous red mohawk—bobbing along in a group of petty thieves and troublemakers now walking past the crowd that waited to get into Asylum. That upright comb of bright scarlet hair, along with his distinctive laugh, had helped earn the delinquent his street name of Rooster.

Son of a bitch.

She hadn't seen the bastard in years. Her blood boiled to spot him now. A known rebel-sympathizer, strutting around with his repeat-offender friends when he should be rotting in a prison somewhere. Better yet, dead from choking on the business end of her blades.

When the top of his red mohawk turned the corner up the block with his four pals, Mira hissed a curse. Not her concern what Rooster was up to. Not her damn jurisdiction, even if it turned out he was up to his usual no good.

Still . . .

Impulse propelled her into motion, even against her better judgment. Rooster was an occasional supplier to human militant groups and rebel factions. And that occasional alliance made him Mira's permanent enemy. She fell in behind him and his friends at a covert distance, her lug-soled boots silent as they devoured the pavement in stealth pursuit.

They shuffled up the block and entered an alleyway door of another place, one that had long ago been a popular dance club in the North End. The former neo-Gothic church was far from holy now, and far less reputable than it had been even a decade ago. Graffiti and old shelling scars from the wars all but obscured the fading "La Notte" sign painted on the side of the old red brick building. No longer pulsing with silky trance and synth music, the current proprietor favored hard-core industrial bands with screaming vocals in the club at street level.

All the better to drown out the raucous shouting and bloodthirsty cheers of the customers taking part in the establishment's underground arena.

It was down to that part of the club that Rooster and his pals now descended. Mira followed. The stench of smoke and spilled liquor hung like fog in the air. The crowd was thick at the bottom of the steep stairwell, thicker still in the space between the entrance and the large, caged-in, steel-reinforced fighting arena at the center of the room.

Inside the cage, two huge Breed males circled each other in bloody combat. Outside, gathered around the perimeter and standing a dozen rows deep, the crowd of human spectators cheered and hollered, bets placed on their favorite. This match had been going on for some time, based on the amount of blood in the ring and the fevered pitch of the crowd outside of it. Mira had seen the outlawed games before, and hardly flinched at the sight of the two powerful vampires wearing only gladi-ator-style leather shorts and a U-shaped steel torc around their neck. Titanium spikes rode the knuckles of their fingerless leather gloves, making each blow a sav-age shredding of flesh and muscle.

Rooster and his friends paused to watch one of the fighters take a hard strike to the sternum. His hooting laughter shot up through the crowd as the combatant crashed backward into the bars. The downed vampire was already in bad shape, pitted against an undefeated fighter who never failed to bring in the big crowds and heavy purses. Now, spitting blood, heaving under the force of this last blow, the losing male scrabbled to reach the mercy button inside the cage. Rooster and the rest of the spectators hissed and booed as the call for mercy temporarily halted the match and delivered a punishing jolt of electricity to the wounded combatant's dark-haired opponent. Unfazed, the immense Breed fighter took the hit as if it were no more than a bee sting, fangs bared in a cold smile that promised yet another win for his record.

The cage thundered with violence as the fight resumed, but Mira ignored the spectacle of the arena. Her sights were locked on her target. Her own need to punish boiled like acid in her veins as she stalked Rooster through the throng.

She thought of Kellan's final moments as she watched the rebel sympathizer cackle and hoot, he and the other humans cheering each terrible strike, frothing for more Breed bloodshed.

She didn't know at what point she'd drawn her blades from their sheaths at her back. She felt the chill of custom-tooled metal in her hands, her fingertips light on the scrollwork of the daggers' hilts. Felt her instincts itching to let the blades fly as Rooster shot a sudden glance in her direction.

He saw her, realized she was coming for him. Something flashed in his eyes as they met hers. Panic, certainly. But Mira saw guilt in that worried gaze too. In fact, his oh-shit look seemed to say that she was the last person he expected or wanted to see. He shrank back behind one of his hoodlum pals, as if that fiery shock of upright hair wouldn't give him away.

Mira felt a snarl curl up from the back of her throat. Son of a bitch was going to bolt. And sure enough, he did.

"Damn it!" She shouldered her way through the thick crowd, trying not to lose sight of her quarry as she maneuvered for a clear shot at him with her blades.

Someone saw her drawn weapons and a scream of warning went up. People scrambled out of her way—just long enough that she saw her chance at nailing Rooster. She took it without a hint of hesitation. Her twin blades flew. They arrowed on an unerring path that hit her moving target and skewered him to the far wall, one dagger buried to the hilt in each of the human's thin biceps.

He howled, no longer amused now that he was on the receiving end of a little pain. Mira shoved a few gawking stragglers aside as she closed in on him, venom hot in her veins. She'd already broken one law here tonight; looking at the rebel ally just beyond arm's reach from her now, she was tempted to add aggravated homicide to the tab.

A strong hand came down on her shoulder.

"Don't do it, Mira." Nathan. He and the rest of the warriors all stood behind her now, disapproval on each hard face.

She realized only now how hushed the club had gone. The illegal contest in the cage was over, the spectators now gathered to watch the new one Mira had started. The human proprietor of the place and some of his Breed fighters moved in from other areas of the club, their mere presence threatening added trouble if things got any further out of hand.

Shit. Mira knew she'd stepped in it this time, but her blood was still on a hard boil and all she could think about was settling the score for Kellan. One less rebel bastard tonight was a good place to start.

"Let it go," Nathan said, his voice soldier-cool and emotionless, the way she'd heard him speak a thousand times before, even under heavy combat fire. "This is not the way you were trained. You know that."

She did. She knew it, and yet she still threw off Nathan's grip and took a hard lunge toward Rooster, who yowled like a banshee, writhing where he was pinned to the wall. Nathan blocked her. He moved faster than she could track him, placing himself between her and the human. "Get out of my way, Nathan. You know who this scum hangs with—rebel pigs. Way I see it, that makes him one of them."

"Somebody help me!" Rooster howled. "Somebody call the cops! I'm innocent!"

Mira shook her head, meeting her teammate's disapproving gaze. "He's lying. He knows something, Nathan. I can see it in him. I can feel it. He knows who's responsible for Kellan's death. Damn it, I want someone to pay for what happened to him!"

Nathan's curse was an airless growl. "For fuck's sake, Mira." His eyes were intense, but tender. Holding her with a pity that she'd never seen before and hated to acknowledge now. "The only one you're making pay for what happened to Kellan is yourself."

The truth in his words hit her like a slap. She absorbed the blow in a stunned kind of silence, watching as the rest of her squad and Nathan's moved in around the two of them.

"Probably not a good idea to linger down here," Webb remarked to Mira and Nathan when neither of them had relaxed from their unspoken standoff. "If we don't clean this up quick, things could turn ugly."

Bal swore low under his breath. "Too late for that."

Pouring into the underground club from the street outside came twenty black-clad officers from Joint Urban Security. The JUSTIS detail stormed in, heavily armed, dressed in full riot gear. Mira could only watch—and blame no one but herself—as the law enforcers surrounded them, their automatic weapons trained on her and the rest of her teammates.

Thirsty for more?
Read on for

A TASTE OF MIDNIGHT

a short story
set in the world of the Midnight Breed.

CHAPTER
One

Christmas music swelled from the tuxedo-clad orchestra, filling the ballroom of the Edinburgh mansion where two dozen beautiful couples danced beneath garlands of crisp holly and fragrant evergreen boughs. High overhead, giant chandeliers dripping with cut crystals and glittering gold accents scattered soft light like diamonds onto the Darkhaven gathering below. It was night outside the eighteen-foot windows that ran the length of the ballroom, daytime shutters folded back from the glass to reveal a pristine, moonlit spread of rolling Highland hills blanketed in wintry white.

The scene was as picture perfect as a page in a glossy magazine.

Elegant, urbane. Utterly enchanting.

Danika could hardly stifle the urge to scream.

She didn't belong here. Coming back to Scotland for the holidays and to this Breed social gathering tonight—both at the insistence of Conlan's well-meaning relatives—had been a mistake. Two days in Edinburgh and already she was itching to book the next flight home to her quiet life in Denmark. She'd been in her high-heeled sandals and black cocktail dress only two hours, struggling to make small talk with a hundred people she didn't know, and more than half that time she'd been eyeing the mansion's front door with a longing she could scarcely hide.

"Are you having a nice time, Danika?"

God, it was all she could do not to pivot and bolt.

Instead, she smiled politely at the young woman beside her. "Of course. The party is lovely, Emma."

"You see? I knew you'd enjoy getting out for a while," the petite redhead said. She was the Breedmate of one of Con's distant cousins, a mere child in her twenties, still fresh with the shine of unspoiled youth and glowing with the promise of the eternal bond she shared with James, the handsome Breed male at her side. His dark eyes were tender on Emma, his strong arm holding her protectively at his side. When he smiled at his pretty mate, it was impossible to miss the press of his emerging fangs behind his lip. Desire transformed his gaze too, his·irises flashing with heated sparks of amber.

The couple obviously adored each other, and it was hard for Danika not to envy them their future. Hard to remember what it was like to be newly blood-bonded and so in love, looking forward to time together without end.

Danika glanced away from the pair and smoothed the scarlet silk mourning sash tied around her waist. She'd forgone the traditional white widow's gown, but even a year and a half after Conlan's death in Boston, she found it difficult to give up this last symbol of her loss. Being in Scotland—Con's homeland—only made his absence more obvious. They'd forged a history together here, in the Highlands. Centuries of time bonded as one, living a peaceful existence, until Con's sense of duty and honor took them to America some hundred years ago, where he'd pledged his sword in service as a warrior of the Order.

They'd wanted for nothing, except the child they'd finally decided to have. Their son, Connor, conceived just three months before Conlan was killed on an Order mission gone awry. She'd hated leaving the baby back at her guest cottage with Con's family tonight, even for a couple of hours. He was all she had, her only link to the life she'd shared with Conlan MacConn. Danika glanced out at the sea of strangers all around her, civilian Breed males and their mates, a hundred unfamiliar faces in an unfamiliar place. She looked at them all, never having felt so alone.

"Will you excuse me for a moment?" she asked the couple beside her. "I should call the house again, make sure everything is all right with Connor."

"But you just checked in on him five minutes ago . . ."

Danika let the comment trail off behind her, already moving toward the quiet perimeter of the ballroom and fishing her phone out of her little evening clutch. The update from the guest cottage where Danika and Connor were staying was the same as it had been every other time she'd called. Everything was fine with the baby, no need for Danika to worry.

She thanked the Breedmate watching Connor and ended the call, knowing it was wrong to wish for a reason to leave the party and rush back to her child. She was supposed to be having a nice time tonight. Since she was stuck there until her companions decided to leave, maybe she should at least make an effort to enjoy herself a little.

Slipping the phone back into her purse, she began a

slow circuit of the room. The red sash around her waist deflected the interest of all but the boldest of the unattached Breed males. Then again, at five foot eleven without the added height of her four-inch spike heels and possessing long blond hair, she realized she was hard to miss. She could ignore the assessing stares of the men at the gathering. It was the pitying looks of the other Breedmates that made her feel the most awkward.

Widowed after so long together? I would rather die myself than lose my mate like that.

Danika briefly closed her eyes as the thought sailed at her from across the room. She didn't know whose mind she'd tapped into, nor could she bar the intrusion. Every Breedmate was gifted with a unique extrasensory talent. Hers was the ability to read thoughts, be it Breed, Breedmate, or basic *Homo sapiens*. Unfortunately, since Conlan's death, that ability had become unpredictable, unmanageable. His Breed blood had kept her youthful for centuries; it had also fed her talent and kept it strong.

Several times already tonight she'd been blindsided by a sudden uninvited mental commentary. Most were mundane prattle and insipid cocktail party drivel, but some thoughts bore sharp edges that zeroed in on her like arrows.

Never would've happened if Conlan had stayed in Scotland where he belonged. Never should've taken an outlander as his mate.

Danika lifted her chin and strode deeper into the throng of Darkhaven civilians. Let them stare. Let them cast their silent blame and suspicion. Let them gape at her like the outsider she was. She had never needed anyone's approval; she sure as hell didn't need it now.

She walked right through the center of the gathering,

her steps unrushed, head held high. Overheard, muffled conversations joined the barrage of unwelcome psychic input, until it was nearly impossible to discern which words were spoken aloud and which were given voice only in her mind. Pointless musings on uncomfortable wardrobe choices and pending holiday plans overlapped with opinionated debates on Breed politics and the dismal economic situation of the human world.

By the time Danika reached the far side of the ballroom, her skull was ringing from the combined cacophony of sensory input. Some fresh air would help clear her head. She made her way toward a closed pair of French doors that opened onto an outdoor terrace.

As she neared, she saw the dark shapes of several Breed males standing outside. Their voices were little more than low rumbles on the other side of the glass. She paused at the mention of a pending live cargo shipment overdue at Edinburgh airport—something expensive, requiring discreet handling. That alone was enough to make her instincts prickle, but it was the next comments that froze her feet to the floor where she stood.

"Does the cargo include anything . . . exotic?"

"Perhaps" came the airless, arrogant reply. "So, be sure to bring your best offers. And your appetites, whatever they may involve."

Low, conspiratorial chuckles answered from the group of vampires. As they continued talking, their voices dropped to a level too quiet for her to make out. But she tried, edging a bit closer to the terrace doors and feigning rapt interest in a hideous painting framed on the wall beside her.

Eavesdropping is a very rude habit.

The thought slammed into her mind from out of nowhere, as deep and rich as molasses and thick with a rolling Scots burr.

Can be dangerous too, lass.

Did she know that thick, dark voice? Even more unsettling, did its owner know her?

Danika sent a quick glance around the gathering, looking for familiar faces among the throng in the ballroom and the smaller groups clustered at its perimeter. Aside from Conlan's handful of cousins and their mates, there were none but strangers all around her.

Yet she was sure she'd heard that slow, sardonic Highland drawl before. She thought about the conspiring handful of Breed males on the terrace outside, and she wondered . . .

Just then, the French doors opened and the four vampires started to file into the mansion. Danika drew back, too late to pretend she hadn't been standing there for more than a few minutes.

The male leading the pack latched on to her instantly with chill, slate-gray eyes. Impeccably dressed in his Armani tux, black hair slicked artfully back from his face, he gave her a thin smile. "What have we here?" The voice that had reeked of arrogance from the other side of the terrace doors now softened with oily charm as all but one of his companions—a towering wall of muscle, broad shoulders, and brooding, dark menace— melted into the rest of the gathering. "To think I might have left the party tonight without the pleasure of being properly introduced to someone as lovely as you."

Danika offered nothing in response. Far from impressed by his attention, she was too busy trying to get a better look at the Breed male standing behind him. Bodyguard or thug, she couldn't be sure. Tall and formidable, he wore more than one firearm beneath the conservative cut of his graphite wool suit coat. His gaze was partially concealed by the careless tousle of his thick chestnut-brown hair, but she could make out the savage line of a knife scar down one beard-grizzled cheek, and the bridge of his nose bore the jag of a poorly healed break. As she stared at him, his generously sculpted mouth turned grim, lips pressed flat and forbidding above his square chin.

Something prickled deep in her veins. The face was all wrong, but the grave twist of that mouth . . .

She knew that dark look. Didn't she?

"My name is Reiver," said the vampire with the dry voice and oily air that made her skin crawl. His gaze traveled the length of her, brows lifting when he noticed the scarlet sash around her waist. "And you must be the widow MacConn. A shame about your man. Dangerous business he was in."

Danika flinched at the reference to her dead mate. In fact, she could've sworn she detected the faintest quirk of reaction from Reiver's menacing associate too. "Conlan was killed doing something he believed in. Dangerous or not, he served the Order with honor."

He lowered his head in a vague acknowledgment. "Of course. And you have my sympathy for your loss."

She might have believed him even a little, if not for the leering glint in his eyes. "I'm not particularly interested in anything you have to offer. Now, if you'll excuse me—"

When she pivoted to walk away, his hand came down firmly on her arm. Danika heard the rumble of a growl but had no time to register if it came from Reiver or the guard behind him, whose body had gone rigid and alert, vibrating with menace. "Such a sharp tongue. The heathen warriors of the Order might find that attractive in a female, but you're a long way from Boston, my dear. A little courtesy would serve you well."

She glanced down to the long fingers that were snaked around her wrist and holding on like a vise. His bodyguard moved forward as though prepared to step in, but Danika refused to be cowed by either of them. "Let go of me."

Reiver's smile became a thin-lipped sneer. "We've hardly had a chance to get acquainted. Stay. I insist."

"I said let go."

He didn't. And in that next instant, the ballroom echoed with the sharp *crack* of her open palm connecting with his face.

It seemed as though the entire room froze in response.

Bodies ceased moving on the dance floor. The orchestra faded into quiet. Conversations halted, heads turned. Everyone stared at Danika and at the vampire who was seething in cold fury, blocked from delivering a return strike by the barricading wall of his bodyguard, who had placed himself between them.

"Danika!" Emma rushed over with James from across the gathering. They gaped at her as though she were a child who'd just poked a stick at a coiled viper. "Danika, what have you done?"

"Get my car," Reiver snarled to his bodyguard. His fury was obvious, glowing in the amber transformation of his eyes and the thinning slits of his pupils. Behind the curled edge of his lip, his emerging fangs gleamed razor sharp. "This spectacle is over. I'm leaving."

"Mr. Reiver," James interjected, clearly anxious. "I cannot apologize enough for this . . . whatever this was about. Please pardon our cousin. She couldn't possibly have intended—"

"No," Danika said. "You don't have to make excuses

for me. I can speak for myself. And if I felt an apology was warranted, I'd give it."

Reiver's bodyguard muttered a curse under his breath while his employer's glare burned even hotter. "The car, Brandogge. Now."

As the big male moved off to carry out the command, Reiver raked Danika with a scathing look that practically stripped her bare. "Perhaps a little time in Scotland will help smooth the coarse edge America has left on you, Widow MacConn. For your sake, I hope so."

Before she could tell him where to stick that suggestion, Conlan's kin steered her away to let Reiver leave the party without further incident.

Bran swung Reiver's black Rolls-Royce around to the front of the Darkhaven and put the sedan in park on the paved half-moon drive outside the entrance. His hands itched on the steering wheel, his pulse hammered hard in his ears. Every instinct was on full alert, telling him to get his ass back inside and make sure the situation didn't escalate with his boss and the widowed Breedmate from Boston.

Not that he had to worry about Reiver. His reputation would insulate him from the worst of the gossip following his public rebuke and the attention it attracted from everyone tonight. Tomorrow it would be all but forgotten, or at least hushed into nonexistence. There were few members of the Breed nation in Scotland who didn't know better than to invite the wrath of Edinburgh's most sinister resident.

If Reiver wanted problems to go away, they tended to disappear quickly. True to the origins of his name, he had long grown accustomed to taking whatever he wanted. No one refused him anything, and no one dared stand in his way. When fat bribes and illicit favors didn't suffice, Reiver had no qualms about resorting to less civilized tactics to ensure his interests were protected.

What might Reiver do if he suspected that his private discussion this evening had been overheard by the Breedmate with a longtime connection to the Order?

It wasn't a stretch to imagine. Bad enough that she'd dented his ego and topped it off with a physical insult in the middle of a crowded ballroom. If Reiver worried that she might know details of his current business dealings, Bran hated to think how his employer would go about securing her silence.

Bran despised the son of a bitch. He felt that contempt simmer through his veins and boil into his vision with amber fire as he watched Reiver come out of the mansion and make his way toward the waiting vehicle. It took some effort to tamp down his hatred and school his features into a mask of professional calm before the other Breed male reached the car and opened the back passenger door.

He slid into the backseat, slamming the door behind him. "That uppity bitch better hope our paths never cross again. Be a shame to ruin such a pretty face, but damn if she's not begging for some hard discipline."

Bran grunted, his eyes narrowed on Reiver in the rearview. "Where to, boss?"

"The club," he snarled. But then the mansion's front door opened and out came the tall blonde and the mated couple who'd come to her defense inside. As they headed for the sea of luxury vehicles parked along the wide driveway, Reiver's seething gaze followed her. "Yes, that's a female in need of a firm hand. Among other things."

Reiver chuckled darkly and Bran's hands tightened to a death grip on the wheel. It was all he could do to resist the urge to reach behind him and smash the other male's face into the bulletproof glass of the back window.

But he had to play it cool.

He hadn't come this far, worked this hard to win Reiver's trust, only to lose it now.

As Bran stepped on the gas and the Rolls eased into motion, Reiver settled back against the leather seat. "If there's one thing I can't stand, it's a haughty female. Even less ones who don't know their place." Demanding eyes met Bran's gaze in the mirror. "I want you to find out all you can about that widow of the Order. Report back to me on everything you discover."

Bran gave an obedient nod, then went back to studying the night road ahead.

He already knew plenty about the woman.

But that was a long time ago—centuries, in fact. Back in a different time, when he was a different man.

And before the beautiful Danish Breedmate had given her heart to his best friend, Conlan of the clan Mac-Conn.

CHAPTER
Two

D anika hadn't gone to the party looking to make new friends, but she surely hadn't expected to have a one-on-one clash with the Breed's most feared crime boss in Edinburgh.

Not that she'd lost any sleep over her run-in with Reiver the night before, despite the terror Emma and James had tried to instill in her after they'd left the Darkhaven gathering. According to them, Reiver's dirty business dealings began a few hundred years ago on the northern border marches, where he acquired livestock, lands, and loyalty at the end of his sword. Now it was payoffs and personal favors that allowed him the freedom to do whatever he pleased. That and his reputation as a man few, if any, dared to cross.

Danika was more offended by Reiver than afraid.

And she couldn't dismiss the troubling conversation she'd overheard. Live cargo shipments arriving any day now. Whispered requests for exotic offerings that would command hefty prices and ignite the hunger of Reiver's lascivious society friends.

The very idea chilled her to her marrow.

Although it was forbidden by Breed law, Reiver wouldn't be the first of their kind to peddle humans as if they were nothing more than cattle meant for slaughter. Skin traders were a despicable scourge, usually ranking among the lowest of the low in Breed society. Base street scum like that generally didn't stay in business for very long.

But if someone with Reiver's reputed power and connections had decided to deal in mortal suffering and death, how many innocent lives would he be allowed to steal and destroy before someone had the courage to take him down?

It was that disturbing thought that had Danika dialing a scrambled phone number in the States while she sat alone inside an Edinburgh coffee shop the next morning.

"Gideon, it's Danika," she told the Breed warrior on the other end of the line, in Boston.

"Hey," he replied. The British-born vampire ran the command center of the Order's compound. "You all right? You need anything? I hope things are good in Denmark."

Normally quick with wry humor, today Gideon seemed cautious, an odd intensity edging his voice. "I'm fine," she said. "Everything's fine. And I'm in Scotland, actually. I decided it might be nice to spend the holidays here in Edinburgh with Connor."

"Ah. That's good." Relief in his answering exhalation. "How is the little guy?"

She couldn't help smiling when she thought of her sweet baby boy, back at the cottage with Emma this morning while Danika ran daytime errands in the city. Her son was Breed; for him and the rest of his kind, sunlight was a deadly threat. "Connor's great. Getting bigger all the time. He's so much like his father already. Calm and good-natured. I'm blessed to have him."

"It's good to hear you're both okay." There was a question in the warrior's slight pause now. "But that's not why you called, is it?"

"No," she admitted. As a fresh wave of customers strolled in to place their orders, Danika got up from her table and walked outside for a little privacy. "Do you know anything about a vampire from the Edinburgh area named Reiver?"

"Let me check the IID." The clack of a keyboard sounded in the background as Gideon tapped into the Breed's international identification database. "Not much on record. Looks like he's been around since the 1700s. Currently holds several properties in the Highlands and a handful of businesses in and around Edinburgh."

"What kind of businesses?" She crossed the street and headed for the car lent to her for the day by Conlan's kin. "Anything out of the ordinary?"

"Import/export companies, couple of antiques shops. And a private gentleman's club on South Bridge. Appears the place has been registered to him for the past century and a half."

She knew that area, a historically notorious part of the Old Town now clogged with tourist shops and pubs. She was only a few blocks away. Danika got into the car and turned the key. "Do you have the name and address of that club, Gideon?"

His answer came in the form of a prolonged silence.

Then: "What's this really about, Danika? You're not being straight with me."

She told him about the incident at the party last night, including the snippet of conversation she'd overheard. "I can't be sure, but I think he was talking about human cargo, Gideon."

"Jesus," the warrior hissed on the other end of the line. "And you put yourself within arm's length of this guy? I don't need to tell you what Conlan would say about that—"

"Con's gone. And I'm fine. I just wanted to make you and the rest of the Order aware of what happened."

"You did the right thing," he told her. "Now do us all a favor and steer clear of the whole situation. We'll take a closer look at Reiver. Don't mention this to anyone— not even the Enforcement Agency. Shit, especially them. The way things are going around here right now, we have to assume that no one can be trusted."

"That bad?"

"I'm not sure how it could get worse, unfortunately." The uncharacteristically grave edge to Gideon's voice had taken on an even darker tone. Although the time she'd been away from the Order had kept her removed from their day-to-day operations, she was still in touch with her old friends and was aware of the war they'd been embroiled in with a powerful enemy named Dragos. The fact that Gideon was unable to make light of that battle now, even to dismiss some of her worry, could only mean bad news. "The compound's location has been compromised. We're scrambling for temporary headquarters, but the whole plan got more complicated yesterday when Dante and Tess's baby arrived ahead of schedule."

Danika wanted to be happy for Dante and his Breedmate, whom she had yet to meet, but she'd been a part of the Order long enough to understand that a newborn was both a blessing and a burden to a group of warriors who lived—and sometimes died—to make the world a better place.

"As if that wasn't enough," Gideon went on, "one of our own is AWOL. Chase disappeared the other night. Based on the way he's been acting lately, we're all dreading that we've lost him to Bloodlust."

"I'm sorry," she said. Of all the warriors, she never would have guessed the most rigid, by-the-book enforcer of Breed law would be the one to fall victim to an irreversible blood addiction. In light of everything the Order was dealing with now, she regretted that she'd called to trouble them with her suspicions about a petty gangster like Reiver. "I wish I were there with you all, Gideon. I wish there was something more I could do."

"Don't worry about us. You take care of you, understand?" She heard him typing something more on the keyboard in his tech lab. "You want me to send someone your way? Reichen's in Europe on a mission, but you say the word and I know Lucan will pull him—"

"No," she said as she turned the corner from cobbled High Street and slowly made her way along the hodgepodge collection of Victorian-era brick buildings and modern storefronts that lined the South Bridge. "It's not necessary, Gideon. I'm perfectly fine. I shouldn't have bothered you."

"No bother, Danika. You're kin, always will be. We all feel that way."

"Thank you," she replied, warmed by the thought. "I have to go now."

"Keep out of trouble," he cautioned grimly. "And you get in touch ASAP if you need anything at all. Right?"

"Yeah. I will." She told him good-bye and ended the call just as the car's GPS announced that she had reached her destination.

Although Gideon hadn't spoken the address when she'd asked him for it, his mind had given up the answer to her ESP talent. The building that housed Reiver's club had no signage, only a bloodred door with a brass wolf's-head knocker.

Danika drove around to a side street where she could park, then walked back to have a closer look. She shouldn't have been tempted to try the front door, but a tentative squeeze of the cold metal latch was too much to resist.

The building was unlocked. Strange. Unless Reiver's business encouraged straying visitors to enter. She eased the heavy door open and walked into the dim vestibule. Interior shutters blocked the daylight from outside as she closed the door behind her, the soft glow of a fluted wall sconce the only illumination inside. She didn't bother to call into the gloom to see if anyone was there. All she wanted was a quick look, something to either confirm her suspicions about Reiver or dismiss them.

She ventured farther inside and tried one of the interior doors toward the rear of the vestibule. It was shut tight, bolted. Another door appeared to lead to a stairwell, but it too was locked. So much for a quick look around.

Danika released a pent-up breath but sucked it short when movement sounded from somewhere inside the building.

She wasn't alone here.

She pivoted and raced back to the front door. It was locked now. She struggled with the latch, but it wouldn't budge no matter how hard she tried. "Damn it!"

"What the hell do you think you're doing?"

Danika wheeled around on a gasp.

It was *him*.

Not Reiver, but his menacing bodyguard with the mane of shaggy brown hair and the savagely scarred face. Gone was the dark suit and weaponry. Now he stood before her in nothing but loose jeans and bare feet, looking like he'd just rolled out of bed. It jolted her, seeing his naked, muscled chest and strong arms. Breed *dermaglyphs* tracked across his torso and over his bulky shoulders in swirling arcs and flourishes. As he moved toward her, the color of those genetic skin markings deepened from the golden tone of his flesh to dark shades that broadcast his displeasure.

His overlong hair drooped low into his eyes, but she didn't need to see his narrowed gaze to know that it was fixed on her in growing, dangerous anger. She glanced away from him, throwing an anxious look at the locked door behind her.

"You don't belong here, lass."

Maybe it was the fact that he was out of her line of sight in that moment, but when he spoke just then—when he called her lass—she realized she knew that gravel-and-velvet voice. She'd heard it in her head at the party, when he'd sent a chiding thought her way for eaves-dropping on Reiver. Yet he hadn't outed her to him when he had every chance to do so.

And there was something else familiar about him, she realized now.

Something that spoke to her from a distant yet unde-niable place.

She looked at him again, trying to see past the bearded jaw and battle-scarred face that hid behind the thick fall of his hair. "Do I know you?"

"No."

His curt answer should have been enough to convince her. Instead it only made her study him more. She stared at him, trying to make sense of what her instincts were telling her. "Mal . . . ?"

The hard line of his mouth pressed flat, unreadable. "My name is Brannoc."

She didn't think so, despite the forbidding glower he pinned on her. "Brannoc what?" When he didn't answer, she tried a different tack. "Reiver called you Brandogge last night. Is that what you are to him, his personal watchdog?"

"When need be." He took a step forward, the bulk of his huge body crowding her back against the door. The roll of his Scottish accent deepened with each syllable. "It was unwise of you to come here. You're trespassing, and my employer does not tolerate intruders in his place of business."

The closer he got to her, the more the air seemed sucked from the room. He was heat and danger and dark menace, a storm pushing her to retreat. Danika held his simmering gaze, mere inches between them now. "Just what kind of business goes on in here?"

He didn't answer, merely took more space from her, his gunmetal gray eyes throwing off sparks through the tendrils of dark hair that hung into them.

"Reiver's running a blood club, isn't he." Not a question, because her earlier suspicion had now hardened into a cold certainty that settled like ice in her stomach. "You know this, and yet you can serve him? What kind of man could willingly protect someone like Reiver and turn a blind eye to the way he makes his living?"

"We all make choices in life. We do what we have to."

"At the expense of your honor?" she challenged hotly. "Even at the cost of your own soul?"

He stared at her for the longest moment. Then the lock on the door behind her sprang free with a sharp metallic *snick* that made her flinch. "Go back where you belong, lass."

She didn't move. She didn't care now whether she knew him or if he was simply the hired guard dog of a skin-trading thug. Contempt for what he stood for—for what he was able to condone—put a defiant spark in her veins. "If you think I'll walk away without doing something about this, you're wrong. I won't be silent knowing innocent people are being hurt—"

His answering snarl cut her words short. "Yes, you bloody will be."

Suddenly she was pressed flat against the carved wood panels of the door, his body scorching hers everywhere they made contact. Which was too many places to count. She felt each contour and muscled bulk, from the unyielding planes of his naked chest and iron-clad abdomen, to the blatantly sexual heat of his pelvis and thick-hewn thighs.

"You *will* be silent," he commanded her tightly, full lips drawn back off his teeth and fangs. Fire crackled in his eyes now, but there was more than fury or threat in his wild gaze. There was concern in that hard look. A concern that bordered on desperation. "You'll say nothing to anyone, Danika. Do you understand?"

She gaped at him as the realization of how she knew him finally settled on her. It was an old memory—as old as her love for Conlan. Older, still, for she'd known this man even longer. Might have been tempted at one time to give him her heart, if she hadn't feared he'd leave it crushed under his boot heels one day. "Oh, my God," she murmured, reaching up to touch the grizzled, battle-worn face that had once been so handsome and bold. "It really is you . . ."

He didn't let her fingers light for more than an instant on his cheek. His grasp was firm, his mouth grim as he gave a slight shake of his head. Danika couldn't breathe. She felt as if she'd been knocked to the ground and lifted high aloft, all at the same time. A tangle of emotion swamped her as she struggled to accept what she was seeing, what she was feeling in that moment.

But where she was awash in confusion and a hopeful sense of relief, the man she knew to be Malcolm MacBain projected utter control. Cool and deliberate, devoid of any tenderness, he guided her hand back down to her side and held it there. "Forget what you heard. Forget Reiver." He let go of her, but his eyes still trapped her in their penetrating stare. "Forget me too."

He reached past her then and freed the latch on the club's front door. A gust of cold, damp December wind sifted in around them. Street noise intruded, an unwelcome savior that jolted Danika out of the stupor that gripped her as she stared up into the face of someone she'd once considered a beloved friend but who was now worse than a stranger.

"Go," he said, and stepped back to give her space and keep himself out of the wan daylight that was reaching into the vestibule.

Danika looked at him one last time, searching for words that wouldn't come. Then she turned around and numbly walked back into the bustle of the street outside.

CHAPTER
Three

"Boss wants to see you in his office, Bran. Doesn't look happy."

Another of Reiver's personal security detail, Thane, leaned against the doorjamb of Bran's quarters at the club. The vampire was built like a tank, tall and immense, his massive shoulders and arms straining the fabric of his dark suit, the muscled bulk of him filling the doorway. Tonight, his shoulder-length black hair was pulled back in a short queue, the vee of his sharp widow's peak and slashing ebony brows giving his cool green eyes a hawkish quality as he watched Bran finish cleaning his pair of Glock 20s. The guns didn't need the attention, but after the day he'd had, if Bran didn't keep his hands busy, he was liable to punch someone. Starting with the bastard he worked for.

Taking his time on the weapons, he angled a scowl in Thane's direction as he reassembled the second of the pistols. "Tell the boss I'll be up in a minute."

"And tempt him to shoot the messenger?" Although

he gave a low chuckle as he said it, Thane's shrewd eyes showed no humor. "You got a problem with Mr. Reiver, you take it up with him yourself, man."

Bran casually inspected both of his service weapons, then shoved them into the cross-body holsters that rode over the top of his graphite-gray shirt. "I've got no problems with him."

"You sure about that?" Thane stared, letting the question hang between them.

In the seven months since Bran had entered Reiver's employ, Thane had proven the hardest of the other guards to read. Tough, smart, hardcore when needed, if anyone were to suspect Bran's true motives where Reiver was concerned, it would without a doubt be Thane.

Bran stood up and crossed the small room to retrieve his black suit coat from the back of the wooden chair where it hung. He felt Thane's eyes on him as he shrugged into the coat, completing his thug's uniform, and prepared to face his boss.

"I don't know how you do it, man. Living here at the club, day in day out." Thane studied him. "Don't you have a place of your own, or kin somewhere to take you in?"

Bran cast a bland look at the thin cot and sparse furnishings of the room that had been his home since he'd come on board with Reiver. He shrugged. "I have a place to lay my head. I don't need anything more."

Not for now, at least.

Not until he had what he came for: vengeance.

Then, perhaps, he would return to his true home. Try to find some way to live again, in the empty place where Reiver had left nothing but death.

He brushed past Thane into the hallway. "The boss say what he wanted?"

"Nope. Just told me to find you and send you up to see him." The big guard crossed his arms over his chest. "Better hope you've got nothing to hide."

Bran ignored the warning and strode through the main floor of the club, past the members' lounge and gaming tables, where a few of Reiver's wealthiest clients had recently arrived to begin their night of deal making, debate, and discreetly arranged debauchery. Reiver's office was upstairs, a lavish suite that spanned the entire third floor of the building. The pair of vampires posted at the door admitted him with expressionless nods.

He walked in and found Reiver standing in front of a large flat-screen monitor, remote control gripped in his hand. "You sent for me?"

"Yes." The word was little better than a hiss. When Reiver swiveled his head to look at him, his face was hard with displeasure. "I've been informed that roughly an hour's worth of security camera feed from inside the club today has been damaged irreparably."

"Really." Bran feigned a measure of surprise, even though he'd been the one who destroyed the video surveillance footage personally. Right after Danika's appearance in the building.

Reiver grunted. "What's the use of keeping a watchdog on the premises if he isn't aware of everything that goes on in here at all times?" He set the remote down on his desk, his movements too deliberate. Too calm to be trusted. "Did anything unusual happen today, Brandogge?"

Bran bristled at the insulting nickname but kept his head. Just one more means of Reiver testing him, goading him to see what he was truly made of. "We had a visitor this morning," he said. No sense in denying it; he suspected Reiver already knew anyway and was testing his loyalty. "The female from the party last night."

"Danika MacConn." The sound of her name on Reiver's lips made Bran's pulse spike with a contempt he fought hard not to show. "I did some investigating of my own after Thane recovered a backup feed from the lobby this morning. Would you like to see it?"

Bran gave a nonchalant shake of his head, his suspicion confirmed that he was being tested and judged. Leave it to Thane to throw him under the bus. But what was worse was the fact that Danika's appearance at the club today had only heightened Reiver's interest in her.

"Apparently the meddling bitch is in Scotland only temporarily, staying at the little cottage near the river on the MacConns' lands."

Jesus Christ. He knew where Danika was and how to find her. Details that could prove more than dangerous in the hands of a heartless bastard like Reiver.

"The question is, what was she doing nosing around my place of business today?"

Bran shrugged dismissively. "She didn't say what she wanted, but since you saw the camera feed, you know she didn't get far. And she won't be coming back anytime soon. The way I left things with her, I don't think she'll pose any further problems for you."

"No," Reiver said, all too readily. "No, I'm certain she won't. I saw to that myself a few minutes ago."

All the blood in Bran's head made a swift, cold rush into his boots. He held the flat stare of his employer, careful to betray none of the dread he was feeling. "What do you mean, you saw to it?"

"I sent a couple of men over to the MacConn lands to look in on the woman. I'm sure they'll be able to persuade her that she might be more comfortable staying out of my affairs. Unfortunately, Edinburgh can be a very dangerous place for a strong-headed woman."

"Who did you send?" The words were dry in Bran's throat, his limbs wooden as he waited to hear the answer.

"Kerr and Packard."

Two of his most brutal henchmen. Where Thane and some of the other Breed males in service to Reiver were threatening in their own right, Kerr and Packard were reserved for only the ugliest jobs. They were the bone-breakers of Reiver's stable, the ones dispatched when he wanted to make his point with someone in the bloodiest of terms.

It was all Bran could do not to leap on Reiver and tear out the son of a bitch's throat right where he stood. But killing him now wouldn't spare Danika the pain that was heading her way. There would be time to deal with Reiver later—time for Bran to see his vengeance through as he'd long planned.

Right now, all that mattered was reaching Danika.

Before Kerr and Packard had the chance to do their worst.

Bran cleared his throat to dislodge the icy knot that had settled there. "If there's nothing else you need from me . . ."

"No," Reiver said, casual despite the fact that he'd issued a likely death warrant for an innocent woman. "That'll be all for now, Brandogge. I'll send for you if I have need of anything further."

Bran inclined his head, then pivoted to make his exit. Each calm stride was a test of his self-control as he made his way back downstairs and through the now-bustling club.

He had to get out of there. He had to get to Danika, and fast.

Hell, it might already be too late.

As he cleared the members' lounge and turned the corner down a stretch of empty hallway, his steps hastened. Worry and rage snarled in his gut when he thought about Reiver's evil touching someone else he cared about. He couldn't bite back the curse that boiled out between his teeth and emerging fangs.

"I gather it didn't go well."

Bran paused, swung a dark look over his shoulder at Thane. The guard stood behind him in the hallway, one beefy shoulder pressed against the wall, his booted feet crossed at the ankle. His expression might have been mistaken for boredom, if not for the glint of suspicion in his eyes.

"Something went wrong with the surveillance camera feed today. But I guess you already know that," Bran said, wrestling his concern and fury into a semblance of curt frustration. And it didn't escape him that the best defense was often a good offense. "Thanks for not telling me that my ass was on the line with the boss."

"Wasn't my place to tell you," Thane said. "You going down to the control room to have a look?"

"Yeah." Bran nodded, well aware that there was a back exit to the building down there too.

Thane started walking toward him. "I'll go with you."

Bran scoffed. "You've helped me enough for one night, don't you think? Why don't you do something useful and send a few of the girls up to the boss for a while, tell them to take good care of him, make him real happy. Pick the best ones too, the ones with the most skilled mouths. Maybe if we keep him busy, he'll lay off the rest of us for the night."

Thane stared at him, unsmiling. "All right, Bran. You do what you have to. I'll handle things with Mr. Reiver."

Bran might have questioned the cryptic response, but all his focus was zeroed in on one task now. He stalked toward the club's security control room, casting a quick look behind him as he neared the back exit. The hallway was empty. Thane was gone.

Bran punched open the door and stepped into the bracing wintry chill outside. Too risky to take one of Reiver's fleet vehicles and hope it wouldn't be missed. Besides, he was Breed. He'd get where he was going even faster on foot.

He summoned the speed of his preternatural genetics and vanished into the night.

CHAPTER
Four

Danika got up from the rocking chair and gently placed little Connor into the nest of blankets in his crib, careful not to wake him. His face was as innocent as a cherub's as he slept, sated from his evening feeding at her wrist. She savored these tender moments with her baby.

Watching the small bundle nestled in the center of the delicate crib, it was easy to forget how fierce and unbreakable he'd be one day. How bold and courageous his father's noble Breed blood would make him. In just a few years' time, by the age of five or six, Connor would be old enough to hunt his own prey. A short decade more and he would be full grown, lethally so, a Breed male ready to make his mark on the world. Would he accept a civilian life, perhaps find a Breedmate to give him sons of his own and centuries of peaceful existence? Or would he follow in his father's footsteps, pledging himself to a greater purpose?

In her heart, Danika knew the answer to those questions, difficult as it was to accept. Each time Connor grasped her finger in his tight little fist, his innocent eyes far too knowing, too fathomless for a mother's peace of mind, she knew. Her son would be a warrior, like his father.

And it killed something inside her to think she might lose him one day too.

With a soft kiss to Connor's velvety head, Danika drew away from the crib to let him sleep. She retrieved her empty tea mug from the table beside the rocking chair, then clicked off the bureau lamp on her way out of the bedroom, her gaze lingering on her child as she quietly closed the door.

Even before she turned around, she realized she and Connor weren't alone anymore.

"Nice little place," said one of the two vampires who stood inside the living area of the cottage. "Cozy, ain't it, Kerr?"

"Secluded too," murmured his companion with a leer that threatened more than simple violence.

Her fingers tightened around the earthenware mug in her hands. There was no need to wonder how the pair got in. Locked doors were nothing but a moment's mental effort for a Breed vampire who wanted something on the other side. As for the two thugs who dripped melting snow from their boots and dark menace from their every pore, there was no doubt where they'd come from.

Reiver.

For what wasn't the first time that day, Danika regretted her visit to his private club. She was still sick to have discovered that someone she once knew—someone she had cared for—was part of a despicable organization like Reiver's. Whatever Malcolm MacBain was calling himself now, and for whatever reason he seemed determined to deny his true identity, Danika hadn't been fooled. Not even the scars that marred his face had been enough to convince her that he was someone other than Mal. But knowing his name and face from the past was not the same thing as knowing the man he'd become.

And as she stood before these two terrifying intruders now, part of her wondered if it was Reiver who'd sent them or his loyal guard dog back at the club, who'd demanded her silence with a cold fury that had left her shaken to her core.

"What do you want?" she asked them, lifting her chin to face this threat, even though her legs felt like sand beneath her.

"Mr. Reiver asked us to come and see you," said the one named Kerr. His big hands were gloved in black leather, sinister mitts that looked large enough to crush her skull. "He wants you to know there's a storm could be heading your way. He thinks it best if you don't stick around to see it arrive."

"Is that right?" As the pair of them stalked toward her, Danika edged away from the bedroom door where Connor slept. Whatever might happen to her tonight, she didn't want to give them any reason to search the rest of the tiny cottage.

"Mr. Reiver's of the mind that Edinburgh's going to prove inhospitable to you if you stay any longer." As Kerr spoke, the other thug aligned himself with the path she was subtly taking, moving so that he could block her if she had thoughts of making a break. "My associate Mr. Packard and I are here to help you. Come with us now, and you can avoid what's sure to be a very bad situation."

"A painful situation," added the second vampire, his lips splitting in a chilling grin, baring sharp white fangs.

Their minds were black with awful intentions, thoughts so brutal she found it hard to breathe as she watched them close in further. She didn't need her extrasensory talent to understand that the odds of her surviving this confrontation weren't good. Even if she agreed to go with them and swore never to speak Reiver's name to another living soul, she knew the trip would end with her death.

The idea of Connor being left without his only parent or, worse, dragged into this impossible scenario along with her was more than she could bear. She flung the heavy mug at Packard and bolted into action in the instant his attention was diverted.

The kitchen was only a few feet away, but she barely made it there before Kerr was on her with hard, punishing hands. She fought his bruising hold, crying out as her skull knocked sharply against the unforgiving edge of the stove. Her arms swung out, hands flailing, scrabbling and searching for any means of defense.

As she struggled with Kerr, Packard came at her now too. He tossed off his companion with an otherworldly growl. "Leave her to me," he snarled, fangs dripping saliva, eyes wild with amber fury.

Danika fumbled in a blind panic, hissing when her fingers brushed the hot copper of the teakettle. It was heavy with water on the stove, still scalding from the tea she'd made a short while ago. She grabbed the handle and swung it at Packard with every ounce of strength she possessed.

He howled when the pot connected with the side of his head. Hot water exploded from out of the spout and the opened lid, dousing his face and neck. A nasty gash bled at his temple. He wiped it with his fingertips, then pierced her with a murderous glower. "You'll pay for that in shredded pieces, bitch."

Danika backed away in utter terror. She had nowhere to go, nothing else to use against them. No hope of anyone hearing her screams.

Packard wheeled on her like an animal moving in for the kill. He lunged, and Danika closed her eyes. She waited to feel his huge body collide with her, but in the next instant the entire cottage seemed to erupt into total chaos.

Cold air swept in from outside in a frigid gust. And with it came a dark shape, moving so fast she could hardly register his movements.

It was Malcolm.

Danika watched in stunned disbelief as he leapt on Packard and slashed the vampire's throat open with the edge of a wicked blade. The guard went down in a bleeding heap, and then it was Kerr who felt Mal's fury. The fight was swift and brutal, fists and knives and flashing, deadly fangs. When it ended, Malcolm's breath was sawing from between his lips, his eyes throwing off fierce sparks as he let go of Kerr's dead bulk and stepped over the body like forgotten rubbish.

"Malcolm," Danika whispered, aware only then of the shudders that were racking her from head to toe where she stood.

In the hard, heavy silence that followed, a muffled cry rose up from behind the closed door of the bedroom.

Mal's wild gaze narrowed on her. "You have an infant?"

"My son, Connor." Her eyes were moist, her voice choked with fear for what might have happened to them. Might still, if the searing look Malcolm pierced her with was anything to go by.

He raked a hand over his scarred and grizzled jaw, then expelled a vivid curse. "Get the child, Dani. It's not safe for either one of you now."

Two of Reiver's guards were lying lifeless in pools of blood inside the cottage.

A widowed Breedmate with an infant son—the family of his one-time best friend and a member of the Order besides, for fuck's sake—were waiting in the dead men's car parked behind him near the end of the snowy driveway.

And in his hand, a locked-and-loaded pistol aimed at the front window of the small guest house several hundred feet away, its chamber ready to release a hail of rounds and ignite the stream of gas that was leaking from the pipe he'd disconnected on the stove.

Bloody hell.

He'd spent half a goddamn year serving a criminal he hated with every ounce of his being, hiding who he was, burying his past and the future yanked out of his grasp, all for one purpose: so he could prepare for the ideal moment when he could take Reiver and the rest of his untouchable cronies down in one fell swoop.

Only to risk throwing it all away, right here.

Malcolm MacBain exhaled a low oath in rusty Gaelic. Then he pulled the trigger and turned to stalk back to the idling car.

Glass shattered behind him. An answering vacuum sucked in some of the chill night air from around him as he walked, pulling with it a flurry of snowflakes that danced on the Highland breeze.

The world went quiet, but only for a second.

Then the cottage exploded and the ground beneath his boots shook with an earth-rattling *boom*.

Malcolm felt the destruction in his bones. He saw it reflected in the windshield of Reiver's fleet sedan, bright orange flames shooting skyward, the light from the blast illuminating Danika's awestruck, horrified face behind the glass.

He slid into the driver's seat without comment and threw the car into a sharp reverse turn. As he roared away from the burning house, he felt Dani's eyes on him. She held her baby close to her breast, shielding his head protectively with her hand. "Malcolm, what have you done?"

"The only thing that could be done." He kept his focus on the dark road ahead, knowing they had to get where they were going before the fireworks brought all of Conlan's clan out to see what had occurred.

"Where are you taking us? Why don't you want Con's family to know what happened back there?"

He felt her ability prodding into his skull. He scoffed a rough curse and slanted a sharp look on her. "Stay out of my head, lass. Leave my damned thoughts alone."

"They're going to worry about me. I need to let them know that Connor and I are all right—"

"You'll do no such thing." His voice grated out of him, harsher than he intended. "What I did just now was buy you time. Time you'll need to get as far away from Scotland as you can. And it will all be for naught if anyone—even Conlan's kin—know that you and the baby are alive."

Danika was staring at him, shaking her head. "It's cruel to let them think anything else."

"Two of Reiver's worst enforcers are dead inside that

blaze. He sent them to kill you, Dani. Don't think for a second he won't retaliate on you or the rest of the Mac-Conns if he has even the slightest cause to suspect you might have walked away from this thing tonight."

He let her answering silence fill the quiet of the car as he drove deeper into the night, farther into the rolling hills and wilderness plains of the Highlands where he was born. "As of right now, you're dead, Danika. You have to trust me. It's the only way."

"Where will I go?"

"Somewhere he won't think to look for you."

She went quiet beside him again, murmuring soft words to her baby as the bundle in her arms began to fidget and fuss. Malcolm couldn't keep his gaze from straying to her now and then as the miles fell away behind them. She was lovely still, with her pale blond hair and smooth-as-cream skin.

Time had made him forget how regal yet feminine her Nordic features were, but seeing her now was like looking through a glass to all those years that had passed—the centuries, in fact. Danika MacConn's beauty hadn't faded even a little, despite the faint shadows riding under her eyes that hinted at how long she'd apparently gone without a fortifying taste of Breed blood.

He regretted the loss she'd suffered with Conlan's death. Losing one's blood-bonded mate was the worst kind of suffering. Con was the lucky one, relieved of the grief Danika had to carry without him.

And watching her interact so tenderly with her baby son opened up a deeper ache inside Malcolm—the ache of a recent loss of his own. It was an anguish that had nearly destroyed him but now gave him reason to breathe. To have patience. To avenge.

The last thing he wanted was a vulnerable female and

baby in his care. All the worse that it should be *this* female, at this time . . . in this place.

Steeling himself to the consequences of his actions that night, Malcolm turned the sedan onto a rambling path that could hardly be called a road. They bumped and jostled through a thick heath, following the line of an old cow fence of tumbledown stones. The fortress dominated the vista up ahead, looming as dark as pitch against the wintry night sky.

Danika leaned forward in her seat, peering out the windshield. "I know this place," she murmured softly.

"Aye," he agreed. "You should know it well enough, I reckon."

She was quiet for a long moment, staring straight ahead as he slowed to a stop in front of it. "This is the castle where Conlan first asked me to be his mate." Danika's face glowed milky white in the lights of the dashboard as she turned to look at him now. "Malcolm . . . this is your castle."

CHAPTER
Five

The fifteenth-century stone tower house had been modernized extensively inside. Cold gray stone walls had been coated with white plaster and adorned with contemporary paintings and black-and-white art photographs of the surrounding Highlands. Rough-hewn plank floors were now gleaming hardwood, warmed by thick wool rugs. In place of tallow candles and mounted torches spewing soot and smoke from their open flames, Mal had turned on beautiful lamps to chase away the shadows of the castle's interior.

But it was the room he'd brought Danika and Connor to on the second floor that gave her the most unexpected jolt of surprise. A nursery. Unfinished, by the look of it. A wooden crib stood empty in the center of the cozy chamber. A tall chest of drawers stood against the wall to her left, beside a basket overflowing with a menagerie of stuffed animals and plush baby toys that looked like they'd never been moved. On the far wall, someone had begun painting a whimsical mural—

grinning lions and monkeys, wide-eyed elephants and giraffes, frolicking together on a colorful, half-completed landscape of jungle trees and tall green grasses.

And, draped with a pale sheet in a forgotten corner of the charming little chamber, a rocking chair sat alone in the gloom like a specter.

"There are blankets and pillows in the chest," Mal said from beside her. "Use whatever you like."

When she turned to thank him, he was already gone.

A few minutes later, after settling Connor in to sleep, Danika made her way back down the curving stairwell through the heart of the castle. She could hear Malcolm in the kitchen at ground level, boots moving over the slate floor, cabinets being opened and closed. Warm yellow light seeped out from the open doorway as Danika approached.

Mal had his back to her as he scooped something out of a bowl on the counter into a plastic zipper bag. His black suit coat and leather weapon holsters were draped over one of the four chairs at the table in the center of the kitchen. Without looking at her, he asked, "Find everything you need up there?"

"Yes. Thank you." She stepped inside the rectangular kitchen. She looked around at the curved white walls, granite-topped cabinets, and glistening stainless steel stove that outfitted the place. "I remember when this room was just a vault and open fireplace hollowed out of the stone. You and Con would sit down here for hours, arguing philosophy and bragging of your varied conquests. As I recall, yours were often female related."

He grunted. "A long time ago."

"Doesn't seem that long, now that I'm here again," she said, marveling at how true that was. The span of time evaporated further when he turned to face her now, his stony gray eyes sober with concern. The sight of him here, in this place, after the danger they'd faced together just a short while ago, made her heart constrict. He walked toward her, holding the filled plastic bag in his hand. It dripped water off one corner, the snow inside already beginning to melt.

"No ice in the house, so I collected some snow while you were upstairs." He gestured to the table and chairs. "Sit, Dani. Let me have a look at that bump on your head."

She did as he asked. He walked with her, sinking down onto his heels as she took a seat facing him. She hadn't realized she'd been hurt until she felt the cold touch of the homemade compress against her brow. She winced, sucking in a sharp breath. In reflex, her hand went up to her forehead, where Mal still held the ice pack in place. His skin was warm beneath her fingertips, the feel of his strong bones and tendons burning instantly into her brain.

The touch lingered, too long.

Too heavy with unspoken, unbidden, meaning.

They were too close like this, intimately so. He crouched before her. She with her legs spread on either side of his large body as he leaned in to tend her. His face was level with hers, near enough that she could see the first glimmer of amber burning into the cool gray of his irises. Near enough that she could feel the air crackle in the few inches that separated their bodies, electrified with a palpable tension neither of them seemed to expect.

With a scowl, he pulled his hand away from her, placing the compress of melting snow onto the table behind her. "This wasn't a good idea."

Danika swallowed, her throat suddenly dry. "You mean helping me tonight, or . . ."

"All of it," he replied tersely, a thick growl that rasped through his teeth and the lengthening points of his fangs.

But he didn't withdraw from where he hunched before her, and his eyes remained fixed on her face, tormented and stormy. Smoldering with the same dark longing that had begun to kindle inside her. He snarled a curse, low under his breath. "I have to go. I have to get back to the club before Reiver notices I'm gone."

"Don't," she blurted, shaking her head when he started to move away from her. The thought of being left alone, just Connor and her, after the night they'd already had put a chill in her veins. And she couldn't bear the idea of Reiver possibly finding out what Malcolm had done for her and meting out punishment. "Don't go back there. How can you even think of going back now?"

"I have a job to do, Dani. Simple as that."

"Reiver is an animal," she reminded him. "He's a beast who trades in human lives. You said yourself he would've had me and my child murdered in cold blood."

"Yes," Malcolm agreed tightly. "Reiver is all those things. Worse, in fact. A pity you didn't realize that sooner, before everything went to hell tonight."

There wasn't much blame in that accusation. Rather, a stark dread. A fear in his eyes that his anger didn't quite mask. She searched that haunted gaze, hurting for him, wanting to understand who he'd become. "What happened to you, Malcolm? What happened to your face, to your name . . . to the man you used to be?"

"He's gone, as dead as you are now." His mouth was a grim line, a muscle ticking in the side of his savaged, beard-shadowed jaw. "A hell of a lot can happen in a few hundred years, lass."

"Yeah," she said. "I guess it can. I never thought I'd see the day that Malcolm MacBain tossed away his honor and his good name in order to serve someone like Reiver."

"We all make choices. And I have my reasons," he murmured. With that hissed reply, he finally did withdraw from her. Dark lashes shuttering his gaze, he rose to his feet.

She stood with him, nose to nose, refusing to let him shut her out. "Tell me."

"Let it go, Danika." The words were a deep rumble, coming from his chest.

But she couldn't let him walk away. She stared at him harder, pushing her wayward talent in his direction. "You hate him."

He didn't answer; but then, he didn't have to. His big body radiated loathing.

"It's not loyalty that makes you serve Reiver," she said. "It's rage. Isn't it?"

His thoughts answered her like a reflex: *He took something precious from me. Everything I had. I will stop at nothing to make him pay.*

Danika closed her eyes as the grief of that pledge sank into her consciousness. "Mal, I'm sorry."

He roared a dark curse, and then his hands were on her arms, gripping her firmly, hauling her into the shadow of his powerful body. Into the face of his fury. "Goddamn it, woman! Stay out of my thoughts." His grasp held tighter, his eyes bright and wild now, lips peeled back from his enormous fangs. "Why couldn't you have stayed the bloody fuck out of my life?"

Danika had never cowered before a man, not Conlan

or any other Breed male. Not even Reiver, or the brutal messengers he'd sent to her cottage earlier that night. But Malcolm's fury was a storm that slammed into her, stripping her of her courage. Buffeting her with a ferocity that left her shaking, breathless.

He was a dangerous man. Even more so because he was wounded, deep down. Festering with a hatred that was eating him alive. She saw that now. And something more in the searing amber fire of his eyes.

Desire.

The interest that had sparked between them before was burned away now. Turned into something far more consuming as Malcolm's hot gaze bore into her, then slowly settled on her parted lips. Another thought arrowed from his mind into hers, uninvited this time, dark and startling in its carnality.

She could have told him to release her. As formidable as he was, as volatile and strong as she knew him to be, he would have taken his hands off her in an instant if she'd wanted him to.

But that wasn't what she wanted.

And he knew it as well as she did.

"Danika," he rasped thickly, eyes flaring hotly. Then his mouth was on hers.

The contact was explosive, staggering. It had been so long since she'd been touched, kissed, desired. Malcolm's lips seduced, demanded, claiming hers with a passion that stole all the breath from her lungs. She hadn't realized how much she'd missed the feeling, and even though a part of her had not let go of Conlan—might never fully let him go—the part of her that was still vital, still alive and warm and female, could not deny this need for comforting. For physical, intimate contact.

The fact that it was Malcolm kissing her now, his

hands stroking her arms and throat, strong fingers slipping into the fine hair at her nape as he pulled her deeper
into his embrace, deeper into his dizzying kiss, only
made her need quicken even more.

He dragged his mouth to the sensitive skin below her
ear, breath scorching, voice gravelly and dark. "Christ,
lass. You shouldn't feel this good. I shouldn't want you
like this."

She moaned her reply, lost to the same overwhelming
need. For Malcolm. For the feel of his strong hands on
her, familiar and yet so very new. No stranger could
have stirred her the way he did now, and she let him
sweep her into the current of his passion.

The edge of the table pressed into her backside; Malcolm's hard, masculine body hemmed her in from the
front. Even through their clothes, the heat between
them was undeniable. The thick jut of his arousal was a
heavy demand against her hip, a delicious friction that
ground into her in a primal rhythm, his palms and
fingers stroking her breasts over the soft knit of her
sweater.

Her hands craved to explore him too. She ran them
up his broad chest, following the taut slabs of muscle
that felt like iron beneath his dark T-shirt. The *dermaglyphs* on his bared biceps surged with the colors of his
need. Dark wine, burnished gold, and deepest indigo
pulsed like living tattoos, intensifying with each fevered
beat of his heart.

When she lifted her gaze back to Malcolm's face, she
found his expression fierce, his fangs stretched long and
sharp, his pupils transformed to catlike slits, all but
eclipsed by scorching pools of amber. That light flashed
hotter when he reached between her thighs and rubbed
the seat of his palm against the aching core of her body.

Danika arched into his touch, panting as he stroked her, every nerve ending exploding in waves of hot need.

"Tell me to stop," he whispered thickly against her mouth, the sharp points of his fangs grazing her lips. "Tell me you don't want this."

But she could say no such thing. Her cry of mounting release was all she could manage as a dam inside her crumbled away like rubble under the skill of his touch. She broke apart, gasping his name and holding on to his thick shoulders as he pressed her spine down onto the table and covered her with his body.

Clothing came off in a rush, flung away in mere seconds.

And then they were naked together. Skin to skin, hands roaming over bare flesh. Mouths teasing, testing, taking.

Malcolm's thick sex cleaved the wet petals of her body, a heavy demand that made her thighs part wider to take him. He entered her with a curse huffed coarsely between his lips. His long thrust filled her completely, made her arch beneath him in boneless pleasure. His cock invaded and coaxed at the same time, aggressive yet careful, steel sheathed in softest velvet. In that fevered moment, she couldn't get enough.

Although they'd never kissed before, never touched— certainly never as they had tonight—he knew just how to move with her, when to push her to the edge and where to let her take control of their tempo.

She opened her eyes and saw a man she knew, a man she trusted with this fragile, needful reawakening of her body. "Malcolm," she panted, reaching up to caress his rough jaw and savaged cheek as he rocked into her with a relentless rhythm. "Oh, God, Mal . . ."

She didn't know what she meant to say to him. She

didn't know if there were words. But then he kissed her and the need to speak left her. He drove harder, deeper, until another orgasm raced up on her and swept her over a steep ledge. He came with her. His shout of release was raw and possessive, taking with it her need to think, or to question how they could have ended up like this, together after lifetimes apart.

Naked and burning in each other's arms.

CHAPTER
Six

It wasn't until the roar of his orgasm subsided that Malcolm felt the full weight of what he'd done.

Sex, with Danika.

The widowed Breedmate of a male who'd been like a brother to him all that time ago. The woman who'd put herself in Reiver's crosshairs and was liable to derail Malcolm's entire purpose for living. A female he had no right to desire, let alone seduce—least of all at a time when neither of them could afford the distraction.

It hadn't been his intention to have Danika naked beneath him tonight. Far from it, in fact. Yet he couldn't muster the good sense to regret what had happened here.

Carnal, fevered, incredible sex.

And his greedy body only wanted more.

He stared down at her, laid out before him like an offering on the kitchen table.

Christ, she was beautiful. Milky skin and long, lean limbs. Supple curves in all the right places. He stroked his hands over her perfection. Brushed his fingers across her breasts and down her abdomen, where a small red birthmark in the shape of a teardrop and crescent moon stamped her as a Breedmate—a female meant for his kind, capable of bearing Breed young and bonding to one of his race eternally through blood. Only death could sever it.

The sight of that diminutive mark on Danika Mac-Conn sent a jolt of possessiveness through him—unbidden, but hard to ignore. His fangs were still filling his mouth from the passion he'd shared with her. Now a darker need put a throb in his gums, made his amber-hot eyes burn brighter in his skull . . . made his pulse quicken with the urge to feed. To take her delicate throat in his mouth and pierce the pretty vein that ticked there.

To drink from her and bind this female to him at last.

That urge boiled past his lips on a low growl.

Danika's dusky blue gaze lifted to him, and he could only hope her ability hadn't betrayed his thoughts to her. "Come, lass," he rasped, disengaging from her heat to take her into his arms.

He lifted her up and carried her away from the table, striding naked with her, out of the kitchen and up the castle stairwell to the master bedroom on the second floor. His bedroom. The one he hadn't set foot in for months.

Not since he'd buried the ruined pieces of his old life and his quest to destroy Reiver began.

He brought Danika into the room and set her down on the king-size four-poster bed. The thing was a relic, only a couple hundred years younger than he was. Its headboard, canopy, and carved supports were made of tooled black walnut, its thick down mattress cloaked in creamy sheepskin coverlets and wool blankets woven in MacBain red and black. Danika looked sexy as hell in the middle of it, propped up on her elbows, one slender leg bent at the knee.

Malcolm wanted her all over again.

Still.

Her heavy-lidded gaze raked his naked body and she gave him a knowing smile, all the invitation he required.

He prowled onto the bed and covered her, sank back into her welcoming warmth. He made love to her slowly this time, properly, the way a woman like her deserved to be pleasured. When they were both slicked in clean sweat and sated again, he stretched out alongside her and gathered her close. He stroked her pretty breasts, caressed her delicate throat and jawline. Tried to will his eager, all-too-obvious erection to heel. An exercise in futility when Danika reached down to touch him, wrapping her fingers around the shaft and tenderly petting its length.

He groaned, savoring the feel of her hands on him. His curse was raw in his throat, as dark as the guilt that was suddenly rising up on him. He'd been able to push it aside so long as his senses were consumed with need, but now it gnawed at him.

Danika's touch went still. She was looking at him in concern now, forehead creased. "What is it, Mal? Am I doing something wrong?"

"No." He cursed again and brought her hand up to his mouth to place a kiss in her palm. "Nothing you've done is wrong. As for me . . . Christ." He met her searching gaze, hated that he was making her think she was at fault somehow. He couldn't keep his hands from seeking her out. His fingers craved the feel of her the same way his cock longed to be back inside her. "I feel like

I'm betraying Conlan when I touch you. I'm betraying him by wanting you . . . now, as I did then."

She stared at him in silence, a flicker of surprise in her eyes. "You wanted me?" She gave a small shake of her head, dismissing the idea with a quiet laugh. "As I recall it, through all your travels and exploits at the time, there was hardly a woman you met that you didn't eventually charm out of her virtue."

"But not you. And you were the only one I loved," he confessed, too late to bite it back.

He and Conlan had been friends for years, neighbors for even longer. They'd defended their lands together, rode into battles as a single force, as brothers. But as close as they'd been on the field and in duty, the two Breed males couldn't have been more different. Malcolm craved adventure and was always ready to chase it. Conlan was the steady one, the reliable one. The one most deserving of an extraordinary female like Danika.

Mal could still picture the night he and Con first saw her—the golden, Nordic beauty and adopted daughter of a powerful Darkhaven leader from Copenhagen. She was in Scotland on sojourn, independent even then, a mere girl of eighteen, staying with Breed relations in Edinburgh. Mal had wasted no time making introductions, seeking to impress her with stories of his travels all over the world and his dangerous exploits.

But it was Conlan who eventually won her over. Calm and considerate, steady Con.

"You were so unsettled, always unpredictable," she remarked now. "You would have broken my heart."

"Probably," he admitted. "But I was an idiot then. I didn't realize what you meant to me until Con confided that you and he were to be mated."

She swallowed, scarcely breathing now. "I never knew."

"Would it have made a difference if you had?"

Her eyes fell away from him for a moment, considering. "No, it wouldn't have. Conlan was a good man, a good mate to me through all our time together. I loved him completely. I always will."

Mal nodded, even though the words tasted bitter. "He honored you well. As I knew he would."

Danika reached for him now, her fingertips light on his clenched jaw. "Con's gone, and I'm still alive. I still mourn him, but I can't tell you that my heart isn't glad to be looking at you now, Malcolm. I won't deny that it feels good to be touching you, to be lying here with you, like this. I didn't realize how alone I've felt this past year until I had your arms around me." She stroked his scarred cheek, the pad of her thumb brushing tenderly over the poorly healed knife wound. "Conlan's not the only one you feel you're betraying here tonight, is he?"

He turned his head to avoid the contact, wishing he could avoid reliving the failure that earned him that brutal gash. Before Danika had a chance to prod his mind for answers, he mentally slammed the gate down hard on his past. Locked it behind a wall of cold fury. "I don't want to talk about that, Dani."

"You have an unfinished nursery upstairs," she murmured, sitting up with him when he started to move away from her on the bed. "You obviously don't live here anymore, or haven't in quite some time. And even though I can tell you're blocking me from your mind right now, downstairs in the kitchen, your thoughts gave away that you lost someone you loved. I know you're grieving and angry—"

"I said I don't want to talk about it," he snapped harshly. "All of that is personal."

She exhaled a quiet scoff. "There's nothing more personal than what we shared tonight. How can telling me about your past—about the mate it's obvious you loved and lost—be more intimate than this?"

"Because the less you know, the safer it will be for you." He swung his feet to the floor. "I have to go. I've been away from the club for too long."

Danika swung off the bed before he could, putting herself in front of him. Her hands were on his shoulders, her eyes searching his. "How long have you been plotting to kill Reiver?"

Mal hissed a curse. "Just drop it, Dani."

He felt her push harder at his mind. A determined prod, and then she was inside his thoughts, pulling the truth out of him against his will. "Seven months," she whispered, staggering back on her heels. "You've had to look at him, work for him . . . all this time. Why?"

"Because I needed to get close to him," Mal ground out. "I needed to get in deep enough to destroy him, not just kill him. God knows that would've been easy enough to do by now. For what he did to Fiona, I want to destroy him and all of his cronies who hide behind their wealth and connections, feeling themselves above any law. All I've been waiting for is the chance—and it's coming. I've never been closer to having this thing done."

"What happened to your Breedmate, Mal?" Danika reached out, smoothed her hands over his scarred, broken face. "Have you told anyone at all?"

He shook his head, mute for a long moment as the memories swelled, black as acid. "I hadn't planned to take a mate. I'd been alone for so long, I'd gotten used to my freedom. I fed from human females, found pleasure with more than a few. But I made it my habit to steer clear of the women with this damnable mark," he said, tracing the edges of the Breedmate birthmark on Danika's trim belly. "But then I met Fiona. She was sweet and gentle and innocent—just a girl of twenty-two. Everything was fresh to her, everything a new adventure, something magical. She looked at me in much the same way, like some kind of goddamned hero from a fairy tale. I had centuries of living behind me, battles won and lost. I looked at Fiona and realized I'd forgotten what it was like to be so carefree and open."

Danika gave him a tender, wry smile. "You were never either of those things, Mal. Brooding and enigmatic, yes. And devastatingly charming, in your own grim way."

He nodded, unsure why it should come as such a surprise that Dani would know him so well, even after all this time. His mouth quirked with humor, despite the gravity of his memories. "I tried to keep that cynical, world-weary side of me away from Fiona. Figured I'd let it out a little at a time, lest I scare her off too soon."

"But she didn't scare away," Danika said, holding him in a gentle gaze.

Mal shook his head. "No, she didn't. We were together less than a year when I found myself falling in love with her. We blood-bonded, making our home together here at the castle. It wasn't long before she asked me to give her a child. She was only a few months pregnant when . . ."

Danika's breath hitched in her throat. "You lost them both at the same time? Oh, Mal."

"She'd gone to Edinburgh to pick up some custom-made bedding—something to match the mural she was painting on the nursery walls." He grunted, throat still rough with regret. "It was morning, so I stayed home. As it was, I'd been working on a surprise for her that I hoped to finish while she was gone. The rocking chair was almost finished when I felt a jolt of terror through our blood bond. Fiona was in danger, in pain. And I was trapped in this bloody fortress by the sunlight burning outside its walls."

Danika swore softly, pulling his head against her breast. "I'm so sorry, Malcolm."

"I called her cell phone," he murmured, remembering all too vividly the fear that had gripped him in those frantic first moments. "I called six times, a dozen . . . it rang unanswered. I had no choice but to go out and look for her."

Danika's heart thudded beneath his ear. "In broad daylight—knowing it would kill you?"

"I didn't care. I went on foot to the city, the fastest means of reaching her. I followed her through our bond, into the crudest of Edinburgh's slums. It was near noon, and my skin was turning to ash. But she was alive, and I still had a chance of saving her." He shook his head. "I wasn't in the city more than a few minutes when I felt our connection go still. It severed, and I knew she was dead. I'd failed her."

She sat down next to him on the edge of the bed. "You did all you could, Malcolm. More than anyone would expect."

"No," he said. "Not yet. But I will do right by her. I don't know how long I stood there in the street after she was gone, sensing my flesh was burning but feeling only the emptiness of loss. But then dark clouds moved in and a heavy rain started. It bought me time, which I used to search the city. I looked for her until I found a drug dealer who'd heard of a pimp scoring large off finders' fees for pretty young women—even some men and children—in demand by a client of particular tastes."

"Live human game," Dani breathed. "For Reiver and his blood clubs."

Mal nodded. "I never knew such rage as I did when the pimp who took Fiona coughed up Reiver's name. It was the last thing he did. He admitted attacking her that day. He'd grabbed her a few blocks away from the shop she'd visited and took her back to the filth of his flat, where he'd arrange for her sale. But she fought him. She fought for herself and our baby. The pimp had a knife. She tried to get away, and he stabbed her through the heart."

"Oh, my God." A tear streamed down Danika's cheek.

"The bastard used that same knife on my face in the moments before I crushed his skull in my bare hands," Malcolm said, his voice flat in his ears. "Part of me wanted to go after Reiver right away. I wanted swift, brutal justice. But Fiona was more important. I couldn't leave her in that place, with that human garbage. So I brought her home. I buried her here that same day, and I swore to her that Reiver and all those who funded his operation would pay with their lives. I won't rest until I've destroyed them all."

"And so you've forced yourself to serve those same men. All this time." Danika was looking at him, sorrowful, almost pitying. "But at what cost to yourself, Mal?"

"At any cost." He got up hastily, tension riding him for the unplanned, unwanted baring of his soul. "It's late, Dani. I can't risk more time here. I want you to stay put at the castle while I'm gone. I'll try to come back before daybreak."

He didn't wait for her to agree. He stalked toward the adjacent bathroom, willing the shower on with his mind, leaving Danika in silence behind him.

CHAPTER
Seven

Reiver was waiting for him when Malcolm arrived back at the club.

"Busy night, Brandogge?" Reiver was in the public room of the establishment, reclined on a leather sofa, his dress shirt and suit pants unbuttoned. With him was a topless brunette under one arm, a blonde scantily clad in a red lace bra and panties under the other—club regulars whom Reiver kept in frequent rotation in his own personal stable. The women were in his thrall, puncture marks still faintly visible on their necks and limbs, hands roaming all over him as he watched Malcolm with shrewd, untrusting eyes. "I looked for you a couple of hours ago. Thane mentioned he thought you went out for a bit. An important errand or something, he guessed."

Thane, the ass-kissing bastard. Was he worried Mal might be his chief competition as Reiver's right arm? Little did the other guard know what Mal had in store for their employer. And if he got in the way when the

time came for Mal to make his move, he wasn't op-
posed to taking Thane out too.

At least he'd sent the feminine diversion as Mal had
asked. For that alone, he was tempted not to wish the
guy dead in the fallout yet to come.

And whatever Thane's intentions, Mal knew better
than to let Reiver think he had him caught in a lie or
betrayal of trust.

"I went out to check on Packard and Kerr," he volunteered. "I didn't tell Thane where I was going, since I
wasn't sure you'd want anyone else privy to your instructions where the woman was concerned. I figured
Thane would know if you wanted him to know."

Reiver grunted, toying with a lock of the brunette's
long hair. "There was a house fire reported on the Mac-
Conn lands tonight. Packard and Kerr haven't come
back."

"They're dead," Mal replied flatly. "By the time I got
there, things were already going south. The woman
wasn't about to go down easy. Turns out she had a child
to protect too. She was putting up a hell of a fight. It
was getting messy."

He didn't have to fake the bitterness of his report. It
echoed a similar one that had occurred seven months
earlier, in the filthy hovel of a pimp's dank flat. Only
Malcolm hadn't reached that altercation in time to
make a difference.

He muzzled his hatred and channeled it into a mask
of cold indifference. "Packard and Kerr were botching
your orders. I had no choice but to finish things as
cleanly as possible and obliterate the evidence."

"The Breedmate and her child?"

Malcolm shrugged, nonchalant. "As was your concern, she would've been a persistent problem. So I made

sure the situation was snuffed out permanently. Packard and Kerr were collateral damage."

Reiver's dark brows lifted as he considered the account. Then he chuckled darkly and got up from the sofa, bringing his pair of human playthings along with him. He walked over to Malcolm and cuffed his shoulder. "Good work, Bran. No doubt you've worked up an appetite taking care of so much important business for me." Reiver shoved the blonde at him. "She's yours to do with what you will. Never let it be said I don't reward my loyal hounds with a juicy bone when they've earned it."

Malcolm caught the woman as she stumbled into him, dazed and unsteady from her service tonight. She reeked of liquor and narcotics, sex and blood loss. Mal's stomach recoiled, but his revulsion centered on the vampire who watched him closely, waiting to see how Malcolm would respond.

He had no thirst that needed slaking in this place, least of all when it would come from Reiver's leavings. But in seven months of indenture to his vow of vengeance, he'd passed worse tests than this. He'd be damned if he failed now, when Danika and her son were in his keeping, their lives in his hands.

It was rage for what Reiver had ordered tonight that made Mal's hands rougher than intended on the whore tossed at him. It was thoughts of Danika, the impulse he'd felt to pierce her pretty, unspoiled throat and bind her to him, that brought his fangs out to their full, razor-sharp length.

And it was stone-cold determination—a chill and hollow resolve—that made him latch on to the human's neck and swallow gulp after gulp of her fouled blood while Reiver held his gaze, chuckling with sick amusement.

Mal drank until Reiver was gone. Only then did he set the woman away from him, a sweep of his tongue sealing the wounds he'd made before he eased her down onto the sofa, where she fell into a hard sleep.

He wiped the back of his hand across his face, cursing a string of crude Gaelic between his gritted teeth and fangs. The taste in his mouth was rank, bitter. He spat some of it out, startled to hear a throat clear behind him.

Malcolm wheeled around to find Thane in the room with him. "What the fuck are you looking at?"

The black-haired vampire glanced from the limp form of the human female, back to Malcolm. "Don't mean to interrupt, but we've got a couple of patrons causing problems with some of the girls on the main floor. Slapping them around, getting too rough. I told the boss but he says he ain't running a public relations firm in here."

"Yeah?" Mal countered, still vibrating with unvented violence. "What are you telling me for?"

Thane lifted one of his massive shoulders in a vague shrug. "Boss said he doesn't want to be bothered with club issues tonight, so I was thinking I'd go down and dole out some etiquette lessons to the assholes. Wondered if you might feel like joining me."

Mal narrowed a look on the guard, trying to get a read on him. He didn't know if this was yet another test of Reiver's making or some trap of Thane's own. Somehow, he didn't think so. And at that moment, he didn't care.

"Let's go," he snarled, leading the way.

* * *

In the hour before dawn, Malcolm arrived back at the castle. Danika was dozing with little Connor in her arms, nestled together in a large, overstuffed chair in the great hall on the first floor. She woke when Mal entered, heard his booted footsteps, his long-legged stride, coming up the short flight of the stairwell from the tower house's entrance on ground level.

He paused in the arched entryway, his dark brows furrowing as his eyes lit on her and her sleeping son. "After the way we left things between us, I half expected you to be gone when I got here," he murmured.

His face looked so weary and grim, his expression so bleakly tormented, she had no choice but to ask. "Expected, or hoped?"

A quiet scoff, then a slow shake of his head. "Both, maybe."

He started walking farther up the stairwell.

"Mal, wait." She tucked Connor into a secure cocoon of blankets and pillows on the chair, then went to follow Malcolm. "Where are you going?"

His deep voice rumbled from the floor above. "To wash off the stink of Reiver's club."

By the time she reached him, he was already in the master bedroom, already stripping off his weapons and clothing. In moments he was naked, gloriously so. Thick muscle rippled as he strode across the floor toward the adjacent bathroom. Danika reached for his hand, forcing him to pause. The copper tang of human blood was ripe on him.

"You've been feeding tonight." She looked at his fisted hand, so large and powerful, heavy in her grasp. The knuckles were tinted dark with bruises, recent contusions not quite healed over. "You've been fighting. What else did you do tonight?"

He stared at her for a long minute, then drew his hand out of her hold and raked his battered fingers through his hair. "It's a job, Dani. Don't make me explain how I have to do it."

As if that was all he needed to say, he stalked into the bathroom and flipped on the shower. He stepped under the spray, began a vigorous scrub of his body.

She watched him for a moment, stung by his dismissal. And more than that, she worried for what his need to avenge his loss was doing to him. She dreaded what it might cost him.

"I think I have a right to be concerned about you, Mal. It's not as if we're strangers, after all." He didn't answer her, just kept up his furious scouring of his skin. He shampooed his dark hair with equal anger, then doused the suds from his head and body under the steaming hot water. "I care about you, Malcolm. I'm afraid for you."

"Don't be." His eyes blazed as he cut off the shower and pulled a towel off the wall hook outside the tiled alcove. "If you want to fear something, be afraid for yourself if Reiver realizes what I've done. Now more than ever, I need to bring that bastard down."

She shook her head, understanding only in that moment how consumed he was with the hatred he felt for Reiver. "This quest for revenge is destroying you, Mal, not him. How long can you brush up against evil and not come away stained with it yourself?"

"My problem. Not yours." He dried off hastily, then tossed the towel aside to step past her. "Don't worry about my life when you have your own and your child's to think about."

"You arrogant jackass." She glared at him, hating him for his self-sacrifice as much as she loved him for it.

Oh, God. Yes, loved him. Some part of her probably always had. "There was a time I considered you among my dearest friends, Malcolm MacBain. And now—"

"Now what?" His voice shook with a tightly leashed rage as he wheeled on her, eyes blazing. "We had sex, Dani. Great sex, I'll grant you, but your timing sucks. My life is in motion. I'm on this path, and there's too damned much at stake here. I won't put you any closer to the fire than you already are."

"And I can't stand by and watch you burn." She swallowed past the icy clump of lead that sat in her throat. The feeling sank as she stared up at him, the cold settling heavily on her heart. "I've lost one man I loved, Malcolm. I can't put myself through that kind of pain again."

Only then did his face lose some of its hard line and vicious tension. A muscle ticked wildly in the grizzled side of his jaw, and now his eyes smoldered with a darker, less terrifying fury. "Danika, I . . ." He scowled abruptly, blew out a raw curse. When he reached out to her, his hand shook a little. His fingers found her cheek with aching tenderness, curved around gently to cup the back of her neck. He brought her to him, placed a heart-breaking kiss to her lips.

She melted into him despite the hurt and anger that tore at her inside. His embrace was firm and warm, his mouth a soothing balm when all she wanted to do was rage at him, demand things she had no right to expect from him.

His fangs grazed her lightly as he let his mouth drift away from hers, then lower, to the sensitive skin of her throat. She held her breath with a needful anticipation, her veins calling to him, hearing his own heartbeat—his unspoken thoughts—echoing through every electrified nerve ending in her body. Her head tilted as though pulled on invisible strings, granting him access to the throbbing of her pulse. He kissed her there, tender and sweet. Teased the delicate spot with his tongue and teeth and fangs. A moan escaped him then, guttural with denial.

"I can't," he murmured against her lips. "I won't turn the mistakes I've made with you into something irreparable, Dani." He drew back, pressed his forehead to hers as he held her against his naked body. "Time was never on our side, was it? Fate gives us nothing more than a taste of what might have been."

She couldn't speak. Couldn't deny him as he kissed her once more and led her toward the bed. They made love in a breathless tangle, no promises or denials. No words at all. Only passion.

Danika wept for the pleasure he gave her, and for the inescapable fact that these would be the last moments they had together.

Because she'd meant what she told him: She could not stand by and watch his hatred for Reiver destroy him. Her heart couldn't bear another loss.

So as he slept beside her in a heavy doze, Danika slipped out of bed to make a cowardly call on his cell phone from downstairs. "Gideon," she whispered when the scrambled number in Boston connected. "I need to get out of Scotland, and I need the Order's help."

CHAPTER
Eight

It was harder than he cared to admit, leaving Danika that evening at sundown so he could be back at the club before Reiver showed up and wondered where his suddenly straying "Brandogge" had been all day. Malcolm bristled at the role he'd been forced to play. His collar was beginning to chafe—all the more so when he couldn't shake the feeling that it was costing him something he hadn't expected to crave so deeply.

Saying good-bye to her a couple of hours ago had a queer feeling of finality to it. Her kiss had been too resigned. Her embrace had been too tender, too lacking in demand.

He was losing her.

Hell, he'd practically pushed her away himself.

It should have come as a relief in many ways. Romantic entanglement was the dead last thing he needed. He'd been so careful to avoid even casual dalliances since he'd buried his innocent mate and unborn child. Months of work hammering the molten iron of his grief and rage into a resolve made of cold, unbreakable steel.

He'd had it all under his control. Until three nights ago, when he'd chanced to spot the pale, beautiful light that was Danika MacConn, standing mere yards away from him at the Darkhaven party. If only he hadn't seen her. If only he hadn't made it his mission to follow her all night with his gaze, torn between wanting to avoid her notice and wanting nothing more than to place himself in front of her and see if she would remember him. If she would know him, through the mask of his scars and the shield of his false name.

Calling her out that night through his knowledge of her talent had been a reckless move. An arrogant one that he'd known, even then, he would be unable to call back.

Now it was much too late to wish he'd kept his distance.

Too late to think he could go back to what things were like before she arrived in Scotland.

Too late to try to convince himself that he didn't care for Danika . . . that he couldn't possibly have lost his heart to her all over again.

He loved her.

There was a part of him that always had.

The realization hit him with such staggering force, it was all he could do not to storm out of Reiver's damnable club and tell Danika exactly how he felt about her. Words he should have given her already today, when she was kissing him good-bye and he was trying to convince himself that he couldn't keep her. That it wasn't killing something inside of him to consider what he might be throwing away with Dani by holding on so tightly to the need to avenge his dead.

Malcolm cursed roundly and sent his fist into the side of a priceless Roman urn in one of the club's private salons. The ancient objet d'art exploded, shattering into a thousand tiny airborne shards.

"That's gonna cost you heavily with the boss."

Thane chuckled from behind him, and at the sight of the other guard, Malcolm lost it. He flew at the vampire on a roar, fangs erupting in his rage. In truth, no one was more deserving of his fury than himself, but he was ripe for a fight and Thane was the closest target. Besides, the son of a bitch had been giving him about a hundred good reasons lately to kick his ass. Mal snarled with violent intent. "You picked the wrong damn time to be in my face, Thane."

"I didn't come in here to pick a fight with you," he snapped back. "I came to tell you Reiver's drafted us as security for tonight's gathering."

Malcolm narrowed a glare on him. "What gathering?"

Thane gave him a shrewd, knowing look. "Reiver called from the airport. His cargo came in. He's moving it to one of his country estates as we speak." He shoved Mal's arm away from him, hissing a hard curse as he straightened his rumpled dark suit coat. "Since Kerr and Packard are no longer in service, that leaves you and me to head up security tonight. Reiver's expecting his top-tier clients at this thing, so he wants total discretion."

Blood club.

Malcolm knew this moment would come one night, but it still took him aback. This was it—his shot, at last, to take out Reiver and all of his untouchable cronies in one fell swoop. "When do we leave?" he asked, hoping the tight edge of his voice would not betray his eagerness to Thane.

"The boss wants us out there right away."

Mal nodded. Malice coursed through his veins like acid. He met Thane's inscrutable look and gave the guard a cold smile. "So, what the hell are we waiting for?"

Half a dozen gleaming luxury vehicles sat parked outside Reiver's hunting estate, as if their owners were gathered inside for a black-tie event, not the sick, bloody game soon to take place on the snow-covered grounds.

And there would be blood tonight, Malcolm silently vowed, as he and Thane walked up to the front of the palatial Highlands residence. His jaw was clamped tight, veins vibrating malice as another of Reiver's guards opened the door to permit them inside. "This way," said the Breed thug with a jerk of his head. "Mr. Reiver has been waiting for you."

He was in a lavish salon, its high-ceilinged walls paneled in dark mahogany and adorned with painted masterworks depicting all manner of hunting scenes. Graceful stags being felled by medieval archers' arrows; small red foxes on the run from a pack of brown-and-white hounds and red-jacketed gentlemen on horseback; a majestic lion snared and surrounded by spear-wielding natives before a white-skinned adventurer toting a long black rifle. The room was a celebration of slaughter, and assembled within it stood Reiver and the nearly dozen members of his privileged, secret cabal of savages.

"Ah," said Reiver with a thin smile. "About time you arrived. We're just about to view the evening's game selection." His bloodthirsty friends exchanged eager looks, but Reiver's gaze stayed rooted on Malcolm with cool scrutiny. "Shall we get started?"

Reiver touched the frame on the fox hunt painting. In response, from behind the group of elegantly attired vampires, a doorway on the back wall of the salon opened into a dimly lit corridor. With a look that bade Malcolm and Thane follow him, Reiver strode through the center of the throng to lead the way.

Inside the long corridor was still more violent art. Here the depictions of hunter and hunted became more gruesome, scene after scene showing all manner of human degradation and bloodshed. It was horrific art, a profane collection no doubt intended to inflame the basest Breed appetites. Malcolm paid it little mind. All of his focus was centered on Reiver, senses taut and at the ready, waiting for the prime opportunity to lodge his offensive strike on the vampire and his cronies.

As they neared the end of the corridor, Reiver touched another hidden panel on the wall. Cold air gusted in as a thick wooden gate lifted, revealing a covered walkway leading to the outside grounds of the estate. Flanking both sides of the walkway were iron-barred kennel cages, but the cells did not contain animals.

"My God," one of Reiver's cronies breathed from behind Malcolm. "Just look at them all. One more tempting than the next."

Reiver chuckled, so full of himself. "As promised, something for every taste."

The humans were bound and gagged inside their cages, upwards of twenty men and women, all shapes and sizes and ages. They shivered in the wintry night air, eyes wide and fearful. Bile rose in Malcolm's throat as he glanced at the terror-stricken faces. He could not let this sick game proceed any further. Reiver and his blood club associates would die tonight—here and now.

He started to reach for his weapons, prepared to unleash hell on the whole lot of them.

"Oh, but there's more," Reiver announced, snapping his fingers at one of the other guards, dispatching him in unspoken command. "Tonight I have something very unexpected to offer you, and most certainly . . . exotic. Brandogge, I think you'll have particular interest in this."

Malcolm went stock-still at the remark, a cold dread locking down his senses even before he glimpsed what the guard had gone to fetch.

Danika.

Unlike the others, she wasn't shackled or muzzled. No, the pistol pressed to the back of her head was enough to ensure she didn't fight or flee her captors.

Her long blond hair hung limp over her face as she shuffled ahead of Reiver's thug, little Connor held tight in her arms. Malcolm's heart lurched as her stricken gaze lit on him through the crowd. There was apology in her moist blue eyes, a regretful twist to her pale lips.

Before Malcolm could react—before he could calculate the terrible risks of wheeling on Reiver and his associates and hoping to take them out before the guard with the gun on Danika pulled the trigger—Thane and two other guards pounced on him. Dani screamed, and it nearly undid him to hear the terror and worry in her voice. Worry for him, when it was his personal need for retribution that brought them both to this awful moment.

The cold metal nose of Thane's loaded nine-millimeter jabbed hard and ready to fire into Mal's temple. "Don't do anything stupid, asshole."

Malcolm roared, but it was impotent rage. He couldn't attempt to throw off his captors. He couldn't do anything—not so long as Danika and her baby were at equal risk as he. "Thane, you goddamn bastard. I'll kill you too, before this is over."

The guard seemed unfazed, keeping a steady hand on the weapon poised to blow Malcolm's brain out of his skull. One of the other guards stripped Mal of his Glocks and pocketed them.

While Reiver's associates inched away, he strode forward, slowly shaking his head. "You lied to me. You betrayed my trust." He paused in front of Malcolm, seething with thinly held malice. "You could have risen far in my service. I thought that's what you were aiming for, Brandogge. So, the only question I have is, why would you be so fucking stupid to cross me now?"

Malcolm growled his reply. "I'm not your dog. I've never been your anything, you arrogant son of a bitch." He could see the flicker of confusion in Reiver's dark eyes, and he kept going, glad to finally voice his intentions. "I've been waiting for the chance to kill you and your blood club cronies ever since your pimp in Edinburgh told me your name."

Reiver's confusion deepened, turned to uncertainty and a sick look of surprise. "My pimp?"

"Aye," Mal ground out. "The human rubbish who'd been supplying game for your sick gatherings. The same human offal who grabbed a young woman off the street in Edinburgh seven months ago for the purpose of selling her to you."

Reiver scoffed. "Am I to fret over every ant that gets crushed under a boot heel? Or mourn every beast sent to the abattoir? This is no different, except it's us on the top of the food chain, not mankind."

"She was a Breedmate," Malcolm hissed. "And she was newly pregnant. She put up a fight with your supplier. He killed her. My mate, my unborn child."

Reiver's bark of laughter erupted out of him. "All this for a female, Brandogge? And a dead one besides?" His cruel gaze slid to Danika. "And now this other one too? What does she mean to you?"

"Leave her out of this," Mal snarled. "She has nothing to do with it."

"Oh, but she does." Reiver's eyes turned brutal, sparking with amber. "She matters to you, and that means she and her brat will suffer worse than you now. Pity you won't live to see that." He glanced to Thane. "Kill him."

The icy metal of the gun bit harder into Mal's temple, Thane's finger on the trigger.

Then, in a blur of movement and speed, he pivoted, firing instead on the guard holding Danika.

The guard went down, head blasted apart. Chaos erupted. Reiver's cronies scattered as Thane shot one of the guards on Malcolm and Mal snapped the neck of the other.

"Dani, run!" he shouted, grabbing his weapons from the dead vampire and wheeling around to fire a hell storm of bullets into Reiver.

Too late.

Reiver was already on her.

Malcolm's vision burned amber hot as he raised both loaded Glocks and aimed them in the center of Reiver's sneering face.

Except it wasn't Reiver's face he saw down the barrels of his guns . . .

Ah, Christ.

It was Danika's baby boy, wailing and squirming,

dangling by the pudgy little arm that Reiver clutched tight in his fist. In his other hand, Reiver held a fistful of Danika's hair. She struggled against his brutal hold, her eyes wild with horror, hands reaching for her squalling child.

Reiver's smile was a deadly baring of his fangs. "You lose, Brandogge."

CHAPTER
Nine

Danika could hardly breathe for the fear that gripped her as she watched Connor flailing in Reiver's cruel grasp. Her own pain meant nothing, her own panic and regret—none of it mattered when her child's life literally hung in the balance.

And Malcolm.

Oh, God . . . Mal.

She'd thought things couldn't have gotten worse when Reiver spotted her and Connor arriving at the airport earlier tonight for the flight Gideon had arranged for them back to Denmark. Reiver and his thugs had been there to pick up a live cargo shipment at a private hangar—that same cargo she'd overheard him talking about at the Darkhaven party, a night that seemed a year ago now. They'd grabbed her and Connor and tossed them into the vehicle with the rest of the people intended for Reiver's sick hunting party.

Danika had dreaded what Reiver had in mind, not only for her and her child but for Malcolm as well.

Most of all, for him. Reiver had been unable to hide his fury at having been deceived by Mal about the fact that she was still breathing. Still able to create trouble for him and his sinister business dealings.

And so she *had* created trouble for Reiver—at least, she hoped so, now more than ever.

Her call to the Order had been about more than just arranging passage out of Scotland for Connor and her. She couldn't bear the thought of Malcolm's life in danger, even if it meant interfering in his quest for personal vengeance. She'd brought the Order into the situation. Although the compound in Boston had been thrown into chaos since she'd last talked with Gideon, his immediate inquiries to an Enforcement Agency ally of the Order's revealed that an elite squad of Agents in London were already aware of Reiver and working to bring him down. They even had one of their own embedded in his organization, working as one of his bodyguards.

Danika glanced at the dangerous-looking Breed male with the black hair swept back in a disheveled queue at his nape. The guard called Thane, who'd defied Reiver to help her and Malcolm both. Several of Reiver's cronies lay dead thanks to Thane, the rest having fled, some back into the mansion, others across the snowy expanse of the back lawn.

And now the undercover Enforcement Agent stood as cautious and still as Malcolm, both of them understanding how precious Danika's baby was to her; neither willing to give Reiver the excuse to bring little Connor harm.

"Drop your weapons, both of you." Reiver's voice was otherworldly, a gravelly snarl of menace. "Drop them, or I'll tear this child's arm from its socket and feed it to his mother while you watch."

"Oh, my God," Danika moaned, unable to keep the horror from erupting from her lips. "Please, don't hurt my baby. Please . . ."

Even though it was the only solution she could see, she didn't know what was more terrifying: Reiver's heinous threat, or the fact that it made both Malcolm and Thane slowly disarm and set their guns down on the ground.

"Now back up. Keep moving until I tell you to stop."

They obeyed, both Breed males' eyes simmering with amber fire. "Let them go," Malcolm growled. "Goddamn it, you sick fuck . . . let them go."

Reiver chuckled. "As you wish."

The fist in Danika's hair loosened and suddenly she was pitching forward, a violent shove with a force so punishing she felt as if she were flying. Malcolm moved in a flash of motion, catching her before she fell.

But Reiver wasn't finished yet.

Danika sensed her child was in danger even before Reiver sent Connor airborne. She swung her head around and there he was—her baby, her heart itself—flung aloft like a rag doll as Reiver pivoted, then vanished into the night to make his escape.

Danika screamed as she stared up at her helpless child, her chest exploding in abject terror.

Malcolm jolted into action.

With a running vault, he leapt to catch Connor in midair, bringing him down safely in the cradle of his arms. Danika was on her knees, holding her face in her hands and shaking as Thane stood nearby, making a feeble attempt to console her.

"Dani," Mal murmured. "Danika, it's all right. Connor is safe."

She lifted her tearstained face and sucked in a hitching sob as she took the crying baby out of his hands. "Oh, Mal." She wrapped one arm around his neck, pulling him into her embrace along with her precious child. "Malcolm, thank you. Thank you for saving my son. You saved us."

He kissed her brow and hugged her close, never loving her more than in those terrifying moments when he thought he might lose her to Reiver's fury. "It's all right," he assured her. "You're both safe now. But you have to get out of here."

He helped her to her feet. However, inside he knew he couldn't go with her. Not yet. Not after what Reiver had done here tonight.

Thane, the guard who was no guard at all, gave Mal a grim look. "Reiver won't get far. Neither will his cronies. The Agency is aware of what was going down here tonight. My squad will be here any minute, if they're not waiting outside right now to round everyone up."

Malcolm gave a slow shake of his head. He couldn't trust anyone else to finish this. Not after everything he'd been through. He couldn't rest for a moment thinking Reiver or his murderous colleagues were still walking free, able to hurt more innocent people.

Able to hurt Danika or Connor, the two people who mattered more to him than anything else in his life.

He looked at Dani, his heart squeezing with a love so profound it rocked him. As determined as he was to see Reiver dead, there was only one thing that could keep him from pursuing that goal now. Danika could stop him. With a word, a tear, a pleading look.

But she held his gaze with a steady courage. A faith that humbled him, even as it gave him new resolve.

His strong, beautiful female.

His Breedmate, once this was finally over.

He knew what her courage right now cost her. It was written in her haunted blue eyes as she gave him a subtle nod of permission, of stoic understanding.

Malcolm gathered her close and brushed his mouth against hers in an unrushed kiss. "I have to finish this."

Her reply was quiet but resolved. "I know."

It was a struggle to let her go, but he released her and glanced to Thane. "Keep her safe. I'm counting on you."

The other Breed male gave him a solemn nod. "You have my word."

Mal couldn't take his eyes off Danika. She held his gaze, her own unwavering, as proud and stalwart as the regal Nordic princess she truly was. "Go and finish this, Malcolm. Then come back to me, and never leave me again."

EPILOGUE

He came back to Danika two nights later, haggard and worn, but the most welcome sight she'd ever seen. She opened the door of her little farmhouse in Denmark and there was Malcolm, standing on the cold front stoop in the December moonlight, snowflakes dancing all around him. Her heart swelled so swiftly, she couldn't speak. And while the urge to throw herself into his arms was a need that arrowed through her as basic as the need for air, she held back, trying to read his grave, unsmiling expression.

"Reiver is dead," he told her. "The others too."

She exhaled the breath she'd been holding. Relief flooded her, not so much for the final justice Malcolm had delivered on his enemies but for the simple fact that he was standing in front of her now, whole and hale, safe and sound.

Mal didn't move. He cleared his throat. "Thane tells me his contact in Boston, an Enforcement Agency director by the name of Mathias Rowan, has alluded to big trouble brewing over there. If things get as ugly as Rowan and the Order seem to feel they will, Thane and his men may be called on to help them out."

The news worried her deeply. She'd been trying to get in touch with Gideon since she'd arrived home, but the private number she had for the Order's compound in Boston was out of service. Which had never happened in all the time the direct line to the warriors had existed.

If the Order was off grid—by their own choice or by force—and gearing up to combat something awful, she hated to imagine what that could mean.

"Thane's offered me a place in the Enforcement Agency," Mal added. "He wants me to be part of his team."

Danika's heart sank like a stone. The two days he'd been gone had been torture, but she'd made it through. She'd had faith because she knew he'd come back once he'd done what he had to do. She'd endured his absence because she trusted that when he returned, he'd be back to stay.

But she put on a brave face as she looked at him now. "When do you leave?"

"I turned him down, Dani." He took a step closer now and caught her face in the warm, callused palms of his hands. "There's only one place I want to be, and that's with you."

Elation filled her, but she couldn't celebrate if it was her fear for him that was holding him back. "Don't do this just for me, Mal. I know I've told you that I can't bear the thought of you in danger, and it's true. But I don't want to be the one keeping you somewhere you don't want to be. I can't ask that of you."

"You didn't," he said, caressing her cheek with his

thumb. "Thane and his offer will wait, but this won't. I love you, Danika. Be with me. At my side, as my mate."

She held his intense gray gaze, love swelling inside her, filling her up with joy and hope. "Yes, Malcolm. I will be with you. As your mate, your partner, your friend."

He pulled her against him as an amber fire began to spark in his eyes. "My everything, Dani."

She gave him a happy nod. "Forever."

"Starting now," he said, possession raw and thrilling in the deep growl of his voice.

He kissed her passionately, the sharp points of his fangs grazing her lip with dark promise. Then he swept her into his arms and carried her into the house and up to her bed, where their forever was about to begin.